Dedication

Sheet of Skin for Lebensraum is dedicated to Adolfo Kaminsky who boldly risked his life during World War II while forging documents under the noses of the Nazis occupying Paris. The faked documents were provided to thousands of Jews needing to flee ahead of the lupine German hunters who, with the aid of the French government, were rounding up innocent victims and shipping them to *Third Reich* killing centers.

Dr. Leo Szilard, conceived the concept of a nuclear chain reaction while a member of the University of Berlin faculty. Like many other scientists, he escaped to England to avoid Hitler's assault on Jewish scientists. In England, he worked diligently to help other German Jewish scientists find safe harbor out of the insane asylum that had become their homeland. He also wrote the letter to President Roosevelt, which Einstein signed, that resulted in the formation of the Manhattan Project and the building of the atomic bomb. When it became known that the military was considering dropping the atomic bomb on civilian cities in Japan, Szilard drafted a petition strongly advocating that a demonstration of its power precede any attacks with the lethal weapon. Had the U.S. government followed his advice, the hundreds of thousands of men, women, and children living in Hiroshima and Nagasaki would have escaped the atomic blast that incinerated them, or the deadly radiation that spread through those cities on August 6 and 9, 1945. Szilard is the little known originator of the anti-nuke movement. For his service to humanity, Dr. Szilard shares the dedication of this book.

Also sharing the dedication is my beloved cousin, Thayne Oldfield Ellis, who was a strong but unannounced feminist and persistent influence on my life. The completion of this novel is, in part, due to her generous and continuous encouragement.

i

Sheet of Skin for Lebensraum

❧

Rose O. Hayes, Ph.D.

Sheet of Skin For Lebensraum
Copyright © 2018
Dr. Rose O. Hayes

Comments:
roseohayes@aol.com

ISBN: 978-1-941069-87-5

Cover Design: OBD

Published by **Prose Press**
Pawleys Island, South Carolina
prosencons@live.com

Synopsis

Presented to the reader from the point-of-view of
a medical anthropologist
highly schooled in nuclear enigmas.

Taking the reader through a complex riveting plot full of red herrings and cliffhangers, *Sheet of Skin For Lebensraum* weaves historic fiction into the fabric and hazards of atom splitting to produce nuclear weapons and energy. Those are just the beginning of the end point; a deadly, indestructible, radioactive poison produced to exterminate a list of Nazi war criminals who escaped conviction and execution following World War II.

The story begins with Dr. Cecily Suderman, an American nuclear scientist at the Reardon National Nuclear Laboratory, looking down on a rotting sheet of skin that has been fished from the depths of the Red Sea. To her horror, analysis reveals that it is laced with the deadly poison, Polonium 210. If ingested or breathed in, Polonium 210 delivers the slowest and most agonizing death imaginable, melting the internals organs while dissolving the bones.

As the tale unfolds, Suderman meets with another nuclear scientist, Dr. Mousaff al Shariff, at the UN compound on the banks of the Suez Canal in Port Said. Shariff's small team of Egyptian nuclear scientists produced the poison. Suderman is there to find out how, and how much Polonium 210 was produced. She must convince him to give it up.

Until she meets Shariff, she is clearly on the side of good, a dedicated and respected government scientist. But, as he tells her of the path he has traveled to kill the victim whose skin ends up on her lab table, the thin line between good and evil becomes blurred.

He reveals that they manufactured the polonium to right a terrible wrong, the slaughter of victims caught in World War II

Nazi death camps. It was not a one off. Alois Brunner, a former Nazi official, was only their first target.

The team is in possession of a list revealing the names and locations of other prey, nineteen more Nazis who were also guilty of exterminating hundreds of thousands of Jewish and other victims in the *Third Reich* killing centers. The list was obtained from a former Israeli *Mossad* operative.

To commit the murders, they had acquired a hijacked U.S. Navy submarine on the black market, parked it at the bottom of a lagoon off the coast of Sudan, converted the sub into a nuclear production facility, and burned its enriched uranium fuel to irradiate Bismuth and create the lethal Polonium 210 poison.

The catalyst for their quest was the discovery that one of the Nazi victims was Shariff's long lost love, Rosslyn Ford. Rosslyn, an art historian caught up in a Nazi sweep of the Warsaw Museum, had been sent to *Ravensbruck*, Hitler's camp for women prisoners, located 35 miles north of Berlin. Rosslyn had been subjected to heinous medical experiments, rape, brutal beatings, and finally gassed and incinerated. It was Shariff's intention to extract the cruelest possible revenge for her murder.

When it was hijacked, the sub which they acquired was armed with 16 Polaris-14 missiles that were removed before Shariff's team took possession. The missiles packed more explosive power than all the bombs dropped in World War II.

In the course of their mission, the team discovered a terrorist plot to attack the cooling pools of nuclear power plants outside heavily populated American cities, using the hijacked sub's Polaris missiles. The bombings would cause the cooling pools to go critical. Indian Point, 35 miles north of New York City will be the first target of a launch from an offshore submarine. In the resulting deadly inferno, all New Yorkers will be incinerated or exposed to fatal levels of radiation. The surrounding area will be rendered uninhabitable for millions of years. Other heavily populated cities will suffer the same fate with the remaining missiles and, ultimately, over 80 percent of the U.S. population will be annihilated.

Shariff, honor bound to return the sub and warn the UN of the threat against America, brought it into a berth at Port Said. In exchange for full pardons of any transgressions his team has committed, he offers information on the terrorist plot, as well as the location of the missiles.

He is not, however, offering up the remaining Polonium 210, a gram of which could kill twenty million people.

As Shariff justifies the team's murderous plan, his story peals away the raw horrors of German death camps, beginning with the original system in the Germany colony of Namibia, Africa. There, indigenous tribes were exploited and systematically slaughtered as German colonizers took over their lands and resources. The Namibian colonization was designed after the plan for American Indian reservations.

The inhumane system of German colonization evolved from an ancient demonic thread in the fabric of Teutonic culture. It is known as *Lebensraum*. *Lebensraum* holds that Germanic peoples are destined to expand onto the lands of the "lower races" in order to grow food for an emerging mythical, genetically cleansed, and superior Aryan race with perfect bodies and mind sets. *Lebensraum* also drove the development of "genetic cleansing" in the 20th century Nazi killing factories known by the nicer name of "concentration camps".

Shariff argues that he is not a monster because of what he has done, and plans to do. He is just a man of his own destiny. Hearing his saga, Suderman is left to wonder whether he is monstrous or heroic. His epic journey also leaves her unsure about the standards by which she has judged the world, God's management of the universe, and whether cultural traits such as *Lebensraum* have a temporal component or do they slither into hidey-holes, waiting to re-emerge and hunt again? Are such traits universal expressions of the human animal's natural tendency toward aggression? Could any nation, including America, become another Nazi Germany?

As the story progresses, the Polonium 210 in Shariff's possession becomes a minor issue when a plot is discovered to manufacture, on an industrial level, enough Polonium 210 to pollute the world.

In the end, Suderman follows Shariff from Port Said to Nubia, then Cuba, and finally far up the Amazon River to Urubamba on the *Ucayali*. There, at a secret facility located deep within the canopy of the Peruvian jungle, an international team of nuclear scientists will work to develop an antidote to the polonium. The team has been waiting for Shariff to deliver Suderman. She is needed to determine the necessary strength of the antidote by establishing the permissible exposure limits of Polonium 210. They had been waiting since she approached Shariff in Port Said. He had not only convinced her of his cause, he had won her heart.

Author's Note

Events behind Hitler's barbed wire death camps can never be sufficiently understood. Behavioral scientists have no proven theoretical models to explain the brutal and methodical slaughter of the millions who died at the hands of the Nazis in their killing factories, which were assiduously constructed for optimal efficiency.

Even descriptions of the massacre will remain incomplete. Any attempts at historical restoration must be multi-leveled. The camps were compartmentalized so that the experience of one group of victims was not the experience of another group. The exact number who died in the *Third Reich* slaughterhouses, and took their stories to the grave, will never be known.

As a social scientist, I see Germany's bizarre *Third Reich* "racial hygiene" plans as scientifically organized barbarism. It was a form of genetic insanity that grew out of the intent to hygienically cleanse an expanding German race. It was also an extension of the slaughtering conducted by the *Second Reich* during colonization of what was then called German South-West Africa, now Namibia. The genocide practiced there, where thousands were manacled in iron chains and tossed to the sharks in Walvis Bay, followed by second-person cannibalism when the sharks were subsequently caught and consumed, was based on the ancient concept of *Lebensraum*. *Lebensraum* is Germany's Camelot, calling for a racially pure Teutonic world in which the lands of the "lower races" are taken over to feed a growing Aryan race of humans with perfect bodies and mental sets.

Another quandary begging explanation is how German civilians could have had no knowledge of what was happening in the death camps. Thousands of military and non-military employees worked there. Human fat coated the windows in nearby villages as the crematoriums incinerated the bodies of death camp victims. Mounds of bodies were piled in fields when the slaughter in the gas chambers outpaced the processing capacity of the Nazi ovens. Other bodies were tossed into the rivers. Not knowing would have been incomprehensible. And, why were Jewish people like catnip for the Germans.

Today, there are those who argue that the *Holocaust* is in the past and should be finally put aside. There are no acceptable reasons for dropping those pages of human history. Crimes of that magnitude against humanity must always be fully exposed and addressed, else how are we to prevent their repetition.

There must finally be an explanation of the genesis; an explanation of why Hitler was allowed to rule. Individuals, corporations, and Germany's social institutions were and still are responsible for the cultural values and practices that underlay what went on behind Hitler's barbed wire.

Putting aside this chapter in human history, will not serve us well.

Richard Seaver wrote the Forward for the book, Auschwitz: A Doctor's Eyewitness Account. In that Forward he mentions Bruno Bettelheim's statement that the events which occurred in the Nazi death camps, "though gruesome, need to be told and retold until their meaning for our times is accepted."

It is frightening that so much of this book is based on the facts. It seeks the meaning of the Nazi's monstrous deeds by reconstructing them inside a tale of historical fiction and hard science, while offering the concept of *Lebensraum* as a guide to the madness of the *Third Reich*.

Acknowledgements

I am eternally grateful to Dr. Gary Senn of the University of South Carolina's Ruth Patrick Science Education Center at Aiken. Dr. Senn patiently taught the writer how to unravel some of the mysterious requirements and capabilities of an Apple and, more than once, over-rode the many errors in judgment made while this work was in progress.

Contents

Chapter

One. The Corpse, July 1970 1

Two. Dr. Shariff, August 1970 11

Three. The Dragon. 1969 29

Four. The Path Forward. 40

Five. The Vineyard in the Negev 48

Six. Assembly Line of Death 59

Seven. Belzec: The Extermination Model 89

Eight. BAYER and Zyklon B 103

Nine. Ravensbruck 113

Ten. The Mossad List 123

Eleven. The Ancient Mariners 148

Twelve. Kineococcus radiotolerans 165

Thirteen. The Mountain Called 179

Fourteen. The Run For Cuba 198

Fifteen. The Sierra Maestras 212

Sixteen. The Dark Ops Program 225

Seventeen. Run From The Mountain 251

Appendix 278

1
The Corpse, July 1970
The sea giveth.

I stared down at the gruesome foul smelling remains lying on the cold metal lab bench. It was repulsive. Flesh that once covered a body, but now devoid of organs and a musculoskeletal system, had been reduced to a shrunken gelatinous remnant of water logged skin, almost unrecognizable as human. The owner had been male. Vestiges of a penis were left.

The rotting limp grey mass had been snagged and dragged from the depths by a trawler in the Red Sea, and ultimately delivered to the U.S. Department of Energy's Reardon Ridge National Lab. The lab is part of the massive Reardon Weapons Complex where the pits (code for triggers) in the nation's nuclear warheads are built. The complex spreads across a large plateau in the Northern Rockies of Montana.

The horrid fleshy thing before me had landed in my department because, upon inspection, it had proven to be highly radioactive, and I am the resident Permissible Exposure Limits (PELs) expert. Actually, I am the country's leading expert.

At 14,000 feet, the working environment at Reardon is a desolate rocky moonscape. Everything outside the complex of buildings is cold and barren, devoid of plant and animal life. One does not awaken to bird songs at Reardon. Even in the summer months, when it is warm in the sunlight, it is winter in the shade.

The shimmering impoundment of water in the nearby lake is inviting, but forbidding. Repeatedly sucked in and out to cool the site's seven nuclear reactors, it is radioactive and lethal. Heated more than 30 degrees, the elevated temperature has killed all aquatic life.

The almost lifeless landscape around Reardon is a constant reminder that man's existence on our planet evolved under incessant bombardment by cosmic rays and radiations from the primordial radionuclides in the earth's crust. Through the eons there was a balance between radiation and life forms. Now, however, atom splitting has forever upset that balance by producing excessively radioactive materials that are deadly to humans, and their environments.

❧

Scientists at the lab, entirely male but me, know a little something about radiation since Reardon is one of the dirtiest sites in the Department of Energy's nuclear complex. As a consequence of producing the plutonium pits, millions of gallons of liquid waste has been generated and held in aging storage tanks or has seeped into the lake. The waste is the most toxic liquid on earth; highly radioactive spent nuclear reactor fuel and other residuals.

Underground plumes of escaped lethal poison from the old corroding tanks are slowly clawing their way toward the site boundaries and the valley below. If one of those plumes escapes the site, the drinking water of every town and city on the valley floor below will become permanently toxic. At Reardon, we staffers are 24/7 warriors playing radioactive roulette while battling to do what the navy calls "Hold what you've got."

Even with their hard-core experience, the rest of the staff was clueless about dealing with the anomaly lying on my lab bench.

I wasn't unfamiliar with soft tissue exposures to radiation, but handling and smelling the rotting remnants spread out before me made my skin crawl. I was often tasked with resolving radiation enigmas for the U.S. government, but this was a first. Then again, it would be a first for any other forensic anthropologist.

∽

Forensic work had not been my first choice. In med school I had pulled my thick rust-colored hair back in a severe chignon, peered out through wire-rimmed glasses, and made no attempt to exude sexuality. Then, I was all about becoming an Internist. That changed when I met Mr. Wonderful. I let my hair down, got contacts, and switched my major to medical anthropology so I could trek off to study culture and ecology with him in the upper reaches of the Amazon River.

Warren Jackson was daring, strapping, handsome, forceful and virile. He awakened a part of me that I did not know existed. For the next three years I lived in a world that was a heady mix of riverine villages, choking vegetation, poisonous plants and reptiles, and hot sex.

Warren went native almost immediately, enjoying the *machismo* camaraderie of the *riberenos men* living along the torrential river. I did not make the transition so easily. The *riberenos* called me Senora Rufescent, named after the Tiger Herons in the area because of my long legs, *rufous* colored hair, dark brown eyes, and fish diet. I would not eat the bush meat in the local's diet, including monkey meat and lizards. I remember my embarrassment when I cringed and jumped away from a snake one man brought in for lunch. Warren, on the other hand, would kill and eat anything.

After three years of rigorous field work in the disease-ridden watery world of Amazonia, following him deeper and deeper up the river on the *Ucayali* branch, my attraction to his world peaked.

Everything on the river seemed knarley. *Shangri La* had become humid, fetid, and heavy, including Warren. I could no longer bear his touch. A curtain dropped. It was over. It happens.

In Amazonia, weaverbirds are everywhere, and they always build their nests on the west side of trees. The west side began to beckon me, too, and I moved to the dry, barren, volcanic uplands of the river. In the uplands, I established a base camp to study the medical disorders associated with uranium mining on the *Macusani Plateau.* Not realizing it at the time, but the  mines there were to be a turning point in my life.

Two years of studying the medical afflictions of natives working the mines, and living in the polluted environment associated with the extraction and milling process, set me on a path I had never anticipated; the permissible exposure limits of radioactive elements. It was there that I became all too familiar with the impact on human health when up close and personal with uranium ore, radon gas, and the dust associated with ore extraction and milling. That path ultimately brought me up against one of its end points; the Reardon Ridge National Lab, and production of all-plutonium pits, the triggers of nuclear warheads.

Among the assortment of physical failures found in the *Macusani* workers, the worst was lung cancer. Macusani mine workers had a lung cancer rate six times higher than the general population of Peruvian workers. Everyone up on the plateau was sick, about to become sick, or dying.

My life became absorbed by the deaths and dying of the mineworkers. Intermittent trips down to the river to see Warren became further and further apart. I used my research as an excuse. He never made excuses for not leaving the river. Warren gradually became my husband in name only.

4

One thing led to another and on my last trip down to his river camp, wanting out but also wanting to be the injured party, I told him, "You just play at science now. Staying here is not your vocation. It is your vacation. You have abandoned ecology and our marriage."

My aim was wide of the mark and I knew it, but it was the cathartic I needed for the guilt I felt. I had failed to make the transition he made, into a jungle trekking scientist of the Amazon, unhampered by the lack of amenities in the bush. While he was completely at home with his life there, I no longer wanted to be a part of it so I closed the chapter on Peru, and Warren, and returned to the U.S.

And now, dressed in full radiological control gear, I was standing over a putrid sheet of human skin that would have to be moved to a room where I could set up an "off limits" dissection lab. I signed my name to Form 4491 – Dr. Cecily Suderman – requesting space on the "hot cell" side of the facility. Attached to the request was a long list of equipment needed for the dissection work and spectrometric analysis.

In any federal agency, getting such a request through the required signature levels that normally obstruct the needed clearance is a Herculean task. Apparently, management intended to pull out all stops to get this one done. The paper work made it through channels almost immediately.

৵

Left alone with the fetid remains in what was to be my new lab, I began considering the options. Ordinarily, I relied on what medical anthropologists trained in forensics use as standard biomarkers on skeletal material to tell the story. Public bones are always helpful to establish gender but, in this case, the flaccid penal flesh indicated that this John Doe was most likely a male.

Under microscopic analysis, a cross section of a long bone can provide evidence of age, genetics, musculoskeletal diseases and environmental effects. Dentition is also one of the best clues to a skeleton's age, along with epiphyseal ossification (calcification of the growth plates). It's also easy to tell which side of the body a bone comes from, and some 140 markers of bone remodeling are known occupational stressors. I had none of these to use so, we were not likely to ever know who John Doe actually was unless we learned of the circumstances under which his skin became so radioactive.

He was now just a sheet of deteriorating epidermis that no longer covered his musculoskeletal system and organs. And, because the bits of dermis left clinging to the underside of his epidermis gave off a high reading of radioactivity, genetic markers would be suspect. Radiation at high levels plays havoc with the construction of your genes. Whoever this poor bastard had been, he suffered an excruciating death, apparently dissolved from the inside out.

Hours of analysis identified the source of radiation. To my horror, it was Polonium, named by Marie Curie to commemorate her Polish homeland. This particular form was the deadliest poison on earth, Polonium 210. It brings a death far worse than a thousand cuts. Polonium 210 is a toxic stew of chemicals that can enter the body and eat it cell by cell. One gram could kill millions if dispersed in a nation's aquifers, reservoirs, food chain, or pharmaceutical supply system. Anything involving ingestion or inhalation.

It is also one of the deadliest national security threats in the world due to the form in which it can be delivered. An amount sufficient to eliminate a nation's population can be suspended in several small vials of water and hand delivered to targets. *It takes so little to kill so many.*

Polonium 210 is always on the radar of every U.S. agency tasked with repelling attacks on the U.S. It's a global moving target because any nuclear nation with stock piles of high-level uranium can produce it if they have the will, and all nuclear nations have tons of high-level uranium. It is the feedstock for their reactors.

I put down my ten-blade scalpel for a moment and stared at the skin before me, trying to read it for any clues. *There are over 400 nuclear reactors operating at any minute in the world. Where did the uranium required to produce the Polonium 210 that killed this guy come from?"* The skin gave me no clue, but it would.

In the Pentagon War Room, the possibility that some nation would have the will to build an arsenal of Polonium 210 is often a subject of speculation. It would be the mother of all weapons, a chemical weapon on steroids. Given the world's current preoccupation with nuclear warheads, the chemical killer could be quietly produced while the world focuses on the red herring. Theories of Polonium 210 containment are always floated in War Room meetings but, in truth, there is no defense against such an attack, and no controls over its effect.

While it can be safely handled with care, if you ingest it or inhale it, it goes cannibalistic once inside your body. Your organs will begin to melt, and the bones of your skeleton will start dissolving. After an agonizing few days, death will be merciful.

As I continued to study the data, it was beginning to appear that the Polonium 210 that killed John Doe originated in the type of high-level uranium-235 used to power U.S. nuclear submarines. *Impossible. If the polonium had come from inside a sub, or from one of the sites that store excessed sub reactors or the fuel for those boats, how had it been processed into Polonium 210?.*

I was familiar with a few cases involving Polonium 210 exposure. It was rumored that the Russians had developed their own brand in a secret Cold War chamber and then used it to surreptitiously dispatch a few unsuspecting enemy agents. There were also documents describing a program, implemented during the Manhattan Project, when the U.S. Atomic Energy Commission had funded human experiments involving polonium. *

In those secret experiments, hospitalized patients with incurable diseases were injected with the poison and upon their deaths, autopsies revealed high concentrations in the liver, kidney, and testes.

Since then, the scientific community had been told the silent killing power of the poison was considered so insidious there had been no known attempts to add it to any nation's chemical arsenal. Certainly, there were no reports on Polonium 210 being produced inside submarines.

However, checking the National Nuclear Safety Office's database, there had also been no reported cases of missing Polonium 210 from any of the federal repositories. So, that left the most likely source as the inside of a submarine.

In a way, that was good news. If it had come from a submarine, that made it the Navy's problem. Not mine.

Even so, I couldn't quit thinking about the exposure factor. Nuclear submarine reactors are flawlessly designed to withstand the vibration, pitching, and rolling of a ship operating in heavy seas. But, the reactors can still be hazardous since they are not built to shut down using gravity control rods, like land-based reactors. Salt-water corrosion is also a constant maintenance problem.

In the event of an onboard reactor failure, submariners can get exposed to deadly radiation, but not Polonium 210. It would take extraordinary circumstances inside a submarine to produce the form of polonium that killed the subject on my lab table. Its production requires equipment and skills not normally found aboard subs. Aside from the boat's reactor and high-level uranium fuel, it would require the production of Bismuth, sophisticated centrifugal pumps, and other special high-tech machines.

*Described in Biological Studies with Polonium, Radium, and Plutonium, National Nuclear Energy Series, Vol. VI-3, Chapter 3. McGraw-Hill, New York, 1950.

However, there is also the fact that any nuclear submarine is a nuclear proliferation risk because of its onboard enriched uranium fuel supply. Big target for terrorists. *Could the guy in our lab have been the victim of some kind of terrorist attack involving the hijacking of a U.S. submarine and Polonium 210 production?* There was no record of that kind of attack but the Navy might have kept the record for "eyes only". The situation was fraught with potentials, most of which are beyond my job description.

I completed all the test protocols and sat down at the gray metal government issue desk in my otherwise colorless lab. Reviewing the data, the thought that some part of the case was in my domain would not go away. But which part of this mystery was my job? Scanning the numbers again, I decided, *It's unlikely that the corpse was a submariner because a submarine crew would not have the capability to produce Polonium 210 from their boat's fuel. That would require intense laboratory extraction work. Not a sailor's strong suit. That suit belonged to the guys trained in nuclear physics.*

As much as I would have liked to leave it on the Navy's side of the net, the stuff can be a powerful poison, and even suspended in water. Like it or not, John Doe's skin signaled a huge public health and safety threat. That put the case firmly back in my court. *Someone is playing a dangerous game. That someone has to be a monster, and the monster must be found and stopped.*

I filed a report stating the cause of death was Polonium 210 exposure. In the <u>Conclusion</u> section I noted that, based on the destruction of the interior organs and musculoskeletal system from within, death was most likely due to ingestion, inhalation, or absorption. I also noted that nothing was left of the corpse but the epidermis. Since Polonium 210 does not easily penetrate human epidermis, the probability of casual or deliberate external exposure should probably be eliminated.

In the <u>Action</u> section, putting it firmly on some Navy admiral's desk, I wrote, *If it is determined that the polonium originated in a*

U.S. nuclear submarine, there is an obvious national security risk and a national security advisory should be issued.

I added, *In all likelihood, the victim was murdered.*

Since my bailiwick is public health hazards, I transmitted a Hazard Communication Warning.

As for the time of death, cellular decomposition of the skin indicated biological termination occurred approximately four weeks earlier, although with floaters, especially those exposed to radiation, time of death is always a scientific wild ass guess.

2

Dr. Shariff, August 1970

Crime on the high seas.

A month later, with John Doe's sheet of skin in cryogenics storage at Reardon, we learned how the polonium had been extracted and converted into a lethal weapon. The plot did involve a U.S. nuclear submarine, which had been hijacked. It was one of the most creative and daring attacks the Navy had ever experienced. Except, until my discovery that a nuclear submarine's fuel had been used to extract the Polonium 210 that almost completely dissolved John Doe's body, the Navy wasn't even aware their boat had been hijacked.

It was not difficult to determine from which sub the polonium in question came. All uranium has a unique footprint and every supply of submarine fuel is carefully characterized and cataloged. The fuel in question had come from a sub commissioned as the *Scorpion*.

Official records indicated that on May 22, 1968 *Scorpion* went down on the second day of her maiden voyage. It was during a practice deep dive. She was an SSN-589 Skipjackclass, powered by her forward nuclear reactor. Presumably, she took the crew of one hundred men down with her, disappearing into the deep depression of the Atlantic's North American Basin. But her hull hadn't been found in the watery complex of currents that twist and wind around on the sea floor.

According to the records, there had been two final communications from *Scorpion*. The first indicated she was nose up and blowing ballast, trying for the surface. The second was too garbled to translate. But it was assumed the crew was still "riding the boat". Then, silence.

It did not surprise me that her disappearance had not been considered a unique occurrence. Plenty of sunken subs lay in the depths of the planet's oceans.

What was surprising was the ship's inventory. When *Scorpion* went down, she was one of the world's most powerful killing machines, carrying sixteen Polaris A-1 nuclear ballistic missiles. Her killing power exceeded all the bombs dropped during World War II and she was a swift and stealthy stalker, an imminent threat to anything in the water, or on land. She could run ahead of her prey, turn, and fire directly into them. Naturally, an extensive hunt followed, prompted more by national security than concern for the crewmembers, who were presumed dead.

As it turned out, the Navy had missed the lurking variable in the bureaucratic quicksand of government contracts, procurement policies, and practices that had taken *Scorpion* down. There it was, in the records, in black and white. She, and those of her kind, carries the seeds of their own destruction.

❧

August is Egypt's hottest month. I had been sent to interview Dr. Mousaff al Shariff at Major General Alden Lloyd's headquarters in Port Said on the banks of the Suez Canal. General Lloyd headed up the UN peacekeeping force at the canal. Shariff had been the leader of a group of Egyptian nuclear scientists who acquired *Scorpion* on the black market in the spring of 1969, a year after her hijacking.

As reading material for the long flight from Montana, the CIA had provided me with a copy of his dossier. Shariff's profile was interesting. It kept me occupied while I read under the barely sufficient light above my airline seat and careened across the United States, the Atlantic Ocean, and North Africa's Sahara Desert, in a silver missile moving through the friendly skies in excess of 500 miles an hour.

I could not have known that my world would be changed forever by that flight. I was about to be confronted with a moral dilemma brought on by the actions of Shariff and the events that led him to those actions. The thin sharp line that, for me, had always delineated good from evil was about to become blurred.

&

Day 1. Arriving at Cairo International Airport, I found the driver of my reserved limo patiently holding up a sign bearing my name. He was standing at the entrance to the customs and immigration area. Finding him was something of a miracle in the mass of humanity that seemed to fill every vacant foot of space and suck up all the air in the terminal. His name, of course, was *Osman*. In that world if you call, "*Yah, Osman,*" at least a dozen nearby men will answer.

A lot of grief is saved by having a limo meet you at Cairo International, one of the largest airports in the world. Arabic is the dominant language, and the rule of the land is *In sha Allah* (if Allah wills it), so nothing is exactly logical, predictable, or on time by Western standards. The limo driver can purchase your visa sticker, find your checked bags, wait while you go through the immigration line (no mean feat), and most importantly, somehow keep finding you. Grabbing a taxi there is not recommended for the uninitiated.

Taking *El Orouba Road,* Osman cut in and out of the amazing myriad of vehicles along the route: a river of taxis, lorries, busses, cars, and trucks, along with horse and donkey-powered wagons. Pedestrians, burdened with baggage, food, and all manner of wares for sale, walked dangerously close to the passing traffic. Some stepped into the roadway, waving unidentifiable objects in the unlikely event passing motorists would pull over to buy them. They seemed indifferent to the prospect of death.

The fleeting blur of architectural landscape held my attention. When I last rode along *El Orouba,* the drive was through a corridor of densely packed, one-storied wattle and daub houses divided into compounds of extended families. Like everywhere else in the Nile Valley, the nondescript houses blended colorlessly into the desert landscape. But a decade had passed, and the route had transformed into one of tall multiple storied structures, still wattle and daub and colorless. Now, however, the extended family compounds were stacked up six and seven stories high, reflecting the population growth and urban sprawl that characterizes Cairo.

Strangely, the buildings all remained unfinished, with rebar  jutting skyward from the top floors. Among the construction debris and spikes of rebar, strategically located TV dish antennas could be seen on most roofs.

Osman explained that the rebar signified a building remained under construction. "It is customary," he said, "due to the tax laws. As long as a building is unfinished, the government does not levy taxes. We are a people too poor to pay taxes."

The strange apparitions were a beacon of the country's poverty. Looking down the alleyways of the underserviced areas was a stark

reminder of how millions of people on the planet live.

Cairo's city center and the Hilton Ramses on *Nile Corniche* was only sixteen miles from the airport, but the drive took almost an hour, miraculous speed given the mix of transportation modes and prevailing practice of treating traffic lights and stop signs as suggestions. Confusion reigned at every intersection, and I grew increasingly grateful for the air conditioning inside the limo. Outside, it was dusty, and over 110 degrees.

After checking into the high-rise tower overlooking the river and seeing my luggage to the room, I decided to take a stroll before grabbing a bite to eat in one of the hotel's four restaurants. It would then be time for the traditional mid-day nap, jokingly referred to in the Nile Valley as Egyptian P.T. (physical training).

General Lloyd would be sending a car for me when the afternoon heat had passed and the city once again came to life.

⁊

It was a short walk to the Egyptian Museum where I ducked in to take a look at the famed golden mask of *Tutankhamen* and the even more ancient *King Narmer* palette. On the palette, *King Narmer* is shown

15

wearing the crown of Upper Egypt and grasping the slain king of Lower Egypt by the hair. The slain king wears the crown of the lower delta lands. The scene signifies that around 3,000 years before Christ, *Narmer* united the two lands and ruled both, forming one of man's earliest civilizations.

One's perspective changes while studying the palette. Egypt might currently be considered underdeveloped but it was one of the earliest and greatest civilizations on the planet and survived vicissitudes for almost 5,000 years. Realizing that I come from a country that is not yet 300 years old gave me pause for thought about the assumed superiority and resilience of modern First World nations.

Having taken in a measure of Egypt's cultural history, I decided to opt for street food in the *Tawfiqiyya Suk*, rather than an upscale sit-down dinner back at the hotel. *Tawfiqiyya* street cooks are known for producing the best *Fiteer*, a sort of pizza made of layered phyllo-type dough and savory toppings. The Egyptian bean dish, F*uhl*, and little fried *Taameya* sesame breads can be found there, too. The decision to go native picked up my spirit and shed some of the jet lag.

Later, in my room at the luxurious Ramses, I was awakened from a deep nap by the ringing phone next to my bed. The polite clerk at the desk informed me that a car was on its way from Port Said and would pick me up in about an hour, *In sha Allah*.

By Cairo time, it was just past five in the evening. The car would arrive around six and by the time we made the return trip to Port Said it would be nine o'clock. The sun would have set on my first day in Egypt, but there was nothing unusual about such a late hour meeting. When the sun is at it's highest, all activities are curtailed and begin again after a late dinner when the gripping heat starts releasing its hold on life.

Reluctantly, I crawled from between silky Egyptian cotton sheets, crossed the room on a thick south Persian carpet, and made my way into the bathroom. It was stunning, with walls and floors of pale pink granite quarried at the Nile's third cataract where ancient workers had cleaved boulders for the Giza pyramids and their colossal statues.

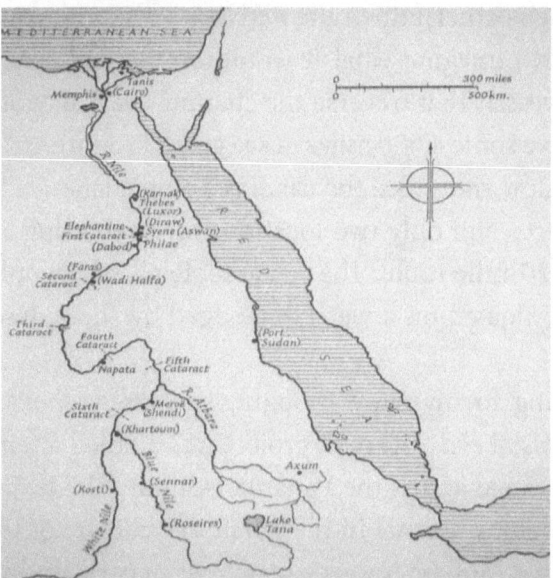

Stepping into the shower, I let the cool water slide over my body, washing away the dust and smell of the streets. While toweling off, I caught a glimpse of my image in the long mirror on the back of the door – still toned, with smooth tan skin.

Back in the bedroom, I found *shai sada sucre tahqil* (strong black tea with sugar) waiting for me on a table in front of the sofa. Energized from the cool shower and sweet tea, I dressed, collected my things, and called for them to be taken downstairs.

The rest of this trip would be spent in lesser digs at the UN compound on the banks of the Suez. I was excited to see the canal. It had been at the forefront of world affairs for thousands of years, connecting the Mediterranean and Red Seas.

I remembered reading somewhere that over the centuries ancient Egyptian kings and queens had tried and failed to dig through the Isthmus of Suez to open a passage for goods from the east African coast. The Romans tried to make a cut through the isthmus for the spread of Pax *Romana*. Completion of the canal had to wait on the necessary technology. In 1869, Ferdinand de Lesseps finally managed to open a shallow, artificial waterway running from Port Said at the Mediterranean, south to the city of Suez on the northern tip of the Red Sea.

I tried to imagine what it would be like onboard one of the nearly 50 vessels that traverse the channel every day of the year in order to save some 4,000 miles of sea travel around Africa. It would be a long slow ride since the canal is a single lane sea level course with no locks and only two locations for overtaking slower ships along its 120-mile route. The remarkable passage would take days as the ship floated on a waterway edged by sheer desert on each side.

Laughing to myself, I thought, *de Lesseps should have quit while he was ahead.* His next project was a failed attempt to build a sea-level canal across the Panama isthmus. The technology that allowed opening a canal in the harsh dry climate of the Suez was no match for Mother Nature's plague of malaria and yellow fever in the jungles of Panama.

⚜

Arriving at the Canal Authority complex, I was greeted by General Lloyd and his 'prisoner', Dr. Musaff al Shariff. The *Scorpion* had been in his possession for the past year. I needed to interview him since it had been determined that the Polonium 210 in play, that had ravaged the John Doe in my lab, or what remained of him, had been generated using *Scorpion's* reactor fuel. Shariff had brought the sub back, but he also brought along non-negotiable terms for information he possessed about her missing Polaris missiles. Powerful people were prepared to see that his terms were met.

He bore no signs of being treated as a detainee. Obviously, his custody was a mere formality. His handsome face was inscrutable, giving nothing away. My sense was that he could be either delightful or dangerous, depending on your relationship with him. As some of my male counterparts have been overheard saying, 'He probably pisses ice water when needed.'

According to his dossier, he held a lot of high cards, at least one of which involved a public health and safety hazard, Polonium 210, my wheelhouse. I studied him closely, thinking, *Everyone has doors. I wonder what is behind his doors.*

The dossier I had read on him contained a detailed description of his life, from early years as a youth in *Sharm el-Sheik* at the southern tip of the Sinai Peninsula, to the day that he appeared at the UN complex on the banks of the Suez a few days earlier. I had flipped through the pages during my flight to Cairo. They revealed a fascinating life, painting a picture of a man who lived by the philosophy, "Tomorrow is not promised".

"… family genealogy dating back a thousand years … teenager … cranked up an old beat up motorcycle and spent days exploring the Nubian desert of Egypt's southlands . . . Scuba diving in the Red Sea . . . knows both areas well." A picture was clipped to one page showing a strikingly fetching young man proudly seated on an ageing English Triumph."

"1936 . . . completed doctoral work at Oxford . . . promising nuclear physicist in the new field of fission research . . . scientific world in a race to develop power of sustained atom splitting . . . game changer . . . all chasing the elusive atomic chain reaction."

" . . . joined Enrico Fermi's staff at the University of Rome . . . team steadily peeling back secrets of nature's atomic powers . . . became Fermi's lab manager . . . they built world's first functional research reactor."

The last pages indicated that circumstances beyond his control altered his career path, forcing him to return to his homeland in 1939. With Hitler on the rise, Europe had morphed into a cauldron of danger, especially for nuclear scientists.

The file brought to mind my undergrad history classes. By the late 30s, Adolph Hitler was becoming the Agent Orange of German politics, poisoning a country that had once given rise to some of the world's greatest philosophers, artists, and scientists. Following defeat in World War I, Germany became riddled with fear, discontent, and resentment emanating from a yoke of deprivation strangling its economics. The yoke had been placed there by the Allied victors who had converted the nation into a potato field. Hitler, a testosterone-infused demagogue with a disordered personality and messianic pretentions, fed on that ideological kaleidoscope and used it as his vehicle to become ruler of the *Third Reich.*

I remembered descriptions of his mad ravings and hate mongering. The spoilage and resultant *Teutonic* anguish from losing World War I spawned an ethos that jelled into a pack mentality of 'kill or be killed'. Germany happily followed mad Adolph into a second world war, rolling full tilt over the borders of its neighbors. Robbing, raping, and butchering.

I have always felt that the world would have benefitted if his mother had killed Baby Hitler.

Returning to the dossier, it indicated that Egypt was not yet involved but Shariff watched the gathering storm with a wary eye. As Hitler rose to power, many gifted scholars, especially Hebrew nuclear scientists, were forced to run ahead of his lupine Jew hunters. Fermi, by then a Nobel Prize laureate, was compelled to flee Italy with his family. His wife's mother was Jewish, which left the whole family at risk of being put to death after Mussolini passed his race laws and began shipping Italy's Jews to Nazi concentration camps. Fermi, Laura, and their children escaped to America.

Without Fermi, the Rome lab could not continue to function so Shariff ran for the cover of *Bilad es Sudan* (the terrible Sahara). Returning to Cairo, he was quickly appointed to the university's faculty of science and tasked with setting up a nuclear research lab.

After that, the dossier was sketchy for the next two decades, as he hid behind the veil that always separates the Islamic and Western worlds.

He resurfaced on the pages of his dossier in the late 50s, which described a remarkable series of events. "By 1958, . . . hot-cell laboratory in the Nile River delta at *Inshas* . . . lead scientist . . ."

As I read that last page of the CIA's report on Shariff, I realized that he had been involuntarily forced on a journey that would eventually gain him attention from the movers and shakers of the world. His story was a real curtain raiser.

The Cold War had caught Shariff between the two horns of a dilemma and circumstances well beyond his control. Following the scourge of Europe and destruction of Japan in 1945, the world was left to face the unspeakable prospects of nuclear warfare. By the early 1950s, Egypt and 190 other nations had signed President Eisenhower's Nuclear Non-Proliferation Treaty (NTP). The naïve NTP goal was to give each signatory the so-called "peaceful atom" and prevent such wars. In exchange for receiving nuclear technology, each signatory nation committed to using it for civilian purposes only. Predictably, promoted by the so-called Big Five (America, France, the UK, Russia, and China), the 'atoms-for-peace program' turned out to be a proliferation conveyor belt of nuclear terrorism.

By the late 50s, and under orders from the Egyptian government, the *Inshas* team was burning highly enriched uranium and illegally extracting upwards of six kilograms of plutonium each year, enough for a nuclear bomb. Egypt's goal was the kind of firepower needed to deter Israel from launching its nuclear weapons, which the world knew they had.

Over the course of my career, I had become deeply concerned about nuclear weapons and energy, and rigid about policies and practices involving public safety and health, especially permissible exposure limits to radioactive material. Nuclear warfare would bring wide spread radiation poisoning.

❦

In 1946, Churchill had described the rift between the U.S.S.R. and the other Allies as an "Iron Curtain". That verbal curtain took material form on August 31, 1961 when Russia began erecting the Berlin Wall.

Two months later, the Soviets upped the stakes by dropping the Tsar Bomb over the Arctic Ocean. The bomb was a 57-megaton hydrogen bomb thousands of times more powerful than the atomic bomb dropped on Hiroshima in 1945, the largest man-made explosion the world had seen.

The first nuclear battlefield was located 90 miles off America's shores. While the U.S. and Russia stared down each other's missiles during "détente", Havana became friendly with Russia after Castro's guerilla forces toppled the Batista regime. When Cuba negotiated a trade agreement with Russia to import Russian crude, the American owned refineries in Cuba refused to process it. Castro retaliated by nationalizing the refineries. Eisenhower responded by cutting Cuba's quota for exporting 7 million tons of its sugar to the U.S., a critical blow to the Cuban economy. Castro retaliated by nationalizing all American owned properties in Cuba. Diplomatic relations between the two countries was canceled.

The right to the pursuit of happiness was then put on hold while the world focused on the U.S./U.S.S.R. hostilities escalating under the Kennedy administration. Secretary of Defense Robert McNamara advocated the chilling prospect of nuclear war that would target only Soviet military targets, not cities.

Following the Tsar bomb test, American U2 flights confirmed that Russia had missiles in Cuba, 90 miles from Key West. A quarantine and blockade of Cuba ensued, followed by a tense standoff at sea and then negotiations between the U.S. and Russia, which largely left the Cuban government out of the loop. In a political slight of hand, the Kennedy administration negotiated a step-down agreement whereby Russia removed its Cuban missiles and America removed its "secret" missiles from Turkey, leaving the false impression that Kennedy was victorious in the scuffle.

By 1964, McNamara had introduced the chilling concept of Mutually Assured Destruction (MAD) as a step-back policy that presumably ensured neither the U.S. nor Russia would start throwing their nuclear arsenals at each other. All this occurred against the backdrop of a U.S. engagement in Vietnam from the mid-fifties to the mid-seventies to stem communism in Asia. In 1961, the U.S. also entered into a space race with the Soviets after the Russian astronaut, Yuri Gagarin, became the first man to orbit the earth.

In that same year, China detonated its first atomic bomb.

The world teetered on the brink of a potential nuclear winter, and broadcast news gave nightly reports on impending doom. Every adult with half a brain was scared stiff and young students were taught how to duck and cover under their classroom desks.

What I was to learn in the meeting with Shariff was that when President Nasser unexpectedly decided to attack Israel in 1967, he and his team of nuclear scientists knew they could not let their *Inshas* work fall into the hands of Egypt's military command. To prevent the Middle East from entering into a nuclear dogfight, they quietly moved the *Inshas* high-level uranium and weapons-grade plutonium to a safe place further south in Nubia, one of Shariff's old haunts. Later, when the theft was discovered, Egypt unobtrusively put a bounty on their heads.

Now 62 years old, and enjoying the hospitality of the United Nation's complex, Shariff held the upper hand, having the ability to blackmail his government. He could tell the UN's International Atomic Energy Administration (IAEA) where Egypt's processing site was located. He could reveal that the Egyptian scientists had been ordered to illicitly enrich uranium and illegally produce weapons-grade plutonium. He could also tell what the Egyptian government intended to do with the unlawful plutonium, and where his team had stashed it in Nubia.

Another of his high cards was telling the U.S. Navy how to hijack one of their nuclear submarines and convert it into a uranium processing lab. He might also be able to tell the U.S. Department of Energy's national laboratory at Reardon Ridge, and me, to whom the cadaver remains in the lab had belonged and how it came to be heavily polluted with Polonium 210. Shariff's war chest probably contained more powerful trade-offs than a long-term Washington politician's. No doubt he was going to get the non-negotiable request for his team's immunity in exchange for what he knew, and others wanted to know.

Looking at him, it was immediately apparent that if he did not get what he wanted, there would be no deal. He was clearly a man who exuded authority and was at ease with pressure and power, nuclear or otherwise. It was also clear that he did not consider his actions as breaking the rules. He just did not accept the rules.

Could he also be a monster who murdered with radioactive materials?

✑

After introductions, the traditional little glasses of *shai sada sucre tahqil* , and polite chitchat, General Lloyd excused himself 'to attend to an issue at the canal'. I was left alone with Shariff.

He was olive skinned, athletically framed, and the most breathtakingly handsome man I had ever seen. He also projected a quiet air of authority carried on a six foot three inch frame. The nuclear guru wore a black Ralph Lauren polo shirt with a jauntily turned up collar. White linen trousers outlined his long fit legs, and on his feet were tasseled saddle-brown Gucci loafers. His thick black hair was greying at the temples and his large brown eyes seemed to be intently listening to me while a slight twinkle said he was simultaneously wondering what it would be like if we were together under other circumstances, whether I was accessible.

Twenty years my senior, everything about him was simply eye

candy. But, appearances can be very deceptive and I made a mental note not to let his sex appeal get in the way of my mission.

Telling him about the cadaver remains back at Reardon, I asked if he had any knowledge of how it became loaded with Polonium 210, which had been extracted from *Scorpion's* fuel. Without hesitation, he admitted he did, but he also said, "It's a long story, best started after we have had a good night's sleep. Let's meet again in the morning."

Flashing a wide charming smile at me, he indicated that he would be free to talk after he conferred with some UN officials who had also arrived at the Canal Authority that evening.

I took his meaning. The immunity papers he had requested for himself and his team were being handed over. Then, we could discuss the former inhabitant of the radioactive skin, and how the victim had met his demise.

❦

Leaving Shariff, I longed to take a stroll along the canal or the Mediterranean beach. But the night was still very warm and, in addition, there were some pretty nasty night hunters that are best given a wide berth in Egypt's desert. One of the worst is the Egyptian cobra. It is highly territorial and will track and attack interlopers, including humans. A relentless hunter on land, it is also known to swim in the sea, presumably stalking fish.

Death from the cobra bite is excruciating. The long sleek copper and black reptile can deliver 300 mgs of venom loaded with neurotoxins (toxic to nerve tissue) and cytotoxins (toxic to cells). Its poison quickly begins tracing through muscle tissue, spreads into the bloodstream, and is absorbed by the body's vital organs.

I remembered watching a man die from a cobra's bite in the Sudan. We were deep in the *Bayuda Desert* and had no anti-venom. Within a short time the victim's nerves ceased to transmit signals, leaving his muscles limp and unable to contract. His tongue, lips,

25

and facial muscles became paralyzed and his vision was blurred by widely dilated pupils. Dispersion of the poison was also accompanied by profuse sweating and convulsions. Within half an hour his heart and respiratory muscles no longer functioned and death came in agonizing waves. *I hate snakes!*

Another dangerous customer in the area is the large Deathstalker scorpion, which can also deliver toxins that cause paralysis, progressing to death by pulmonary edema. The curator at the Cairo Museum told me that *Serket*, the ancient Egyptian goddess and guardian against venom and snakebites, was closely associated with the Deathstalker. In the Valley of the Kings, she is often depicted on tomb walls wearing a Deathstalker on her head, especially when she is guarding the great god *Osiris*. In pictographic writing, her name translates to "closing of the throat".

Remembering that the night belonged to the snake and the scorpion, I shuddered and decided to settle for a short walk within the security of the UN compound. I stepped out into the courtyard and down the three steps onto a brick patio. The desert night air was clean, welcome relief from the exhaust fumes left by the vehicles clogging the streets of Cairo. I took a deep breath and thought about the intriguing man I had just met.

While I stood enjoying the moment, I caught sight of a feral cat. They roam across every acre of Egypt. It was in stalking mode, suddenly leaping into the air and pouncing on a black-winged sandpiper not two yards from me. The bird struggled to escape the cat's jaws but the cat clung on with its sharp claws and began ripping into its body. Even in the darkness I could see blood. Instinctively, I ran at the cat, screaming. Being wild, it released the bird and scurried away.

Looking down at the carnage, I could see that one wing was nearly ripped off and a leg was torn away. The sandpiper flopped about, trying to gain the safety of altitude but its ability to become air born was long since gone. Death, one way or another, was certain.

If I left it there, the cat would return to finish it off, clawing it to death and ripping it apart with its teeth. I reached down and picked it up from the ground. Ants were already crawling over it. Along with the cats, they are everywhere in the Sahara. Brushing off the ants, I quickly made a decision that flew in the face of all my training and natural inclinations. In my job, I often handled the dead, not taken life. But, this was a life that would end violently without my intervention.

Just inside the door of the room where I had been talking with Shariff was a table. On it was a vase holding fresh cut lotus flowers. I opened the door, quickly grabbed the vase, dumped out the flowers and water, and walked to the edge of the patio.

Gently laying the poor creature on the bricks, I raised the vase and smashed it down on the sandpiper's head. I felt the skull shatter under the blow. Still warm, its body went quiet. The struggle was over.

Nausea overwhelmed me and I vomited. For the first time in my life, I had felt the energy that courses through live bodies leave its host. It left me stunned, suddenly too close to the cold reality of my own mortality.

In response to my emotional stress, I broke into a cold sweat and quickly returned to my room inside the building. Exploring the area could wait until daylight.

The second floor guest quarters were Spartan but safe, clean, and comfortable. Exhausted, I fell into bed and slept late the following morning.

৵

Day 2. After showering and dressing in a light cotton outfit, I grabbed breakfast in the well-appointed dining hall on the building's ground floor and then found Shariff. He was settled into a deep leather chair in the lounge just off the dining hall. I took the matching chair on the other side of an intricately carved black mahogany tea table.

What passed for air-conditioning kept the room relatively cool at that hour. The lounge, a large room about 40 feet long and half as wide, was extravagantly appointed. Unlike the basic furnishings upstairs, the décor of the building's lower floor lent itself to the accommodation of heads of state who continuously visit the canal, anxious to view the waterway so vital to the commercial health of their respective countries. Walls were a warm cream color. Tall windows with heavy crown molding were draped in sapphire blue silk, always drawn after lunch to block the harsh desert sun and heat.

In deference to the Muslim prohibition against creating naturalistic images of living beings, the walls were bare of art. Architecture is the art of the Islamic world, graced with magnificent mosques bearing towering minarets from which a *muezzin* calls the faithful to prayer five times each day.

Since it was still morning, sunlight streamed through the windows and across the stone floors. Here and there, the hard stone was softened by a covering of richly colored *Sashavan* Berber carpets, rare by any standard. Punt wood tables sat by sofas and chairs arranged in conversational groupings throughout all the lower rooms, including the lounge where Shariff and I sat.

Along the north wall, a bank of windows, graced by intricate ironwork that served as part of the complex's security system, afforded a beaucolic view of the Mediterranean. There were similar windows along the east wall that overlooked the canal. Bird songs drifted through the glass panes, interspersed by the cries of disgruntled seagulls.

Breaking the ice, Shariff asked how I had slept and told me that his meeting with the UN representatives had gone well. Again, I took his meaning. He was now free to talk about Polonium 210. Then, he began telling a story that was the stuff of Hollywood Oscar Awards.

3
The Dragon. 1969
How to steal a U.S. Navy nuclear submarine.

It began with his team's reason for acquiring *Scorpion*. They were on a mission to perform evil deeds with Polonium 210 in order to right horrible wrongs.

He asked me what I knew of the Sikh religion and, not waiting for an answer, he said, "Sikhs are renowned for religious tolerance. Yet, they have a reputation for being fearless warriors and wear daggers hanging from cords around their necks as a symbol of their belief that in order to be a good Sikh you must protect yourself and all others."

I was startled. *My god! He is the one? He is the monster responsible for the fleshy mass I had analyzed back in my lab at Reardon? He intends to justify what he did. What could be so horribly wrong that poisoning a man with Polonium 210 righted it, balanced the scale? And, how could such a deed protect others?*

Shariff calmly started his remarkable tale by explaining that *Scorpion's* kind had both a soft underbelly and an *Achilles* heel, fatal flaws which allowed her to be tracked and forced to the surface.

He said, "The fire in her soft underbelly came from the onboard nuclear reactor which generated electricity and drove electric motors connected to her propeller shaft. Without sea

29

water continuously pumping through her reactor's core, it would overheat and saturate the ship's quarters with high-level radiation."

While he spoke, he kept a steady eye on me, assessing me. The eyes are supposed to be the window of the soul. His dark eyes suggested a kind soul that was one with the universe, but his words were inconsistent with his penetrating look. "Pumping the coolant was necessary even when *Scorpion* was not moving. That produced a "thermal scar" of low density warm water which ascended to the sea's surface." The scar, he said, "was her *Achilles* heel, a foot print observable by thermal imaging. Additionally, the pumps could be heard on SONAR. With the right technology, she was an easy target."

His incredible good looks and the self assured manner in which he spoke was distracting. It was difficult to think of him as a man of evil, a monster, and yet, he seemed to admit he and the others had intentionally set out to do evil using a poison so deadly that it can eat you alive from the inside out.

I had to ask. "Do you believe that using Polonium 210 to kill is the act of a monster?"

Laughing softly and shaking his head, he answered, "I do not normally engage in cruelty of any kind. Under other circumstances I would have no truck with those who do. I am not a monster. Just a man of my destiny. Listen to my story and then decide for yourself."

He continued describing the bureaucratic spider's web of government procurement practices that produced *Scorpion's* vulnerability. "Although her keel was laid at the boat yard in Groton, her vital organs were not produced there. They were the products of outsourcing to an ocean of suppliers which make a living responding to U.S. government requests for proposals (RFPs)."

As a bureaucrat, I knew all too well the pitfalls of government outsourcing and low bid acceptance, but did not interrupt to say so as he went on. "When the RFP went out to procure *Scorpion's* pumps, the contract was awarded to a pre-qualified manufacturer. It was a 'sweetheart contract'. Theoretically, such contracts are awarded when only one single supplier is capable of delivering the required goods or performing the service. In spite of this restriction, and in the snake pit of D.C. political back scratching, sweetheart contracts are widely used and abused by the powers that be to award hugely profitable deals to friends and associates."

His comments smarted but I knew he had that right.

Smirking, he said, "Down stream, of course, there is a healthy return on the investment for the bureaucratic benefactors."

This adulteration of the competitive bid process, he explained, was how Scorpion fell prey to hijackers. "The fortunate manufacturer who received the sweetheart award for supplying *Scorpion's* pumps only assembled and delivered the pumps it marketed. The parts needed to assemble the pumps were acquired from off-shore subcontractors who, in turn, acquired their inventories from lower level contractors even further down the line."

He shook his head in dismay. "Some of the lower level contractors were not even aware there are regulations governing the quality, control, and acquisition of parts for federal programs. Even more stunning, there are often no regulations in place to ensure that they know."

As Shariff continued the description of *Scorpion's* downfall, I was struck by the chilling reality that the stepladder of federal acquisition practices was actually exposing all U.S. subs to the same fate. *Our contracts and procurement policies are back doors through the Navy's security system, the very system meant to keep ship locations concealed, and the fleet safe. It never occurred to me because, to most bureaucrats, the contracts and procurement departments are like "add ons". You never know anyone there. It is just the office to which an endless river of forms flow and from which all supplies emerge – from file cabinets, computers, and printer paper to contract personnel and military equipment.*

In Scorpion's case, he said, "when her pumps were eventually delivered to the Groton boat yard, they contained defective valves that had been ingenuously engineered to fail at precisely 4:00 pm Greenwich mean time two days after she left port and submerged to run silent. At that hour, *Scorpion* passed directly under a secret satellite in geosynchronous space orbit, launched to track her kind.

When the pumps failed, the spreading radiation throughout her compartments forced her to surface. *Scorpion* was a sitting duck. She broke from the depths inside a ring of vessels carrying an army of black market pirates dressed in radiological control suits. Their weapons were aimed at the sub crew forced up onto the deck to escape exposure to the deadly waves emitting from the reactor."

At this point, I asked how his team had come to know this.

He replied, "We learned of the pirate ring through a fellow Russian physicist who told us about losing one of the Soviet's nuclear subs to that cartel. The cartel is made up of pros who strand such boats at sea using a sophisticated satellite and other technology built to disarm any military security system on the planet."

His earnestness was disarming and I felt my shield gradually lowering as he continued. "*Scorpion* was quickly commandeered and her failed pumps replaced. Fake transmissions were then sent out to NAVCOM, the first indicating that she was trying for the surface and a second one too garbled to translate, leaving the Navy to believe she had gone down. She had not. She was sold into a black market weapons system that can provide any high tech military equipment to a buyer with deep enough pockets."

Then, he gave me a meaningful look. "Like her hull, the whereabouts of her crew remains shrouded in a cloak of mystery, but there are rumors that the cartel also engages in human trafficking."

⚶

A servant entered the room and Shariff paused to speak with him in Arabic. It was time for mid-morning tea and cakes.

By nature, and always in command, he treated ordering food as though it was his responsibility. Without asking me, he ordered for both of us. On him, the act was manly, paternal in a sexy way.

When the servant was gone he continued disclosing how, in the fall of 1969, his team had acquired *Scorpion*. At this point, *a sly smile crossed his handsome face. He could see the question forming on my lips. "*Scorpion's* price? Quite high. It was paid with much of the enriched uranium and plutonium stolen from the nuclear research facility at I*nshas.*"

Against all better judgment, I found this amusing but checked myself when it occurred to me that he was attempting to recruit me and he had just said that, in addition to the Polonium 210 I was after, I now had to report proliferation of Egyptian radioactive materials. *If Scorpion had been paid for with 'much', but not all, of the stolen Inshas material, where was the rest of it? Was it stashed with the Polonium 210?*

Even though his story was gaining traction, I could not be drawn into this web of intrigue.

Sensing my reaction, he gestured with his hands. "We saw ourselves as the good guys. Our actions would have a three-fold effect. By stealing and moving Egypt's radioactive materials, we prevented the breakout of a nuclear dogfight in the Middle East.

Because of information that came to us after we moved the material from *Inshas* , we acquired *Scorpion* and planned to use her uranium fuel to produce Polonium 210. The polonium was needed to go after escaped Nazi war criminals, righting a small part of the terrible wrong the Nazis committed against humanity.

We produced the polonium, of course, by using Scorpion's uranium fuel supply to irradiate bismuth and create the poison. We could have acquired it from Russian or U.S. sources we knew about, but those were easily traceable."

His voice grew saddened. "We were also avenging a woman named Rosslyn Ford."

To me, that reasoning did not exactly compute. I asked, "If you were intent on doing good, why would you provide black marketers with enriched uranium and plutonium? They would obviously sell it to a rogue nation, or terrorists. That material will be lethal and must be safely stored and kept out of the environment. The form of plutonium produced by burning uranium in nuclear reactors will be a deadly threat to humans for over 200,000 years. Sooner or later, if not controlled, the nature of nature will have its way."

He watched me closely as I went on. "You must also know that, in producing Polonium 210, you have admittedly produced a poison that can become a chemical weapon on steroids, a poison so powerful that only a minute amount can kill millions. It is my job to persuade you to hand the poison over to me so I can ensure that it is dispositioned to a secure environment. I also need to report the whereabouts of all the stuff you took from Inshas."

I also wondered, but did not ask, *Who was Rosslyn Ford and what happened to her. What did she have to do with Nazis?*

When I had finished, he continued his story, obviously aware of the dilemma caused by his 'sale' of uranium and plutonium, as well as his possession of polonium. However, it was also clear that being aware of the dilemma had not given him reason to change course. "The dealers we bought *Scorpion* from were dancing with the devil inside her. They could not sell the sub without including her uranium fuel. To remove and sell her fuel separately required containerizing it, a very complicated, time consuming, and expensive process, not to mention deadly. We played that card in negotiating the price. In Nubia, we had highly valuable radioactive material already oxidized, containerized, and ready for transit. We offered to swap some of it for *Scorpion* and her onboard uranium fuel. They took the deal."

While I stared at him in disbelief, his smile turned into raffish laughter. "We did not tell them, and since they were not nuclear scientists they did not know, that the *Inshas* material was too hot to containerize and move to Nubia without being down blended. Prior to packing and transporting it, we mixed it with pure low-level uranium ore to reduce its energetic power. It is now useless as weapons-grade material until it is enriched again by reversing the dilution process. The cost and complication of doing that takes it out of the realm of the terrorist trade."

Laughing loudly he said, "When they find out, and if they find us, there will be hell to pay."

I could tell that he was not really worried. He was not a man easily threatened.

Nor had he worried that there would be an Egyptian target on his team's back. Amused, he reminded me that even though their actions were technically illegal, Egypt could not afford to file a report on the incident to the UN's IAEA. Having ordered the production of illegally enriched uranium to produce enough plutonium for construction of a nuclear weapon, Shariff said, "Egypt quietly closed *Inshas* when it was discovered that the illegal material, along with the facility's nuclear scientists, had gone missing. Of course, without international immunity through the UN, our team still could be locked away and forgotten as international terrorists, or for transgressions against an arm of the American military, or for both."

It was obvious by any logical stretch of the imagination that he and his team should be locked away. His cavalier assurance was not a game changer. I was a medical anthropologist and forensic specialist, responsible for preventing public exposure to toxic materials, especially nuclear material. Downblended or not, any uranium and plutonium is a health hazard if not secured in a tightly controlled environment. Trading it to pirates on the high seas did not qualify as a tightly controlled environment.

However, I had no idea how we could get the stuff back. I had no reason not to believe that he had sufficiently diluted it. By now, it was probably widely distributed among the array of terrorist cells who entertain murderous ideas about blowing up the world. *Ideas that we will apparently have to be on guard against forever. I can only concentrate on finding and containing the Polonium 210. And where is it, with the rest of the stolen Inshas material?*

∽

The tea and cakes arrived and Shariff paused again. The waiter asked, "*Hena?*", pointing to the carved tea table between our chairs.

Shariff nodded and politely thanked him. "*Shukran*"."

Setting the tray on the table, the man quickly left the room after citing the traditional Arab valediction, "*Ma' a salama*".

Apparently, pouring tea is Egyptian women's turf and he waited for me to do the honors. As a liberated western woman, it made little difference to me who poured. As I served, his wonderful dark eyes followed my movements.

He was definitely checking me out.

When our glasses were full and we were nibbling on *Lukeumades* (Greek donuts), Shariff returned to the story of *Scorpion's* acquisition. There was no further mention of Rosslyn Ford.

His team had given *Scorpion* a new name. They called her *Dragon*.

The irony of the novel name amused me. It reflected the ever-present duality in the world, no doubt deliberate on the team's part. While Western mythology holds that dragons are evil fire-breathing monsters, Eastern cosmology holds that the dragon symbolizes beneficence, good. Seemingly, the two are mutually exclusive.

He reminded me that ancient Egyptian dogma explained this duality, and its resolution, through their lore about the two-headed snake, *Nehebkau*. "The snake could strike in both directions at once, creating evil and world chaos, or creating good. To maintain a balance between the two, *Nehebkau* was controlled by the sun god, *Atun*, who kept his fingers on both of its heads."

Not too subtly, he was implying through that ancient lore explained and justified his team's actions.

Remembering American literature's contribution to the dichotomy, I brought up the 1851 book authored by Melville, which explored the phenomenon in a story about a whale named *Moby Dick*. "The whale saw the world's duality through his widely spaced eyes on opposite sides on his giant head. Literary dogma holds that Moby Dick's legend teaches us good has an evil side and evil has a good side, bound together in eternal struggle. But, I wondered how the leviathan would have seen your production of Polonium 210 and the trade you made with the pirates who hijacked Scorpion.?"

It was at this point that he explained the morally questionable reason for his team's actions. "I think I can sway you over to my side when you hear all the facts, why we became 'international terrorists.'"

I waited for him to continue. He stopped to take a drink of his tea and the last bite of his *lukeumade*. "It is a long and complicated saga. Naturally, our quest involved what we did best, processing radioactive material. In addition to *Dragon's* blood, her enriched uranium fuel and submersion capability were also critical. It allowed us to convert her into a hidden processing lab. After months of training to man the sub, we took her to the bottom of a lagoon, *Shaab Ambar*, in an isolated archipelago of the Red Sea. We made the necessary conversions, burned her uranium fuel, produced Bismuth, and extracted several grams of Polonium 210. That's the simplified version, of course. We needed the polonium for our plan to exterminate certain men who had committed evil deeds."

My expression of suspicion did not go unnoticed, but he resumed. "The archipelago was off the coast of Sudan, and near the Nubian desert location where we had stashed the stolen *Inshas* material. The Red Sea is known for its strong winds, unpredictable local currents, high temperatures, and warm 80-degree water. However, in the bottom of the sheltered lagoon at *Shaab Ambar*, our team lived in another environment. *Dragon* lay quietly out of reach of these elements so our work went smoothly and was quickly completed."

I wondered how long they had been able to stay down. He answered my question before I could ask.

"One month after setting her down on the bottom of the lagoon we were ready for the final stage of our mission. And, we were definitely ready to see blue skies again, even though it meant facing the vagaries above the womb which had sheltered us while we cooked our deadly brew."

He went on. "Since nuclear subs are sent out on missions to run silent and deep for six months or more, they leave port crammed with supplies. The passageway to the galley tapers to a narrow aisle of boxes containing enough food to sustain a crew of 100 or more."

He laughed. "The deal we negotiated for acquiring the sub included all the provisions we would need until the end of our mission when the larder would be empty. Our team enjoyed an abundance of the best chow available, excellent cuts of meat, smoked foul and fish, high quality dehydrated vegetables and fruits, a garden of veritable delights for desserts, and an enormous supply of 100% Columbian *Supremo* coffee."

He stood and I watched him walk to the eastern wall of windows looking out over the canal. "We surfaced one night to begin the final leg of our mission. Four of us would go ashore to hunt our first victim. The other three would take *Dragon* back to the bottom and wait for our return. We planned to repeat this action until all our intended victims had been dispatched. Then, when our mission was complete, we intended to offload our gear and send her to the bottom of a deep canyon further out in the sea.

Her final resting spot was carefully chosen. She was to be scuttled in the central portion of the Red Sea where a 1949 deep-water survey off Sudan indicated the presence of hot saline brines and metalliferous muds. The hot solutions (140 degrees Fahrenheit) emanate from active subsea floor fission. On occasion, volcanic explosions occur there. The deepest part of the area where *Dragon* was to be scuttled is some 7,000 feet, in the Red Sea Rift. The rift is a continuation of the Great Rift Valley running north along Africa's eastern shore. Combined with the depth, heat and mud at the bottom, the rift is the perfect environment for ensuring that a hijacked sub will remain undetected and her reactor unretrieved."

He crossed the room and resumed his seat across the tea table from my chair. "As it turned out, we did not scuttle *Dragon*. I have returned her. My team is now scattered across the sands of Egypt. I have surrendered to Major General Lloyd and offered crucial information to the UN regarding *Dragon's* fateful journey. My cooperation was contingent on the condition that we receive total immunity for the numerous national and international transgressions of which we stand guilty."

I asked why the immunity was given.

His look turned very serious before responding. "Part of the information I am offering concerns the remains that were scooped from the Red Sea, which is what brought you to the room where you now sit in Port Said. I am aware that your government cannot disposition those remains until it has more data on the origin of the Polonium 210 that was the poisoning agent."

I added, "...and the whereabouts of any remaining Polonium still at large from your vendetta."

He smiled, and nodded. "However, I have a lot more information to trade, crucial information on matters of international security."

As it turned out, because of what this man knew, he could pretty much get anything he wanted from any nation on earth.

Drinking the last of his tea and then, setting the glass back on the tray he said, "We found out what became of the Polaris missiles that were onboard Scorpion when she was hijacked, and how they are going to be used. Having that information puts us at great risk. Now, we need protection, and the world needs us alive.

4

The Path Forward.

Malevolent hunting and brutal killing may avenge evil.

I was stunned. If what he said was true, it was a miracle he and his team were still alive. I asked, "Where are they?"

He looked at me for a moment, as if deciding how much to tell me. Apparently, he decided on the long version.

"You need to know the whole story. It's lengthy, and convoluted, writ long, but it should answer all your questions."

The thought crossed my mind, *He would not be taking so much time to explain all this if he was not trying to recruit me.*

He settled back into the deep leather chair, stretched out his long legs, and crossed his ankles. He looked as comfortable as a man can get, a man clearly at home in his own skin. And, he was about to tell a tale that, if it had been fiction, would have been a Pulitzer Prize novel.

"When we acquired *Scorpion* we had in our possession a list of the Nazis we sought, as well as their locations. Let me begin by telling you how they became our prey."

His relaxed posture, his dark good looks, the way his white linen shirt and pants hung on his lean frame was distracting. He was the most alluring man I had ever sat across from. I had to keep reminding myself why I was sitting across from him, to remain totally objective, and to keep my shield raised against his sensuality.

"Our Nazi prey were living as escaped war criminals do, in the shadows, with false identities and reinvented histories. We intended to teach them that escape from the long arm of international law had put them in much greater jeopardy than facing their accusers in a war crimes tribunal. Once they were captured, in revenge for the millions of Nazi death camp victims, we intended to deal them an agonizing demise with the Polonium 210 we extracted from *Dragon's* blood. After, all, the Nazis were all serial killers. Executing them should be sanctioned."

His voice dropped, saddened, and he paused for a moment. "We also sought revenge for Rosslyn Ford."

Then a sly smile crossed his lips. He began to tell how they administered the toxin. "Following extraction of the deadly isotope, we suspended it in small glass capsules of water. For good measure, the capsules were protected by overpacks lined with lead, although that was overkill. As you know, unless inhaled, ingested, or absorbed, Polonium 210 can be safely handled. Our intention was to pollute bottles of *Altbier*, Dusseldorf's famous lager, as we needed it. Being mildly bitter, any adulteration of its original taste is masked. Mixed with the Polonium 210, our beer's level of radiation is so toxic it will melt any victim's internal organs and dissolve their bones within a few days. Their last breaths will be a welcome gift from the agony."

Hearing this, I realized the cause of death was as I had reported, ingestion of the stealth toxin. I now knew how and why they had used *Scorpion's* uranium fuel. I was left to wonder a lot more. *Who was Roslyn Ford, and what role had she played in this turbulent tale. How much more Polonium 210 exists, where is it, and where is the remaining Inshas plutonium and uranium?*

I could not help staring in amazement. Sitting just across the tea table from me sat the perfect example of how, given the right cause, civilized men can be drawn to the dark side, become malevolent hunters and brutal killers. I voiced my reservations aloud. "While committing evil, men can become heroes in their own view and rationalize their actions. It happens to men in war. It happened to the brilliant scientists who worked on America's Manhattan Project to build the atomic bomb. They set out to do good for a cause, strayed from the path of scientific neutrality, and committed evil on an unprecedented scale by giving the secret of atom splitting to a government and its military. Man is so arrogant that we never quite get the nature of nature. Aren't you also rationalizing your actions?"

Shariff nodded in agreement. "What we did was on a much smaller scale, although I recognize my defense as a rationalization. The Manhattan Project scientists who set out to save the free world ended up inventing nuclear science's version of the two-headed snake. Good men who probably did not intend to commit evil, but they stand guilty. Their work unleashed a force so powerful that one stupid rationalizing man can now throw the world into nuclear chaos."

I could not resist thinking aloud. "Could you be such a man?"

He nodded again. "You know by now that I probably could. We tossed aside our moral compasses when we set out to kill with the Polonium 210. Men can always rationalize violence. It's their genetic nature to hunt and kill. So, there is the likely prospect that I would slip far enough into the dark side of my genetics to do that. Throughout history, many have, and still do."

∽

Hearing him admit such a large measure of truth about himself somehow made him less of a candidate for being a monster. A part of him was evil personified if he could do what he admitted he had done, and what he still might do. Yet, the acknowledgement about his reality was disarming. Not all men are so brutally honest about their darker natures. There was also the issue of what had driven his actions. It was tempting to accept his justification, even though they were against all the religious and legal tenets of my world.

After a pause, he turned away from the darker aspects of his nature and metamorphosed into a gentle romantic; describing how he met Rosslyn Ford and what she meant to him. It happened while he was completing his Ph.D. at Oxford. She was working on campus in the Egyptian antiquities department of the Ashmolean Museum.

His life was changed forever, he said, when he caught sight of her tall slender body and thick golden hair through one of the glass display cases. It housed a powerful Nubian rewrap bow that he was studying. The artifact's belly was lined in horn, and its formidable strength had made Nubian archers famed and feared throughout the ancient world.

She was intently surveying the thumb rings next to it. The archers wore them to avoid injuring the tendons in their fingers as they drew the powerful bow's string.

Always a hard charger, Shariff had stepped around the case to see the real woman and instantly knew that he had to have her as his own. And he did. "For the next seven years Rosslyn was my candle of light which men seek in the darkness."

So, I thought, *He loved her, still does. But, what happened to her, and what did she have to do with the Nazis?*

His voice became quiet as he recalled memories of her. "It was a passionate affair of romantic escapades and love making. After Oxford, I worked in Rome. We often met in the capitals of Europe, surveying the museums and cathedrals. She always made me laugh with her observations about art. She told me that early religious art was the beginning of the horror movie industry. When she showed me a color plate of Van Eyck's *The Last Judgment*, I was convinced."

"Our favorite meeting places were in the lavish Egyptian hotels of Cairo, Luxor, and Aswan. In those days, members of Europe's elite, who were not spending the cooler months on the Riviera, 'wintered on the Nile'. It was the era of grand hotels, and the grandest of them all was Cairo's infamous Shepheard's."

Recollecting the times, he smiled wanly. "We liked to sit with other guests on the hotel's terrace overlooking *Kamal Pasha Street.* Two meters below the terrace, an amazing and seemingly endless circus passed by. In the circus were traders, snake charmers, funeral processions, overdressed tourists, every imaginable form of transport, and all manner of other interesting sights."

"We sipped Pimms and Shendi while unabashedly watching the passersby from handsome oversized rattan chairs. The chairs were arranged around tables laden with gourmet delights. My favorite was Scotch Eggs. Rosslyn's was Montrachet goat cheese on little rounds of Russian black bread.

The entertainers on the street stared back at us with equal interest. It was theatre-in-the-round, captured hundreds of times in pigment, ink, and film by famous painters, celebrated authors, and popular travel writers."

"The hotel guests, of course, included the who's who of the world; kings, princes, renowned stars of stage, screen and the literati. From time to time there were also generals who were heading up the latest invasion of North Africa."

Shariff's forehead wrinkled slightly as he began to describe one such famous guest. He asked, "Have you heard of Chinese Gordon? Apparently, he was one cocky son of a bitch. Before the Suez Canal was built, Shepheard's was on the Overland Route to and from Bombay. Passing through, General Charles 'Chinese' Gordon stopped over for a few days of leisure. Then, he continued on his way up the Nile to reclaim Khartoum from the *el Mahdi's* army. He ended up decapitated by the *el Mahdi's jihadists,* who hung his head from a tree in front of the British headquarters building. Beheading was the barbaric Arab national past time, strictly frowned on by indignant Europeans."

Then he scoffed. "Europe had practiced decapitation with abandonment through all manner of political and religious wars but likes to dismiss that chapter in its history. Now it takes the high road on the gruesome issue. It's funny how nations are built by aggrandizing onto other's lands, enslaving and slaughtering the indigenous, and then adopting a high moral profile after settling in."

He smiled again, recalling Rosslyn's love of the hotel's opulent interior, which had entrances and halls, designed to emulate every famous monument on the planet. "There was the Karnak Temple room, a Moorish Hall, and even one lounge fashioned after a *Faberge* egg. Floors were covered with plush Persian rugs, and Tiffany stained glass crowned the tall windows. The passageways were wide enough to turn a four-horse coach."

Rakishly laughing, he described the famed Long Bar, "For chaps only. It was never opened to the fair sex except on New Year's Eve. Rumor had it that the 'Suffering Bastard' was invented in that hallowed bastion of bombastic claims and elevated testosterone."

"Another of our favorite past times," he said, "was sitting in the establishment's reception area. Staking out a seat in that area provided its own theatre. Over the decades, Shepheard's was refurbished, rebuilt, and enlarged to 500 bedrooms. The numbering system became so mystical that, without a guide, most of the new arrivals had no prayer of finding their quarters. Lost souls repeatedly circled back to the reception desk seeking directions, and their luggage. Rosslyn and I would make bets with other registered guests on how many times new arrivals would return to the lobby."

"Other grand hotels of the era provided equally entertaining past times." He described their picnics atop the Giza pyramids while staying at the famed Mena House. "We also liked to dine in the Mena House garden café because it included an *al fresco* dance floor. While dancing is not one of my favorites, I would do anything that allowed me to touch her, hold her body close to mine."

His smile faded as he told me that after his work at *Inshas* began, it increasingly tied him to the Egyptian delta. Rosslyn's work became an endless and wider search for indigenous antiquities needing restoration and storage in the controlled environments of the world's great museums. "Eventually, life got in the way. We drifted apart, and our worlds gradually rotated out of each other's orbits."

Even so, he said he never stopped loving her and always knew that someday they would be together again. He often drifted off to sleep thinking of her, longing to hold her. Leaning forward in his chair, he shook his head as the illusion of pain and lost love saddened his face. "Speaking about her is difficult."

At that point, Shariff suggested we take a break. A walk along the port pier seemed in order. He had something to show me.

I was more than ready.

We left the Canal Authority complex and began to stroll past the huge container ships, supertankers, and tall handsome luxury liners gliding along through the water. The air, almost always blowing from the north, was fresh and smelled of the sea.

Suddenly I saw her, tied up in a berth just off the canal's shipping lane. It was *Scorpion,* now Shariff's *Dragon.* She was being returned to the U.S. Navy in exchange for full pardon and immunity from any illegal action born out of having "borrowed" her. I was stunned by her size, and her magnificent presence. As a symbol of awesome power against the free world's enemies, she brought tears to my eyes.

He laughed and took my hand. It seemed to be a familial gesture, but it sent a warm wave through me. "We have enjoyed our time with her. She is majestic. Fast, stealthy, and powerful beyond belief. Only one of her kind could wreak more havoc than you can imagine. Of course, she no longer carries her nuclear arsenal since it was gone before we acquired her. But, because I now have the misfortune of knowing where that arsenal is, I have brought her back."

Continuing, he said, "The U.S. Navy is on its way to reclaim her and, naturally, they do not recognize any claim I have. Last night was my final night aboard. She will be gone by morning, put back to sea, and the Pentagon will pretend this never happened.

Although, they do want to sit down with me and unofficially talk about how it did. I thought you might enjoy seeing her here in Egypt, while she is still mine."

I was overwhelmed and could only say, "This has been quite a walk. Thank you."

My reward was a hearty masculine laugh, showing perfect white teeth. Then, he tucked my arm under his and began guiding me along her length, explaining at various points the structure and function of each section, both inside and out. It was clear he had deep feelings for her. The Navy might take her away, take back her name, and send her again to secretly and silently roam the seas, but Shariff would always know where *Dragon* was. She held a place in his heart.

5

The Vineyard in the Negev

*The cold black ink of Third Reich arrest
records and Rosslyn's fate.*

Tucking my arm in his, next to his body, sent a strong warm
surge through me, intense sexual chemistry, and a warning.
I pulled away. Pretending to look back along the pier, I said, "We
need to return to the compound so I can finish my report. The
U.S. government is waiting on an explanation of how that sheet of
disintegrating grey flesh, retrieved from the Red Sea and now in
cold storage at Reardon, came to be loaded with Polonium 210."

I thought, *Knowing the polonium was sourced from Scorpion
also gives rise to another critical issue. She was supposed to have
gone down in the Atlantic. How could the Navy have missed her
hijacking? Was the rest of the fleet at risk?*

Returning to the lounge off the UN dining hall, we sat in the
deep leather chairs while he resumed telling me about the events
leading up to the acquisition of *Scorpion*, his *Dragon*. However, his
demeanor was different now. He had enjoyed telling how *Scorpion*
had been hijacked, and proudly showing her to me. But the rest
of his story grew more personal, and hurtful. He was not a man
to show emotion, but his eyes revealed the impact of the sojourn
that brought him to the berth where *Dragon* now sat tied up in
Port Said.

It began when Egypt mobilized along Israel's border in the Sinai Peninsula in early June of 1967. Nasser thought he had an ace up his sleeve. Somehow, he had convinced Syria and Jordan to enter the fray at the beginning of the misbegotten scheme and, to their detriment, they attacked Israel on June 5.

Shariff scoffed. "It really turned out to be an embarrassing marked down war. Israel plowed through the Egyptian military like it was a goat rodeo. By June 8, Israel had conducted pre-emptive airstrikes that destroyed two-thirds of Syria's air force and pulverized Egypt's airfields, almost destroying its poorly organized defensive infrastructure. At the same time, the Israelis invaded the Gaza Strip and by June 10 their army had taken the Golan Heights, the West Bank, reached the Suez Canal, and rolled down the entire length of the Sinai Peninsula to capture *Sharm el Sheikh*, Egypt's beautiful resort city and my home town on the southern coast. It took Israel only six days to walk up and knock on Nasser's door."

He shook his head, acknowledging the embarrassment. Meanwhile, realizing that no one could win if nuclear weaponry came into play, he said " Our *Inshas* team determined to try and prevent Egypt from upping the game."

"We knew full well that Israel, assisted by France, had secretly built nuclear weapons at their Nuclear Research Center in the Negev desert. Nuclear scientists talk across political boundaries. We called the Israeli nukes 'their bombs in the basement'. We also knew that the Israelis were prepared to strike back in kind should any of their neighbors be so foolish as to launch weapons carrying nuclear payloads."

Leaning back in the leather chair, he sighed and said, "At *Inshas*, we were caught on the horns of the dilemma. The 'peaceful atom' had turned the Middle East into a potential nuclear cataclysm. We had to take responsibility for the atom splitting we had performed at *Inshas*, so we moved the highly-enriched uranium and weapons-grade plutonium."

Nodding at the attaché case on the floor beside my chair, he said, "As my CIA dossier indicates, if attacked, Egypt planned to retaliate in spades."

Surprise showed on my face. *How had he known that I had his dossier?*

Watching me with now dark, unfathomable eyes, he smiled. "You thought I did not know? Little that the CIA does around me goes unknown, at least not here in the Middle East. This is a world of village intrigue. There are no well kept secrets."

Besides, I am watched over by an organization far more powerful than America's CIA."

Again, I was stunned. *What organization could he be referring to?* I had to ask. "Shariff, what are you talking about?"

He thought for a minute, grew pensive, and began to describe an extensive network of protectors and power brokers at work in the world. "This may take a large leap of faith on your part but you need to believe me. It is a different history of mankind than the one you are familiar with. Scientists have documented the emergence of mankind's progenitors from a primordial soup of vertebrate stew. Books abound with descriptions of the marvelous and magical civilizations that gradually emerged due to man's destined superiority over all the other animals. But, what has not been documented is the interruption of the moral balance and social harmony that was meant to obtain as a constant of the world. Over time, the resulting imbalance and disharmony gave rise to evil conglomerates driven by misguided ambitions of greed, and avarice.

I stopped him. "Are you talking about a version of good versus evil?"

He nodded. "Yes. But, this is the actual version. There are constant battles waged across the planet with forces of good pushing back against dark forces in order to maintain balance and harmony. In the abstract, these opposing forces are referred to as good versus evil, but there is nothing abstract about them. Evil is an omnipresent reality, always seeking opportunities to create chaos.

It has morphed into a power, roughly formed by conglomerates of morally bankrupt organizations; giant corporations, military establishments, and politicians wielding authority at the highest levels. Combined, they seek to control the planet for self-aggrandizing purposes. These dark forces are collectively known as the *Tripartite*.

Those of us who soldier on the side of good, the *Guardians*, always win when combatting the *Tripartite* because our own conglomerate is omnipresent, beneficent and inherently stronger. Even though the battles are sometimes hard fought, and the prices are high because evil can be so prodigious, the end is inevitable. Good wills out."

I said, "Shariff, what you are saying sounds more like an adult fairy tale that an actual record of human history. But, go on."

He continued. "Over time, the *Guardians* became the keeper of formidable knowledge about universal laws governing the structure and function of planetary energy and matter. Our organization tenders the body of knowledge that has evolved to underlay mankind's great civilizations and inventions. Members of the *Guardians* have given the world benevolent science, chemistry, physics, physiology, literature, and peace.

From time to time, *Tripartite* forces have stolen from the great body of knowledge to create chaos. But, the *Guardians* are always vigilant and recover from the assaults.

He stopped speaking for a moment and regarded me. "Cecily, we are all constantly impacted by actions of the *Guardians*, on many levels."

I sat looking back at him, trying to absorb his explanation of how balance is maintained on our planet. There was no doubting his sincerity but it was difficult to settle for the simple explanation that some force of good is continuously creating order out of chaos caused by an entity called the *Tripartite*. I had always opted for a form of apathetic denial that assumed chaos just eventually wore out and dissipated. Most of us do.

I nodded for him to continue and he resumed describing the events leading up to his acquisition of Scorpion.

"As I've told you, we moved the *Inshas* uranium and plutonium for the salvation of the Middle East. My dossier should also say we later risked our lives by crossing Israel's southern border to secretly meet with our counterparts at their nuclear center in the Negev. We sought the cooperation of the Negev scientists to take the same preventative measure we had taken."

Then, he laughed. "Actually, traveling through the Negev was not much of a risk for us. After all, we Egyptians are at home in sand. We have dwelled in the Sahara for thousands of years. However, it was risky business telling the Israeli scientists that Egypt did not presently have access to its own weapons-grade nuclear materials. On that point, we were shooting craps with the devil. Fortunately, the Negev scientists proved to be honorable men and were easily convinced to join our conspiracy and containment plan."

The dossier did not say that. He had my full attention, but as a career bureaucrat working for the U.S. government, I was disturbed by the way Shariff and his team had played fast and loose with his state's nuclear material. No doubt, they had seriously transgressed against Egyptian state policies. Certainly, they had trampled on international prohibitions surrounding nuclear material.

He continued. "We hoped that our mutual actions would limit the war to the traditional bunker busters. We were willing to risk our lives to prevent the use of nuclear nation busters which have come into vogue, far more powerful than the atom splitting bombs dropped on Hiroshima and Nagasaki."

I remembered that on June 11, a cease-fire was finally signed to end the Egyptian/Israeli six-day war. By then, 20,000 Arab forces were dead. Less than 1,000 Israelis had been lost, and the world was left to try and comprehend Nasser's zany decision to poke the Zionist bear. Not only had Egypt lost the war at a tragic price, it turned the entire region into a powder keg.

Listening to him, it was growing harder to assign guilt for his team's actions. At least, for stealing Egypt's radioactive material. I had to acknowledge that what they did would be considered heroic in many quarters.

However, for them, the theft turned out to be a double-edged sword. They were left with a huge inventory of weapons-grade nuclear material that was not only stolen from the Egyptian government but also accountable to the UN's IAEA. There was also the danger they faced if caught by the mercenaries they had paid with useless radioactive material.

I quickly reminded myself that, technically, stealing the weapons-grade material from Egypt's lab to prohibit nuclear warfare in the Middle East, using it to pay for a black market hijacked U.S. Navy nuclear sub, and employing the sub's high-level uranium in an international extermination plot, even if against escaped Nazi war criminals, made them international terrorists.

Yet, his attempt to sway me to his side was increasingly compelling, and I was beginning to understand that behind the screen of his smooth dark good looks, there was a lot to admire in this man. A lot.

Still, he disturbed me on several levels. His perspective of the many transgressions that he and his team had committed blurred the lines of what I had always held to be irrefutable truths. Good is exclusive of evil. Government policies are not to be broken without proper authorization. The sixth commandment is sacrosanct; thou shalt not kill.

And yet, I realized, everyone has blood on their hands when it comes to World War II. Germany started it by aggrandizing against its neighbors, then engaging in bestial genocide against the Jews and other ethnics. Italy and France joined Hitler's ranks and began shipping their Jews to *Third Reich* killing centers. Japan conducted a surprise attack on America's fleet anchored in Pearl Harbor, then brutally slaughtered its way across island after island in the Pacific. America built a weapon capable of such carnage that it will forever stand alone for the death and destruction it caused in the Land of the Rising Sun. While the intent of using it was to end the war, dismissing the option of demonstrating its power, rather than incinerating two Japanese civilian cities, gave the term 'dangerous' new meaning.

⋙

Shariff stood and again walked to the window. For a few minutes it seemed as though he might not continue his story. Then he collected himself, returned to his chair, and began. "It was during the covert meeting in the Negev desert that my team and I learned where the Nazis who had escaped trial for their war crimes were now hiding, scattered across the globe. By then, I also knew where Rosslyn had been all those years."

The pain of telling what he had learned showed on his face and he stopped again to check his emotions. Calling for the attendant, he ordered two Shendis. The cool English beer, topped with lemon soda, was welcome relief.

We switched to idle chitchat while we enjoyed our drinks. Then, he tried to continue talking about Rosslyn but could not hide the anguish it brought. His male pride sought a way out. Instead, he suggested that we go in search of lunch in Port Said. I was relieved. Watching a strong man in emotional agony was gut wrenching.

⋙

Port Said is a cosmopolitan city. It is perched on the western bank of the Suez Canal where waters slip between the Mediterranean Sea and the Indian Ocean. The city's allure is infectious. Rudyard Kipling said of it, "If you truly wish to find someone you have known and who travels, there are two points on the globe you have but to sit and wait, sooner or later your man will come there: the docks of London and Port Said."

We headed for the *Corniche*, a glorious 8 km walkway of

wharfs, piers, and boardwalks along the harbor. It was dotted with restaurants, markets, and historic sights. Our first stop was a bookstall where I turned up an early publication describing battles fought in the area by ancient Egyptian armies led by mighty pharaohs. In it were marvelous sketches of war chariots and 25th dynasty Nubian Kings charging into battle with their war lions running beside them, while the famous and feared Nubian archers threw up curtains of iron tipped arrows from behind.

Shariff was delighted with the sketches because they showed the same powerful re-wrap bow that he had been admiring on the day he first saw Rosslyn. I bought the book and gave it to him.

Walking along, we came to an outdoor restaurant that smelled like seafood heaven. We took a table and stuffed ourselves with Nile perch that had been lightly slipped in an egg and flour batter and then quickly fried in peanut oil. The usual fresh baked *esh* (flat bread) was served, along with steaming bowls of *ful mudammas* (mashed and spiced Egyptian beans). For our drink, Shariff ordered Greek Plomari *ouzo* from *Lesvos*, usually imbibed slowly over several hours of leisure socializing. He certainly knew how to take a gal out to lunch.

By the time we finished our meal it was two o'clock, when the entire country shuts down for Egyptian P.T. My head was swimming from the combination of heat and *ouzo* so I was happy to return to the Canal Authority compound.

Stopping at the desk in the guest rooms' wing, I asked for my key. While the clerk turned to pull it from the board behind the desk, Shariff leaned over and said softly in my ear, "I hope they have another room now that I have lost my bunk on *Dragon*." He gave me a long meaningful look and brushed my cheek with his lips. Men seek refuge from their troubles in that way.

A shock wave ran through me at his touch. It was tempting but I thought, *No way, Dr. Shariff. If I cave in to this temptation, the wheels will come off my wagon. He is definitely not in my job description and definitely not worth my career.*

I left him at the desk after we agreed to meet back in the lounge at six that evening.

∽

Arriving in the lounge promptly at six, I found him already there. Pausing in the doorway for a moment, I studied his profile through the branches of the potted palm tree next to his chair. His linen shirt and pants looked fresh. No doubt he had showered since I left him. I pushed that vision out of my mind.

Still playing the role as my host, the *taameya* breads and tea he had ordered for us were sitting on the carved tea table. As I approached, he rose and I asked if there had been a room for him.

Predictably, there had been, probably a suite judging from his treatment by the staff and the deference paid to him throughout the compound. Our luncheon break seemed to have fortified him and while we ate the delicious little fried sesame cakes and washed them down with tea he continued the story where he had earlier left off.

The horrible reality of what the victims suffered who were caught up in the Nazi's Holocaust had been presented to him at an estate owned by a wealthy Israeli; Amnon Schroeder. Schroeder lived near the Negev nuclear center. While Shariff's team met with their Israeli counterparts at the center, he had invited the Egyptians to take their meals and sleep at his nearby and magnificent chateau in the midst of his vast vineyard, the largest in the Negev.

"At first, he was pretty reserved toward us," Shariff said, "But he did join us for drinks and dinner each evening when we returned from the center. In the twilight of the third evening, while we drank wine at a heavy wooden table in the midst of his vines, he began to loosen up."

Shariff smiled. "The wine we were drinking was delicious, made from his Chardonnay grapes. He told us Chardonnay grapes originated in Jerusalem and drew their name from the Hebrew

SHEETS OF SKIN FOR LEBENSRAUM

phrase, *Sha'ar Adonai* ('Gate of God')."

I was puzzled. "How did the name of the grape get changed?"

Clearly, the Egyptian had been impressed by their Israeli host and as he answered, he waved his hands as though dismissing any argument on the subject. "Supposedly, the grapes were taken to France by the Crusaders and the name became bastardized as Chardonnay."

He was also reflective as he described the man. "Schroeder was tall and lank, approximately my size and age, in our early sixties." Shariff ran his fingers through his thick black hair, his brow creased, and he shook his head slightly. "Unlike mine, his hair had gone completely grey. He had seen too much of the dark side of life."

Pausing to take a sip of his tea, Shariff put his glass back on the table before leaning back in his chair. "Although viticulture was the source of Schroeder's immense wealth, it turned out, that was not the most interesting thing about him. He was a former Israeli *Mossad* operative. After the tumultuous events of his life, he had evidently sought sanctuary as a passionate wine producer with a reverence for the Land of Zion's ancient plants. To him, watching his vines grow and bear fruit each year there in the harsh desert, was symbolic of his people's survival. He named his vineyard *Yeshua*, the Hebrew word for salvation.

Joking, he told us that the fermented and intoxicating fruit of the Israelites had apparently played an important role in the *Pax Romana*. Ancient Rome imported huge stocks of it, transported in clay *amphorae* that were the common containers for the time.

Then, Schroeder's handsome face darkened and his smile disappeared. He reminded us that during World War II, Italy broke ranks with its past and shipped its Jews off to Nazi death camps."

∽

Reaching out and picking up the plate of *taameya*, Shariff offered me the last one. When I declined, he popped the little bread into his mouth. While chewing it, he looked into my eyes and then let his own run down until they stopped on my breasts. I blushed. He was unabashed. Then he continued, "Wine talk in the vineyard was always followed by a late dinner. On the third night, the discussion turned to events in his shrouded past, and Nazis. Having become one of Israel's most renowned Nazi hunters, Schroeder's knowledge of their concentration camps was extensive.

He had also been trained to easily dispatch his prey, enemies of Israel who could not be brought to trial because they were ostensibly hidden deep inside anti-Semitic communities around the globe. But the *Mossad* had ways of finding them and, while his good looks had turned many a woman's head, he could just as easily break a man's neck. He had. Many times.

While he talked, I came to understand that the carefully trellised vineyard was his way of putting those dark chapters of his life in the past. He tries to keep the reality of his proclivity for violence, and the horrifying Nazi sins, buried in his memory banks."

Taking a last sip of his tea to wash down the *taameya*, Shariff placed his empty glass on the table between us before continuing to speak. His voice grew edgy. "Schroeder said the stories behind the cold black ink on *Third Reich* arrest records could only be understood against the backdrop of Germany's racial philosophy, its genetic hygiene programs, and the death camps in its history. Asking our indulgence, the former *sayanim* ("helper") began carefully explaining what the chronicles revealed about the genetic insanity and path to the murderous plan for annihilating millions of victims in 20th century Nazi extermination centers."

6

Assembly Line of Death

*The Nazi death camp was invented
on Africa's Skeleton Coast.*

Although it was now past seven in the evening in Port Said, the temperature outside was still oppressive, leaving the building's inner walls warm to the touch. *God bless air conditioning, such as it is in Egypt..*

In contrast, Shariff's voice was ice cold as he began the next part of his story. "Schroeder told us that Germany's soil is soaked in blood from a century of assembly line butchering that did not actually begin with the plot to slaughter Jews. And, according to him, the *Third Reich* carnage was not a result of penalties levied on Germany in 1918, following its defeat in Word War I."

I was confused and interrupted him. "Shariff, all the history books I have ever read indicate that WWII was Germany's response to the economic deprivations it experienced as a result of those penalties.

He shook his head. "Schroeder contended otherwise. He argued for an earlier source of the death camp pattern that runs deep in Germanic culture and history and extends beyond the European continent. Schroeder said the cultural madness and godless bloodbaths committed by the 20th century *Third Reich* grew out of Germany's *Second Reich*. Biological termination was part of their colonial policy in Africa. The genocide they practiced there began in the 19th century and , like the 20th century butchery, was the result of a Teutonic cultural component known as *Lebensraum*. The *Lebensraum* concept purports that the German people must rightfully expand living space at the expense of the lower races."

Sitting there in the lounge of the UN complex on the banks of the Suez Canal, listening to Shariff's discourse on the evolution of systematic biological termination by German governments was mentally unsettling. I dreaded where he was going, thinking, *Apparently, he is going to make a case for the relationship of that rotting sheet of skin in cold storage back at Reardon and aspects of German culture.*

I wanted to ask that he stop and get to the point. But, the scientist in me wouldn't. The tale was too gripping. So, I listened and took notes as he continued.

"It began in the mid-1840s, during what was politely termed the "colonization." of the Dark Continent (actually an era of invasion, plundering, enslavement, and racial genocide). Under Kaiser Wilhelm II and during the *Second Reich*, Germany raised its flag in an area deemed unfruitful by the other European invaders. The land under the German flag was dubbed German South-West Africa (Deutsch-Sudwestafrika, DSWA)."

I realized he was talking about the area now known as Namibia and asked, "Wasn't it a part of South Africa?"

He nodded in agreement. "It was, but in 1966, the United Nations General Assembly reassigned Namibia as a 'post' to resist its illegal occupation by South Africa due to the disapproval of South Africa's apartheid policy.

Apartheid began when the first government of the Union of South Africa started adopting pro-British, white-unity, racist policies. Although 75 percent of the country's population is black, there is no place for them in the new Union. Blacks are denied voting rights and a barrage of discriminatory laws emerged that has reserved 93 percent of the land for white-only ownership. Thousands have been evicted from farms and driven onto overcrowded impoverished 'reserves'. Many migrated to low-wage jobs in the cities and mines for survival, and to pay their colonial taxes."

Thinking about it, I said, "Apartheid mirrors the policies of Germany's 20th century *Third Reich.*

He studied my face for a moment before speaking. "Yes, and German goals in Namibia were similarly anchored on prospects for more *Teutonic* living space. That's the pattern of aggrandizement that emerges from *Lebensraum.*

I hope it does not offend you when I say that America was also a player at that table. The concentration camps in Namibia and Germany, and apartheid policies in South Africa, took a page from the Indian Reservation policies of the U.S. Let's not forget that America was built by declaring war on the indigenous peoples of the New World, looking upon them as lower races, taking their lands, and herding them onto reservations. Killing them was socially sanctioned when it was deemed necessary. The so-called white man's burden occurred under the concept of *Manifest Destiny,* the doctrine that justified the expansion of Europeans throughout the American continents at the expense of the people already living there. Except for the magnitude and conformation of the genocide involved, *Lebensraum, Apartheid,* and *Manifest Destiny* are not far apart.

I did not respond, not wanting to put a dog in that fight. But, his point hit a mark.

He took my meaning and continued with the description of German aggrandizement. "The *Huns* do not restrict the concept of *Lebensraum* to non-European populations. *Lebensraum* also underlay German aggression against Poland and Russia under the *Third Reich.* There was a plan, known as 'The Hunger Plan', which was to eradicate the farmers in those two countries and replace them with Germany's own. The exported German farmers would toil to feed a genetically perfect Aryan race in a greatly expanded *Teutonic* empire. What happened during World War II was not just a Jewish *Holocaust*, it was another chapter in the *Teuton's* drive to conquer and rule a genetically cleansed world.

But, first, you need to understand the Namibian roots of the Nazi death camps. Apartheid was taken to another level there."

He paused and gave me a long look before continuing. "This will be hard to hear. Are you sure your are up to it?"

As a scientist, charged with bettering society, I had no choice. I nodded yes

Turning somber, the Egyptian resumed telling how Schroeder described the evolution of Nazi death camps. "There were a lot of authoritarian players in the *Third Reich*. Herman Goering played a major role in the establishment and management of the camps. He had been groomed for that job from childhood, taught skills by his father for developing the savage slaughter behind *Third Reich* barbed wire.

Dr. Heinrich Goering served the Kaiser during the *Second Reich*, helping to establish the African colony of Namibia. He was a committed racist and imperialist and a proponent of *Lebensraum*. He foresaw a time when African lands could become additional living space into which the German race might expand and the indigenous people there used as cheap farm labor.

In the Namibian colony, German imperial ambitions to which Dr. Goering was committed involved mass murder and multiple other atrocities. His son later followed in his father's footsteps, overseeing a massive slaughtering system in Nazi Germany.

When the dominant tribes in Deutsch-Sudwestafrika, the Herero and the Nama, rebelled against German rule and exploitation, death camps were established to eradicate them. At a place called Shark Island, a rocky ridge just across Walvis Bay from the town of *Luderitz*, more than three thousand Africans were systematically murdered, their bodies tossed into the nearby bay. Their bones, some held together by rusty metal manacles, can still be found under the waters of the bay. No doubt, the bodies provided a buffet for sharks and other sea life that, in turn, were caught and consumed by the *Teutonic* heathens in charge of the human slaughter. It was a form of second hand cannibalism. The Germans wasted nothing.

In the Namibian capital of *Windhoek*, a mass grave exists under the sidings of the railway station. Further north and west, in the seaside resort town of *Swakopmund*, there is another mass grave. Even the national museum is built over the site of a former concentration camp. To understand the underlying ideas and philosophies of 20th century Nazis, and the murderous programs that came to be conducted under Hitler's *Third Reich*, one must know about the genocide in Namibia under Kaiser Wilhelm II .

Again, he gave me a searching look that said, *Are you up for more?*

Reluctantly, I nodded yes and he resumed telling what they had learned from the former *Mossad* agent about the phase of *Lebensraum* that followed colonization in *Afrika*.

"The *Third Reich* also murdered their own to cleanse the country of those with deficiencies. In the spring of 1940, the *Reich* set up a Chancellery department in the Berlin borough of *Tiergarten* to recruit German physicians for another extinction program labeled 'Useless Eaters'.

Under the 'Useless Eaters' program, physicians were paid to identify patients who were 'incurably sick'. In addition, all hospitals were ordered to turn over their 'unproductive patients'. Either a 'mercy death' was administered to those patients or they were transported to the gas chambers built for their elimination at *Grafeneck* and *Bernburg*. Strangely, German men of medicine found such assignments within the defined roles of their profession, which tells us volumes about the mental set behind the wanton lack of humanity in the subsequent concentration camps."

Shariff's voice grew softer. "Orphans, disabled, the elderly --

over 70,000 of their own people -- were exterminated. The rest of the world knew little of the diabolical and methodical genocide of Germany's innocents."

His brow creased as he remembered his team's reactions. "We were all stunned by the description of the heartless massacre of people in need of kindness. Dumfounded, our team listened in silence as Schroeder continued describing Germany's inhumane approach to caring for their disadvantaged."

"At first," he told us. "the 'Useless Eaters' were only to be annihilated, but the doctors eventually deluded themselves into believing that experimenting on the 'patients' was within their medical oaths. Over 100 psychologically depraved Nazi physicians and scientists began participating in unspeakable research to create a superior race in Germany; the mythical blonde, blue eyed Aryan species with perfect bodies and mental sets. Horrible procedures were performed on their victims as they experimented with trials that might purify and increase such a home-grown species."

Shariff shook his head as though still in disbelief. "Retarded orphan children were especially subject to the research of these mad men. Their innocent little victims would be closely observed under various circumstances, then given experimental drugs or starved. Their dead bodies would be dissected so the organs and brains could be studied. When the doctors had finished their ghoulish investigations, the children's body parts were sent to teaching hospitals."

Unsure that I could listen to more of the horror, as a diversion I halted the discussion long enough to pour more tea into our glasses.

Shariff studied me for a moment, deciding whether to continue. I nodded for him to resume, and he did. "Dr. Josef Mengele, a German medical anthropologist, wanted to develop procedures that would produce twin births in order to boost the German population growth rate. At his hands, cruel experiments ranging from starvation to excruciatingly painful internal examinations and surgical procedures, were conducted on twin children. At *Auschwitz,* one set of twins, teenage boys, was subjected to having their internal organs examined through their extended rectums. Their agonizing screams could be heard for days throughout the camp compounds. Mengele later transferred his research to the concentration camps where he was known as the 'Angel of Death'.

Eventually there was a public outcry and in 1941 Hitler was forced to declare the 'Useless Eaters' program cancelled. But the cancelation was a lie. Most of the physicians were reassigned behind the wall of the German military where they continued their macabre experiments on the disabled. They were labeled 'T-4' doctors, after the street address of the *Tiergarten Chancellery.*"

Shariff shook his head in disgust, exclaiming. "The doctors who took part in the program later justified their work at the Nuremberg trials, claiming it was to prevent diseases and disorders. Schroeder told us the warped bastards took pride in their hellish work."

Stopping to drink from his tea glass, he continued. "I will always wonder how Germany came to that point. Why did 20ᵗʰ century Germans fall under the spell of an avaricious and deranged Austrian monster? It was a nation claiming a genealogy based on bursts of creativity leading to Western civilization. It spawned Bach, Beethoven, Kant, Goethe, Schiller, and the likes of Einstein."

He asked me, " How did they devolve from such civility to barbarism?"

Not expecting an answer, he continued. "Apparently, *Lebensraum* lurks just beneath the surface of German culture and its society. But, how could we have reasonably predicted the unthinkable to stop them?"

Again, not waiting for an answer, he returned to Schroeder's description of events leading up to the *Holocaust.* "Schroeder claims that the Nazi concentration camp program became the 'Useless Eaters' program on steroids! After morphing full blown into the *Holocaust,* twelve million men, women, and children, whose only crime was having certain genetic or social traits, were methodically and savagely obliterated."

The story was becoming more than I could bear. The visual images evoked by the tale of abused and butchered children was making me nauseous and I asked to be excused. Making my way across the hall to the ladies room, I pushed open the door and barely made it to the latrine where I heaved what remained in my stomach from lunch.

When I had rinsed my face and collected myself, I looked into the mirror. My face was ashen and my mascara smeared. *It will be embarrassing to go back looking like this.*

Pulling a towel from the rack on the wall, I wet it and rubbed away the mascara. For another minute I held the towel against my face, letting its coolness sooth my frazzled nerves. The color began returning to my cheeks. Taking a deep breath, I pushed open the door to return to the lounge.

Shariff was waiting outside in the hall, and putting his arm around my shoulder, he suggested that we stop talking about Nazi death camps.

Embarrassed by my unscientific demonstration, I declined his offer.

We made our way back to the lounge, his arm still around my shoulder. He helped me into the deep leather chair and lightly kissed my forehead before taking his seat. Then, he continued.

"The deranged Mengele would select young victims in the disrobing rooms of the Nazi crematoriums, including infants. He wanted them for study after they had been gassed. To ensure that their little dead bodies were not inadvertently cast into the ovens before he could dissect them, their chests would be marked. Once dissected and examined, their eyes and organs would be provided to researchers their for further studies."

"Mengele also selected children from orphanages for transport to Auschwitz-Birkenau where they became slave laborers. One young survivor remembers that upon arrival some children were selected to work but others were sent straight to their deaths. He was disrobed, shaved, and showered, then given a striped suit and tattooed. After that, he was assigned to work as an agricultural laborer. Part of his work was ploughing fields and then fertilizing them with ashes from the crematorium. He recalls how he could feel bone fragments in the ashes he spread."

Walking back to the window, Shariff stared out into the evening light. The telling of the tale was obviously taking its toll on him, too. I studied his profile and could see that the vein in his temple throbbed.

A huge tanker was sliding by on the blue waters, held back by the engineered banks of the canal. Since it was the summer season and the water flow was southward, the northbound tanker was going against the current. Ahead of it, two pilot ships attached to the behemoth by thick lines, kept it moving down the middle of the single-lane waterway. It rode low in the water, heading to Europe with shipping containers piled high on the aft deck.

As a momentary distraction from discussing the killing centers, he began to describe the traffic on the canal. "Eighteen thousand vessels traverse the Suez each year. It's a continuous conveyor belt – products of every description floating between the continents of the world. Did you know it is so critical to international commerce that passage during times of war is guaranteed by the Convention of Constantinople?"

Again, not waiting for me to answer, he resumed the story while still standing at the window. I think he needed to draw strength from the life on the other side of the glass pane. "The *Third Reich* was an evil plague tearing across Europe, led by a satanic monster more malevolent than the devils in Milton's Paradise Lost."

He then turned to the argument that Germany should no longer be held accountable for the sins of its past. It was an argument that he vigorously opposed, revealing that in addition to a darker side, he had a deep humanitarian bent.

In that role, Shariff evoked an image of the dedicated scientist he had been before his life ran off the track and entered the dark and mysterious path he now followed. In that moment, I was drawn to him. Then a warning bell went off in my head. *I must not want this.* I looked away.

When I looked back, he was watching me, with more than impersonal interest. There was chemistry between us, and it was becoming distracting. He finally looked away, but not before he made his point. He would be pursuing.

But, what of Rosslyn?

Shariff was shaking his head, and said "You do not have to be Jewish to understand that if Germany is excused from its history, if the slate is just wiped clean, there is no assurance that the Namibian colonization, the 'Useless Eaters' program, the Hunger Plan, or the *Holocaust* won't be repeated somewhere. We need to always remember the reality of that netherworld, that a nightmare rose up from the bowels of the Deutschland that held a threat for all mankind. At the heart of the nightmare was a quest for growing a legendary superior race of people called Aryans. That superior Germanic race would rule the world, and for that to happen, the rest of us would have to go the way of the Jews."

Laughing derisively, he exclaimed, "The ironic part of it all is that no such Aryan race ever existed. It was just postulated by early philosophers and debunked by later scientists. The leader of the Aryan quest was an ignorant, mentally deranged, dark-haired, physically puny, failed Austrian artist, who could not have qualified as a member of the mythical race which he espoused."

Turning, he left the window and, as he walked past me to his seat he brushed the back of my neck gently with his hand. I felt a charge.

Once he was seated across from me he warned, "Good humans must always be on guard. German narcissism has gone to ground but it can always crawl out of its hidey-hole and begin to hunt again. The slaughter of the Jews was just a stone in the road to that Aryan world."

Listening to him, chills ran through me. I also had an

epiphany. I could find no argument against his condemnation, and the basis for what he had done. I thought, *There would never be enough Holocaust museums in the world to heal that wound.* In that instant, the horrible death that Shariff and his team inflicted on one of the Nazi perpetrators did not seem so immoral. I thought, *I am standing on the line I have drawn between good and evil. He is recruiting me.*

Seeking relief from the frustrating doomsday scenario he had just pronounced, he cast his eyes along my body and I watched his anger transform to more carnal interests.

A warm wave swept through me. It was becoming increasingly difficult to resist him, and he could tell. But, there was a wall between us; Rosslyn, my career. I stood and excused myself.

Walking across the hall, I asked a waiter in the dining room for a glass of water. "*Fi moya?*" While he poured the water, I cursed my role as Shariff's interrogator. I cursed the entire situation. *Under other circumstances I would be deep into an affair with this man. And I would not be spending my time here in Port Said listening to him detail the bloodthirsty acts of Germany. Rudyard Kipling had described the port as one of the world's 'must' destinations, not a place where the telling of brutality trumped lust.*

By the time I returned to the room where he waited, I was under control. Understanding my dilemma, he changed the subject to neutral grounds. "It just occurred to me. You may want to include something about my team in your report."

He smiled. "They are not discussed in my dossier, although your intelligence community is aware of them. As I said, they have taken to the sands of the *Bilad es Sudan*, the terrible Sahara desert. While they wait for finalization of their pardons, they are keeping a low profile. For the record, I won't name them but I can at least describe these remarkable men."

His smile broadened as I stared at him, taken aback, amazed at his familiarity with a dossier that was highly classified; code word. Was there nothing in the dossier I had been given that he did not know about? It had never left my possession, so obviously he had a copy. Maybe he even wrote it. *Who the hell knows, given the intelligence community!*

He smiled again. "Have you forgotten what I told you about the *Guardians?*"

He began describing a team of remarkable talents. "One, a nuclear physicist, is highly published, has discovered the secret to technologically imitating the process that radioactive elements undergo in nature to eventually become stable and safe, like lead. You are probably familiar with the process of transmutation.

Another team member is a gifted nuclear chemist. He contributed to the transmutation research in our lab.

The nuclear industry, of course, is not inclined to pare down their profits by spending money to clean up the garbage they leave behind so they are opposed to transmutation technology. Their power plants are constructed like buildings without toilets. They create a waste that has no place to go and will take thousands of years to transmute naturally.

There is no repository in which to store it and it cannot leave the site where it is generated until there is a repository. The government pays billions of dollars each day to keep it in storage at the plants. That is, the taxpayers do, so no skin off the nuclear industry's back. Besides, they don't want the waste destroyed because it is their savings account. When good uranium becomes unavailable, scarce, or too expensive, they will move to reprocess the waste. Again, at the taxpayer's cost.

I felt compelled to come to the defense of the nuclear industry. "Shariff, you are dismissing the fact that there are computer models which project that nuclear waste can be safely stored in a deep geologic repository for thousands of years. Also, nuclear energy is an energy source that is not carbon based and not an environmental pollutant. Nor is it a depleting resource like coal and petroleum. I don't think you are being objective when it comes to nuclear energy."

He shook his head in denial. "Many experts in the biological and earth sciences say the long-term predictions are unreliable. And, they are not verifiable. The idea that nuclear waste can be stuffed into metal containers and stored in what earth scientists call open systems is scientific voodoo. All environments are composed of energy and matter, components that are continuously interacting and therefore changing their environs. It is impossible to predict and control the conditions in which the nuclear waste would supposedly be contained over time. You know the phrase, 'We do not know what we do not know, that we do not know.'

There are other severe limitations of earth science predictions that must be realized before we begin shoving deadly materials like nuclear waste down rabbit holes like geologic repositories. Petrologists contend that desert rock, formed from volcanic rock called tuff, is 10 percent water. Its principal chemical constituent is silicon dioxide. During drilling and emplacement of waste in such repositories rock pathways are formed for water to enter and leave.

There can be other pathways for water seepage into repositories. For instance, as heat generated by the high-level waste intensifies, it will evaporate or boil off the water trapped in the repository rock. Water vapor or steam will form and can travel tens of meters before condensing in fractures in cooler areas. The condensed water could dissolve small quantities of minerals lining the pores and fractures of the rock. In turn, those may travel and precipitate other dissolved minerals. After repeated cycling hundreds or perhaps thousands of times, the structure of the rock's pores and fractures will be modified. There will also be expansion and contraction in response to the intense heat of the waste. Water could begin moving through the rock at an altered rate."

I could see where this was going and it was having the same effect on me as his explanation of how government procurement practices resulted in Scorpion's hijacking.

He continued. "Those processes will result in the water changing the rock chemistry, which will change where the water moves. That will change the chemistry again and again in a chain link system. These continuous reactions could increase the opening of the cracks and produce a natural drainage system. The drainage system would inevitably lead to the water table, no matter how far below. In time, the water could even pond and enter the containers of the stored waste."

He paused for a minute, in thought, and then slightly shook his head. "Another cog in the wheel is the problem of containerization. How do we make containers that will not corrode or be weakened by natural elements over the life of nuclear waste, hundreds of thousands of years?"

He smiled broadly. "I understand that radiation exposure is your wheel house. However, you are also a career bureaucrat and that biases you, clouds your vision. If you are truly honest you must also realize there is a dark side to nuclear energy and the waste it produces. Why else does your government spends billions each year on federal scientists like yourself and the engineers who are assigned to constantly monitor the lethal poison stored at the power plants?"

Now he was really touching a nerve, . "Sir, Are you suggesting that we are part of the problem, rather than part of the solution? Getting hot under the collar, I waded in and struck my colors. "Nuclear energy is cheap, safe, and clean as long as it is managed correctly. My job is to see that it is."

Raising a hand to quiet me, he said, "I'm sure that to some extent it is managed. Otherwise everyone in your country would be regularly exposed to lethal doses of radiation. However, your claim that the waste is cheap, safe, and clean is totally without merit. The public is led to believe that it is cheap because they are only told how little it costs for wattage output at the plants, compared to other forms of energy. The industry leaves out the up stream costs.

It costs billions of dollars to mine and transport uranium ore. More costs are sunk into extracting that minute part of the ore that can be enriched into a fuel form for a reactor. The fuel form is so inefficient that it must be exchanged every year or so after only five percent of its energy has been used. Millions more are spent on that process. We've already covered the storage costs."

He looked long and hard at me. "You know that it is not a clean form of energy. Granted, it is not carbon based but it leaves behind a residual that, in the end, may be more destructive to the human race than ozone damage. Nuclear waste is deadly to humans and their environments and cannot be neutralized. No technology exists that can do that, so once produced in a reactor, it belongs to us for hundreds of thousands, even millions, of years.

There is another aspect to the environmental costs of nuclear energy, of producing energy by splitting atoms. We can exactly measure that cost. Water. Available water, potable or otherwise, is already becoming increasingly problematic. Some even predict water wars in the future.

To produce electricity, nuclear reactors require millions of gallons of water to be continuously sucked in and spewed out every minute of their operation. In the process, water is warmed and leads to biotic sterility. In addition, every power plant has to maintain a 30-day emergency water supply in case of a reactor meltdown. During an accident, 10 to 30 thousand gallons per minute may be needed for emergency cooling. That's a lot of water to withhold from farming and human consumption needs."

I thought about the lake near the Reardon lab and how barren of life it had become as its water ran in and out of the site's reactors. I also thought, *In some ways, the reactors at Reardon had also sucked the life out me.*

Continuing, he said, "Fish & other wildlife get caught in the plant intake structures. It is estimated that a single nuclear facility can kill 3.5 million fish per year (32 times more than the combined impact of all other energy plants)."

Even though he could have skipped lecturing me on the subject, hearing his concerns for the risks presented to the environment was heartening. I liked relating to him on that level.

No dilemmas there.

And lastly, he went on, "Nuclear waste is not safe. That is why the government spends all that tax money, billions of dollars, to maintain controls around the stuff. If the controls are removed the earth's air, water, land, and seas will become toxic for humans."

His smile became a sarcastic laugh. "There is another side to the cost of nuclear waste. No one ever lost money investing in the nuclear industry because, in one way or another, all aspects of it are subsidized with public funds. The generating plants are subsidized during construction. Production of their product, energy, is subsidized. The cost of storing the deadly waste that accrues during the production phase is paid for by the government. The costs of all the subsidies are passed on to the ill-informed public through federal and state taxes and usage rates. When a plant fails or is decommissioned, the owners get to walk away and leave tons of radioactive spent nuclear fuel in the plant's cooling pool and dry cask systems. More millions of tax dollars are spent."

He laughed. "Cheap? Talk about getting people to buy a pig in a poke. They not only put a lot of lipstick on that pig, they even put a prom dress on it before it's taken to market."

Again, he studied me for a moment, assessing the impact of his attack on nuclear energy. Correctly guessing that we were not having a moment of camaraderie, he returned to the description of his men.

"But, I digress. Another member of our team is a nuclear engineer with an uncanny affinity for machines and can solve any problem involving a nuclear reactor. And, another was one of the earliest nuclear scientists to begin the work of processing uranium at *Inshas*. But make no mistake, he is first a defender of humanity and would guard against any wrongful use of nuclear power with his last breath.

"We also have two of the most gifted petrologists in the world on our team. They are like hawks and the desert is their hunting grounds, reading it and tracking without the aid of maps."

A wicked smile crossed his mouth. "One is uncommonly handsome and his dark brown eyes run down every woman crossing his path. He is descended from a long line of *Tuareg* nomads and could easily have been a warrior instead of a scientist. The other is of royal descent and chose to split atoms instead of working on stone monumental works."

Moving off point, his eyes swept me again and I was beginning to take his measure. Clearly, if not for nuclear science, Shariff might also have been at home warring and womanizing. Normally, I would have found this offensive, and it bothered me that I did not. He was peeling away layers of my persona that had been suppressed since my early days in the Amazon with Warren Jackson. I wondered, *What was life like for Rosslyn with this man?*

For a moment, he seemed to study our glasses sitting on the table between us. Then he asked, "Did you know that at a point, the American government was funding research on transmutation?"

That got my attention. As a radiological exposure expert I am well versed on most aspects of nuclear waste research but was completely unaware of any federal research on transmutation. I asked, "Are you sure about that?"

He nodded. "It's true, but those researchers were turned out to pasture. Since the U.S. had that technology, but suspended the program, I assume the industry convinced the feds to round-file it and, instead, store nuclear waste as a savings account."

I had my doubts about his reasoning. "Why would the federal government cancel a program that could lead to elimination of nuclear waste and opt for storing it? The cost of storing it is running in the billions."

He leaned forward and spoke seriously. "Cecily, you and I know that big business and politics always trumps science. Think about it."

I took a long look at him and he continued to dismantle the nuclear industry's claims that their product is clean, cheap, and safe. "The storage costs are minor compared to the return on investment down stream. At a point, good grade uranium ore will become scarce, expensive, or even unavailable. At that point, the waste, spent fuel from the industry's own reactors, could be retrieved and reprocessed. While that process is too expensive now, there will come a time when it is an economic feasibility."

I still had my doubts. "How would the industry benefit? By law, the spent fuel, once it is removed from the reactors and becomes waste, is the property of the federal government."

He waved off my argument. "Of necessity, the government will become the nuclear industry's business partner, not that it isn't now. Industry will be allowed to take the stuff off the government's hands at a highly subsidized pricing schedule. Then, they will reprocess it in facilities they build for that purpose, also highly subsidized.

Once the fuel has been reprocessed they can run it through their reactors again, and again charge the ratepayers. What a business plan. You take something that nature provides, use it to produce a subsidized product for which you charge arbitrary usage rates, and leave behind a deadly garbage pile that accrues as you produce your product. As your garbage pile grows, you get the government to store it. Then, you get the government to give it back so you can sell it again. You and I are in the wrong end of the business."

I thought, *What a novel concept.* I had thought for a long time that the toxic waste from producing nuclear energy was becoming a paramount public health problem and a major concern of the government. It had not occurred to me that the nuclear industry and its puppet politicians did not want the waste destroyed because it could eventually become a valuable commodity.

He was saying, "The downstream costs are equally staggering. When a plant is decommissioned it costs billions. Then, tens of thousands of tons of reactor spent fuel, lethal nuclear waste, remain behind at the old plants, cooling in giant pools of chemically controlled water.

I reminded him that it could be removed to cement casks.

"Agreed," he said. "But years have to pass before it is cooled enough for that to happen and it still has to be kept at the site in those thick cement casks for thousands of years to prevent human contact or environmental pollution. And who knows how long it will be before nature finds a way to intrude into the casks? Look at the ancient Egyptian pyramids. They are made of solid granite and after only a few thousand years they are decomposing. Some elements in nuclear waste last millions of years."

On an intellectual level I knew that, but until Shariff began stressing it as one of the down sides of the nuclear waste problem I had not really thought of the impact on the hundreds of sites where nuclear waste now sits. My focus was narrower, exposure.

Thinking aloud about the physical characteristics of the waste, I said, "I should have thought more carefully about the social costs of atom splitting for nuclear energy. I knew that the communities where nuclear plants are built are forever at risk of radiation exposure. When the plants have produced beyond their licensed life, they have to be decommissioned, torn down. Contaminated parts are shipped away for burial in some other community's backyard where their deadly energy will hopefully not contaminate and kill. Those parts that cannot be shipped are either transformed or entombed on-site in millions of gallons of cement to prevent radiation leakage, at least until the forces of nature invade them. But, the waste will never be safe for mankind. It will sit in America's backyards for eons. Science has no way to eliminate the lethal poison that the production of nuclear energy leaves behind. My job has been to see that exposure has been confined to permissible limits. Until now, I have not given a hard look at the long-term consequences."

At this point, Shariff decided to drop the discussion of nuclear waste, stretched out, crossed his arms behind his head, and returned to the description of his men. My eyes ran down his lean body. A charge ran through me before I collected myself. He noticed, but continued. "All told, my team is a tough crowd, men of science who not only can handle the powerful secrets of nature, but much of the rest of the physical world, including manning stolen submarines. These are the men with whom I crossed the Rubicon."

I watched him closely as he spoke of his men, clearly with affection. I was thinking, *They might be a tough crowd but I'm guessing their leader is even more indomitable. He is definitely both the iron hand and, in bed, I'd guess, the velvet glove. I wondered if he would ever cross back over the Rubicon.*

⮾

I took a last drink from my water glass and Shariff asked if I wanted more. His gaze conveyed concern. As an alpha male, he was genetically programmed to care for the physical and mental state of women in the presence of violence, even the verbal violence to which his story was subjecting me.

He resumed describing the discussion of the *Third Reich* in Schroeder's vineyard. "Schroeder told us that when Hermann Goering authorized the preparation of a strategy called *Die Endlosung der Judenfrage* (the Final Solution of the Jewish Question), T-4 doctors were tasked with finding expedient biological termination procedures for eliminating massive numbers of the 'racial defilers'. They were also tasked with developing processes for eradicating the evidence of Germany's genocide program.

Schroeder then paused and looked down at the table, seeming to study the grain of its cedar planking. After a moment he told us that Goering had many roles in the *Third Reich* -- ace pilot, commander-in-chief of the *Luftwaffe* (Germany's air force), and leading member of the Nazi Party. He became the second most powerful man in Germany when he founded the murderous *Gestapo*. For that brutal work, he was awarded the coveted *Pour le Merite*, better known as the 'Blue Max'. He fell from grace when the *Luftwaffe* failed to stop the Allied bombing of German cities."

Shariff scoffed. "Like anyone could have stopped the combined power of the Allies."

He went on. "Goering was the most avarice of the lot. Schroeder told us that after he fell from power, he withdrew from the military and political scenes and turned to legalized robbery. The ghoul began acquisitioning property and artwork from the homes of Jewish *Holocaust* victims."

Another sly smile appeared on the Egyptian's lips while he sat across from me in the deep leather chair. "How Goering crashed and burned was an amusing tale. Schroeder confided to us that in April of 1945, when Goering was informed that Hitler intended to commit suicide, he actually sent the *Fuhrer a* telegram asking permission to take control of the *Reich*. The paranoid Hitler considered his request an act of treason and ordered him arrested. Goering evaded the SS and lived to be convicted of war crimes and crimes against humanity at the Nuremberg trials."

The sly smile broadened. "Although the tribunal sentenced him to death by hanging, he mysteriously died of cyanide poisoning at the age of 53, the night before his sentence was to be carried out. Schroeder's *Mossad* team administered the cyanide. It was a well deserved and ugly death."

Previously, there had never been a reason for me to evaluate the laws on their merits of applicability to situations. Now, Shariff's attitude toward vigilante style retribution was causing me to think about law's immutability.

As I listened to his cold description of Goering's end, I began to wonder about the degree of separation between the sanctioned hanging of the Nazi criminal and what the *Mossad* had done to him. And, after the tortuous treatment of death camp victims how could an appropriate measure of pain be established when terminating a Nazi war criminal? Who had more right to terminate Herman Goering than the Jews? On balance, Goering's death could be a wash in a reordered value system. An eye for an eye.

Looking away from Shariff, I began recalling what I learned in

Anthropology 101 about the first known codified laws, written by King Hammurabi. I asked Shariff if he was familiar with the Code of Hammurabi.

"Refresh my memory," he said.

"He was an early Mesopotamian king who wanted to expand his small kingdom, only some 50 square miles in territory. To do so, he needed a form of social control over the diverse people he planned to conquer."

Laughing, Shariff said, "Of course. Rulers cannot exert authority without such restraints because we humans are biologically independent animals inclined to practice freedom with abandon. Ruling over large groups of us without social controls is like trying to herd cats."

I nodded in agreement and continued my description. "All rulers seek to interpret or impose laws to their political advantage. While laws don't necessarily make subjects want to do their happy dance, once socially sanctioned, they are powerful elixirs. Realizing this, the king issued the Code of Hammurabi in 1750 BC. To seal the deal, he claimed he was given the almost 300 codifications by the sun god *Shamash*. His Code laid the early foundation for coupling the will of God and the authority of leaders and courts with the cloak of moral sanctity."

A slight frown formed on Shariff's forehead. He said, "As I recall, some of the codifications were severely cruel, such as mutilation and beheading for crimes like stealing a loaf of bread. They also laid the foundation for many of the religious tenets by which we live today. The concept, "An eye for an eye", emerged from Hammurabi's Code.

Turning to look at him, I thought, *Actually, it could be argued that he and his team, and the Mossad operatives, had taken even less retribution than an eye for an eye.*

Once again, he read me, and said, "Take the religious and legal prohibitions against killing. Mass murder gets committed during war, even remote killing like dropping the atomic bomb on civilian cities. But, killing your enemies in warfare is sanctioned. Self defense, if demonstrable, is sanctioned. Where did killing Nazi war criminals fall in this paradigm? And, if all that killing can be socially sanctioned, couldn't the killing of the victim whose skin you handled back in the Reardon lab be justified under 'an eye for eye'? Can't that killing be seen as a continuation of war and a sanctioned elimination of the enemy?"

Shariff clearly saw he and his team standing on moral principles. With every hour spent listening to him describe the terrible realities of *Third Reich* concentration camps, I could find fewer and fewer objections to the biological termination which the *Mossad* and Shariff's Egyptian team had committed. *A few eyes for untold millions.*

❧

With that, he turned to the evening of their fourth day in Israel. "The team had again gathered around the wooden table in Schroeder's vineyard, having spent the last ten hours in the Negev research center laying out strategies to keep Egyptian and Israeli nuclear warheads out of combat. We were tired, hungry and thirsty but Schroeder joined us for another round of discussions on *Third Reich* genocide.

He filled our glasses while women from his house arrived with trays of fruit and sugar-glazed sweet cakes. They also brought a welcomed platter of buttery-colored goat cheese made from the *Shami* herd raised there at the vineyard. The cheese got its color from being bathed in the vineyard's wine as it aged inside its protective rind. Fresh baked bread was placed on the table to go with the cheese, along with glasses for more of Schroeder's favorite wine.

The women took only minutes to place the refreshments on the table and pour drinks for the guests. Schroeder had waited to speak, an acknowledgement that many Israelis, especially the women, did not like to hear of or speak about the brutalities inflicted on

81

their kind in the concentration camps. We all nodded thanks and Schroeder continued when the women had retired.

He began describing another of Germany's monstrous aggrandizement plans, the 'Hunger Plan'. It was another piece of maniacal German empire building."

Shariff shook his head in amazement. "We couldn't believe what he was telling us. There seemed to be no end to the Nazi's insatiable cannibalistic appetites. He described how Germany intended to mount their own Diaspora by expanding its territory and growing its population onto Russian soil. Under the 'Hunger Plan', 30 million Russians in conquered territories were to be eliminated through starvation. Their food supplies were to be diverted to the German army and German civilians. Cities in the targeted areas would be razed and the land would either be allowed to reforest or be settled by German colonists."

Listening to Shariff, I was torn between two conflicting emotions. On the one hand, I was sickened over the reality of how the world had allowed millions of innocent people to be caught in the surreal Nazi web of death. On the other hand, I was mesmerized by the brutal tale he was sharing with me. It was a horror story unlike any other. *Hollywood couldn't write this stuff.*

As he continued, I felt shame for my morbid fascination in the details he was sharing. "Laying out another piece of the *Third Reich's* expansion strategy and 'racial cleansing' goal, Schroeder told us that in 1942, high-ranking Nazi officials held a meeting in the Berlin suburb of *Wannsee*. At the *Wannsee Conference*, plans were formalized for the final and total eradication of all Europe's Jewish population, some eleven million people. Jews would either be worked to death, killed by firing squads, or murdered in gas vans that were ostensibly en route to concentration camps."

Shariff leaned forward in his chair. "According to Schroeder, it was when these methods proved to be inadequate for the scale of the *Wannsee* operation that the Nazis began setting up the mass killing centers; Auschwitz, Treblinka and the other extermination camps, following the pattern established by the *Second Reich* in Namibia. Every man, woman and child brought into one of those centers was circling the drain as soon as they had been processed.

The *Third Reich* methodical system of slaughter involved utilizing the technologies that T-4 doctors had first developed to eliminate the 'Useless Eaters'. The Namibian genocide, the 'Useless Eaters', the "Hunger Plan", the *Wansee* campaign, and the *Holocaust* were all part of a monstrous master plan for a Teutonic ruled world. *Lebensraum*. The system was like a fire that sucks in air and burns hotter as it grows."

He paused here and seemed to be assessing my reactions, deciding whether I could handle so much raw truth. The other factor was that we both understood he was using the story as an objectification for employing Polonium 210 as a murder weapon. Then, he resumed the tale. "Schroeder said *Mossad* records indicate that in some of the death camps, prisoners arrived in trains and were immediately marched to gas chambers. According to witness testimonies, those who were quickly gassed were the lucky ones. It was the kindest death the Nazis offered their victims."

Again, he paused and looked at me before going on. He was monitoring the emotional impact that the ghastly details were having on me, were going to have on me. He was now in protective mode. "Even so, it was an agonizing death. One thousand people at a time were gassed at *Auschwitz*. First, they were tricked into disrobing in the 'changing room' by arch liars who told them they were being packed into the 'water therapy room' for sanitizing so they could be sent on to work camps. The water therapy rooms, of course, were the gassing chambers."

Shariff looked toward the window, as if to be reassured by the life outside. "The rest of Schroeder's story was darker than evil personified. Once packed into the 'water therapy room', pea-sized grains of Zyklon-B crystals were released into the chamber's vents and quickly transformed into gas. As the gas spread through the air, workers outside the chambers heard piercing screams, wailing, moaning, and futile banging on the bolted double doors."

He shook his head. "There was no escaping Zyklon-B. The deadly gas immediately causes an excruciating irritation to the throat and intense pressure in the head before leading to paralysis of the respiratory system and, finally, its lethal effect. The victims were trapped and going to their deaths like cattle in a slaughter house."

Turning from the window, he again gave me a long look, a protective look. "Schroeder said there was a pattern to the way the bodies were stacked when the chamber doors were finally opened after fans had dispersed the gas. The deadly vapor first spread at floor level and then rose to the ceiling. For this reason, the bottom layers of corpses were always those of the children, the old, and the weak. Middle-aged men and women were the next layer, and the tallest and strongest lay on top. Often the dead were intertwined in each other's arms or holding hands. Their mouths were frequently wide open and their faces turned blue. The heads of babies still in their mother's wombs were usually crowned, while the legs of women not pregnant were streaked with menstrual blood.

I was turning white with horror, the nausea returning. Tears began running down my cheeks. He rose and took my head in his hands, kissing my forehead. "It's over. It can never happen again. We must see to it."

His touch was comforting and the nausea began to pass, replaced by a feeling of warmth from his touch. At that moment I loved this man, not for any romantic interest but because he was a good man and my psyche needed someone good as a backdrop to the horror and reality of what had happened in Germany while the world looked the other way. I also knew that I would never again feel safe. If it happened once, when and where would it happen again?

He sat back down in his chair, still watching me with dark seeing eyes, but continued where he had left off. "After the doors had been opened and the corpses dragged to the crematorium rooms by straps around their limbs, their bodies were hosed down to wash away the urine, excrement, and other body fluids. Then, before they were shoveled into the ovens with iron forks, fillings in their teeth were wrenched out, eyeglasses, artificial limbs, and dentures removed, and the women's hair cut off. These remnants of human life were added to the massive pile of kindling that fired the *Third Reich's* war machine."

At this point, Shariff said Schroeder's face was rigid and ashen but he continued, telling us that the horror of death in the gas chamber actually spared them from what otherwise lay in store at the hands of their butchers. "In *Auschwitz* and *Ravensbruck*, gruesome experiments were conducted on the genetically undesirable: Jews, Roma (Gypsies), and others. Efficient and inexpensive procedures for mass sterilization techniques were tested to further the crazy Nazi goal of 'racial hygiene'. The women were also raped, battered, starved, and worked to death.

The Nazi genocidal procedures varied from camp to camp. One constant was the Nazi ovens, which burned day and night to eliminate evidence of their demonic program.

Prisoners at *Natzweiler* and *Sachsenhausen* were subjected to phosgene and mustard gas to test for possible antidotes. Other procedures were used on the prisoners to determine how different 'races' withstood various contagious diseases.

At *Dachau*, physicians from the German air force and the German Experimental Institution for Aviation used prisoners as guinea pigs to conduct high-altitude experiments for the *Luftwaffe*. Prisoners were placed in pressure chambers to determine the maximum altitude from which crews of damaged aircraft could safely parachute. Autopsies were then performed on the brains of the subjects who died during the experiments."

I could only imagine the fear and screaming as their victims were tortured and flayed and my nausea returned, but I nodded for Shariff to continue. "There were also freezing experiments to find effective treatment for hypothermia and tests to evaluate various methods of reviving aircrews shot down at sea. Some prisoners were used to try and determine how to make seawater potable."

Then, he said the Israeli began to describe another player in the mad Nazi pillage of humanity. "Like Goering, Schroeder said *Mossad* reports proved that Himmler was also one of the most powerful men in Nazi Germany, and one who was most responsible for the *Holocaust*. Hitler had appointed him Commander of the Home Army and General Plenipotentiary for administration of the entire *Third Reich*, Germany's version of national suicide.

Schroeder told us that although it had taken sixteen years, Himmler developed the SS from a small 290-man battalion to a million-strong paramilitary group of feared thugs. They controlled the Nazi concentration camps he built and oversaw. As such, he was responsible for the murder of an estimated eleven to fourteen million people."

Shariff said, "Schroeder had scoffed at the memory of the man, telling us that he and Hitler were a matched pair. Both mentally warped. Himmler practiced occultism. Neo-pagan beliefs drove his obsession with the racial policies of Nazi Germany. However, his mental deficiencies did not prevent him from sharpening the skills he needed to survive in the snake pit of the *Third Reich*. When he realized that the war was lost, he betrayed his benefactor by secretly attempting to open peace talks with the Allies. Hitler discovered the betrayal, ordered him arrested, and dismissed him from all his posts in April 1945. During his attempt to go into hiding, Himmler was detained and then arrested by British forces."

A smirk crossed his lips as Shariff paused for a moment and then said, "A dark shadow passed over Schroeder's face as he told us about Himmler's last moments in prison. According to him, those moments were not pleasant. The official story was that on May 23 the Nazi had committed suicide. The *Mossad* operative still carried in his memory banks the sound and feel of Himmler's neck snapping."

I was horrified at the description of Nazi brutality in their death camps, but I also found Shariff's sardonic attitudes on *Mossad* vengeance unsettling. It was emotionally destabilizing to think of so much evil in the world without an opposing force of good. His seeming sarcasm left me with an uncertain understanding of whether he belonged to that force, which camp he belonged in.

Having finished his description of Himmler's death, Shariff said, "Schroeder simply passed the cheese plate, urging the others to try it with the baked bread. I studied him carefully while we enjoyed the food, wondering how he could live with such intimate details of Nazi carnage and still smile sometimes, enjoy his vineyard, and the culinary delights that issued forth from the kitchen in his chateau."

In juxtaposition, I sat there wondering how Shariff could have come away from learning all this and still have tenderness left in his soul. Yet, he had shown me tenderness when I needed it. No wonder people try to forget that such savagery occurred. It shakes your world to know it did and that those who could have stopped it did not. *The civilized world is not supposed to work that way.*

He continued to describe the conversation around the vineyard table. It got worse. "When the plate had made its way around the table, Schroeder began speaking about the evidence of ghoulish experiments found when *Buchenwald* was liberated. He provided a detailed description of the disgusting brain research. According to him, subjects had been euthanized and their crania sawed open, cut clean in half from top to bottom, exposing the two sides of the brain's soft tissue and the 22 bony structures of the skull and face. Some heads had been cut all the way down along several of the upper cervical vertebrae, exposing the spinal cord.

Buchenwald was not the only place where ghouls could be found. The camp commander at Bergen Belsen was Joseph Kramer. His nickname was 'the Beast'. One report described a scene in which Kramer lost his temper and with a single stroke of his truncheon, split a female prisoner's skull in half. Guards at the camp were also ghouls. One famously cruel female guard, Herta Bothe, would shoot at the women prisoners and beat them with wooden sticks. Starvation and crowding turned the camp into an epidemic hotbed. In 1945, Anne Frank died there during a widespread outbreak of typhus.

When the British liberated Bergen Belsen in the spring of that year they found some 10,000 dead bodies piled up right to the front gate. The crematorium had broken down and the stench was overwhelming. The remaining prisoners, 40,000 or so, were scarecrows, so ill that even after their liberation, 400-500 died each day. Amazingly, Kramer was still in camp when the Brits arrived, arrogantly burning documents. The scene was so shocking the Brits made a film to document the conditions.

7

Belzec: The Extermination Model
How could people be duped into walking to their deaths without rebelling.

S hariff stopped and watched me. "If this is too much for you I can stop."

As much as I wanted to say yes, my inner scientist would not let me. I needed to hear the gory details. I could not, in clear conscience, shut this nightmare out, opting for denial like so many did, and still do.

He read my thoughts, nodded that he understood, and continued. The tale became even hoarier, leaving me little room for condemning him, and his team's actions. I began to understand that his sarcasm was, at once, both because he was now jaded and also because he was deeply wounded by the terrible wrongs committed in Germany that can never be undone. His sarcasm was a mask to hide his pain.

He said that Schroeder, by way of driving home the methodically planned butchering system, which the *Third Reich* strategically developed, began to describe the template tested, and modified at *Belzec*. "That particular camp was the prototype for optimal slaughter efficiency. The result was mass annihilation techniques.

Mirror images of the *Belzec* model were then constructed at the other killing factories. The Nazis needed resourceful and rapid methods for handling transports of prisoners from the time of their arrival until their murder and cremation or burial.

He continued to describe camp processing procedures meant to dupe the victims into believing they were being selected for forced labor, procedures meant to hide the belly of the beast. During transport, prisoners were given the impression that *Belzec* was a transition camp. As they were unloaded from the trains they were rushed from one processing area to the next with such speed there was little time to look around and comprehend what was actually happening to them."

Shariff read the doubt on my face. He stopped me from expressing it. "To understand how so many were handled in this manner by so few is impossible, but it happened. The mass psychology in play will never be understood. I can only believe that the horror in which the Nazi victims found themselves had to be replaced with denial."

Shariff then described how they were confronted with one of the survivors. "One of Schroeder's workers joined us, a man named Aharon Rohrlich. He was a *Belzec* survivor and Schroeder asked him to tell us about it.

Shariff's continence was noticeably sad as he described Aharon. "He was gaunt, almost starved as a consequence of disease and malnutrition. His skin was an unhealthy pale in appearance and his jaundiced, sunken eyes looked as though they had stared into Hell. He had the demeanor of a man who no longer cared about living but just could not seem to die."

The tale Aharon told about *Belzec* made Dante's Inferno pale by comparison. He took a place at the table with us, his slender hands folded before him on the table, and his face expressionless, the face that camp survivors had learned as an endurance mechanism while watching others go to their deaths. He began to quietly speak, telling us how, as a young boy, he had arrived at that unearthly acreage of northern Poland in the first rail wagon of condemned Jews. It was in March of 1942. His family had been packed into the carriage like cattle on the way to the slaughterhouse. As it turned out, that was exactly what they were."

Shariff's voice was choked with emotion as he continued, a side of him I was surprise to see. "Speaking of that day clearly opened a raw wound that never healed. Aharon paused for a moment, collecting himself. Then, resuming the frozen mask that was now his normal continence, and the screen he used to hide the old agony always eating at his insides, he continued as Schroeder had asked.

He said that his family had been arrested for the crime of being Jewish. They were told that, along with all the other Jewish people in the village, they were being transported to a work camp. He was only11 years old.

When the transport train stopped at the *Belzec* railway station, the men were quickly separated from their families. They were put in lines and marched off five abreast by armed SS guards. Other SS guards began to interrogate the women.

From an early age, Aharon had been a gifted pianist and, when asked what kind of work the family members could perform, his mother told them about his talent. He said he knew she did that to try and save him. He was then separated from her and his two sisters.

They were taken away with all the other women and children. Jewish children were annihilated along with their parents. His voice dropped as he told us that it was Nazi policy they could not be adopted because they had the 'bad blood'.

At that point Schroeder, obviously protective of the man, reached for the glass in front of Aharon, refilled it, and placed it in his shaking hands. After drinking half of the glass, Aharon continued his story, the story that he tried to forget every waking hour.

He never saw his family again. Within minutes of arriving at

Belzec they all disappeared and he was left alone, among armed and menacing Nazi SS guards and strangers who were hostages like himself.

They were assigned to a bunkhouse; adults and children still alive because they had various skills useful to their captors. His duty became playing the piano, day and night and often in the officers quarters across the road from the camp.

At this point, Aharon spread his fingers on the table and studied them as though recalling how he had played the lilting compositions of German composers while Nazi victims marched past him on their way to their cruel deaths. Then he looked out across the green vineyards, at the canopies of verdant green leaves weighed down by clusters of Chardonnay grapes, the 'Gate of God'. In many ways, I think he had already passed though that gate.

A moment went by before he began describing the camp itself. He said it was surrounded by high fences of barbed wire, screened from the road by trees. The officers were housed in a building outside the fences, not surrounded by enclosures. As he came and went from his duties there, leaving the camp through guarded gates and crossing the road, he passed by the railway platforms on the spur that had been built for delivery of the prisoners. He came to know all too well the procedures for handling the arriving victims, and their fates. They would never leave *Belzec*. They would die and be burned to ashes, while he played for them."

⁓

Shariff stopped at that point and announced that it was now dinnertime. He suggested that we delay our business until the following day and seek out more of the seafood to be found along the piers of the canal.

Relived at the prospect of escaping into the night air and leaving the horrors of the *Holocaust* behind for a few hours, I quickly agreed. I was not even sure I had the appetite for dinner. Like the rest of the world, I wanted to forget the *Third Reich* happened.

As we walked, Shariff tucked my arm in his. It was not the familial tuck of the morning when we walked along *Dragon* in her berth. It was a more personal touch. I was not sure what to do about it so let it go for the moment. Then, it began to feel too comfortable and I withdrew my arm. Among the many other things he was, he was a man I needed to keep at a distance.

Eventually, we came to an enticing seafood restaurant at the beach, El Borg. Shariff asked for a table with a view of the sea and was quickly accommodated. He ordered giant scampi for us, served over a bed of spiced couscous chocked full of local vegetables. Good wine, sea air, and his charming dinner conversation claimed distance from the gut twisting tales back in the UN complex lounge. They made for a gold star evening. Being with him turned me on, and it was not supposed to be that way. But the man had an electrifying effect.

After dinner, we walked along the *Corniche* and I let him tuck my arm under his again, for a while. His body was hard and warm. The feeling was seductive. I wanted this man, but it could never be. He was my target. Any other relationship would cost me my career. And he might still be involved with a woman named Rosslyn Ford. I withdrew my arm again.

Back at the compound, and the door to my room, he pulled me close and bent to kiss me. I turned my head and his lips brushed my cheek. It sent high wattage electricity through me but I quickly dodged the bullet. Kissing his cheek and pushing him away, I whispered "Thank you for a lovely evening. See you in the morning. I'll meet you in the lounge after breakfast."

Safely behind the door of my room, I leaned against it and drew a deep breath. *This situation could get out of hand. There will be no more dinners. And, this does not go into my report!*

෴

93

<u>Day 3.</u> The following morning I joined him in the lounge. True to form, he had already ordered hot coffee and *ligamatte* (Nile Valley doughnuts). During the night and all through my morning shower I had developed a firm resolve to get this interview over with and get out of harm's way. I started our day by asking him to finish his story so I could file my report on the Polonium 210 that had killed the cadaver remains now in the Reardon lab cold bay.

He gave me a long look with those wonderful dark eyes, which drilled right through me, but I stood my ground and he took my meaning. However, we both understood that he was not going to be side railed

The story began where he had left off, at *Belzec*. "The sun had set over the vineyard but we continued to listen intently as Aharon described the horrors he saw behind Hitler's barbed wire fences. As background, he told us why the camp was originally set up.

It began as a labor camp, which housed Jewish workers who were building the so-called Otto Line, a series of fortifications along the Soviet border. The site was eventually selected to be the model for Hitler's death camps because the railway station in *Belzec* connected with the railway center in the Ukraine where all the main lines converged. That made it easy to expedite prisoner transports.

The station was next to the camp's main gate. Once inside, there was a jungle of barbed wire everywhere the prisoners turned. Tree branches, woven into the barbed wire, camouflaged the outer fence. Inside the outer fence was yet another fence of barbed wire, and the space between the two was filled with rolls of barbed wire. Any attempt to escape the grounds would cut a person to pieces. He said he still saw the wire in his sleep.

I watched Aharon as he continued the description of the camp. He obviously slept little. Schroeder told us that his sleep came at different points of the day, never when it was dark. His deeply sunken and jaundiced eyes, and his continence, seemed devoid of emotions. Clearly, there was no gas left in our man's tank and he was just waiting for the journey of life to be over. The remnants of the human before us were symbolic of the polluted horror the *Third Reich* had brought to Europe.

He spoke in the same monotone as the day before, telling us that guard towers were built at each corner of the camp, protected by aprons of still more barbed wire. Another tower was located in the center of the camp overlooking what was called 'the sluice', which was a barbed wire pathway between the two sections of the camp: Camp I and Camp II. Along with its barbed wire apron, the center tower was equipped with a heavy machine gun and searchlight.

Aharon paused for a minute before continuing, as if struggling to remember the camp layout. I wondered if, mercifully, he was beginning to forget some details of his unspeakable nightmare at the hands of the Nazis goons.

When he began to speak again he said that Camp I included the railway ramp, where the arriving wagons of prisoners halted on a spur line. As with his family, the frightened and bewildered passengers emerged from the wagons and were quickly herded into what was called the reception area. Over a loud speaker, the newly delivered victims were told that their stay at *Belzec* was temporary and they would soon be moved to work camps where their skills were needed. Their possessions were taken from them and sent to warehouses outside the camp.

From the reception area, prisoners were rapidly steered into two barracks for undressing; one for the men and one for the women and children. Guards told them all this was necessary before they entered the next barracks, 'the bathing houses', where they would be showered and disinfected before being selected for work. Those terrible lies maintained a modicum of order as the duped victims were led closer and closer to the slaughter house."

Shariff leaned forward at this point and looked down at the floor while speaking. "We were all sickened by the picture Aharon was drawing for us of the cold blooded and methodical process followed by those Nazi bastards. As scientists, we are all schooled in the harsher realities of life and death on our planet, but what we were learning there in that vineyard was something no man can hear without being punched in the gut.

Watching Aharon was almost as hard as hearing what he had to say. He did not make eye contact with any of us as he spoke, just stared down at the table the whole time. I remember how vacant his eyes looked and how non-committal he seemed. Life had been sucked out of him.

With no show of any emotions he then told us that Camp 2 was the extermination area, including the gas chambers, crematoriums, and huge burial pits. The 'sluice' was actually the pathway from the undressing barracks in Camp 1 to the gas chambers in Camp 2. A camouflage net stretched over the gas chambers to prevent aerial observation.

The gassing chambers, complete with false showerheads, had signs at their doors indicating that their purpose was bathing. Water pipes were installed along the walls and in the floors. Each chamber was also outfitted with a 250-kilo stove. The pipes and stove gave the appearance of providing water, warmth, and comfort to the nude 'bathers'.

However, they had another purpose; mass murder. Zyklon-B had not yet been supplied to the killing camps. Since the gas used at that time did not efficiently asphyxiate the captives until room temperatures reached 81 degrees Fahrenheit, the stove was necessary to heat the water in the pipes which, in turn, warmed the room to the necessary temperature for delivery of the poisonous gas.

Once the thousand or so prisoners had been herded into the gassing chamber, and the big double doors locked on the outside, the gassing engine was started. Piercing screams could quickly be heard from the chamber as the lethal vapor filled the room. Within 20 minutes the screaming stopped, everyone was dead, and the engine was turned off.

Doors along the sides of the gassing chamber opened outward onto ramps built to overhang a narrow-gage railway. After each extermination procedure, the doors were opened and working prisoners rolled the bodies onto the ramps, then tossed them down to the ground. After each corpse was searched for valuables, straps were fastened to them and their bodies were dragged onto train trolleys which ferried them to the crematorium or to one of the massive burial pits."

Shariff stopped for a drink of water. He needed a moment before continuing. Then he said, "The *Belzec* survivor halted his tale and Schroeder reached over to squeeze his shoulder, knowing what came next.

We all exchanged looks, wondering how much worse it could get. Then Aharon's eyes teared, an actual emotion from this seemingly emotionally dead man, and we knew it was going to get a lot worse."

Shariff shifted in his chair and his voice was choked as he told me what the Belzec survivor said next.

"He told us that not all victims received the gift of gas. One day a transport of children arrived. Hundreds of children. The prisoner workers were made to dig a huge pit and the children were tossed down into it. They were then covered with dirt, buried alive. The earth moved and rose for days, until they had all suffocated."

Shariff said Aharon had paused and, for the first time, looked at the others. "His eyes conveyed an unfathomable inner agony as he told them that the dying, the butchering, the slaughtering, the Hellishly grotesque scenes, were accompanied by orchestra music. He was made to play in the orchestra. Day after day they had played favorite songs and requests of the SS staff, such as *Drei Lillen*. *Drei Lillen* was a marching song about three lilies growing on a grave and a passing rider who stopped to pick them.

He then stretched out his long slender fingers and seemed to gaze down on them in wonder. Shaking his head, he said that he still could not bring himself to touch the keys of a piano.

Slowly folding his hands again and resting them on the tabletop, Aharon continued, now speaking of the early phase of the extermination plan. It had proved impossible to make the gassing chambers airtight. Sand had to be piled up around the doors to prevent the gas from leaking into the rest of the camp and then the sand had to be shoveled away again after each extermination. The barracks also became inadequate in size as the Nazi's so-called 'Final Solution' expanded across Europe.

The smell of death and rotting flesh hung over the camp like a dark pall but the transports kept coming. By June of 1942, three months after he had arrived with his family, the *Belzec* slaughter machinery was overwhelmed. New chambers with enlarged killing capacity were necessary so a larger, more solid structure was erected. To continue the illusion that the victims were entering a bathing facility, a big bed of colorful flowers was erected in front of the new gassing chamber. Written on the wall were the words '*Bade und Inhalationsraume*' (bath and inhalation therapy rooms).

In August, to further increase the extermination capacity at *Belzec*, Zyklon B had been introduced. That gas was first tested in America for delousing incoming Mexican immigrants. The I.G. FARBEN cartel had acquired its patent and then licensed it to various other companies, as well as providing it to the *Third Reich* through lucrative contracts.

Zyklon *B*, converted to air born gas, soon proved to be an efficient lethal poison that could kill in minutes. Its use was then extended to most of the other death camps, reaping huge profits for I.G. FARBEN and its subsidiaries.

The extermination program was a lucrative business, benefitting a wide circle of participants. SS officials shared in the redistribution of the murdered victims possessions. They received jewelry, leather goods, furs, silks and expensive shoes, which they regularly sent home to their wives and relatives. The packages also contained welcomed teas, coffee, chocolates and canned goods confiscated in the "disrobing" rooms. Prison workers stashed into their own pockets what valuables of the dead they could find.

At the height of the hot 1942 summer around 100,000 victims a day, mainly Jews, were being murdered in the death camps with the new gas. However, its efficiency proved to be a problem at *Belzec*. After asphyxiation in the gassing chambers, the corpses were still thrown down to the ground through the sliding doors along the outer walls. But, there were now so many they couldn't be removed fast enough. Neither could the crematorium keep up with the loads of bodies brought there. Flea-bitten, putrefying corpses piled up in the heat. Additional burial pits had to be excavated.

When the pits became full, bodies were stacked in fields. Decomposing remains gradually transformed to denuded, disarticulated skeletal bones. Skulls, mandibles, femurs, vertebrae -- every one of the 206 bones to be found in a human body -- randomly scattered across sites where corpses had been left to rot.

Most mandibles were missing teeth since fillings, especially gold, had been extracted. Fractures and blood staining on many bones were evidence of brutal pre-mortem beatings. Other bones were scarred by the gnawing of vermin that invaded the sites to feast on the harvest of protein found there.

In November, Himmler issued an order directing the camps to eradicate all remains of the mass slaughter. Jewish workers were forced to exhume and burn the bones and corpses, while the orchestra played on.

On December 11th of that year, the final transports arrived at *Belzec*. Stepping out of the transports was a walk into Hell. By then, the whole area lay under a cloud of black oily smoke. A digging machine was in use for exhuming bodies from the giant burial pits. The putrid remains, dug up by prisoner work units, were being soaked in heavy oil, set ablaze on pyres by Nazi pyromaniacs, and the ashes re-buried in mass graves. Human fat clouded the windows of the barracks inside the barbed wire fences, as well as those in the adjacent village. In an effort to further destroy evidence of their crimes, a bone crushing machine had also been brought into the camp."

Shariff paused in thought for a moment. Then he said, "When I was very young, my father took me to the Hermitage in St. Petersburg. I remember studying two small painted panels by Van Eyck, *The Last Judgement*. The 15th century diptych portrays the eternal punishment of those who failed to obey God's and the church's laws. Bodies are flayed down the middle. Demons knaw on thrashing sinners. Giant serpentine tentacles wrap around the condemned. Earlier, in the 13th century, Jigoku Soshi gave the world his Japanese version of a *Last Judgment*. His scroll portrays Buddhist Hell, where anguished, naked souls are brutally bludgeoned and tossed into a giant, fiery-red inferno by demons. Both are supposed renditions of the worst that can happen. Hitler's evil and frenzied genetic cleansing program managed to make these renowned masters seem like a big yawn."

He leaned back in his chair and crossed his strong sinewy arms over his chest before continuing. "Decommissioning *Belzec* began in the spring of 1943. Aharon said the entire elaborate system of barriers, barracks, gas chambers and crematoriums were quickly dismantled. By summer, firs and wild lupines were planted where before there had been only a demonic hellhole, a stronger version of Milton's Paradise Lost. In less than one year, hundreds of thousands had been annihilated in that unearthly place where the German's had perfected assembly line death.

During that year, the Polish underground had leaked two reports to the Allies revealing the camp's crimes. An earlier report had also been published in the Polish Fortnightly Review on December 1 of 1942.

At this point, Aharon clenched his bony hands and pulled them down in his lap. He seemed to be drawing into himself, seeking the only safe place left in the world for his tormented soul. He spoke without emotion, saying that in spite of the leaked reports, no one came to stop the slaughter. He wondered how the world could have stood by knowing that behind

Hitler's barbed wire millions of innocent men, women, and little children were being callously murdered.

He stopped for a long moment, and then looked at us. He asked where we thought God was then. None of us had an answer."

Uncharacteristically, Shariff did not try to hide the emotion that telling Aharon's story was costing him, saying, "Aharon then put his hands back on the table, spreading his fingers as though covering two octaves on the keys of a piano. His story was ended. Standing, he politely excused himself and, as Schroeder said he always did at that time of day, walked into the vineyard to be alone and seek solace. Sleep never came to him in the night but the screams in his head were quieted when he stood in solitude in the midst of the old vines and the life they bore, the Gate of God."

Shariff sat quietly for a while, deep in thought. Then he said, "I wonder if Aharon was still searching for God, looking for him in the Gate of God."

I reached across the tea table and touched Shariff's hand in a gesture of comfort. It was to be the catalyst that changed my life. He rose, came around the tea table, pulling me up into his arms. A wave of warmth swept through my body and his embrace became my world. I could not bring myself to push him away.

Our lips met, overwhelming me with desire. I could feel the lust in his loins. He slipped his hand inside my blouse and cupped my breast. My knees went weak.

I suddenly realized that this could go no further. We were standing in the lounge of the U.N.'s Suez Canal complex, a very public place. He read me, as usual, and started pulling me toward the stairs leading up to our bedrooms above.

As we began ascending the stairs, my ardor cooled enough for a moment of clarity, and my inner scientist took over. "We can't. And, you know why."

He gave me a long smoldering look, continuing to hold me. After a few minutes he reluctantly released me, acknowledging my logic. Any relationship we could hope to have had to be put on hold until the polonium problem he had created was resolved. If I gave into my physical urge toward him I could lose my job and my career, a price I was not willing to pay. And, there was still the issue of Rosslyn.

Loudly sighing, he slipped into evasive mode, returned to his seat, and motioned for me to sit. Then he continued where he had left off before I touched him. It was a thin veil but, for now, it was all that stood between us and a path we would live to regret if we lifted that fragile barrier. "After watching Aharon walk off into the vineyard, Schroeder stood and suggested that we continue our meeting the following day. The women had prepared dinner up at the house and he hoped we would find the goat meat and couscous to our liking.

It was spicy and delicious. Again, the women had also prepared rooms for us."

8

BAYER and Zyklon B
The Nazi slaughtering machine and the corporate world.

A servant appeared in the doorway and asked in Arabic if he should take away the tea and uneaten cakes. Shariff replied, "*Menfudlikh*". (please). When the man had gone, he asked, "Can you bear with me while I continue detailing what else the *Mossad* records reveal, or do you just want the short version now?"

Like a moth to the flame, by then I was drawn to the painful ugly details. Aharon's question haunted me. How could the world have ignored the slaughter going on in those camps? If nothing else, the magnitude of the extermination program would have made secrecy impossible and it should have been grist for the mills of the press and inner sanctums of world leaders. Seeking an answer that I knew would never come, I asked Shariff to continue, and he began again.

"On the fifth morning, we congregated around the table in the vineyard as usual. It had been set for breakfast with colorful *Rosenthal* porcelain. An assortment of fruits, cheeses, breads and sliced meats had been left for us. As we began to eat, women appeared with pitchers of juices and pots of strong hot coffee. The day was still cool and, for the moment, we kept the banter pleasant around the table.

As the meal ended, Schroeder leaned back in his chair and momentarily locked his arms behind his head. While he no longer worked as *Mossad's* leading Nazi hunter, his strong sinewy arms indicated that he would still be a dangerous opponent in a close encounter.

Then he passed around a bowl of *Shamouti* oranges and began peeling one with his knife. He again turned the conversation to the Nazi death camps, saying our meeting at the center could wait. As he neatly peeled his orange I could not help but notice how precisely he slid the knife through its skin and wondered what else he could do with his knife.

Schroeder noticed my study of his knife, since little escaped his attention. But, he chose to ignore it.

He began to speak about the next upgrade of the death camp system when the extermination process was further elevated for efficient utilization of the prisoners, or their corpses.

The practice of selecting prisoners to have their bodies harvested for organs continued. Himmler liked to personally make the selections from incoming transports. Jewish doctors were forced to assist by opening the skulls and body cavities, and extracting the organs for examination.

Zyklon B became the major killing agent throughout the camps due to its efficiency. Some reports indicated that the gas could kill a 150-pound man within two minutes and was so effective that up to 1,200 people could be killed in one gassing.

In this phase of the *Wannsee* scheme, the camps were modified so that gassing chambers were either in or near crematoriums. Following a gassing, ventilation equipment would remove the lethal fumes and the bodies would be dragged out. In some camps, when the dead stacked up too fast for disposal in the crematoriums, they were thrown in rivers, or used as fertilizer."

Shariff said, "At this point the Israeli slowly shook his head. and told us there will never be a true count of all the victims. Then, he again suggested those who were gassed were fortunate.

He studied me for a long moment to see how I was faring. Then he asked, "Did you know that the *Third Reich* also became the largest slave owner in the history of the world?

I shook my head, "No."

He nodded. "Some of the newly arriving victims were designated usable for slave labor. Theirs was a slower death."

Smiling, he told me the Israeli had then tossed the last piece of orange into his mouth and said sarcastically, "If the *Third Reich* had been able to extend their rule over the rest of the world, none of us would have survived. We would all have ended up as slaves and then in Nazi ovens -- Asians, Latinos, Arabs, Africans, anyone who did not have blonde hair and blue eyes and did not fit into their crazy home-grown mold of the mythical Aryan race."

Strangely, Shariff seemed amused by the concept. He said, "Schroeder then laughed and began telling us that, given Hitler's physique and dark looks, he would have gone to the gassing chamber with us. Then, pausing, his eyes grew deep with hatred and he told us that, thinking about it, he would have gladly walked into one of those gas chambers if he could have taken that son-of-a-bitch with him."

Shariff's brow creased. "I knew Schroeder meant what he said. As we listened to him there in his vineyard, I also knew that we were being converted to the dark side of good. Each of us was particularly impacted by the descriptions of the experiments on women prisoners. Men, by nature, are sires and we instinctively protect the potential carriers of our seed. We were all becoming candidates for Nazi hunting. And, of course, I would be hunting revenge for Rosslyn."

Continuing with their morning meeting in Schroeder's vineyard, Shariff said, "The Israeli then returned to the discussion of Zyklon B, explaining that prior to the *Third Reich*, several large German dye-making corporations had merged in 1925, founding the cartel I.G. FARBEN, (Interessen-Gemeinschaft Farbenindustrie Aktien-Gesellschaft). The merger's original purpose was to address the vigorous competition between the country's synthetic dye and chemical industries. Their rapacious rivalry verged on cannibalism."

"Schroeder found their internecine warfare telling. He contended that Nazi Germany was full of flesh eaters, saying anthropophagy was not restricted to the death camps. It could be found in the upper echelons of the *Third Reich*, in Teutonic commerce, anywhere Nazis were found.

He also said that even though three of the industries, BAYER, BASF and HOECHST, had already become the largest chemical industries in the world, there never seemed to be enough market shares for the voracious giants. Teutonic narcissism seemed to loom large in all levels of German culture."

"Schroeder told us that being the largest of the chemical industries was not enough. Merging as IGF, they became the single largest chemical company in the world and the world's fourth largest industry after General Motors, U.S. Steel, and Standard Oil of New Jersey. By 1938, IGF employed over 200,000 workers.

Even that position in international commerce was not enough. The *Third Reich* was founded on a military-industrial complex. IGF joined the club and the Nazi camps became their outposts of pharmacological research. They courted and partnered with the *Reich*, opening even wider avenues of revenue generation. The cartel first became a huge contractor and major supplier of synthetic petrol and rubber for the Nazis. Following that, in the planning stages to occupy Czechoslovakia and Poland, IGF closely collaborated with Nazi officials to determine which chemical plants in those countries were to be secured and delivered to its cartel.

The cartel's total disregard for humanity came when they began to build facilities near some of the death camps to take advantage of the Nazi's huge pool of slave labor. Tens of thousands of laborers died working for the cartel.

As well as using the Nazi's captives for free or cheap prisoner labor, IGF scientists also used them in trials of experimental drugs, many of which proved fatal. IGF/Bayer wanted new drugs tested for pharmaceutical markets so they designed and ran IG Farbenindustrie at Auschwitz, a lab for developing special experimental drugs and procedures. Drug companies still have not said whether any of their current products are based on these experiments."

Shaking his head, Shariff said, "Once workers became incapable of labor or useful as human guinea pigs, many were killed with phenol injections into the heart."

"The cartel became so economically and politically powerful that a post-war investigation by the U.S. War Department concluded IGF had full knowledge of Germany's plan for world conquest and had insider knowledge of *Third Reich* attack plans. When the war ended, many IGF officers were tried as war criminals before the Nuremburg Military Tribunal and imprisoned or executed. The IG FARBEN TRIAL was 7th of the 13 Nuremburg trials."

Shariff recalled that Schroeder claimed their punishment was a fig leaf. "You would think that after their cities lay in ruins, five million of their soldiers lay dead, and their country now occupied by four armies of the Allies, the German people would have looked upon the *Third Reich* as a national calamity. But, most of the cartel directors who had been sentenced to prison were released and quickly restored to their directorships. Boosting arrogant disregard for sin and humanity to its ultimate height, some of them were even awarded the Federal Cross of Merit."

I stopped him at that point, saying "I will never understand what went on there. Not just the Nazis, the whole population of Germany. Its like it was a parallel universe in which the ethics and values of civilization was nonexistent. Another, inhuman like, ethos existed."

At that point, Shariff said he had interjected and asked Schroeder, "Do you think the post-war awards raise a prudent question? Some argue that Nazism was an aberration, a discontinuity in German culture. But, where were all the good German people during the earlier planning to butcher native Africans and Germany's own disabled citizens? Where were all those supposedly good and uninformed citizens as the Nazis announced and implemented their chilling Final Solutions for genetic cleansing? Where were they during the war when millions were being slaughtered like farm animals and thousands of German citizens should have become resistance fighters instead of employees in the death camps? Where were they after the war when there should have been outrage at the revealed guilt of military, corporate, and medical officers, rather than rewards? Where had all the people been who later claimed to have no knowledge of the death camps?"

Sitting across from me, Shariff waved his hand in a gesture of dismissal. He knew there would never be an answer.

Then, he said , "But, Schroeder had a response. He looked around the table at each man, staring at us across the political divide that kept our countries from working together to build a better world. Nodding his head sadly, the former Mossad operative quietly replied that the world is ruled by those who show up. In the case of the *Third Reich*, the rest of the world did not show up, or arrived too late. He said that even the Heavens had abandoned their victems."

At that point, Shariff said he asked what became of the cartel? "Schroeder's answer was even more disturbing. He told us that in the Russian occupation zones, IGF assets were seized by the Soviets and declared reparation payments. In the Allied sector things went differently. Ostensibly, the Allies had considered the cartel too morally bankrupt to continue existing so it was supposedly broken up and liquidated.

However, politics and big business trumped morality and justice. IGF was too deeply entangled with giant American corporations to be mortally wounded, especially the successors of Standard Oil. So, in reality, the cartel was only fragmented. Then, in the late 1940s, it was rebuilt as a shell company and continued to do business. In 1951, the cartel was again rejoined into its original constituent companies, and the largest of those bought out the smaller companies. AGFA, BAYER, and BASF once again became some of the largest chemical and pharmaceutical companies on the planet. The world did not seem to care."

Shariff laughed sarcastically and ran his hand through his thick black hair. "So, we now have the Nazis to thank for better living through chemistry!"

He shook his head. "It gets even worse. We learned from Schroeder that over the years, IGF was vigorously criticized for failure to provide compensation to those it killed or used as slave laborers in the Nazi camps. Remarkably, their defense was that the issue was still the object of ongoing legal disputes. Imagine, the bastards hid behind the law and looked to the courts for justice!"

Shariff's face and voice hardened. "Schroeder posed the question, 'If millions were tortured and put to death; if hundreds of thousands were illegally used in forced labor; if thousands were experimented on with drugs produced in death camp labs; if still more were maimed or killed in unthinkable medical trials; if properties were stolen, people were dehumanized, women were randomly and repeatedly raped; and babies and children were starved or butchered like lab rats, what restitution was even feasible? What standard could be used to determine an appropriate financial compensation?"

The Egyptian the turned to BAYER's role in the death camp system. "BAYER raised the bar of immorality. Its Board member, Fritz ter Meer, was sentenced to seven years in prison and then, in 1956, was elected head of BAYER'S board. Under his leadership, the corporation went on to try and pull off one of the greatest hoodwinks in history. It claimed that it was exonerated from the charge of crimes against humanity since BAYER, doing business as part of IGF, did not technically exist between 1925 and when it was re-formed in1952. Apparently, BAYER saw its membership in the cartel as a hiatus that got it off the hook. What a morally bankrupt stance, advancing that claim as grounds for not being accountable for its criminal conduct during the war. They were actually suggesting that the civilized world give them a pass!"

Shariff again turned to study me for a moment, then asked, "Did you know that the corporation finally admitted using slave labor during the war and joined 12 other German companies in a payout to those who survived? The companies paid one billion pounds in 'reparation funds' intended to forestall a flood of group actions going through U.S. courts. They feared a boycott of German companies, whose wartime conduct was under scrutiny. A BAYER company spokesman announced the corporation felt the millions it donated to the fund had settled the score. I think they were studying squid in their laboratory at Auschwitz to learn how to evade their pursuers by squirting dark ink."

He threw up his hands in exasperation. "The scrutiny of German corporate actions during the war revealed so many other horrible surprises, like the revelation that Deutsche Bank, the largest in Germany, provided financing for construction of Auschwitz."

The vein in his temple was throbbing again, a tell I had learned to recognize. It was sensual and alluring, manly. While listening to his condemnations, my eyes were drawn down the length of his outstretched legs. The outline beneath his white linen pants was a distraction from the chilling details of the *Third Reich's* depravity. He caught my gaze and smiled wickedly at my embarrassment.

More than embarrassment, I was stricken with guilt at having been distracted by his physical prowess when we were deep into a discussion of Nazi bestiality.

In addition to my physical attraction to him, it was becoming more and more difficult for me to find fault with the retaliatory measures that he and his associates had taken in revenge for Holocaust victims. The line between good and evil had all but disappeared. But my inner scientist held sway. And, once again, I vowed to keep my *id* under control and keep him at a distance, for now.

My mission was to unravel the mystery of the decomposing and highly radioactive sheet of skin now in cold storage at Reardon. And, if possible, I had to recover the polonium involved. His condemnation of what the Nazi's had done did not change my mission, and yet, it was increasingly altering my view on the parameters of the death penalty. Formerly, I had held the belief that it was only the state's domain. Now, after listening to the lurid descriptions of the Nazi serial killings, I was not so sure that court ordered biological termination was the only appropriate course of action.

Shariff had turned to causal analysis. "I agree with Aharon's assessment. What the 20th century Nazis did cannot be explained by simply defining it in terms of the human capacity for violence or sanctioned killing by warring nations. What was done in the Nazi death camps was so twisted, so monstrous, that there is no fit with civilized society's understanding of the human capacity for inhumanity. The Germans did not just commit genocide. They did not just enslave people. They were not just conducting territorial war over political, racial or religious differences. What they did in their African colony and European concentration camps was so inhumane it cannot be explained by any extant theory of *homo sapiens* behavior."

He fixed me with a hard glare. "The Nazis were another kind of animal, and those that are left should be found and exterminated. They are a threat to the force of good in humanity, the embodiment of evil. And, if BAYER and the other cartel members are excused for their war crimes then nothing is learned from that salient moment in mankind's history. Humanity will not be well served by rewriting the story to purge Germany or the IGF cartel of guilt. We will be no better for knowing what was done. The world should be better for knowing, painful as it is."

He was also defending the cold murder of Brunner. I knew it, but in the face of everything he had told me about the Nazi massacres, I could no longer find the taking of Brunner's life too significant.

Shariff's voice then softened. He said, "Schroeder began explaining how his operative team worked and why the *Mossad* had such extensive records of the camps. He said not everyone had the stomach for their work. Some of what they had done, and some of what they knew, was not for the feint hearted."

I had already guessed that.

Shariff continued describing what Schroeder told them about *Mossad* tactics. "As an example of their work, he told us about Adolph Eichmann's fate. It was his team that kidnapped the war criminal in Argentina and secreted him to Israel where he stood trial for his crimes. *Third Reich* records proved that Herr Eichmann bore responsibility for the design and development of the Nazi extermination camps and for the death of millions. Not only was he guilty of the charges against him, he was especially proud of his role in the slaughter of Jews. Convicted on hundreds of charges, the Israelis hanged him on June 1, 1962.

Schroeder happily watched the Jew killer's neck snap when he dropped from the gallows and swung for hours. He told us he stayed there, at the gallows, to watch survivors of the death camps pass, seeking some closure to their personal nightmares."

Shariff smiled sarcastically and said through stiff lips, "The former *Mossad* operative also told us that Joseph Mengele died a kinder death than he deserved. He said they spread rumors that he drowned after suffering a stroke while swimming in the pool of a plush Brazilian resort. Mengele did drown from a stroke in the pool of that resort, but it was from a stroke of bad luck. Schroeder's *Mossad* team caught up with him."

9

Ravensbruck.
The Women's Death Camp.

As he continued to describe the scene in the Negev vineyard that morning, the handsome Egyptian again ran his fingers through his thick black hair. "Everyone around the table was quiet. Even though religious dogma prohibits actions like the murder of Mengele, Schroeder was suggesting the evil that German war criminals had committed justified *Mossad* actions. It was hard to argue that they were vigilantes.

Aharon's question about where the rest of the world was while the Nazi's were butchering the innocents in their slaughterhouses painted a picture of compliant indifference by the world. The question brought forth a large measure of truth; that indifference was inexcusable. It bordered on condoning what happened in those camps. We were all shamed and it forged our future.

Looking at each other, we mutely agreed on our path forward. We were going to commit terrible evil in order to do good. We were going to do it because, as men of science, we could. And, we understood there would be no turning back for us."

As I listened to Shariff, I realized that he was now turning me. He was crafting a justifiable rationalization for the gruesome murder of someone whose fleshy remains had ended up in cold storage at the Reardon lab. That murder had brought me to Egypt.

By all moral standards, what he had apparently done to the victim was the act of an immoral cold-blooded killer. But, while the standards and practices of my profession called for me to remain totally objective, my inner scientist was becoming overwhelmed by personal emotions. I found less and less fault with his reasoning and the terrible deed that ended with that slab of fetid skin on my lab bench. It seemed so long ago.

It wasn't just his dangerously seductive sexuality at work. Hearing the horrid realities of what the Nazis had done to the innocents was seducing me toward the dark side. I was beginning to accept that some evil deeds are for the good.

∽

He leaned forward, his elbows resting on his firm thighs, his dark eyes unfathomable. Then, he began to tell me about Rosslyn Ford. "I chose that point to tell Schroeder what I had heard about Rosslyn. After I left my lab at *Inshas,* I worked on a project in Sudan, which I will tell you about at another time. While I was working there, a woman named Jadwiga Lapinska was brought from Israel to tell me about the woman I had loved for many years. Rumors had come to me that Rosslyn was caught up in a Nazi sweep of the Warsaw museum where she was working with a fellow art historian. I had always harbored the hope that she had been released when they realized that she was Canadian, not a Pole."

I shot him a dubious look. Since there had been no contact between them for years, it was clear to me that he had been living in denial. *Where did he think she had been?*

He continued. "I was telling him about her because of the extensive *Mossad* records on Nazi arrests and asked if he could get me any reports accounting for her arrest. Jadwiga claimed that she had met Rosslyn when they were both prisoners in the women's concentration camp at *Ravensbruck.*

Shariff gave me a penetrating look and said, "I knew that if there was a record, it would finally confirm what I had been told by Jadwiga."

By any measure of fairness, the next part of his story might justify his delivery to the dark side. It left him with mental souvenirs that would never leave. The veins in his temple pulsed as he said, "I asked for the reports even though I was unsure how I could bear knowing for sure that she had been tortured, raped, the subject of unspeakable medical experiments, or worked to death."

As he continued, his voice grew heavy and his posture conveyed the deep pain he bore from what he was about to tell me. "Schroeder obtained Rosslyn's record very shortly. According to the report, the death camp known as *Ravensbruck was* some 30 miles north of Berlin. Himmler had established the camp in 1938, specifically to enslave women. Once within the camp, the women were totally at the mercy of the Nazi brutes, the *Third Reich* war machine, and the corporate parasites that fed on it all.

Rosslyn had indeed been arrested in the Warsaw Museum, where she was working with a fellow art restoration expert. She had brought an ancient Egyptian *stelae* there to get assistance in transcribing the hieratic writing on the antiquity. The transcription had just been completed when Nazi troops swept the museum and arrested the staff, including Rosslyn, for the crime of being 'artists'.

She was also listed as an enemy alien since Canada had declared war against Germany in 1939. Himmler ordered her detained for an eventual swap and she was sent to *Ravensbruck.* There were many held in the Nazi death camps as such hostages; the sister of famous New York mayor, Fiorello LaGuardia, spies, French resistance members, Polish aristocrats and Scandinavian nationals. Himmler planned to bargain them away when opportunities arose. The Nazis raised human flesh pedaling to a science."

Shariff went on. "Records indisputably reveal why Heinrich Himmler, *SS Reichsfuhrer* and Head of the German police, established and maintained *Ravensbruck.* Nestled alongside a small idyllic lake, it became the evil cauldron and epicenter of a vast slave system with 34 satellite divisions. The prisoners were not just Jewish. They came from many walks of life and nations; labeled prostitutes, artists, homosexuals, lesbians, political resisters, a-socials, Roma (Gypsies) and Jehovah's Witnesses. Captured women were secretly shipped from Poland, Lichtenburg, Russia, Ukraine, Germany, France, and other European countries, even some Americans.

They were not only used as forced laborers, they were also used as sex slaves and guinea pigs in unthinkable sterilization and other medical experiments. He began elaborating on the grisly experiments that T-4 doctors conducted on the *Ravensbruck* women. No woman in Europe was safe from the webs cast by the Nazi thugs to trap females for their slave system."

Watching him as he told his agonizing tale, I was not sure he could go on. But Shariff's mettle was of steel. He continued. "Camp barracks built for 250 had to accommodate 2,000. There were no beds. The women slept on the floors with no blankets to cover them in the harsh cold winters. To survive, they had to work the system for clothing to keep warm. Rations were minimal to non-existent. Imitation coffee was served for breakfast and the lucky ones got a bowl of soup for lunch and dinner."

He dropped his head slightly. "If women arrived with children, their children were soon taken way. If they were pregnant, or got pregnant from the constant rapes, the doctors, nurses, and guards forced abortions. Babies born there were butchered in front of their mothers.

Although designed to hold 6,000 prisoners, by 1945 and the end of the war, more than 100,000 women had passed through *Ravenbruck's* gates and into the slave labor system. Records indicate that between 30,000-50,000 died from the cold, starvation, beatings, lethal injections, medical experiments, and the exhausting work. They also died like flies from diseases spread through the camp by a plague of lice and filthy water. The areas around the bathrooms quickly became septic as five hundred women at a time used three trenches that sufficed as toilets."

What he told me next seemed unthinkable but it was an affirmation of what the human survival instinct will drive people to. "Some women became *kapos*. Throughout the system, the death camps depended on the cooperation of these trustee inmates to carry out the will of the Nazi commandants and guards by supervising the forced labor of their fellow prisoners.

As an enticement, *kapos* were given quarters separate from the general prison population, and beds. Extra food and warm clothing was also one of the special privileges they were given in exchange for their collaboration.

Slavery was a critical commodity in the *Reich's* economy. Many imprisoned women were forced to work in the on-site SS-owned factories where they converted confiscated clothing and furs for the *Reichstag*. In addition, corporations were quick to take advantage of the high return on investment available through use of *Third Reich* prisoners. Prisoners were leased out as free or cheap slaves to work in huge factories built adjacent to some of the Nazi camps.

German corporations, such as AEG, Daimler-Benz, Siemens Electric Company, Bayer, BASF, and Hoechst happily participated in the forced labor system.

Other prisoners were assigned to work gangs, constructing buildings and roads. When working on the roads, the women would be hooked to massive rollers like draft animals and forced to pull the equipment until they collapsed from fatigue.

Still others worked in sub camps manufacturing aircraft components, weapons, munitions, and explosives. When they could, they sabotaged Siemens rocket components."

Shariff clinched his jaw. "Himmler ordered whippings and torture as punishment for poor performance of the harsh work."

As he continued, the story summoned up visions that turned my stomach.

"The less fortunate were used as subjects in horrifying medical experiments planned by the corporate officials, and conducted by the T-4 doctors and Joseph Mengele. Drugs needed testing for IGF's immense pharmaceutical markets. Although the SS had no pharmaceutical interests, per se, they welcomed research results that would advance treatment of soldier's wounds in the field and speed their return to battle. Of course, the *Reich* also supported experiments that might further their goal of racial cleansing. So, bestial experiments conducted by the doctors inside the corporate facilities were overlooked.

Societal conventions and laws prohibited use of humans for the kind of research the chemical and pharmaceutical corporations planned with the help of the Nazi doctors. However, using captives in the death camps as guinea pigs, including those at *Ravensbruck*, removed such constraints. Experimental drugs for their immense markets were tested with impunity.

Nearly a thousand women at *Auschwitz* and *Ravensbruck* had their uteruses ravaged and destroyed by the gynecologist, Dr. Carl Clauberg. He exposed them to strong X-rays to see if large doses would produce sterility. Clauburg also performed uterine injections with various chemicals in an effort to induce such scarification that the uterus would be 'glued shut'. All this was done to devise methods to support the Nazi genetic cleansing goals.

After the war, and until his arrest in 1955, Clauberg was allowed to resume his work at a clinic in West Germany."

Polish and Roma women were particularly singled out for hellish tests. The Polish women were referred to as rabbits and mutilated in horrible medical trials at the camp's 'hospital'. Those women were kept in the bloc call the 'Rabbit House.'

Nazi doctors would cut deep wounds in the leg muscles of the Polish women and pack them with deliberately infected bacterial materials, dirt, shrapnel, glass and other material. The wounds were then sutured shut to promote infection and test new drugs for their healing efficacy. Sometimes gangrene gas was injected into the wounds and bone cavities. When the wounds became puss filled and necrotic, the doctors would amputate the limbs and try transplanting body parts from other prisoners."

Shariff recalled one particularly ghoulish account that Schroeder found in the *Mossad* records. It described a Polish woman who was housed on the 'Rabbit Block'. "Her limbs had all been amputated by the Nazi doctors in those unspeakable transplant experiments. Jadwiga lost her legs that way."

Most of the women died due to the experiments. Some were murdered afterward so that their bodies could be further studied during autopsy. Women who somehow survived these monstrous trials were horribly disfigured and crippled.

Ravensbruck women were also repeatedly raped, exposed to all forms of sexual abuse, impregnated, and given socially transmitted diseases. Both Nazi personnel and prisoners were given access to those women as a reward for meeting or surpassing production quotas. The babies born in the camp were deliberately starved to death or butchered in front of their mothers."

He shook his head. "It is hard to believe that it could get any worse, but it did. The next form of *Ravensbruck* hell came when the camp began training female SS supervisors who learned to torture and murder the inmates before taking their new skills to other camps in the system."

At this point, a waiter brought in a pitcher of cold water. Shariff paused while the man filled two glasses on the tray. I got the feeling that he, and probably others on staff, had been listening to Shariff's grizzly tale beyond the doorway. He poured and handed us our glasses as though in commiseration.

I thanked him and nodded to Shariff to continue. "According to records found by the *Mossad*, in the early winter of 1945 the barracks in the camp were so overcrowded and unhygienic that a typhus epidemic broke out. Then, a gas chamber was constructed near the crematorium. The Nazis began to systematically use it to annihilate those who became too ill, old, or weak to work."

Shariff's frown deepened as he recalled a particular point in the Mossad report. The stench of the crematory was overwhelming and the women prisoners who were not sent to the crematorium looked like walking skeletons.

It all ended in the spring of 1945 when an order was given to evacuate the inmates ahead of the advancing Russians who were coming to liberate the camp. Almost 25,000 prisoners were sent on a death march to purge all evidence in the camp of the Nazi crimes."

He shook his head in dismay. "The next part of the report seemed like a cruel joke God played on the women of *Ravensbruck*. It turned out the Russians were almost worse than the Nazis, raping everyone, in the camps, in the villages, on the roads. The women who could, marched to escape the Russians even after their German guards had abandoned their posts."

At this point, Shariff paused to take a drink of his water and steady himself before continuing. "I finally came to the part in the report which described Rosslyn's fate. I steeled myself against what I knew was coming.

Rosslyn was especially interesting to the T-4 doctors in the experimental building. She was fair and had very golden hair, which Nazis fancied. But, her eyes were dark brown. She was therefore considered genetically defective."

At this point, Shariff's face seemed to turn to stone. "The Nazi doctors used her and others in experiments to determine if eye color could be changed. They would inject dyes into prisoners' eyes from the lab at Auschwitz. The dyes caused extreme pain and eventual blindness."

Then his voice finally broke. "When Rosslyn's eyes became very infected and no longer useful for the optical experiments, her legs were broken and then her fibula and tibia bones were surgically bound together at the fractured points. The doctors wanted to see whether calcification would bond and reinforce them. They were looking for a technique that could be used in the field to quickly get soldiers back on their feet and into battle.

She was also experimented on to see whether her body would

replace bone after sections were surgically removed. When they were force marched from the camp, Rosslyn was spent and could no longer see or walk."

He said, "I will carry the next words to my grave. The report said that if I want to visit Rosslyn I should go to *Ravensbruck*. The Nazis quickly sent women to the gassing chambers who were too weak to march, and then baked them in the ovens. They wanted none of their victims left behind as evidence of their crimes.

Tens of thousands of women died at *Ravensbruck*, either from the living conditions, slave labor, medical experiments, or the gas chambers. The scene of their horror is now replaced by one that is picturesque. But those who survived revealed that there in the bottom of the village's beautiful little lake are the ashes from the bodies that were cremated in the *Ravensbruck* ovens. Rosslyn's ashes are with her sisters."

I watched him as he continued but could not find the words to convey the horror I felt for his tragedy. Instead, I asked how the Mossad had discovered the gruesome details.

"Schroeder told me that, strangely, the Nazis kept meticulous records on the prisoners,. These were not destroyed. That is how so much is known about the lawless evil behind the barbed wire of their death centers. Even though the records revealed so much, the truth about *Ravensbruck* flew under the radar until recently because it was largely off limits to the public after its Russian liberation. *Ravensbruck* became part of Russia's Cold War antimissile program."

Shariff then leaned back in his chair and grew silent, as though exhausted. The silence became deafening, swallowing the room, and his private pain shown clearly on his face, betraying his anguish. He was a million miles away at that moment.

Outside, the rising heat was slowly eating away at the engineered cooler air inside the building. Tension began stifling me, and I could feel my pulse pounding in my eardrums. Ghosts of the women trapped in that hellish place, that Nazi freak show, clouded my mind and, for relief, I began concentrating on the sounds from across the hall. It was lunchtime and I heard the sound of dishes rattling as the tables were being prepared for the diners.

And then the visions pushed aside the sounds from the dining room and flooded my mind again, visions of starving women without dishes rattling, without clothes in the icy winters, ridden with lice, beaten, tortured, raped, robbed of their humanity. *Too horrible to have happened in the civilized world I know. It was like a parallel universe.*

When I could no longer bear the visions and Shariff's silence, I finally asked him, "Did you go to *Ravensbruck*?"

I knew the answer that was coming.

He leaned forward and held his head in his hands. "Yes. I blamed myself for losing her, letting her go, putting my work at *Inshas* before our relationship. I should have married her, changed the course of events that caused her to die such a brutal death in a Nazi extermination camp. I had always thought that one day I would turn a corner in Paris or Cairo, or somewhere on the planet, and look up to see her walking toward me."

He rose and walked to the window. "Some things change you forever." Looking out, he said softly, "Life is only a gift for some of us." Turning, he excused himself and left the room.

Watching him go, I realized that he would always be on that path, the path to revenge her.

10

The Mossad List.
Monsters still walk the land.

Not wanting to go out in the heat, I chose to eat alone in the dining room. When my lunch was finished I walked back across the hall to see if Shariff had returned. He had.

Looking up at me from his seat, he nodded and gestured toward my chair. As I walked past him, his hand reached out and brushed mine. But he did not look at me the same way as before, and his words were stiff and measured. Reliving the tale of Rosslyn's fate had reopened a wound that now lay between us.

He began again to describe the last meeting his team had in Schroeder's vineyard. "We spent time drinking wine and talking about the camps. Then, Schroeder left us. He was gone for the better part of an hour, leaving us to wonder if our meeting was over.

Just as we were about to go, he walked through the vines and sat in his chair at the table. He was carrying a folder. Laying it on the table, he opened to a page which had been paper clipped. Removing the clip, he handed the page to me, saying that it was a list of the Nazi war criminals who escaped Europe before they could be brought to trial, those that were still alive.

He also explained the origin of the list. Dr. Efraim Zuroff,

Chief Nazi Hunter of the Simon Wiesenthal Center in Israel, had generated a list of surviving high-ranking Nazis, then spread across the globe. The Center had also developed a status report on efforts to bring the criminals to justice.

The status report graded countries on their level of effort to locate and try the war murderers within their borders. Schroeder skimmed through the report for us "... The United States was judged to have a highly successful investigation and prosecution program. It has identified suspects and undergone maximum investigations and prosecution ... Canada, Germany, Hungary, Italy, and Serbia have also taken necessary measures to enable proper investigation and prosecution of Nazi war criminals ... Netherlands and Poland, only minimal success has been achieved ... Great Britain failed to make at least a minimal effort to investigate war criminals and failed to achieve any practical results, even stopped efforts to deal with the issue ... Norway, Sweden and Syria refused to investigate or prosecute suspected Nazi war criminals, claiming statute of limitation laws or ideological restrictions ... complete failure to investigate and prosecute suspected Nazi war criminals in Australia, Austria, Estonia, Latvia, Lithuania, and the Ukraine ... no known suspects in Bosnia-Herzegovina, Costa Rica, Croatia, Czech Republic, Finland, France, Greece, New Zealand, Romania, Slovakia or Spain ... Argentina, Belarus, Belgium, Denmark, Luxemburg, Russia, Slovenia, Columbia, Paraguay, Uruguay, Bolivia, Brazil, and Chile did not even respond to the center's request for information and clearly did not take any action to investigate suspected war criminals."

Schroeder finished by telling us that the *Mossad* has tracked the movements of the escaped rats on the list. Their whereabouts are recorded as they slink from one warren to another, like evil insidious troglodytes. He also said, with a sardonic smile, that the list had once been much longer but the *Mossad* had 'bumped into many of them'. Then he rose, turned, and walked through the vineyard toward his chateau."

Shariff shook his head. "I glanced at the names, stunned, and struggling to absorb the fact that some of those bastards were still be alive, and probably living well."

Alois Brunner – Syria
Dr. Aribert Heim - ?
Ladislaus Scizsik-Csatary – Hungary
Gerhard Sommer – Germany
Vladimir Katriuk – Canada
Hans (Antanas) Lipschis – Germany
Ivan (John) Kalymon – United States
Soren Kam – Germany
Algimantas Dailide – Germany
Milhail Gorshkow – Estonia
Theodor Szehinskyj – United States
Helmut Oberlander – Canada

I wondered if any of them were the ones who personally inflicted the pain and torture Rosslyn endured at *Ravensbruck*. "God, how I would like to get my hands on that one. I am a scientist, trained to unravel the intricate details of the world and respect the life forms that pass across its stage. However, deep hatred and a thirst for blood consumed me. All humanity had been ground out of me. Like Schroeder, my heart had turned to stone."

Finally, finding my tongue, and thinking aloud, I said, 'There is something so strange about a people who would torture, rape, mutilate, gas, and burn victims in ovens as the solution to what they perceived as a social problem."

He nodded. "That group, or what remains of them, have no right to a place on Planet Earth. Standing, I declared to my team that the world must be rid of such scum and reminded them that we had the power to make that happen. We had the skills to develop a witches brew that would cause such brutal agony its victims would pray for death. I did not care what that made me, made us, feeling

125

that some good had to be snatched by the deaths of such evil."

"My men understood."

Shariff waited a moment for all that to sink in before he continued. "It was then that we decided to conduct our first hunt in Syria where Alois Brunner was known to be hiding. He had been there for decades, safe because Syria refused to cooperate with efforts to prosecute him even though he had been convicted in absentia by France.

Brunner deserved to be first on our hit list because he had been Adolf Eichmann's key operative. He was responsible for deporting 47,000 Jews from Austria, 44,000 Jews from Greece, 23,500 from France and 14,000 from Slovakia. All were sent to the death camps that Eichmann had established for their extermination. The Simon Wiesenthal Center considered Brunner to be the most important unpunished Nazi alive and he was on the Most Wanted List of Holocaust Perpetrators. The world did not need Alois Brunner."

I sat quietly, at a loss for words. The description of Rosslyn's abuse, torture, and death still left me dazed and sick to my stomach.

Shariff had paused to take a last drink from his water glass. I watched his strong hands grip the glass and wondered what they had done to Nazi's necks that he caught up with.

Continuing with his story, he said, "After Schroeder left the vineyard, we followed his path to the chateau and found him sitting on the western veranda. The sun was setting and I stopped to watch the spectacle with him. It hit me that the golden orbit had disappeared into the horizon only a few times since our arrival, but it seemed like a lifetime. I spoke for the team."

"It is clear that your score with Germany's war criminals has not been settled. We have highly enriched uranium, which we stole from the *Inshas* lab to prevent the use of nuclear warheads by Egypt's military. That is what we are here to discuss with the Negev scientists. We stored it where it can do no harm. Now, we will access it and use it to seek revenge for Rosslyn and the other victims of the Holocaust. We're going Nazi hunting. Will you join us?"

"Schroeder rose, saying, that he would relish joining us in the hunt, but today's political environment prohibits such direct actions by Israelis. They are now forced to act in consort with other nations, always taking care not to give their enemies an excuse to unleash their dogs, and their nuclear bombs. Israel watches and waits as the escaped war criminals sneak from hidey-hole to hidey-hole. Then, nodding his head at the list in my hands, he said it is now ours to do with as we see fit.

Finally, he shook my hand and said he could not know what actions we take but believed that we went with God.

I asked him if, after all that had occurred, he still believed there is a God. Not answering, he turned and re-entered his home.

We all understood that the conversation that had just occurred on his veranda 'had never taken place'.

And that was how we ended up at the bottom of the lagoon in *Shaab Ambar*."

∽

I watched him carefully as I asked, "When do we get to the part about the sheet of human skin that ended up on my lab bench back at Reardon?"

He studied me for a minute, deciding how much to tell me, and then said, "As I said, since Alois Brunner's name was the first one on the list, we decided to start there. But, we did not plan for Brunner's death to be a one-off. At least, it was not supposed to be. After Brunner's execution, we planned to track down the rest of the dirty bastards.

As it turned out, we could not follow that path once we caught up with Brunner. In exchange for the antidote to the Polonium 210 we had infected him with, he traded us the location of Scorpion's Polaris missiles and a plan to use them in attacks on the cooling pools in nuclear power plants near American cities. We had to bring that information to the United Nations Security Council.

And that is how I ended up in Port Said."

I gave him a meaningful look. "Where were you between *Shaab Ambar* and *Port Said?*"

He studied me again. "Off the record?"

I knew he was not going to tell me more unless I agreed. Hoping to be able to piece enough of a report together without breaking his confidence, I said, "If that is the only way."

He nodded and began to finish the story of his sojourn from *Shaab Ambar* to *Port Said*. "As I have already told you, we acquired *Dragon* in order to use her fuel and reactor to irradiate bismuth and produce Polonium 210. We had to take that course of action since the manufacture of the poison is restricted to state-regulated nuclear reactors."

He laughed. "But you know there is always a way around government regulations. Polonium 210 is easily obtained if you know where to find it. It is even contained in anti-static fans made in New York. Someone with lab experience can extract enough lethal doses from one of those fans to kill ten people."

Growing serious, he continued. "However, our circumstance was more complex. Polonium 210 from those sources is also traceable. We needed to produce our own to prevent an experienced scientist from tracking it back to us too soon."

I interjected. "It only has a 138-day half-life before beginning to transmute to a stable state, like lead. By measuring the proportion of polonium and lead in a sample, the poison's production date can be established. It also has a fingerprint. By analyzing the impurities in the polonium, the origin of its production can be traced."

He nodded. "By producing our own in a U.S. sub that was presumed sunk, we hoped the path would be twisted enough to throw off the hounds, at least long enough for us to complete our mission. We produced a gram, more than enough to terminate everyone on the *Mossad* list, and millions of others."

Smiling wickedly, he said, "As you know, we traded some enriched *Inshas uranium* for the sub. We also made extra money in the deal and used that to fund our Nazi hunting operation."

Watching him, I thought, *He does not so much break the rules as he simply does not accept them.*

"Our plan" he said, "...was simple. Only about 50 nanograms of Polonium 210 are fatal, starting with the liver and spleen. Before traveling to each location identified on the *Mossad* list, we would suspend lethal doses of the poison in small two-ounce spritzer bottles filled with water we polluted with the polonium and labeled insect relent. Those could be carried through airport security without setting off any alarms. We had any number of options for getting the toxin to our target, but we chose airline travel because our time was limited due to the short half-life factor of Polonium 210. And the hunt for us."

Arriving at our target, we planned to acquire bottles of the German lager, *Altbier*, lace two of the bottles with the poisoned water, and serve those to our victim while we drank others that were not polluted, pretending to enjoy a friendly conversation with a fellow traveler.

To get to our first target, Brunner, we surfaced one night and four of us offloaded into one of the onboard *pangas*, along with two of the contaminated spritzer bottles encased in safety overpacks. We rowed ashore while the other three took *Dragon* back to the bottom of the lagoon to wait for our return. Our intention was to repeat that action, using *Dragon* as our warehouse, until all on the list were dead."

He looked at me and shrugged. "Some would contend that, like the Nazis, we are also serial killers. Many who know the whole truth about the *Third Reich* death camps will overlook our transgressions."

He stopped and studied me for a minute, then said, "By the way, Polonium 210 is very difficult to detect in a patient. The symptoms do not become observable for a few days. Diagnosing the etiology takes much longer. Tracing it to its source is even less likely. There was only a slim chance that some scientist had enough savvy to identify the source of death, much less know that it had to be ingested to kill. We planned to be well away before the contamination was discovered. The perfect crime."

He was amused as he asked, "How long did it take you?"

I chose not to answer, so he continued. "Polonium 210 was also the perfect weapon for putting the others on the *Mossad* list on notice. Word travels fast among that rat pack. We meant Brunner's slow, tortuous and spectacular extermination to send the bone chilling message, 'We're coming for you.'"

Still amused, he said, "Brunner was reported to be masquerading as a retired commodities broker from Brussels and living in a small town in northern Syria so we hired a helicopter in Cairo to get us there. Not wanting to fly over Israeli territory and risk being shot out of the sky, and knowing we would be suspect if we landed in Damascus, we took the scenic route across Saudi Arabia to the Persian Gulf, then followed the Euphrates River to the Syrian town of *Jarabulus* at the Turkish border."

I asked how long the flight lasted, thinking helicopters were not known for their long distance reach. He replied, "We could not make the trip in one hop so we landed to refuel in *Ar Rahmadi*, overnighted, and filled up our bird. Pretending to be Syrian scientists assigned to check the embankment dams along the Euphrates, we knew we could pull off that masquerade for at least 24 hours before checks were run on us through the poorly organized Syrian security system. Water wars between the Middle Eastern nations often see government officials in the area checking on the river system so our presence would bring no special attention for a day or so. It is said in the river marshes that whoever controls the water controls the enemy."

He stretched out his long legs and got comfortable while continuing to describe their journey. "Flying low along the river we were treated to remarkable sights. The Euphrates is a complex of shallow freshwater lakes, swamps, and marshes. Since the climate is subtropical, it is a hot and arid land except along the river, like Egypt. Below us were a continuous ribbon of aquatic vegetation; reeds, rushes and papyrus. When we crossed marshy land there were numerous birds along migratory routes, which we were careful to avoid since our bird's blades and the bird flocks would not mix well. We also spotted wild boar, buffalo and large snakes as the downdraft from our blades parted the phragmite reeds that form towering walls along the hundreds of channels into which the river is divided as it passes through the marshes."

He laughed. "We were not exactly welcome anywhere along the river's course since that is the territory of the Marsh Arabs. They have been badly treated by Sadam Hussein's administration and they suspect all outsiders. The government drained many of the marshes to punish them for their politics. Where once there was riverine forest, south and east of the border, the land now turns into desert, supporting no vegetation except in small pockets. Many Marsh Arabs have been reduced to living in slums around cities such as *Basra.*

Archeological expeditions have recovered remains of palace reliefs from the 1st millennium BCE that depict lion and bull hunts in fertile landscapes in the area. They are similar to our Egyptian reliefs. Then, there were cities with monumental architecture. There was also a wide spread trade system. Apparently, empires sprang up, organized into competing city-states, with many located along canals of the river.

Later sixteenth to nineteenth century European explorers reported an abundance of animal life in the area, including gazelle, leopard and lion. There were also *mangar*, good for sport fishing. The Brits nicknamed them 'Tigris salmon.'"

Shaking his head, he said, "All outsiders are now potential enemies. They watched us closely as we passed over their unique

floating villages and small *mashoofs* watercraft ."

He rose and stretched. I allowed my eyes to run down his sensual body, pausing where his manhood made a slight bulge in his trousers. Then, he again took his seat and continued to describe the trek to hunt Brunner. "When we arrived in *Jarabulus*, we discovered that Brunner had left the area. He was on the run. Putting out the promise of a handsome reward for information on his whereabouts, it did not take long to learn of his new destination. He was now on the African continent, in Namibia.

Backtracking in our bird, we flew to Johannesburg, South Africa and arranged for the rental of two Land Rovers with sand tracks."

The mention of sand tracks brought back memories. He confused my raised eyebrows and said, "The sand tracks are used to throw under a vehicle's wheels when it bogs down in desert sands. They can provide traction."

Rolling my eyes, I told him, "I know what sand tracks are. We often used them when I was working in Sudan and crossing the Sahara.

He gave me a look that seemed to fall somewhere between amusement and amazement. Apparently, western women scientists were an anomaly to him. It had not occurred to me that he might not know we spent as much time doing field research in desolate places as we do in high tech labs.

I smiled and asked him to go on with his account of the hunt for Brunner.

The hunt in Africa required crossing harsh land. "From Johannesburg, Brunner had headed north to a town on the Namibian coast. We took the same road, the only paved route. After fifteen hours of hard driving we made *Windhoek*, the capitol. There, we paid informants who confirmed that our quarry had continued on to *Swakopmund* by the sea. They also told us something that we did not know. Brunner was in the company of many others.

To get to *Swakopmund*, we had to cross the Namib desert. The heat, sand, and blazing sun took their toll. The Namib is the oldest and driest desert on earth. No one survives if they run into trouble between water holes, which are few and far between ."

Laughing, he said, "There is an observable pecking order around the spring fed ponds, and water is so scarce that animals there have learned to survive by sharing it. The big cats tend to arrive first, then the prey animals. If we keep polluting the earth

at the same exponential rate since the industrial revolution, we humans may have to take a page from their book."

I agreed. "Water wars may well be a part of our future. Many areas on earth are already suffering shortages of potable water."

He nodded and went on. "By the time we reached *Windhoek*, we needed rest, and a plan to handle the others in Brunner's company, so we overnighted there. At the dinner table in a restaurant near our hotel, we developed a plan to separate him from his companions.

By sun up we were on the road again, passing, the stranded skeletons of ships that had run aground on the treacherous shifting shoals of the Skeleton Coast. It was another four hours on when we arrived in the seaport town of *Swakopmund*."

"We hit the docks there in time for lunch and immediately headed for the Jetty Restaurant, famous for its fresh oysters and abalone. Having stuffed ourselves on the delicacies of Walvis Bay, we checked in at the Europa Hof Hotel where we knew Brunner was staying.

After washing the desert dust off and changing clothes, we drove over to the main marina to look for a charter. There was a beauty available, a 40 ft. ketch rig Steel Yacht owned by a local fisherman. He had little time for recreation and was happy to let us charter the boat for the week, especially since we were going to crew it ourselves.

Two of our team remained aboard to ready and provision her while the rest of us returned to the hotel to put our plan in play. We needed to cut Brunner out from the herd.

We stalked him for two days and then opportunity knocked. After being out to meet the others he was traveling with, he came back to the hotel and stopped in the bar before going up to his room. I pretended to accidently bump into him, introduced myself as a fellow hotel guest, and invited him to have a drink with me. We talked for an hour or so and he seemed to enjoy having someone with a scientific background for company.

As we were leaving the bar, I invited him to join me for some sport fishing on the yacht the next morning. He gladly accepted, saying he loved to sail and fashioned himself an expert angler."

At seven the following morning, we met in the lobby and took one of the Land Rovers to the marina where the ketch was moored. When the wind is in the east, a foul smell usually wafts across the harbor from the fish factories along the shore but that day there was a westerly wind. The weather was fresh, and Brunner happily predicted the day would bring some good catches.

Little did he know.

Not bothering to run up the sails, we powered out to a likely spot up the coast, and dropped anchor. That done, I suggested we have a drink and went below to get lagers. We had stocked the refrigerator with several six packs of Altbier, two of which had been carefully uncapped, contaminated with the Polonium 210, and recapped.

Those two sat in ominous isolation on the rack of the refrigerator door. The others sat on the two shelves of the unit, safe for the four crew members to imbibe. I picked up one of the polluted bottles from the door rack and one from the unit's shelf.

Leaving the caps on, I climbed the ship's ladder back up into the cockpit. When he saw that they were *Altbiers* he was delighted. I handed him his, along with a bottle opener and then went forward with the rest of the crew, ostensibly to help cleat the anchor line. I had no intention of being within exposure range of the lethal poison when he uncapped his bottle.

Once I heard the cap pop, I knew he would quickly down his *Altbier*, sealing his fate. I gave it fifteen minutes and then returned aft to offer him a second. He promptly accepted my offer and I gave him the other contaminated bottle for good measure. It was a pleasure to sit and watch him swig it. After he had downed the second polluted brew, I invited him to help himself to the others. He did, while we spent the day casting for *kabeljou*. Brunner caught two about 70 cm long. I caught three but they were under the 40 cm minimum and had to go back. It didn't matter. I had hooked the fish I wanted.

All in all, it was a good day. The life Brunner had left to him was circling the drain. Keeping an eye on him brought me great satisfaction, knowing that the poison was eating away at his insides, enjoying the thought that, like his victims in the Nazi camps, he was about to walk through Hell barefooted. The stars had aligned and he was now the victim. His death in a few days would be agonizing, but he suspected nothing. The grim reaper was coming for him, but by the time he began to feel symptomatic there would be no hope. Biological termination would come in slow excruciating waves.

We motored back into port as the sun was setting and Brunner happily accepted my offer to go out again the next morning. I turned in early, fatigued by an afternoon in the heat of the Skeleton Coast and calmed by the successful murder of our first Nazi target."

I sat listening to Shariff in stunned silence. In so many ways, he was everything one could want in a man, but what he was telling me about the cold, calculated killing of another human being was in total contradiction to the edicts of scientific ethics and religious dictates. I said so.

Shariff looked at me for a long moment and then began to steadily justify his actions. "Cecily, where ethics and killing are concerned, the world is a goat rodeo. Everyone has some blood on their hands. We wallow in it. Even our food involves slaughter. It is not as though the steaks we eat come from free range animals that died of old age. In combat, killing is considered justifiable homicide. Self defense is justifiable. Electrifying criminals is socially sanctioned. Julius and Ethel Rosenberg were hanged for espionage in 1951 because, technically, they could not be tried for treason since the U.S. was not at war with Russia. My team and I may have committed murder by some standards while, by others, we performed a public service. That is what the *Third Reich* claimed to be doing in their slaughterhouses; gassing and incinerating millions of men, women, and innocent children as a public service. The line between good and evil is defined by where you are standing and the standards that prevail on that turf. "

Concluding his argument, he said, "My first job as a nuclear scientist was to enrich Egyptian uranium beyond the limits considered legal in the international community. In some places I would have been a criminal but in Egypt, and other Middles East countries, my work was sanctioned at the highest levels, state sponsored in Egypt. In terms of social status, I was in the upper echelon.

That work prepared me for my second job, delivering an agonizing death to Nazi criminals who escaped prosecution. They would have been convicted in the Nuremburg trials and executed. I make no apologies for my past or my present. I am both moral and immoral. We all are."

Dismissing my look of dismay, he continued his story. "Brunner was waiting in the lobby the next morning when we came down from our rooms. He was anxious to put out again. We made our way to the harbor and were underway within an hour.

The morning air over the bay was cool and the water fairly flat.

Kabeljou were running and we soon bagged our limit so we went below to have sandwiches, and more *Altbier*.

My men and I had decided to keep him aboard for several days until he was almost totally debilitated. Then, we planned to abandon him in an isolated spot along the 700-mile Skeleton Coast. Dying, and in agony, he would never walk out.

As we ate our sandwiches and drank the lager, we began to tell him about our sojourn and how we ended up processing *Dragon's* uranium fuel into Polonium 210, a poison 250,000 times more deadly than hydrogen cyanide. When we got to the part about the *Mossad* list and how we were going to use the poison, and the agony it brought, he suddenly sensed he was not among friends.

Asking how we could infect that many men with the poison, I looked at him steadily and answered, "By giving them *Altbier* laced with Polonium 210."

Shariff smiled. "Brunner turned pasty as the realization about what we had done to him sank in. Being a Nazi, he was no stranger to chemical warfare. The Germans used all sorts of chemical weapons during World War II, including hydrogen cyanide, the base of Zyklon B. Our victim quickly comprehended the threat to his life.

He moved from the bunk where he had been sitting and made an effort to climb up to the cockpit, but his legs were too weak. We set him back on the bunk and explained our plan down to the last detail; to watch him dissolve from the inside out and then dump him, somewhat still alive, on the desolate Skeleton Coast. We were not offering the gift of a quick death by Zyklon B, followed by incineration in a Nazi oven. If he were lucky, some of the cheetahs known to hunt along the coast, would ravage and devour him. Otherwise, he would lay there for days in the scorching heat and hyper-arid environment, dying by

inches while his internal organs liquefied, his bones dissolved, and his body steadily putrefied.

Terror gripped him as we methodically embellished on the biological process of death by Polonium 210. I could not tell whether he was becoming too scared to function or the poison was debilitating him. It was one or the other, maybe both.

He lay back on the bunk for half an hour without moving, staring at the starboard mahogany wall, seemingly stunned into immobility. But, he was not stunned. The fiend was thinking.

Finally, he rose up on one elbow, surveyed us with disdain, and announced that killing him would not be in the world's best interest. He said there was supposed to be an antidote for what we had done to him and he had information that was far more important to the world than our plot to revenge a few million Jews. He was willing to trade the information for his life.

Such a claim naturally caught our attention. What could possibly balance the scale against avenging millions of victims in the Nazi killing centers.

In fact, there is such an antidote. We acknowledged that the Brits had developed the chelation agent HOE-TTC (dimercaprol) that, in lab experiments proved to be 90 percent effective against exposure to Polonium 210. However, as far as we knew, it was still in the experimental stage and we had none in our possession. For whatever reason, the Brits did not pursue industrial scale production of the antidote. Probably thought there would never be a need to repel such an insidious chemical weapon."

Still, dying men are easily convinced that there is hope. We lied and told him that we were carrying HOE-TTC onboard the boat."

Continuing, Shariff said that the serial killer had smiled, thinking we had taken his bait. "He began negotiating for the antidote. As the minutes passed, Brunner explained that if we provided him with the antidote, he would tell us the location of the 16 Polaris A-1 missiles taken from the hijacked U.S. sub *Scorpion,* our *Dragon.*

I waved off his offer, telling him we had no dog in that fight. Recovering the missiles was the U.S. navy's problem. Ours was eliminating any remaining butchers on the *Mossad* list.

That was when he cinched the deal. He announced that not only would he tell us the location of the missiles, which were close by, he would tell us the plan to use them against heavily populated U.S. cities. That plan was in play and it was what brought him out of Syria to *Swakopmund*. The others on the list were also in *Swakopmund* to launch the plan.

I studied my despicable prey, lying there on the padded bunk as the ketch gently rocked back and forth with the swell. The sounds of the waves slapping against the hull seemed to tick off the life remaining to him. For the moment, the enjoyment of watching him die was overruled by the need to make him believe that we could reverse the process.

In the distance, the beautiful clear beach of the Skeleton Coast lay to our port and I could almost feel the cold *Benguela* current beneath us. As much as I wanted the bastard dead, wanted to cut out his heart and toss it to the sharks in those waters, I had to convince him that we were willing to collude with him. He had to believe that we were weighing which would be the greater good; removing Alois Brunner from the face of the earth or saving millions of people in America.

Of course, it was never a contest. In the final analysis, we are men of science, good men, whether you think so or not. We could never have entertained the prospect of letting millions die in nuclear blasts and radiation exposure in exchange for the death of the horrible human being we now held captive. But he had to believe we might."

Watching Shariff, and listening to his remarkable story, I could not help but think, *You would have done far worse to him if he had not told you what you needed to know. You make the line between good and evil so spurious. It was not supposed to be this way.*

He continued. "We played our roles well, and convinced him

that he held some high cards in the game. Finally, a bargain was struck. In exchange for administering the antidote to him, he would tell us the location of the missiles, the details of the plan to use them, and reveal the whereabouts of the others in the town. He cunningly suggested that the bargain be based on a gentlemen's agreement. That was never an option. He did not qualify as a gentleman in my estimation so I fashioned a bargain containing a lot of firewalls.

It was agreed that he would first tell us where the missiles were located and the exact location in *Swakopmund* of the others on the *Mossad* list we held. We would motor back into Walvis Bay. One of our crew would put to shore in the ship's dingy and take a Land Rover to verify that the missiles were where he said.

Following verification of the missiles, and the safe return of our man to the ketch, we would inject Brunner with the first half of the antidote. When he had been injected, he would reveal the missile attack plan, including the names of the nuclear plants and cities which were to be targeted and the dates for the planned attacks. All this was to be documented in his own handwriting. After he signed and dated the document, we would inject him with the other half of the antidote and return him to shore.

Anxious to begin receiving the life saving antidote, he quickly began, giving us directions to the site where the missiles were stashed. He also cautioned that the others in *Swakopmund* would be watching anyone returning from the ketch since they knew he had gone fishing with its crew. The watchers would be dangerous."

Shariff sketched a rough map of the area to show me where the missiles were hidden. "About 30 miles inland to the north and east of town, there is a range of mountains. In the mountains are huge veins of uranium. Although, some of the veins were discovered back in the late 1920s, commercial mining did not develop for decades. There were several start-ups through the years but repeated minimal successes resulted in the investors voting with their feet. They pulled out. Their start-ups left a labyrinth of abandoned tunnels.

Once serious commercialization began, the richest beds gradually became an immense open pit mine, terraced down hundreds of feet deep. Blasting tons of ore from the pit each day makes the area highly dangerous so access is tightly controlled.

There is also a health hazard. When the dust from the blasting and rock crushing is breathed in, uranium particles enter the lungs and decay radioactively. The result is a high incidence of lung cancer."

Shariff gestured with his hands, indicating the irony. "The isolated location of the mine, plus the radioactive dust and restricted access to the area, make the old tunnels a highly secure place for hiding contraband."

Nazi use of the mine tunnel had been planned far in advance. "Brunner, and the others waiting in *Swakopmund*, had formed an organization before escaping Europe, and Hitler. The organization, *Nach Lebensraum,* has vast holdings, including a large voting share of the Namibian pit mine. So, members of the organization can enter the area at will. Brunner furnished our man a note granting him access."

Pausing, Shariff smiled and said, "The formation of the organization is an interesting story in itself. It reveals the alliances against the *Fuhrer* in his final days of power as it became clear that he had become a mad man and the war was not ending well for Germany, including anyone affiliated with the *Fuhrer*. Starting in 1943, the rats belonging to *Nach Lebensraum* began planning how they would abandon ship.

In preparation for this eventuality, they started shipping contraband to points around the globe; gold, art, money, stocks, anything of value they could steal from their sectors of control. The men on the *Mossad* list did not exit Germany empty handed, by any means."

"The shipping points became their hideouts as they slipped from under the *Fuhrer's* nose and reinvented themselves elsewhere. In post-war 1945, the contraband they had conveyed from their homeland made them some of the wealthiest men in the world but, being creatures of the dark side, they always kept low profiles. They also approached the *Tripartite* for membership and protection under its umbrella in exchange for a handsome portion of their ill-gotten gains. Of course, they became 'outed' when Schroeder turned their names over to us.

Alois Brunner was the only one in our cross hairs when we arrived in *Swakopmund*. Then, our plan was to work our way down the list after we dispatched him. Until Brunner told us, we did not know that the others were onto us the minute I approached him. Our every move was being watched, although they did not know who we were and had no way of knowing our game plan.

They were waiting on shore for the return of the ketch on that second day, when Brunner and I were supposed to be out sport fishing again. However, when we sailed back into Walvis Bay we did not bring the ketch back to her berth. We dropped anchor off shore. The Nazis had no option other than to wait.

On board, our man returned safe after verifying the location of the missiles in one of the mine tunnels. He had taken pictures to verify Brunner's story. The tunnel entrance where the missiles were stored was well hidden in the main pit.

It was also clear that uranium was being processed at the site, another danger to encroachers. Our man also took pictures of the long trains delivering hydrochloric acid, used in the chemical separation operation, and the stations where they

were unloaded. Because of the activity on the site, and the pollution level, we knew the area would remain off-limits to outsiders for some time. So, for the moment, the missiles were safe in their lair."

I had to ask. "Did you pretend to give Brunner the antidote?"

Shariff nodded slightly. "With the first part of our agreement completed, I injected him with what was supposed to be half of the antidote. We allowed him to rest for awhile before we sat down with him to complete our mutual arrangement and document the plan of attack on America."

The plan, as Shariff described it, was horrific. "The attack involves a coordinated strike by German and Russian subs outfitted with Russian SS-N-3 cruise missiles. When each sub is within range of its target, the missiles are to be simultaneously launched. Their marks are to be the cooling pools of nuclear power plants operating near heavily populated cities. As the nuclear warheads hit, the pools will become incinerated. The radioactive fuel assemblies, carefully arranged in geometric spatial patterns in the pool waters, would be transformed into lethal poisonous clouds that will contaminate everything beneath them.

According to plan, Indian Point, on the east bank of the Hudson River, is to be the main target on the east coast. Ironically, that plant is some 35 miles north of Midtown Manhattan, the birthplace of the infamous U.S. Manhattan Project.

One of the main reasons Indian Point was selected as a target is because, although it is on the Nuclear Regulatory Commission's list of plants most likely to experience a massive earthquake, the plant's cooling pools also have a flaw that makes them ripe for a fire. While Indian Point's three reactors are under an impenetrable steel-reinforced containment dome, its two 40-foot deep cooling pools, where the nuclear waste is stored, are not. And, the pool lacks ability to quickly replenish rapidly leaking water.

The plant's three reactors have produced 2,700 spent fuel assemblies, which are stored in the cooling pool. Indian Point is a firestorm waiting to happen."

I was shocked into a verbal outburst by the prospect of an attack on Indian Plant, or any other nuclear power plant in America. "Standard practice at such plants is to pull used uranium fuel assemblies out of the reactor's vessel when 5 per cent of their radioactive energy has been burned up through irradiation. The remaining 95 per cent, which will instantly kill any human next to it, has to be remotely moved to a cooling pool where continuously circulating chemically treated water protect workers and the public from exposure to its lethal radioactivity. Interruption of the water's circulation will cause the assemblies to heat up and lead to a pool fire. A spent nuclear fuel pool fire is the most dreaded catastrophe in the industry. An inferno on steroids! Such a plan is madness!"

"That pool holds some 230,000,000 curies of radioactivity waiting to be released into the environment. Unbelievably, like most nuclear energy plants, its security system provides no contingency for an attack from the air."

Shariff nodded in agreement. "The area's population density also makes it an ideal terrorist target, with some 2,100 people per square mile. New York City, and every other town in the path of the plume that will spread from a pool fire at the site will leave the area uninhabitable for millions of years."

Continuing, he described Bruner's face as he unveiled the Nazi plan. "It contorted into an evil smile while he reminded us that the technology to control a pool fire does not exist. In addition, everywhere the missiles strike, millions of Americans will either die in the blast or be fatally exposed to high-level radiation. The few who survive will not find land on which to grow food. It will be a terrorist dream come true!

Brunner then named the other nuclear sites and cities that are targeted, named the others waiting for us to return with him, gave directions to their locations, then signed and dated the document.

I injected him again, then we bound him to avoid any attempt to go overboard."

"At that point, we heaved to and headed out to sea, setting a northerly heading along the coast. We sailed all night until we reached a deserted point with a small protected bay. There was no one around for hundreds of miles.

By then, the Polonium 210 was working its evil energy on Brunner's insides because, of course, the injections I gave him were not the antidote. We had had our way with the Nazi, and in the bargain, we saved America. Dropping anchor in the little bay, we threw him into the dingy, rowed ashore, and left him, still bound, wretching in agony, and stranded on the Skeleton Coast."

I was horrified at the cold dispatching of another human being, no matter his crimes. "You just left him there to die?"

Shariff nodded and showed no remorse. "We reap what we sow. Whether by the poison or by predators, his end would be worse than death by a thousand cuts."

Continuing, he said, "Having already broken honor with the German, we decided to abandon our arrangement with the Namibian owner of the boat in the bargain. "We chose to keep the ketch. We needed it to get back to *Dragon*, and by then we were fond of her. She was *yar*. With the others waiting and watching for us, it seemed the better part of valor not to return to *Swakopmund*."

A small smile creased the corners of his mouth. "We set sail to the south, passing *Swakopmund*. On the way, we finished the unpolluted *Altbier*. Beer never tasted so good as we thought of the Nazi laying in agony on the Skeleton Coast, a death well earned.

That evening, under a low riding moon, we dropped anchor off *Luderitz* and slept aboard. In the morning two of us remained on deck and the other two went into town for supplies. We provisioned the ketch well for our getaway.

On some shelves we stored jars of exotic fruit jams, thick cut marmalades, tapenades, and Yorkshire chutneys. There were also tins of shortbreads and English cheddar cheese biscuits. Camembert, chevre, stilton, and taleggio cheeses wrapped in foils and encased in sealed wooden boxes were neatly stacked behind the counter railings to hold them tight during heavy water. A favorite of the crew was buttery *Comte* from the *Jurah* region of France. English honey was included in the larder, along with a large shaker of Palm Island salt.

For lunches and heavier meals, we brought on a range of smoked fish, including Nova Scotia salmon and smoked sable. Cold cuts were also obtained so sandwiches could be made; Black Forest ham, salamis, corned beef, and pastrami.

While in town, one of our crew also mailed the ketch owner a more than generous check. He must have been somewhat mystified but was well rewarded for his contribution to our cause. We owed him that since he would never see his boat again. When we were through with her, we would burn her to the water line so there could be no connection to us."

Shariff's face betrayed a yearning for the freedom that the ketch had afforded them for the next few weeks. "While technically we were now international terrorists, our intention was to live like kings as we made the long voyage around the Cape of Good Hope at the southern tip of South Africa, into the Indian Ocean, and then north up the Red Sea to the lagoon where *Dragon* waited on the sea floor. We ran up the main and Genoa, caught the wind, and headed out to sea."

"Everyone of us put in a lot of tiller time. Had circumstances been different, we might have sailed on forever, like the passage from Lord Alfred Tennyson's *The Voyage*."

> *We left behind the painted buoy*
> *That tosses at the harbor-mouth;*
> *And madly danced our hearts with joy,*
> *As fast we fleeted to the South:*
> *How fresh was every sight and sound*
> *On open main or winding shore!*
> *We knew the merry world was round,*
> *And we might sail for evermore.*

11

The Ancient Mariners
Flight to the Mountain of Fire

As he ended the tale, I continued to stare at him in disbelief. On the one hand, over the last two days I had found him to be a man of great strength and character, definable by his humanity. He was heroic for securing Egyptian uranium to prevent a nuclear holocaust in the Middle East. Someone who, under other circumstances, I could entertain spending a lifetime with, happy in his bed.

On the other hand, what he had just unapologetically described, the diabolical torturous murder of another human being, would be defined by those in the mental health field and most courts of law as the behavior of a full blown psychopath. Adding piracy for the unauthorized acquisition of a U.S. nuclear submarine and a Namibian ketch, left no room in the margins for qualifying his behavior as anything other than seriously abnormal.

He looked me in the eye, seeming to read my mind again. "I see you are not coping well with our treatment of Alois Brunner. What would you have us do with him after all we learned about his role in the Nazi death camps, and Rosslyn's brutal death at *Ravensbruck*?"

My response was quick. "I do not believe that the biblical edict of an eye for an eye transcends the gains we have made in the evolution of civilization. The world has certainly risen above the barbaric acts of the Germans in their death camps. The whole world cannot lose its humanity just because they did."

He considered my words for a minute before speaking. "I do not feel that I lose my humanity when killing Nazi war criminals. I am simply bringing to justice the bestial bastards that got through the nets and avoided the trials at Nuremburg, where they would surely have been sentenced to death. I also do not believe that any of God's edicts should have a place in this discussion. God was noticeably absent in the death camps."

I agreed that the criminals on the *Mossad* list would almost certainly have been found guilty of war crimes against humanity and likely sentenced to death at Nuremburg. However, I retorted, "Their executions would have been carried out using methods deemed civil by society."

I added, "One mark of civilization is the sanction against torture. You and your team not only chose to be judge and jury, you became a lynch mob, and you tortured. Worse yet, you abandoned scientific ethics. You have been given a great gift, training in the power of nature's laws. Scientists are enjoined to use that training to do great good. Those ethics prohibit the use of nature's laws to knowingly cause harm, especially the use of them to torture. At some point you crossed the *Rubicon*. Will you not cross back?"

Leaning forward in his chair, he again went silent for a moment, apparently choosing his next words carefully. "Violence and torture have always been components of civilized society. Human history is ripe with stories of horror. Disembowelment, beheading, the Court of Star Chamber's rack. America has blood on its hands. What do you suppose it was like that day in Hiroshima, or when the bomb was dropped on Nagasaki?"

"Today, in America, criminals are electrified, fried, as punishment for mortal sins. The list of cruel and inhuman treatment is long. Innocent people have been used in painful medical experiments. In fact, from 1943 to 1947, your government sanctioned use of humans as guinea pigs in experiments with polonium. Your government still sanctions the exposure of its citizens to polonium by the tobacco industry. Where the plants are grown using phosphate fertilizers, smoke from their leaves emit Polonium 210 that is deposited in a smoker's airways, delivering radiation right to surrounding cells. One study has shown that smoking 1 ½ packs a day delivers the same amount of radiation as 300 chest X-rays a year."

Fixing me with a hard stare, he said, "Do you think government officials are unaware of these transgressions? Cecily, do you not understand that is how the real world, the so-called civilized world, has always worked. Such acts are overlooked due to political, religious, and financial interests. Taking revenge for transgressions against socially sanctioned behavior, killing in war, all forms of biological termination are a dirty business. Someone always ends up with blood on their hands, figuratively or literally. But it is part of mankind's history.

The term 'civilization' came into being to refer to those early forms of social organization leading to the formation of states with systems of writing. It did not refer to morality. Egypt, Sumer, ancient Greece and Rome all committed socially sanctioned torture. Some of it in warfare and some as pure entertainment. Remember the Roman Coliseum games. If you do not understand these facts of human nature and history, you are living in denial."

We locked eyes. He gave no hint of displeasure at the disagreement we were having. It was also clear that he was not giving ground. On that score, he was apparently unmovable. "Besides, Nazi war criminals are not members of civilized society and do not deserve a kind socially sanctioned punishment for their crimes. While they are human in form, their mentality is of another order, some kind of deranged bestial serial killers. Enlightened morays do not apply to them."

Anxiety spread threw me like naked fear. It was suddenly clear why they had insisted that Brunner direct them to the locations of the other Nazis left behind in *Swakopmund*. It was not for the team's safety. They intended to pick up their trails and keep tracking them. They planned to become serial killers themselves.

Realizing that we had reached an impasse on the subject, I tried to collect my thoughts and take another tack. "Shariff, you know that you will be stripped of all your credentials if what you have done becomes public and if you carry this vendetta any further."

He nodded in agreement. "I know that. We all knew it there in Walvis Bay on board the ketch, when we became the modern version of the ancient Mariner, doomed to sail on forever. Polonium 210 was our crossbow and we used it to kill the Albatross, knowing that in doing so we could never again make landfall. Our intention was to sail on, killing with our crossbow until every name on the *Mossad* list had suffered the same fate.

Ultimately, however, our inner scientists gained the day. We are also men of integrity. Burdened by the information that Brunner traded for what he thought would be his life, we could not in good conscience let the attack on America take place without a warning. So we made landfall. My men are now spread out across the *Bilad es Sudan*, 'the terrible Sahara', our desert homeland, to await benediction for our acts. I have carried the information to appropriate channels."

He gestured with his hand, "Ironically, like Brunner, we traded the doomsday message in return for our lives."

He smiled wanly. "Hitler proved that one man can change the course of the world. Our team has also changed the course of the world by saving the U.S. from the mother of all acts of war. You are correct. We stand guilty of setting our own standards, as he did. However, right is on our side."

Clearly we were using different standards and he considered the discussion over. "We have been given immunity by the U.N. and the U.S. for all our transgressions."

I had to ask. "In addition to returning the Scorpion, providing the location of the Polaris A-1s, and the details of the planned nuclear attack on America, will you turn over the *Mossad* list and tell me where the remaining Polonium 210 is stashed?

It seemed forever before he finally answered. "I will leave it to the CIA to hunt down the rest of the dogs on that list. However, if they do not, I will take my men back to sea and one by one we will hunt them down and send them by way of Brunner. As for the polonium, I cannot give up our crossbow until that book is finally closed."

Again, I stared at him in disbelief.

It was my turn to carefully choose my words. "Shariff, I was sent here for the express purpose of finding that poison and getting it into a controlled environment where it does not represent a public safety hazard. I have to complete my mission."

He rose and again walked to the window, staring out for what seemed like an eternity. "I cannot give up the polonium. If the CIA does not finish our mission, we will go hunting Nazis once more. And now, we cannot go back to Egypt, or anywhere else and be part of the nuclear waste disaster that enriching uranium has become. It is against our ethics. We do have our ethics.

In addition, I will always be haunted by the knowledge of Rosslyn's terrible death and need to revenge her. If I die before that happens, let me die drowning in my own blood. That is who I am, what I have become."

Turning to look at me, he said, "Cecily, I need you to love me in spite of it all."

Tears came to my eyes. His words left me hollow inside, deeply unhappy. I know that the thing about unhappiness is something worse comes along and you realize that the unhappy time was the good time. But it was too much of a sacrifice.

My resolve remained firm. "Shariff, you cannot use love as a bargaining chip. You must tell me where the rest of the Polonium 210 is. We cannot go forward until that is behind us. Please don't let it poison us, as well."

His look softened. Apparently my plea breached the barrier between us and he walked toward me. Picking up the tablet that lay on the table, he wrote something and handed it to me. It said, "What if I take you to it?"

I looked up at him. He put a finger to his lips warning me not to repeat what was said in his note. Then he reached across and took back the note.

He whispered, "Walls have ears in the Middle East."

Stepping past the table, he leaned down and kissed me softly on the mouth. It was like no kiss I had ever had before, pulling me in. My heart beat faster. My blood pressure pulsated against my eardrums. I kissed him back, ardently, and, nodding, I agreed. I wanted Shariff like I had wanted no other man. Also, I had to get the Polonium 210 from him.

✎

Returning to my room, I used the telephone to call Reardon and tell my office that I was changing locations. They thought it damned strange that I could not tell them my destination, but I could not tell them what I did not know.

Just as I put the phone back in its cradle, he knocked on the door and stepped in. I had thrown my things in my bag while on the phone with Reardon. Reaching up to brush my cheek with the back of his hand, he said, "Our transportation is waiting."

The wave of energy passed between us again. His hand dropped to my waist and he pulled me closer. We both knew there was no time for what we were thinking and I stepped back.

Reluctantly, he took his hand from my waist and picked up my bag. As we stepped into the hallway, he whispered in my ear, "Later".

It was mid-afternoon and, knowing there would be no one in Major General Alden Lloyd's office until the heat began to dissipate in early evening, we left the UN compound without announcing our departure. I suspected General Lloyd knew we were going and had more information than I did.

153

A waiting jeep drove us to the Port Said landing strip where a Sikorsky CH53-A, designed for heavy lifting by the U.S. military, was on standby. I had flown in one before and wondered why we needed so much power, including the two machine guns mounted on each side of the bird's fuselage.

As we lifted off, he put his arm around me and yelled over the noise of the engine and blades, "Trust me. It will be all right."

The helicopter quickly gained altitude and soon began tracing the Nile southward, a brown ribbon knifing between the Sahara desert to the west and the Red Sea Hills to the east. Nubia was ahead of us. I watched the water below as it curled across the desert floor. Desolate country. Islands and ox bows along its course betrayed its ancient origins.

Beneath us were occasional villages of mud and dung flat-roofed houses hugging the river banks , and a few verdant looking date palm groves. Little else of significance invaded the sand

colored landscape.

The rhythmic beating of the bird's blades, six on the main rotor and four on the tail, eventually lulled me to sleep. I leaned against Shariff for comfort and was aware that he had wrapped me in his arms.

Five hours later I awoke with a jolt. He was holding me tight. We had just landed in God knows where. He motioned for me to wait and he jumped down, looked around cautiously, then held up his arms to catch me. The pilot had already thrown down my bag.

I jumped into his arms and, ducking under the blades, we made our way out of their rotation. Sand enveloped us while the Sikorsky's engines shut down and the blades slowly came to a halt.

When the curtain of sand settled the apparition before us was breath taking. There in the middle of the Sahara desert, looming a thousand feet above our heads, was a granite mountain.

Scattered about and leading up to the base of mountain were the ruins of an ancient Egyptian temple compound. I judged it to be Middle Kingdom based on what remained of the capitols on the forest of columns behind an imposing pylon.

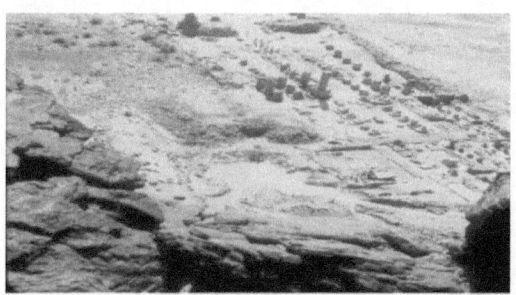

In strange juxtaposition, the nearby Sikorsky was sitting on a landing pad composed of huge stones that had probably once paved the floor of a building in the massive complex. The scene was surreal.

Men came running to take our luggage. They quickly disappeared into the shadow of the mountain. Still looking cautiously around, Shariff took me by the arm and started walking into the ruins. The size of the columns and walls dwarfed us, small humans from the 20th century walking through a page of history that had been written three thousand years earlier. I could not absorb all that was happening; being with Shariff, a ride in a heavily armed helicopter to an eerie place long abandoned by the ancients of a powerful dynasty, and among artifacts crafted by humans like me, but from what seemed like a storybook universe.

Looking to the top of the mountain, he explained, "It is a granite inselberg. On maps, the village just beyond on the riverbank, is called *Napata* and the mountain is called *Jebel Barkal*.

We are near the third cataract of the Nile in northern Sudan, where early Egyptian artisans worked to forge blocks and colossi for the royal pyramids and temples."

Jebel Barkal is not the name the locals give the mountain. They call it *Jebel Kabrit*. Tomorrow, when the sun rises, you will see why. The mountain is made of red granite and glows like fire as the sun hits it."

He took hold of my shoulders and turned me to face east. "See those pyramids in the distance? They belonged to the Nubian kings who ruled all Egypt and Nubia near the end of the Egyptian New Kingdom. Remember the drawings in the book you bought for me in Port Said? Some of the Pharaohs, charging their enemies with war lions running beside their chariots, were 25th and 26th dynasty Egyptian Pharaohs, but also Nubian kings. The Nubians invaded and ruled Egypt for a hundred years and those are their royal burials."

As we approached the entrance to the temple, he veered off to the left and began following the base of the mountain. I was following in his footsteps. A few minutes later, he suddenly stopped, put his hand behind him, and taking hold of my arm, motioned for me to stand still.

I looked ahead of him and suddenly saw movement in the sand. It was the sleek dark body of a large Egyptian cobra, about nine feet long and coiled around the remnants of a stone lion. Its upper body waved above the desert floor a good four feet. The snake had spread the vertebral bones in its upper neck to form a hood, poised to strike. Cobras are night hunters and we had surprised it in the darkness. Its posture was the signal not to come any closer. We were already too close since it could easily reach us where we stood.

Shariff began slowly backing away, pushing me backwards with him, and keeping his body between the deadly venomous viper and me.

When we were finally out of range, he laughed and said to the snake, "Sorry about that. We leave you in peace."

Still smiling, he told me about an ancient legend in the area which held that a giant three-headed cobra lay atop the largest of the pyramids he had pointed out. "That pyramid is called Barkal Five. The snake is said to wear a crown on each of its heads; the crown of Upper Egypt, the crown of Lower Egypt, and the Triple Crown signifying the unification of Egypt and Nubia. Those crowns are used in the pictographic paintings throughout the river valley to symbolize the far-reaching political power of a long line of rulers.

We trekked back through the ancient temple and began circling the mountain further out in the desert. After we had trekked through the sand about a city block Shariff turned and, with me close behind him, again approached the inselberg. At this point there were no ruins indicating any human presence from the past.

Increasing our pace, he warned, "We need to hurry, and watch where you step. Cobras not only hunt prey at night, they are territorial and known to stalk intruders."

When we reached the base, he turned right and walked along the steep granite wall. Shortly, we came to a smooth area that turned out to be a well camouflaged, human engineered, entrance. Pushing aside a hinged sandstone panel to gain entry, he quickly pulled me inside and closed the panel after us.

I could never have anticipated the next surprise the mountain held. We were in a huge chamber, another temple inside *Jebel Barkal* that had been built to honor Egyptian gods. But now the temple had clearly been converted to another use, a highly technical use.

A generator hummed somewhere in the background,

furnishing electrical lighting. Much of the equipment before us was familiar to me; glove boxes for remote handling of radioactive material, a sophisticated centrifuge system for separating lower and higher level radioactive elements like uranium, the duct work of a complex ventilation system, and overpack containers indicating that transportation of some very nasty stuff was in play.

As I turned to Shariff for an explanation, several men approached us, laughing and grabbing Shariff in familiar hugs. We were definitely among friends.

Returning their hugs, he grinned widely and said, "Dr. Suderman, meet the rest of my team."

I had already guessed that. The men took turns shaking my hand and uttering the traditional Muslim greeting, "*Salam Alelkum*" (Peace be unto you).

I had learned the basic tenets of decorum in Arab society and returned the greeting. "*Alelkum salam*" (and to you).

They led us into the chamber's interior where the temple's vaulted ceiling soared into the darkness above. Ancient columns and colossi, perfectly preserved under the mountain for thousands of years, loomed over us like strange apparitions among the 20th century equipment of the Egyptian scientists whose work, I could only assume, had something to do with handling Polonium 210.

Scanning the area and doing a quick assessment, I knew the poison was now separated into a number of containers, the overpacks. Before I could count them, Shariff said, "Too heavy for you to carry."

He knew I had not given up my mission. He also knew when he agreed to bring me to the Polonium 210 that I had no hope of taking it. He had kept his part of the bargain and foiled me in the process.

However, I knew that he also loved me. Love has been many a man's downfall. I was not giving up.

We stepped into a well-lit alcove where a heavy punt wood table was surrounded by ten chairs covered in soft goat hair rugs. The table served as the dining area for the crew. As we were taking seats, two other men began carrying trays to the table. The trays were laden with glasses of *shai sada suker tahgil* and mounds of fresh *tameya* cakes. Welcome fare since we had not eaten in hours. The smell of *foul musseri* cooking somewhere nearby wafted in. I felt like I had stepped through the looking glass with Dorothy, wandered into Emerald City, and was attending the Mad Hatter's tea party.

Shariff was watching me with amusement, measuring my level of cognitive dissidence. Reaching over, he took my hand and said, "Let me make the introductions. Then I will explain all this to you. It's another long story."

He began the introductions by saying, " These men are my army. You fight with the army you've got, and mine is adequate to almost any task.."

One by one the men stood. Shariff explained the role of each after they had introduced themselves. As he did so, I realized that this was a tea party with a remarkable complement of nuclear experts, gifted men of science that could build, dismantle, or destroy almost anything on the planet, especially if it had to do with atoms. Particularly split atoms.

Akeem, sitting on Shariff's left, pronounced his name in a heavy accent. He was short and slightly built, olive skinned with deep-set brown eyes. His hair was silver and beginning to thin on his crown.

Shariff explained that Akeem was the one who was highly published and had discovered the secret to technologically imitating the transmutation process that radioactive elements undergo in nature to eventually become stable and safe, like lead. "The nuclear industry, of course, is not inclined to pare down their profits by spending money to clean up the garbage they leave behind, so they vigorously oppose Akeem's work."

The next team member, Osama, was much lighter skinned than the others and had amber colored eyes. He was also tall and ruggedly built. I guessed his lineage contained a serious injection of European genes. Shariff described him as the gifted nuclear chemist that contributed to Akeem's transmutation research.

The third man had a broad smile on his face. His dark skin color suggested ancestral connections to Nubia and, like Osama, he was ruggedly built. Shoush was a nuclear engineer with an uncanny affinity for machines. And, he could solve any problem involving a nuclear reactor.

Next, Abbas had a stern presence and, according to Shariff, "… was one of the earliest nuclear scientists to begin the work of processing uranium at *Inshas*. Abbas is also a defender of humanity. He will guard against any wrongful use of nuclear power with his last breath."

Then, he laughed and turned to the last two men at the end of the table. "You must meet two of the most gifted petrologists in the world. They were in *Swakopmund* with me and acted as the boat crew when we took Alois Brunner sport fishing, so to speak. They are like hawks, and the desert is their hunting grounds, reading it and tracking without the aid of maps."

One was uncommonly handsome and looked boldly at me as he pronounced his name; Elham. Again laughing, Shariff said, "Careful. Elham is the one whose eyes run down every woman crossing his path. They are his prey. Descended from a long line of *Tuareg* nomads, he could easily have been a warrior instead of a scientist."

Hussein came last. His face and body were angular like the Pharaohs on the tomb walls at Aswan. Shariff explained the he was descended from the *Ramesid* line. He held a strong likeness to *Rameses II*, in both physique and spirit.

Rameses II was known to be a great warrior and builder. He had undertaken the construction of some of the most monumental stone works in ancient Egypt, including his own mortuary temple at Aswan. He was always shown on monument walls charging the enemy with his lions running beside his chariot. If not for wars and weaponry, Hussein would probably have been a great builder of stone like his ancestor but, as fate would have it, he had turned his talents to the power and inherent dangers of atom splitting."

Nodding to all his men, Shariff said, "Our little band is united in our opposition to the ultimate horror predicted by Pierre Curie. In Currie's Nobel Prize speech, he warned that the awesome power of atom splitting, in the wrong hands, could bring disaster to the world. Unfortunately, it has gone beyond Curie's prediction of disaster. It is now a matter of total annihilation. Atom splitting has become a freak show, producing nuclear weaponry that can obliterate in seconds what it took the universe billions of years to generate. Even worse, it has produced so much radioactive waste that it is turning the planet into a lethal radioactive minefield."

Shaking his head, he said, "As you know, nuclear waste, part and parcel of energy and weapons production, cannot be neutralized or destroyed by any existing technologies.

Government claims that it is safely stored are oxymorons. Even if governments funded the research needed to develop a risk free repository, it would require several decades to complete the work. We are already drowning in the stuff. There are thousands of tons in the U.S. alone. Some is the result of building nuclear weapons but most of it is the byproduct of nuclear energy. America is home to billions of curies, waiting in spent nuclear fuel to kill."

He smiled ironically and shook his head. "The nuclear industry may destroy Planet Earth ahead of nuclear warfare. There are hundreds of reactors spewing out nuclear waste across the globe. Unbelievably, governments are continuously licensing more, even though not one country has a reliable plan for permanently storing or neutralizing the waste."

Then he moved to the downside of nuclear weaponry. Not trying to disguise his disgust, he declared, "Government scientists and their military supporters have expanded the power of bombs to the point of insanity. They have developed weapons that can never be used, not because they are needed but just because they could. The hydrogen bomb was the worst decision in a long sad history of bad decisions on the use of nuclear power. Those bombs have the potential of a Dooms Day device. They can be scaled up to a deliverable power of 500 kilotons. As you know, nuclear weaponry has gone from bunker busters to city busters to nation busters in the form of thermodynamic bombs. Imagine the head of a nuclear nation crazy enough to launch a thermodynamic bomb."

He took a drink of his tea while considering what he wanted to say next. "The first thermonuclear bomb was 450 times more powerful than the bomb dropped on Nagasaki. Such weapons are now mounted on intercontinental ballistic missiles that can be launched from submarines, like our *Dragon*. But the U.S. is not the only bull in the arena. At least five other nations have nuclear arsenals, probably thermodynamic, and we are not sure about weapons development in India, Pakistan, Israel, and South Africa."

He shook his head sadly. "Few people understand that our world constantly teeters on the brink of extinction because we have broken nature's atomic code. Man now has the ability to chain nature's atoms together and obliterate the planet in a few short hours. Even if that power is never used, the lethal radioactive waste left behind from building the weapons is swallowing us alive. We are living in a sea of it.

Worse yet, the spent fuel from the reactors producing nuclear energy is essentially the same stuff that we used to produce our Polonium 210. The U.S. knows how. Russia knows how. Sooner or later, a rogue nation or an organized cell of terrorists will figure it out. There will no longer be a need for missiles or submarines. When that happens, the world will be at the mercy of only a few. You know why. That is your reason for tracking me down."

Not wanting to discuss the awesome potentials for a world threatened by chemical warfare in front of an audience, and trying to hide my unease, I looked around at the equipment in the chamber. "What are you planning to do with this equipment?"

He quickly gave me an answer. "We are not using most of the

equipment. It was used for another earlier mission, of which I was a part. That is another long story, which I need to tell you. For now, we are leaving revenge for the victims of the Holocaust and Rosslyn in the hands of the CIA. I have turned a copy of the *Mossad* list over to the agency. As I said, if they fail, we will take up the task again.

We have taken on a new mission. That mission does involve the Polonium 210 we produced. We had planned to leave it here in this isolated and secure place. Unfortunately, current political unrest in Sudan makes it unsafe to do so. Several *al Qaida* cells have formed in the country. Bad actors are drawing attention to the Sudan, including Carlos the Jackal. He is on the run from Venezuelan and French authorities and has taken up residence in Khartoum. Apparently he murdered several French agents.

Carlos was trained in Palestinian liberation camps. Groups from those camps are known as 'Black Septembrists" and they are vicious terrorists. Carlos has also been known to associate with the German Baader-Meinhof gang. His talents range from execution to airliner rocket attacks.

Anyway, Sudan is now in the news and of interest to too many countries and their agents, including the U.S. CIA. We need a place to store the polonium that is off everyone's radar. So, we are shortly moving it to another locale, There is a man in Cuba who will provide us safe haven. He and I were involved in setting up the lab in this temple for that earlier project. That effort also involved committing evil for the sake of saving our planet and its inhabitants."

I had to ask. "But, what is your new mission?"

12

Kineococcus radiotolerans
Don't Play With Fire

His voice softened as he began speaking of a time in the past. "Before I tell you about how our mission has changed, I need to tell you about the earlier work that was performed in this lab. Thirty some years ago, in 1937 when I was a young new Oxford graduate, I had the great privilege of managing the University of Rome's nuclear physics laboratory for the Nobel Prize winner, Dr. Enrico Fermi. Dr. Fermi had a field team in the highlands of Gabon, then French Equatorial Africa.

The team was surveying uranium deposits in the area, searching for high concentrations of U-235. Fermi was building the world's first nuclear reactor in his Rome lab and needed the U-235 for the reactor's fuel. He was trying to find the secret to a controlled atomic chain reaction."

Stunned at the news that a nuclear reactor had been built in Europe preceding the Manhattan project which developed the U.S. atomic bomb, and even more stunned that the dangerous secret to prolonged atom splitting was an experiment in Rome's university lab, I asked, "What did the Italians want with a nuclear reactor and the ability to control a nuclear chain reaction? And who were the members of that team?"

Shariff laughed, flashing his wide smile. "The Italians did not want a nuclear reactor and really had no idea of its significance. Fermi was building the reactor purely for the sake of research. Little did we know that what we were doing in the Rome lab would lead to the atomic bombing of two civilian cities in Japan, the end of World War II, potential destruction of the planet during a subsequent and prolonged Cold War between the U.S. and Russia, an astronomical buildup of nuclear arsenals, global threats of nuclear terrorism, and enough nuclear waste from hundreds of commercial nuclear reactors across the world to poison the planet for our species and its environment. Naively, we were just conducting research for the sake of research.

The Gabon field team included some of the most remarkable people I have ever had the privilege of knowing. While they came from all parts of the world, they had one thing in common. They were a rare breed of gifted scientists who also excelled at work in the wilderness.

Dr. Jacques Belle Jacques was a tall, blonde, powerfully built former quarterback of the University of Michigan's football team. Before completing his doctoral work in nuclear physics at Michigan, he was a trained Navy fighter pilot and spent time aboard a carrier in Asian waters. Jacques met and married a classmate at Michigan but after a short marriage, when she demanded that he choose between her or wandering in the wilds of Third World countries as the head of Fermi's field team, he found himself once again a free spirit.

Another team member, Francesco Pacillo, was an ingenious environmental engineer. He was fearless and seemed to thrive on danger, as well as being the universal indigenous man. Francesco was *Italianate* in appearance, with eyes, coloring, and the accent of *Piedmonte* males. While his lineage was rumored to connect with the early kings of Rome, he was most at home in the wilderness. For reasons that need no explanation, the team nicknamed him the Italian Stallion.

His infectious smile was a veil. Although Francesco was a

dedicated protector of our team, you would never want him for a foe. He could be very dangerous. He and Jacques would have been highly effective soldiers of fortune. At the time, the team had no clue what an extraordinary future was in store for the tall, strapping and classically handsome forty-three year old."

I laughed, instantly intrigued. "Was he a womanizer?"

Shariff smiled. "Back in the day, he broke many women's hearts, but never intentionally. He loved hard when he loved but he could never bring himself to stay the course. The wild was always beckoning and he knew he would make a lousy husband so he spared the gentler sex the heartbreak of trying to tame him.

Dr. Charles Grayson, Charlie, was a sandy haired rugged Oxford man of science. Every inch a geochemist, his wheelhouse became the quantification of matter and energy. He was always measuring something in the environment. Wherever he went, his backpack carried an endless array of devices and instruments for enumerating the world. Like so many of his scholarly predecessors, he left Britannica to wander out to the Dark Continent in search of scientific answers to universal questions.

Charlie was a gentleman but he also had an inner armature of iron when it came to his quests. You know that joke, 'The sun never sets on the British empire, because you can't trust an Englishman after dark'? Well, Charlie could be that Englishman when it came to his work.

England had spawned a lineup of such adventurous seekers. They introduced the world to amazing discoveries; the earliest ancestors of *homo sapiens*, King Tut's tomb, the Rosetta Stone, and the Nubian pyramid fields, among which you now sit.

Charlie had known several stunning women, some from the royal family. But stunning European women were not cut out for the kind of life on which he had set his cap. The life he wanted could not be had in the libraries and laboratories of the civilized world. His future, he thought, held no prospects for marriage and a family.

Then, Dr. Leslie Everly joined Fermi's field team. She was a geophysicist with impressive credentials. The hardships of life in the wilderness, without such amenities as mattresses, indoor plumbing, electricity, and cooked meals, were just part of the job and she did her job with amazing intensity, and *la grace*. She could throw down a bedroll anywhere and, without compunction, sleep soundly next to any of her male counterparts. If her nearness heightened their libidos, that was their problem."

I listened, fascinated by the cast of characters in Shariff's tale of his and Fermi's drive to build the first nuclear reactor in order to control a chained fission explosion. Poor bastards. Talk about good intentions and the road to Hell!

At that point, Shariff looked intently at me and said that what he was about to tell me was highly confidential. Unless I gave my word to never tell another living soul, he would not continue. He locked eye contact with me and held firm.

My options were limited. Unless I gave him my word, he would not tell me the rest of the tale. I needed to hear the rest of the tale, both because of my intense personal interest, and because, from a professional perspective, hearing it might help me acquire the Polonium 210 his team produced in *Dragon's* lab.

Sighing, I turned to look at him. "I give my word."

He nodded and began to finish the tale. This part described an incredible demonstration of nature's awesome power. "Up in the highlands of Gabon, Fermi's team came across the old abandoned Okla mines and accidentally stumbled onto a radioactive enigma that may yet alter the course of human history, as well as our existence on this planet."

I looked at him, speechless. "How could a discovery of that magnitude not be widely known to those of us in the nuclear sciences?'

He raised a finger to silence me. "It is another long and convoluted story that I will tell you if you want to listen."

Want to listen? I was compelled to know what the Hell

happened up in those highlands. As a nuclear scientist, I needed to know about a potentially catastrophic nuclear enigma.

I watched him shift in his chair to get comfortable and was reminded how sensual he looked when he did that back in the lounge of the UN compound on the banks of the Suez. "While taking radiation readings in one section of the mine, the team suddenly ran across gamma radiation hot spots that made their dosimeters jump into the red zone. The radiation levels emitted by the Okla hot spots were higher than any they had ever measured, except when they were around Fermi's nuclear reactor. And, this enigma was not man-made. Somehow, it was a natural freak of nature.

They immediately evacuated the area, but returned later with appropriate rad con suiting to gather samples. The samples they collected were sealed in four small lead cylinders to guard them from exposure to the deadly gamma rays being emitted by the stuff.

He sighed. "Not understanding what a game changer their Gabon samples were, the team smuggled them out through the Gabon airport by wrapping them in hazmat stickers. At the airport they claimed the cylinders just contained normal soil samples that were always marked hazard material to prevent any possible biological exposure to examining airport personnel. Failing all logic, the Gabon security guard, such as it was, allowed the cylinders to go through in the team's checked luggage.

Not until Fermi analyzed them with a spectrometer back in his Rome laboratory did they realize the truly deadly nature of the cylinder's contents. In addition to the high-level radioactivity of the uranium in the samples, there was a passenger, an organic parasite feeding off the energy emitted by the uranium. Actually, it was a colony composed of at least 3,000 different virile bacteria. That colony is the only organism on earth that can survive in a high level radioactive environment.

Fermi instantly recognized that the Okla uranium and its passenger was a unique natural entity with no known enemies.

If released into the environment, it could feed off of, and suck the strength out of, all sources of radiation, possibly even all humanity because the human body contains Potassium 40, which is mildly radioactive."

Alarmed but not wanting to panic the whole scientific world, as well as the public, Fermi quietly organized a meeting with the greatest nuclear minds on the planet; Albert Einstein, J. Robert Oppenheimer, Leo Szilard, and Neils Boer.

Einstein had already immigrated to America because of threats on his life in Nazi Germany due to his Jewish heritage. His high profile following the Nobel Prize in physics put a target on his back.

Szilard, who first conceived the concept of a nuclear chain reaction, had escaped Germany and was living in England where he settled to avoid Hitler's assault on Jewish scientists at the University of Berlin (later renamed Humboldt University). He was working diligently to help other Jewish scientists in Germany find safe harbor out of the insane asylum that their homeland had become. Later, he was to write the letter to President Roosevelt, which Einstein signed, which resulted in the formation of the Manhattan Project and the building of the atomic bomb.

When it became known the U.S. military was considering dropping the atomic bomb on civilian cities in Japan, Szilard drafted a petition strongly advocating that a demonstration of its power should precede any attacks with the weapon."

Shariff was quiet for a moment, then said, "Szilard is the little known originator of the anti-nuke movement."

Another moment of silence while he obviously pondered the role of scientists like himself in bringing the nuclear monster to humanity's dogfights. Then, "Niels Bohr was working at the institute he had founded in Denmark. He could be counted on to attend the meeting and contribute critical insight based on his expertise in atomic structure and quantum theory. During the Manhattan Project era, Niels traveled back and forth to assist Oppenheimer in the design of the A-bomb. However, he was also an advocate of 'science for the sake of science' and spoke openly of the work with Russian counterparts. That got him into political hot water and, at one point, Churchill requested that he be jailed.

Oppenheimer, an American born Jew, could be counted on to travel from Berkeley University in California. Unlike the others, Oppenheimer had never received a Nobel Prize for his work. However, he was highly respected and highly conceited. He could be depended on to provide significant support and insight. He would want his name on a scientific dilemma of this magnitude. As you know, he became known as the Father of the Atomic Bomb.

In a quirk of fate, he was also persecuted during the Senator McCarthy witch-hunt across America. McCarthy was overly fond of holding photo ops with his media fan club and singled out the famous and infamous for his self-promoting campaign. It was a moment of madness in American politics and people like Oppenheimer, who wouldn't play the game, were thrown up on the sacrificial alter.

In terms of the meeting he asked these popes of nuclear science to attend, Fermi made a bold move. For the venue, he selected the University of Kiel. Located in extreme northern Germany, it was not on the radar of the mainstream media hounds. Fermi thought that, although the environment in Germany was increasingly hostile to Jewish scientists, especially Nobel Prize winners, the Kiel area was far removed from Berlin and the eye of the storm. The small university town had not yet been infected with Nazi sentiments and the faculty was still committed to science for the sake of mankind's betterment.

A meeting like he proposed could take place there in relative isolation, and under the noses of the Nazis. Kiel was the last place Hitler's minions and the media would expect the most famous Jewish nuclear scientists in the world to congregate for a meeting."

I thought, *That meeting was not even believable, except it is Shariff telling it.*

He continued. "Even though there was always danger on

171

German soil, if any threat emerged from the Berlin bastion of Hitlerian nationalism, Fermi was sure that they could escape to Denmark by ferry in less than three hours.

Based on these considerations, he penned a letter on August 5 to each man on his personal stationary, rather than the official letterhead of the University of Rome. A letter on his personal stationary would signal to his colleagues the serious nature of his transmittal and the magnitude of his need to meet with them. The letter simply said, *A scientific matter of great import needs to be discussed. Arrangements have been made for a meeting at the University of Kiel on January 4, 1938. Advise you dress warmly for northern Germany weather and possibly Copenhagen. Deepest sincerity, Enrico Fermi."*

As I sat listening to Shariff, I recalled all the times I had pondered the wisdom of dropping the atomic bomb on hundreds of thousands of men, women, and children whose only crime may have been their birth in the Land of the Rising Sun. We know that children were caught in school classrooms. Women were caught in their kitchens. Men were turned to ash while sitting on park benches. *In that moment, America crossed that thin line between good and evil?*

He was watching me as he spoke, probably reading my thoughts again. "The scientists gathered as Fermi asked."

He laughed, " The University of Kiel, hundreds of years old, was constructed to solid German standards. During the winter, northern Germany is icy cold and high winds assault every barrier, although the building where the meeting was held was warm enough."

"The attendees gathered in the faculty lounge on the upper floor of the Science Building. A small group, they constituted the greatest collection of knowledge in 20th century nuclear science. All five sat around the hearth of the massive fireplace in the well-appointed room. A crackling fire, and Germanic fortitude, kept the cold outside at bay.

Within the room's thick mahogany walls, heavy hunter green leather furniture was arranged in conversational groups. Across from the fireplace, a lovely side table seemed to always be set with hot strong German coffee and a selection of tortes and Bundt cakes. Freshly baked, their smell blended with the pungent odor of burning firewood.

It is one of history's ironies that the Germans made this meeting possible. That meeting was to result in a weapon that saved the world from becoming the nuclear holocaust that wrongful use of atom splitting has made possible.

Einstein spoke first, asking what critical issue required them to assemble under the noses of the Nazis, which would likely find them all in a death camp if they were discovered.

Fermi systematically explained the discovery of his Gabon team, his analyses of the ore samples they collected there, and his assumptions based on the analyses. He had named the bacterial colony *Kineococcus radiotolerans* due to its relationship with the high-level uranium and its tolerance of intense radioactivity.

The atomic popes, gathered in front of that fire, drilled him with penetrating questions about his procedures, his lab equipment, his analyses, and the basis of his conclusions and concerns. He answered them all with the facts at his disposal, except for one. That one had no answer. *What caused the high level of radioactivity up there and why was there an organic ectoparasitic colony of bacteria living off the Gabon highlands uranium ore?*

Einstein reminded him the laws of physics denied that a form of organic matter, a bacterial colony, could live in some relationship with an energy field of high-level radiation. The enigma discovered by his team had to have another explanation because such a level of radiation would be lethal to any living organism known to science..

Fermi was determined to convince his colleagues that physics had reached the dawn of a new era. Reminding them that science builds on science, he cautioned them not to dismiss the significance of the discovery his team had made, and the fact that it was now in a safe in Rome.

Shariff spread his fingers on the tabletop to emphasize what he was about to say next. "I knew its exact location because I had put it in the safe. As I have explained, at the time, I was lead scientist in the Rome lab, and its manager. After the team had delivered the cylinders, and unpacked them in the reactor room of the lab, Fermi had directed me to put them in the smaller safe in his office, rather than the larger safe that all lab personnel used. Each time he brought them out for further spectrometric analysis, he asked that I return them to that safe. It was only later that I learned of their deadly nature.

On that fateful day in Kiel, Fermi prompted his colleagues to remember there was a time when science did not even know that radiation existed."

Shariff laughed, "I'm sure you are mindful that much of the current knowledge about radioactivity is due to luck. Wilhelm Roentgen accidentally discovered the X-ray while working with cardboard in his lab and called it "X" because no one knew what it was at the time.

Marie Curie invented the term "radioactivity" but did not realize that she had unlocked the secret door to horrendous atomic power. Unfortunately, the moth flew too close to the flame. She was eventually killed by her fascinating enigma, which she sometimes carried around in her pockets. After her death, they even had to secure her cookbooks in lead lined containers because of their level of radiation.

While he was casually manipulating light atoms by bombarding them with alpha rays, Ernest Rutherford accidentally discovered how to split the atom. The truth is, we often unpeel nature's secrets by playing poker with the laws of the universe."

Continuing to describe the Kiel meeting, Shariff said, "Fermi prevailed and Einstein finally nodded in agreement. There was no scientific basis to refute Fermi's logic.

Oppenheimer remained unconvinced. He argued that it might not be the relationship between the uranium and the bacteria that was the issue. He wondered whether it might be the environment in which they co-existed, and posed the possibility that the uranium and its ectoparasite were sharing some atmosphere that was unique to the Okla mine. Not found anywhere else on earth, one that mutually sustains the high-level radiation and its bacterial colony. The cylinders containing the uranium and the bacteria could also contain part of that environment. He asked Fermi if he had tested for that, a lurking variable. If that was the case, there was low probability that the hot zone, if left undisturbed, presented a risk. 'Oppi' suggested the samples could be put back and the issue put to rest, so to speak."

"Fermi retorted that Oppenheimer's solution would be sweeping the problem under the rug. He argued that it would be one thing for the four of them to arbitrarily brush aside the universal scientific rule of acceptance through collegial consensus. But, for them to capriciously decide to bury a phenomena of that magnitude from the rest of the scientific community would be to deny all the principles upon which the discipline of physics has been built."

Szilard listened quietly while the discussion circumnavigated the potential variables that could be in play. As he sipped his coffee, he was thinking about a threat from another direction, *a lurking variable with long fangs.*

Shifting in his chair, he leaned forward and told his peers that there was another danger, a sidebar that could make the Gabon discovery one of the most critical issues in human history if Fermi was right about the nature of the uranium samples in his safe.

He began reviewing the history of Adolph Hitler's recent rise to power and apparent intentions toward world domination. He started by reminding them that ignorance by itself is not too dangerous. Combined with power, however, it is a toxic mix. In his 1925 book, *Mein Kampf*, Hitler had expressed a pathological

ROSE O. HAYES Ph.D.

obsession with Jews. To the dismay of University of Berlin faculty, in 1933 he was appointed Chancellor of Germany. The lunatic was then turned loose to conduct ethnic cleansing, his personal moral cesspool of racial hygiene. He declared that Jews were not countrymen of German blood and therefore were not citizens who could hold public office or publish in German newspapers. It was not long before he stripped 'non-Aryan academics' from their posts. More than 100 physicists fled Germany, the present company included.

Szilard went on to remind them that they had taken with them the results of their research based on Einstein's formula, $E=Mc^2$. The formula revealed that, given the right technologies, there is a potential for releasing horrific amounts of energy. As in Fermi's Rome laboratory, they had been applying the formula in attempts to harness atoms and create a chain reaction of radiating atomic energy. However, their dangerous work on fission energy was kept secret. Hitler was unaware that he had sent them away with the potential knowledge to create such power.

Unfortunately, other physicists who had also worked on the project were not Jewish, and remained at the university. Szilard warned his colleagues that it was only a matter of time before the *Fuhrer* became aware of the significance of the work.

While the others listened Szilard continued. He cautioned that Hitler could force their remaining compatriots to continue fission research. Since fission is a chain reaction in which an atomic nucleus splits into fragments of comparable mass and emits one hundred to several hundred million volts of energy within a split second, the situation was fraught with possibilities. Terrifying potential in the wrong hands. The *Fuhrer* would have no respect for scientific neutrality. 'Wolves like him are never converted to eating grass in the presence of sheep.'"

"Szilard finished his coffee and looked hard at the others around him. He told them that their Berlin compatriots would also be compelled to make the *Fuhrer* aware that vast quantities of good uranium ore, high in uranium-235, are required for harnessing split atoms in a nuclear chain reaction. If Hitler should learn of the high-grade uranium ore present in Gabon he would invade and take over the Okla mines. Szilard's understanding was that he had already stopped the sale of uranium from Czechoslovakian mines. Sadly, he told them the fact that Germany could build the most powerful weapon on earth was not the biggest problem. If he ordered the mining of Gabon's uranium beds in order to build that weapon, the bacterial colony would be proliferated wherever the ore was shipped."

"Szilard concluded that if Fermi was right, the colony living on the ore would not only seek out any available sources of radioactivity for sustenance, it could also reconstruct itself within hours if decimated. In other words, the world could bomb the hell out of it and its DNA would simply be restored in short order. It was indestructible. It could even be a threat to human biology since the bodies of *homo sapiens* contain radiation. Any government in control of that ore would rule the world."

Fermi had later told Shariff that the others looked at Szilard in horror. Oppenheimer was first to speak and said that surely the test results were mistaken! There could not be an organic colony on earth that could live in a highly radioactive environment and also reconstitute itself after cellular destruction. In the entire history of science, there had been no evidence of such a possibility.

Shariff leaned forward and said, "The group argued all sides of the situation for the better part of the day and finally agreed on an optimal approach for resolving the dilemma presented by the hot zone in Gabon, and the secreted samples I kept returning to Fermi's vault. Another scientific expedition back to the area, though perilous, was critical and timing was crucial.

Fermi's field team would have to return to the Okla mine to survey and characterize the site, measure the magnitude and strength of the radioactivity in the area, and collect additional lab specimens. The scientists at the meeting all agreed to inject their considerable resources into the project.

Before adjourning, Fermi informed them that Hitler's known penchant for violence when disappointed had done the world at least one favor. Fermi's contact at Berlin University had sent word that, like most men called into the *Fuhrer's* presence, the physicists who worked on fission research were fearful of upsetting him. They decided to inform the *Fuhrer* that while the theoretical solutions for developing an atomic weapon were known, the technical problems presented insurmountable barriers to its soon being a determining factor in warfare."

Then, Shariff smiled and said, "In addition, it seemed to be a consensus among the scientific faculty that Hitler appeared intellectually incapable of comprehending nuclear physics concepts. They also assumed that he would never provide the massive economic support required to arm the country with a weapon based on the unproven potential for fission energy. Hitler was always leery of anything that he could not quickly see or touch.

"After hours of examining all the facts Fermi could provide, he waved his hand, dismissing the issue. He told them the winter should pass without further interest by the *Fuhrer.* For the time being he felt they were spared the worry of Hitler immediately discovering *Kineococcus radiotolerans.*

Before they left Kiel he cautioned the others to remember, from that moment on they would be surrounded by strangers where *Kineococcus radiotolerans* was concerned. 'Not a word.'

13

The Mountain Called.
Mission Impossible.

Having finished their meal in the alcove, Shariff suggested that they move outside and enjoy a few beers in the cool night air of the desert. When the sun sets, the Saharan sands quickly give up their heat and the temperature becomes brisk.

I asked about the snake. He laughed. "The snake took umbrage with our intrusion into his territory because we surprised him. He has had time to settle down and is probably off seeking his dinner. It is not in his nature to seek our company."

Chairs were brought out, along with a table that was obviously used regularly for the occasion. The night was gorgeous. Looking skyward, the stars formed an impenetrable blanket, a thousand points of light. As strange as my journey to Africa had become, the moment brought contentment.

Bottles of *Altbier* were passed and Shariff began to finish the tale where he left off inside the temple. "A month later, Fermi's field team returned to the highlands and made the long trek back to the mountain region where they had earlier collected the specimens that were now locked in Fermi's safe. Local natives were hired to carry the heavy equipment the expedition needed to assess the enigma they knew lurked up in the old abandoned Okla mine.

Arriving at the former camp site on the third night, and exhausted from battling the insects, heat, and thick foliage along the upward sloping topography, they prepared the equipment and supplies for the climb they had to make the following morning. After completing the preparations they slipped into the warm soft bags that would serve as their beds while there in the wilderness. As sleep began to overtake them, Francesco's hearty male laugh cut through the silence of the night. He reminded them of the last time they had climbed into the same bags on this spot. On that occasion, as he was preparing to slide into his, he had spotted movement inside the bag. Holding it above the ground, a deadly, hissing Gabon Viper had slid out."

Shariff shook his head, saying, "Francesco had narrowly missed certain and agonizing death."

Then, he began describing their doomed return up to the Okla mine. "The following morning the team was awakened by a chorus of bird songs and gorilla calls issuing from the thick canopy of trees lofting above the camp. The Gabonese cooks, accustomed to the cacophony, paid no mind and began preparing a breakfast of eggs and bush meat which, as it turned out, would be their only meal that day. While they waited for their breakfast, the team sat around a ring fire drinking the usual thick sweet tea while Francesco, returning to the snake incident, reminded them to watch the undergrowth as they climbed and avoid reaching into the tree branches overhanging their path. Gabon Vipers like to wait quietly for the chance to strike, and hang on to their target with large fangs until the victim succumbs to their poison. It's a lethal encounter and brutal death."

"Following their meal, the equipment was loaded and the hike upward began. Each porter carried eighty pounds on his back. The scientists carried the lighter but more critical state of the art equipment. The climb was taxing, steep, and made slippery by ground cover and loose rock. When they eventually reached the plateau on the mountain's top and the land became as flat as a horse's topline, they dropped their burdens for a short recovery period.

At that point, the porters refused to continue further. Local lore held that the god of the mountain wanted no intrusions and made trespassers sick. When the mines were still operating, many workers had become ill and died of the god's curse.

Since the locals would not approach the mine, Fermi's team had no choice but to load as much of the equipment as they could carry onto their own backs. Jacques, fluent in the local dialect, ordered the porters to wait in place.

They did not, of course. As soon as their employers disappeared on the trail, the porters began descending back down to base camp where they anticipated finishing off the bitter local beer which the khawajas had brought."

I could not resist being drawn into Shariff's tale, sitting next to him beneath the starlight of the Sahara desert. The night, and his nearness, stirred emotions in me that could not be denied. He sensed it and moved closer. But for the others, we would have been in each other's arms. Checking his libido, and the energy flowing between us, he continued. "Within half an hour the team covered the last mile and entered the mine tunnel where Jacque's monitor had first soared into the red zone. Stopping long enough to suit up in radiation protection units, they began making their way along the tunnel. As anticipated, it happened again. The reading on the monitor suddenly jumped to an extraordinary level of emissions emanating from the area beneath their feet.

As the monitor screamed at decibel levels that reverberated off the shaft walls, they quickly began collecting data. It was imperative that they outline the footprint of the hot zone, profile its conformation, and collect additional samples of rock from the floor in order to characterize the enigma. They had no way of telling how effectively their rad con suits were providing protection against the gamma rays bombarding them."

At that point, Shariff's voice became slightly elevated, conveying a sense of awe. "The conformation profile outlined by the in-coming data was astonishing, revealing a double-barreled

ROSE O. HAYES Ph.D.

geologic freak of nature beyond any force in the history of science. According to sonar waves and spectrometric readings, beneath the Okla mine, about eight miles down in the earth's crust there is a Precambrian granite basement that registers extremely elevated radioactivity. Some crystalizing ancient heat source formed a rock chamber that encloses high-level radioactive energy. Above the chamber, there is a sandstone layer, about a mile thick. It forms a roof over the granite basement. The chamber was directly beneath them, the spot where the team had gathered their first samples, and gamma rays from the trapped energy were making their way to the surface through fissures in the sandstone cap.

As their equipment integrated the incoming data, the events leading to the formation of the mutant force became outlined. At a time during one of Earth's pluvial periods, concentrations of uranium, which were especially rich in highly fissionable U-235, washed into the area. Eventually, the concentrations became dense enough to go critical and formed a massive natural nuclear reactor that burned for hundreds of thousands of years.

At the same time that the volatile uranium was being deposited, waves of unicellular microorganisms were also washing into the area. The microorganisms eventually formed a biological colony of some 3,000 bacteria. The colony survived the intense heat of the reactor's long burn by mutating into an ectoparasitic organism that feeds on radioactivity. Nothing can destroy it as long as it can find radioactive feeding grounds for its sustenance. The team nicknamed it Godzilla, but Fermi had already assigned it the scientific name, Kineo*coccus radiotolerans*.

Staring in disbelief, I said, "How could such an organic community, capable of surviving in a toxic radioactive environment, exist without my knowledge?"

He smirked. "There are many nuclear secrets that have been closely guarded over the decades, even from nuclear scientists. Decisions concerning nuclear secrets are often made behind closed doors by the powers that be. The public knows only what the secret

182

holders want them to know. Our science is imperfect due to those secrets and the empty spaces in our laboratory-generated body of knowledge. One of the reasons such secrets are kept is to delude the public into thinking there are no unknowns about nuclear power and its safety."

He laughed. "In an effort to remove its stigma of danger, the industry claims it is completely transparent and controllable. We physicists know that we do not know what we do not know that we cannot know. We know that we are dancing with the Devil."

I nodded for him to continue, beginning to feel like Dorothy going through the looking glass.

"When the data had been collected, the team made their way back down to base camp and got a good night's sleep. By morning, the magnitude of what they were dealing with had set in and as they again sat around the fire ring drinking morning tea a heated discussion progressed.

Clearly, science had no intervention strategies for controlling the force under the Okla mine, or the samples they had once more collected in lead-lined cylinders. They all finally agreed that the potential power of the freak of nature had to remain secret and the samples they had collected had to be returned to the mine. The four of them planned to hike back up to the hot zone and replace the samples in the same location where they had been collected. They ate a hearty breakfast and began the upward trek.

While they were trudging back up the mountain, another force of nature was building beneath the sea off the Dark Continent's west coast. The North American and African Plates were continuing their eternal tectonic struggle to pass one another, in opposite directions. As the two edges of the Goliathan plates ground their way past each other a powerful earthquake was triggered. The quake undulated across the sea floor and up onto the landmass.

Forces of the displaced earth hit the Gabon highlands just as the survey team re-entered the Okla mine tunnel. Rolling waves rippled across the mine floor, distorting lentils and twisting them off their support posts. The architecture of the tunnel was violently shifted, tearing at the walls, opening crevices and swallowing whole sections of the shafts. Sections of the ceiling collapsed around the team and filled the tunnel with fallen rock and debris. Earth movement built to a magnitude 9.3 on the Richter scale.

Outside, massive avalanches of the terrain thundered down to the jungle floor below and a choking cloud of dust rose into the air. As the highlands were re-sculpted, the cylinders of primordial uranium and its water-born parasitic bacteria passenger were lost, reclaimed by the mountain.

Swept up in the violent avalanches, the team members were carried down to the ravine at the base of the mountain. Jacques, Charley and Francesco suffered contusions and cuts but Leslie suffered near fatal injuries, buried under heavy rocks and debris. Her right leg and arm were broken, her pelvis cracked, and there were internal injuries. Charley was the first to find and dig her out but the ground was still moving fiercely. Fearing another imminent slide, he pulled her up, slung her over his shoulder, and ran for the cover of the jungle.

Hours later, and a frantic drive over what served as roads in the area, they finally got her to a hospital. She survived several surgeries, with Charley constantly by her side, even in the operating room. A week later, Jacques and Francesco returned to Fermi's lab, empty handed, to report what had happened, and what they now knew about the chamber of horrors up on the mountain. They also told him the avalanche most likely sealed off the area from any further explorations so the chamber's secret was safe. Except for the samples in Fermi's office vault.

Fascinated but still skeptical, I asked, "Where are those samples now?'

He held up his hand, signaling me to be patient. "When the Nazis overran Europe, Fermi was forced to escape with his family to America because his wife's mother was Jewish. Under Italy's race laws, passed by Mussolini, the entire family was subject to deportation. Italy was shipping its Jews to the Nazi death camps."

"Rather than allow the dangerous Gabon samples to fall into Hitler's hands, Fermi smuggled them into America where he had taken a position at Columbia University in New York City. They remained secured in his office safe until he later moved them to Chicago when he joined Oppenheimer's Manhattan Project in a race to invent an atomic bomb ahead of feared German efforts to do the same.

I gave him a look conveying disapproval and said, "What? You do remember Einstein's recommendation that we should look deeply into nature to understand things better. He must have added a warning to his fellow physicists, including Oppenheimer and Fermi, not to mess with Mother Nature's atomic power. But they did mess with it, and as a result they learned to split the atom in a chain reaction. In doing so, they changed the course of human history forever and created a recipe for inevitable disaster."

I turned to look at the others. "Splitting the atom in a chain reaction was a train wreck waiting to happen. The results were atomic bombs, the Cold War weapons race, nuclear weaponry, and thermodynamic warheads secretly carried by submarines that run silent in the planet's oceans waiting to unleash a Hell like no other ever seen on this earth. They crossed a lot of science's ethical lines. Some say they were morally bankrupt and did the world no favor."

The others nodded in agreement. Shariff acknowledged my point, then went on explaining what happened to the four little canisters that had been prophetically filled on that Gabon mountaintop in 1938. "In 1954, when Fermi was dying of radiation induced cancer, he turned the cylinders over to Oppenheimer who, by then, was directing Princeton's Institute for Advanced Study.

Oppi secured them in a heavily lead-lined safe in the library of his home and, on his deathbed in 1967, he directed one of his protégés, Dr. Cris Everly-Grayson to take them.

Cris is the daughter of two members of the Okla mine team that originally collected the samples: Leslie Everly and Charles Grayson.

She grew up in Ann Arbor, Michigan where her mother and father worked in the University of Michigan Physics Laboratory with another member of the team, Jacques Belle. As a graduate student, Cris was trained by Oppenheimer, first at Berkley where he was on faculty, then Princeton,

Cris called Ann Arbor to tell her mother that Oppenheimer had directed her to remove the cylinders, which she had found wrapped in the old style Hazard Material stickers in his library safe. Leslie instantly warned her not to touch them. Years had gone by since they were encapsulated in the cylinders. High-level radioactive material has a way or corroding any container. They might be leaking.

Leslie caught a flight and arrived in Newark the following morning. Cris met her and they drove to the Oppenheimer home in Princeton. Leslie donned a radiation protection suit, removed the familiar cylinders from Oppenheimer's safe, and packed them for transport. She also told her daughter they were being watched by people who did not know what the cylinders contained but suspected that, because of Fermi, Oppenheimer, Szilard, and Bohr's involvement, they had something to do with a radioactive weapon. The watchers were probably willing to kill for them.

The women hurriedly loaded the cylinders and their luggage into Cris's car and headed south on the New Jersey turnpike. To Cris's astonishment, Leslie then revealed that their destination was Key West.

During the long drive south to Florida, Cris learned how Fermi's team had collected the samples up on the Gabon highlands, and what they knew about the freakish anomaly. She was also told that in Key West both she and the cylinders were being turned over to Francesco Pacillo. He was now her only protection from the watchers. He would explain who the watchers were. Leslie also explained that she was being put under Francesco's protection because there was no safer place to be than behind his firewall.

The drive south went without incident, although they had

every reason to think they were being tracked as the hours passed. The trip was also not without its rewards. In Old Town Alexandria they stopped for the night and treated themselves to seafood stew at the famous Fish Market on the west bank of the Potomac. In Savannah they sampled the southern fare, shrimp and grits. On their last night together they ate on the dock in Key West and treated themselves to conch fritters and that most famous of pain killers, the Dark and Stormy.

At sunrise the following morning, Leslie delivered her daughter to the Garrison Bight side of the island where, as planned, Francesco swooped in, pulled along the dock in a powerful 40-foot yacht, and reached down to take Cris aboard, along with the cylinders.

He was thirty years her senior, sensual, exciting, and exuded power. She knew instantly that she was in good hands. She was smitten. Neither could have known at that moment that their shared mission to safeguard the cylinders would also lead to a union that was to last the rest of their lives."

✍

He turned to look at me and his dark eyes scanned my body the way men do when they suddenly experience an elevated testosterone level. Then, he continued. "Francesco sent her below to sleep while he stayed at the helm and sped out to sea through the Florida Straits, bound for Baracoa, on the far eastern end of Cuba. It was too soon to tell her that in the intervening years since the team had survived the earth quake and avalanche up in the Okla mine, he had become enormously wealthy and wielded formidable influence with dominant leaders throughout the world. His associates included heads of state, a large segment of the world's scientific community, wealthy entrepreneurs, and officers of daunting military units. With their support, he had forged an organization that guarded the contents of the cylinders Oppenheimer had placed in her care, along with all who held their secret.

187

The organization also guarded the destructive power of the cylinder's contents, *Kineococcus radiotolerans*. *Kineococcus radiotolerans* was used by the scientists I have just described to build a weapon unlike the world has known. And, it is based on a deep space satellite system to prevent nuclear warfare on Planet Earth. Francesco has always taken the lead in that effort."

I looked back at him in amazement. Nothing was known of such an organization in the nuclear realm with which I was familiar, the scientists in my world. The weapon, which Shariff said the organization protected, was certainly not common knowledge. And my circle was privileged to a lot of secret stuff.

He went on. "The organization protecting the cylinders has a name. It is called the *Guardians*. Another organization, no less powerful, has formed, which is the *Guardians'* arch enemy. They are the watchers that ominously tracked Cris and Leslie to Key West. That organization is known as the *Tripartite*, composed of giant industrial conglomerates, nuclear energy titans, their puppet politicians, and a large military that protects the *Tripartite's* interests, economic and otherwise.

Francesco was left with the unpleasant duty of explaining all this to Cris and the fact that she would have to forever remain under his protection and that of the *Guardians* because the *Tripartite* killers would come for her, as they do for all who might have information on Fermi's secret cylinders."

⋘

I was beginning to shiver. It was growing too cool under the desert stars. Shariff, always watching me, noticed and suggested that we return to the protection of the temple inside the mountain. It is always cool there but warmer than the desert night chill.

Inside, we again gathered around the table in the alcove. Tea was made and two oil lamps were lit which made the alcove cozy. We settled in to listen as Shariff continued telling how the ancient temple had become a 20ᵗʰ century nuclear processing facility, and the uncanny weapon it produced.

"It was not long before the *Tripartite* forces hit Francesco's compound in Baracoa. They still did not know exactly what Cris had taken to Francesco but assumed it had something to do with radioactivity since it came from Oppenheimer's safe. They also assumed that since she had taken it to Francesco, it was something they needed in their possession."

"As usual, they underestimated Francesco. He always planned several evasive options ahead of his enemy. While his forces, well equipped and skilled fighters, held the enemy at the gate, he had his yacht brought around. Loading Cris and the cylinders back aboard, he sped along the coast for several miles and turned into a cove where his next evasive action waited; *Taino* natives mounted on horses specially bred to speed along the steep rocky trails of the *Sierra Maestra*.

The *Taino* are indigenous to the island. Their language is *Arawakan* and their name means 'human being'. At the time of Christopher Columbus's exploration, they inhabited what we now know as Cuba, Jamaica, Hispaniola, Puerto Rico and the Virgin Islands. They were once the most numerous people of the Caribbean but European aggrandizement, and their imported diseases, reduced *Taino* numbers to a few hundred. Those who survive became fierce protectors of Cuba's *Sierra Maestra* mountains, their last foothold on what had historically been a small part of their domain. They now guard Francesco and the *Kineococcus radiotolerans* weapon that was implanted near his ranch.

He had the ranch built at *Pico Turquino*, the highest point above *Comandancia de la Plata,* the headquarters of Castro and Guevara before leading the 1959 revolution against the Batista regime. During the revolution, the *Taino* joined the revolutionary fighters, always ready to fight for a cause that involved freedom from those who attempted to exert external controls over their people and territory. They saw Francesco in the same role as Castro and

Guevara, a brave opponent to those dark forces that had decimated their numbers and confiscated their lands.

The horses they brought to the cove that night were from Francesco's line of *Cubano de Pasos*. He had bred his herd to be short backed, at least sixteen hands tall, renowned for speed, and able to cover ground smoothly and swiftly, even while crossing difficult terrain over long distances. The highly unique breed, which evolved after being abandoned and allowed to become feral by the Spanish Conquistadors, can track at 13-15 miles per hour due to their four-beat lateral gait called the *Marcha*.

The *Taino* natives are expert horsemen, as is Francesco. Cris was a level four dressage rider. However, she was not used to long, hard rides and their next stop was Francesco's ranch, a difficult ride up the eastern slope of the *Sierra Maestra*. He pulled up every few miles and made her dismount to stretch and find some relief from the burning in her knees. She noticed that the two pack horses being ponied had large leather containers tied across their withers. She assumed they held the cylinders she had delivered to Francesco. He always dismounted and checked them as she rested.

After relaxing and regrouping several days at the ranch, they mounted fresh horses and were escorted down the western slope of the mountains by another contingent of *Taino*.

At the base of the mountains, in a tidewater meadow of tall grasses, a helicopter waited to transport the cylinders, Francesco, and Cris across the Caribbean to Belize."

Shariff fixed his eyes on me and paused for a moment before saying, "They were hosted in Belize while arrangements were made for their travel to the place where we now drink our tea. The trip here was arduous. It required traveling across the *Bayuda Desert* from Khartoum to this granite inselberg where they were joined by the other members of the team from the Okla mine event. Eventually, I was brought here from my lab in the *Inshas* nuclear processing facility where our team was illegally enriching uranium and extracting weapons-grade plutonium so that Egypt could build its own nuclear bomb."

He paused while warm tea was poured. Fresh mint leaves were passed and I studied them for a minute, wondering how so many amenities were available in this barren corner of the Dark Continent. The alcove had grown warm from the heat provided by the lamps and the scent of mint combined with the warm air, creating an inviting place to listen to a tale surpassed by few.

Shariff continued. "Francesco suddenly appeared at our lab one day and explained that the enriched uranium and weapons grade plutonium we had been illegally producing was needed for a far greater cause. He asked me to bring the material and join his project at *Jebel Barkal*. Although I did not know the man who had mysteriously appeared at *Inshas* in a Sikorsky helicopter armed like a fortress, he was impressive enough to convince me, and my team, to agree on both counts."

Shariff paused and smiled. "Besides, we got the feeling he left us no choice."

After stopping to take a drink of his tea, he put down the glass and said in an emphatic voice, "You need to understand that Francesco Pacillo is a heroic man, but also the possessor of extensive shadowy powers. He can find anything or anyone he looks for. He is what they call in the military a 'water walker', and apparently there are no secrets safe from him. He lives in multiple worlds and he knew about our illegal activities at *Inshas* which, while sanctioned by the Egyptian government, would have left us legally defenseless before the rest of the world and disgraced in all halls of science. And, his project to utilize the *Kineococcus radiotolerans* for the prevention of nuclear warfare on the planet was humanitarian, of the highest order. My team and I had no personal or ethical alternative but to agree to his request."

Shariff pointed to the equipment outside the alcove. "With the help of those who were on that mountain in Gabon when the avalanche came, we secretly moved Egypt's uranium and plutonium to the lab here in this temple. We integrated it with the mysterious colony of bacteria from the Okla mine to provide the bacteria's feedstock, which it requires for its sustenance. Combined, the Okla bacterial colony and the *Inshas* uranium became *Kineococcus radiotolerans*. When the processing work was completed, we packaged the *Kineococcus radiotolerans* into four indestructible weapons systems which are now imbedded in separate locations around the globe."

It was tempting to believe the next part of his story was fiction and not possibly true. However, having taken the measure of the man, I knew the tale he was telling had legs.

"The four *Kineococcus radiotolerans* weapons continuously communicate through a system emanating from a satellite that had been launched into geosynchronous space for that purpose. Once in place, the governments of all nuclear nations were told of the system's existence and ordered to have their military stand down from using nuclear warheads. They were also ordered to destroy their nuclear waste stockpiles, which are a constant risk for health hazards, environmental pollution, and terrorist attacks. Otherwise, they would be looking at planetary pinball. If released, *Kineococcus radiotolerans* would gradually ingest all forms of radioactive materials on the planet. That would play havoc with the energy and defense systems of every nation. The good news is, *Kineococcus radiotolerans* would also resolve the nuclear waste issue.

Environmental pollution is a constant threat from the nuclear waste generated by producing weapons and energy. There are thousands of tons and millions of gallons of the deadly poison laying around the planet in all sorts of containers, tanks, unlined pits, and cooling pools. Much of it has spilled into waterways or percolated into ground water via plumes.

The waste has also been directly dumped into the oceans and seas. The U.S. has dumped thousands of barrels a few miles off San Francisco's coast and Russia has completely poisoned some sections of the Bering Sea. Who knows what the smaller players in the atom splitting game secretly do with their nuclear garbage."

I knew about the dumping of nuclear waste in inappropriate areas. It was my job to know. But I had never heard about the stand down order of the *Kineococcus radiotolerans* system. *Another closely guarded secret that even nuclear scientists were not privy to.* I had grown up in a world that was always on edge for fear of nuclear warfare. It turns out that nuclear waste may destroy our habitat before nuclear warfare.

He gestured with a wave of his hand. "The *Kineococcus radiotolerans* plan is also a go-no-go system. If any one of the weapons are disturbed, all will lock and fire, releasing their contents. *Kineococcus radiotolerans* will be turned loose on the earth's environment to begin feeding. The colony will infiltrate the strongest, most energetic sources first. Eventually, it will turn to the weaker sources, possibly even the Potassium 40 in humans."

The vein pulsed in his temple, masculine and sensual, but also betraying the level of futility he was feeling. "We were never satisfied with that eventuality but it was our only means to force nuclear nations to control their own military, nuclear waste, and sponsored terrorists. The looming prospect of nuclear warfare, a war that no one can win or survive, or terrorist attacks with dirty bombs, had become an inescapable reality and we saw no other option."

He paused for a moment, a small smile forming on his lips as he looked directly at me. "That is until my team and I acquired the *Scorpion* and used her uranium fuel to produce Polonium 210. Granted, it was developed to murder deserving Nazi war criminals, but when it gained the attention of the *Guardians* another plan for its use emerged.

Kineococcus radiotolerans will be uncontrollable if activated, but Polonium 210 is the perfect solution to that one great drawback. Polonium 210 can target specific areas or individuals without indiscriminatingly destroying all radioactive sources on the planet and possibly innocent human beings. That is our new mission. The world will never have to know that Polonium 210 has replaced *Kineococcus radiotolerans,* so the power of its presumed threat will continue. Between the two weapons, we hope we have found a way to protect our world from nuclear annihilation."

I silently mulled over the horrible prospects he was outlining and began to feel the cold under the mountain of rock above our heads. The world outside seemed even colder, and more threatening, and the air seemed to be sucked out of the little alcove where we sat, leaving it hard for me to breathe. Until that moment I had never really conceived of an actual planetary war in which nuclear warheads rained across the continents, incinerating the earth and all life forms, poisoning the waters, sending a cloud of lethal radiation to exterminate anything that escaped the original blasts. The carnage was unfathomable. Hiroshima times millions.

He was watching me, reading my thoughts, and I returned his gaze, knowing what was happening. I was being recruited. Moments passed and then, gathering my thoughts, I said, "No. I cannot be a part of this. My mission is to safeguard the public from excessive doses of radiation. I am a permissible exposure expert, not a killer. You are asking me to join you in an astonishing act of arrogance, a premeditated campaign of murder by radiation exposure."

I remembered how I have always felt about the surprise attacks on civilian cities in Japan with the atomic bomb. The bombing was much more than a demonstration of its terrifying power. It was a nuclear flash point in human history. "When Oppenheimer, Fermi, Szilard, Bohr and all the others at Los Alamos built the world's first nuclear weapon for the U.S. military by splitting atoms, they were thinking in the same vein as you. They played God, unleashing abysmal destruction on two cities of civilians."

Before he could begin his refute, I continued. "At that moment, the world was split into power and powerless tribes. Some think that was noble, but it changed the fabric of civilized society and got us here today. How do you know that what you are planning is not just raising the bar. Either way, whether you wait for the weapon you built and turned over to the satellite in geosynchronous space to strike, and eradicate us all, or whether you methodically eliminate only those you select and target, you are also playing God. Your plan is not just a course correction. It is astonishingly arrogant and I will not help you."

He waited for my tirade to end, reached out and took my hand. Holding it tenderly, he spoke quietly. "Cecily, remember what Francesco told Cris when he raced with her and the cylinders across the Florida Straits to Cuba? He told her that her life had changed forever. Her old life was ended. Gone. That she would never be able to go back and would forever have to remain under his protection and that of the *Guardians*. It is the same for you."

I shook my head vigorously, denying what he was saying, but he continued. "From the moment you set foot in Port Said you became a target of the watchers because they are always watching me. Anyone who comes near me gets in their crosshairs. I am sorry but you must now remain under my protection and that of the *Guardians*. You will be safe if you do. If you choose to leave that protection, either the *Tripartite* killers will take you for questioning, and then do away with you, or our own guards will end your life to protect what you now know."

I was stunned. This man, who had both revolted me and aroused me over the past few days had just told me that his nearness had caused my entire life to be taken from me. All the time we talked, dined, strolled the docks of Port Said, and kissed, he knew this!

He had to be wrong. "No. You do not understand. I am a scientist in the ranks of the U.S. government. I have knowledge about America's nuclear capacity that is only held by a few with the highest security clearance. If you hold me against my will, you will be pitting yourself against the intelligence and military capability of the most powerful nation on earth. They will come for me and they may not care if I have to die in order to see that what I know is held safe."

Shaking his head, he said, "Do you think I do not know that? Even more reason for you to use the protection I offer you here, and wherever else we have to go to complete our mission. If it makes you feel better, although I cannot reveal their identities, there are people at the highest levels of your government who are dedicated members of the *Guardians*. They will see that we are safe. And once you have time to think it through, you will realize that our cause is right, worth dying for if necessary."

Fear gripped me as I began to understand the logic of Shariff's argument. "You cannot be serious. There is an obvious fly in your ointment. Polonium is a slow killer. Sometimes it takes days for the poison to liquefy the organs and dissolve the musculoskeletal system. That could leave enough time for a terrorist to set off a dirty bomb or the leader of a nation to order a nuclear strike. In the end, you may kill a lot of people, murder them with Polonium 210, and still lose the battle. If I have understood you correctly, *Kineococcus radiotolerans* will load and fire if any nuclear warheads are launched. It is a go-no go system, so if the worst-case scenario happens, there can be no action to reverse its course. Polonium 210 cannot control for that.

He had listened patiently but I could tell from his body language that he was just biding time until I had exhausted my argument. "Cecily, everything you say has some validity. No plan is perfect. However, there is one variable in this scheme of things that you do not know. It is Francesco Pacillo. I know him well. He is not a man who would design a mission impossible, a plan that he would be destined to lose.

Francesco would have left a backdoor open in his satellite communications plan. If I am correct, he can either disarm the satellite or neuter the communication system between the weapons, or both. Besides, we are not evil scientists. Like the power of *Kineococcus radiotolerans*, the threat of releasing Polonium 210 should hold the world at bay. Releasing it is not our goal. We would do everything in our power to avoid that. And, that is why I am confident that Francesco would not have designed the satellite controlled system without building in a back door."

"And what," I asked, "is this back door?"

His response caught me totally off guard. "I do not know. We will have to go ask him."

Again, I was caught off guard. "I thought you said he is holed up in the *Sierra Maestra* mountains of Cuba."

"That is true. He, Cris Everly-Grayson, now his wife, Charles Grayson, and Leslie Everly Grayson, now married to Charles and mother of Cris, all evade the *Tripartite* by staying at Francesco's mountain fortress." He laughed. "There are more nuclear scientists and Ph.D.'s in those mountains than in most major universities."

The laugh faded, "We leave in the morning, with the Polonium 210. It is no longer safe here. As I said, too many players with high profiles are now in this pool; Osama bin Laden, Carlos the Jackal, and an *al Qaeda* cell itching to make the six o'clock news. The polonium has to be moved and we need to take cover on Francesco's mountain for safety. So, we leave for Cuba in the cool of the morning hours."

14
The Run For Cuba
Sheltered at Pico Turquino

He nodded to the others. "If we leave by four a.m., we will be in *Shendi* in time to catch the train, if we are lucky and it is running. We can travel by rail from there into *Omdurman*. A jet will be waiting for us outside *Omdurman*."

I asked, "Assuming the train is running, why would we get off in *Omdurman*? Why not continue into *Khartoum*, which has a decent size airport from which full bodied jets leave on a somewhat regular basis." *I had no intention of joining their flight plan to Cuba since the U.S. government had banned travel to that country for anyone holding an American passport. I hoped that in Khartoum I would either be spotted by American embassy officials or CIA spies. There might be a way to take control of the Polonium 210 before we left Africa. The chance of that happening in Cuba was slim to none, especially up in the Sierra Maestras.*

As usual, he was watching me with that look in his eye, reading my thoughts, watching my body language, rather than listening to what I said. A small tolerant smile creased the corners of his mouth. "Cecily, we are trying to keep a low profile here. In this world nothing goes unnoticed, especially unusual events like Egyptians traveling with a *wahid* , a white woman. Particularly an American *wahid sita* like yourself who wears no *tobe* and is not quiet.

Here, at least in public, men talk and women keep their mouths closed and their eyes down cast. In Sudan, the value of women ranges from zero to a few goats and possibly some chickens. A small select number bring dowries of several *fedans* but even a dowry of such worth does not give a woman much leverage. She is always without the rights and freedoms of men and cannot leave the confines of the walls around her home unless covered from head to foot in a *tobe*, and in the company of male relatives. Sometimes the old grandmothers will act as an escort.

I know these conditions jolt your Western sense of gender equality but the world is what it is. We will meet fewer complications passing through the busy market town of *Omdurman* where all sorts of people are shopping. In *Khartoum*, everyone who isn't a servant knows everyone who isn't a servant. That city is 'village intrigue central' and our presence will draw instant attention."

Turning to Akeem, he said, "Will you show the *wahid* to her quarters and be sure she has what she needs."

Returning his attention to me, he said, "Go with Akeem and get some rest before we leave."

Fixing me with a stern look, he warned, "The sooner you accept your new position in life, the easier it will be for all of us to get to the safety of Francesco's Cuban fortress.

Believe me, you will be safe there. Over the years, the *Guardians* have evolved into a tightly integrated network with very powerful members and other contacts. With unlimited funding and rapid but secret communication channels, they are aware of our position and activities at all times. Like-minded heads of state, politicians, industrialists, military forces, scientists and other reinforcements are always watching over our team. The network spans the globe.

You have no other option for now. When we have left this part of the world you will have fewer restrictions. But wherever we are,

ROSE O. HAYES Ph.D.

you will always need to be a team player, for your own safety and ours. Right now, being a team player means keeping as low a profile as possible."

I was reminded of some prose from one of Edgar Allen Poe's works, "*The Imp of the Perverse.*" That was me, my inner rebel. While I understood what Shariff had just told me about my altered status in life and being a team player, I still had not completely accepted my plight. By nature, I am not easily controlled. At the moment, however, no other alternatives were apparent. I was somewhere in the middle of the Sahara, in a land where my worth was near the bottom of the bucket, my command of the Sudanese dialect in Arabic was slim, and there was only one way out. With him.

Hiding my irritation, I followed Akeem, as directed.

᧔

<u>Day 4.</u> Someone pulled back the blanket from my shoulder and said, "*Menfuhdlik* (please). It is time to go. We must hurry." It was Akeem and it seemed like only minutes since he had shown me where to lay down the night before.

I threw back the rest of the blanket, stretched my legs over the side of the cot, and slipped into my shoes. The pungent smell of tea and mint wafted toward me. One of the others brought a glass of the heavily sugared liquid and, downing it, my head quickly cleared. Within minutes, I gathered up my bag and headed for the alcove where Shariff was giving directions.

"Remember to keep low out of the rotation of the blades. And, cover your faces with your scarves because the blowing sand will be very heavy next to the bird."

He turned and handed me a brightly colored cloth. "Wrap this *tarka* around your head and over your nose and mouth. Also, squint near the helicopter or you will be blinded by the sand."

As I reached for it, he said, "Keep this with you and keep your head and shoulders covered in *Omdurman*. There, all women in

200

public will be covered in their *tobes*. Since it takes practice to keep up a *tobe* when moving, you will have to make do with a *tarka*."

The resentment of my new status in life was growing. He could tell, and a slight smile formed on his lips. *Men can never hide their pleasure at having the upper hand over a woman.*

He couldn't leave it alone. "By the way, the *tarka* is what Sudanese girls wear before they reach puberty so you will draw some looks." The smile broadened in direct proportion to my anger.

We left the alcove and crossed the temple floor. I noticed that some of the equipment was now missing and looked quizzically at Shariff. Walking ahead of me he said, "We are taking what may be needed for the mission. It will follow us on a second bird."

The mission?, I wondered, but there was no time to ask.

Stepping out into the desert, the noise of the helicopter engines and whirling blades drowned out any prospects for further discussion. Shariff suddenly took my arm, pushed my head down, and ran forward. The bird was just ahead, appearing in the blow like a giant insect looking for a kill. As we reached it, he lifted me up to Hussein who pulled me inside the cabin and out of the whirling sand. Even inside, the decibel levels were still ear splitting.

As soon as all the others were on board, the door was closed, and the heavily armed Sikorsky took off. The ground beneath soon disappeared. It was not yet daylight and darkness engulfed us.

Even though I had developed a serious resentment toward Shariff's treatment of me during the past few hours, I leaned against him for security and found his warm hard body more comforting than I liked to admit. Security and Shariff were becoming synonymous.

As the sun rose, I could see that we were following the southward path of the Nile. It looked like a huge brown snake winding and twisting between the banks of the barren rocky Red Sea Hills on the

east and the dry ocean of sand that is the Sahara on the west. The number of islands in the river surprised me.

Two hours passed as we sat watching the scene below, lulled by the constant throb of the bird's blades. After a couple of hours the Sikorsky began settling toward earth and the village of *Shendi* appeared below. As it landed, spiraling sand again engulfed us. My *tarka* almost blew away in the displaced air from the rotors and I grasped it under my throat, unable to use it as a screen over my face. The sand scoured my skin and I could hardly catch my breath in the cloud of Saharan soil that swallowed the team as we ran beneath the blades and jumped into the nearby Land Rovers waiting to take us to the train stop.

Now covered in what passed for soil in the Sahara, I did not appear that different from my companions. Dark or light skinned, we were all Saharan tan.

The ride to the train stop on the edge of the village was short. Arriving at the scene, I was struck by a sensation of cognitive dissidence. An ancient diesel engine sat heaving on its tracks against the backdrop of an unending and largely featureless desert landscape. Attached to the engine was a long line of old coach cars.

Shariff's team encircled me as we left the Land Rovers, forming a screen between me and the other expectant passengers. I could only catch quick glimpses of them by peeking between my protectors. Waiting to board was a myriad of turbaned men, women in *tobes* holding children, camels, donkeys, goats, stacks of burlap bags filled with dates from the groves along the river, and other cargo to be loaded onto the iron behemoth.

Down a few cars, I noticed that Shariff had entered into a heated conversation with the *gaffir* who was collecting fares and issuing tickets.

Returning to our group, he said to the others, "It is settled. She will be with us in the men's car. Take her to the bathrooms now. She will not be allowed to leave her seat on the train."

I was quickly ushered to the building where the women's toilets were and told to use them. The men waited outside.

As it turned out, on Sudanese trains males and females ride in separate cars. Since Shariff refused to allow me out of his sight, and his protection, he had insisted on paying an extra fee to have me at his side in the men's car. My rudimentary Sudanese dialect of Arabic told me he had just paid a lot of *baksheesh* for his *wahid* .

When we finally boarded the train, Shariff selected seats that exposed me as little as possible to our fellow passengers. Our seats faced a bulkhead and he directed me not to turn and survey the car. The other passengers were politely ignoring the highly unusual presence of a woman in their midst. The rest of our team sat immediately behind us and across the aisle.

Uncomfortable as I was, staring at a bulkhead and sitting on a hard surface with little padding, the scales were somewhat balanced by being off the helicopter, out of the sand, and next to him. Whenever he was near, the energy field that seemed to pass through me was definitely sensual.

The train began to move forward and Shariff started rationalizing why I would be more comfortable with him in the men's car. "The women's cars have two bunks on each wall in first class where you would ride. However, the women are always accompanied by their children so there might be four women and thirty or so children sharing four bunks, hardly enough room to even sit. Also, within a short time the heat in the compartments become so intense that the women take turns walking the car's corridor, along with all the children. Sudanese women have few distractions in their lives and you would quickly become a center of attention, and gossip. That would put all of us at greater risk."

"It will take at least seven hours to make *Omdurman*, longer if sand storms have covered the tracks. The train crew and male passengers will have to dig out the tracks in those areas.

If we do have to stop to clear the tracks, and the other passengers in our car get out to assist, you can leave your seat and step into the next car to use the women's toilet. Otherwise, I am sorry to tell you that you will have no access for the entire trip. Think you can endure it?"

My immediate thought was to remember not to drink any liquids, even in this hyper-arid heat. I nodded in agreement, already feeling thirst rising in my throat, and thinking, *I should be getting hazard pay for this. Talk about the training wheels coming off!*

Through the window, I watched an occasional acacia tree go by, the only features in a vast, tan, waterless sea. The monotony soon lulled me to sleep. Hours later, I woke to find myself enfolded in the protective custody of Shariff's arms. He, too, had fallen asleep.

Not wanting the moment to end, I closed my eyes and concentrated on the warmth of his body and the sensation his nearness aroused in me. If it were another time and place, the day would be perfect.

Another hour passed and shadows across my eyelids startled me. Opening them, I saw pyramids sliding by outside the window. This I had to see. When I sat up to gain a better view, Shariff stirred. He removed his arms but stayed close, speaking softly over my shoulder. "Those are the royal burials of the last Nubian kings and queens. This site is called *Meroe* and there are also quite a few temples in the area, including one dedicated to war lions.

I had heard of the war lion temple in Nubia. King Apedamek built it. The Nubians took newborn cubs from their mothers, raised them in the lion temple, and trained them to run beside the royals' war chariots, attacking the enemy. As part of their training, prisoners were bound and fed to them.

Remembering how the Nubians used lions gave me pause for thought.

Another remarkable practice had also occurred in this area. The first practical application of radiation had made its debut here, just across the river, outside Khartoum.

In 1895, there had been a field hospital set up there where bullets that could not be found by palpation in wounded British soldiers were located with a new technology; x-ray. The Brits were fighting to regain *Khartoum* from the *El Mahdi* forces, his *jihadists,* which had driven them from the territory ten years earlier. Rubbing salt in the wound, so to speak, after ousting the English troops in 1885, the *jihadists* had beheaded General Charles Gordon and hung his head from a tree in *Khartoum's* main *suk.*

Sudan eventually devolved to be the third poorest country in the world and little threat to others. However, atomic research evolved from that first appearance in mankind's history to atom splitting. It had taken only three quarters of a century for atom splitting to lead to the most lethal threats in human history; nuclear waste and thermodynamic bombs.

I wearily thought, *Jihadists are now the least of our concerns. Sudan is lucky to be sitting in the backwater, away from it all.*

Turning to Shariff, I asked, "How much further to *Omdurman*?"

Moving even a little closer, he said, "We are a good 3 ½ hours from *Omdurman*, about 125 miles. Are you thirsty or hungry?"

Not until he mentioned thirst did I realize how dry my throat and eyes were. The heat in the car was an oven. The nearness of his body was suddenly unwelcome. I shifted in the seat to put distance between us.

He reached out and picked up my arm, inspecting it. "Here, you do not experience   perspiration. It is too dry. In the winter, the temperature gets down to around 110 degrees and the only rain comes during the first two weeks in June, if it comes at all. You have to watch for the buildup of salt on your skin. That is how you monitor your perspiration level. If you begin to see salt on your skin, or have muscle cramps, you must drink salted water."

This was a new dilemma for me. A proud western, career

205

oriented woman, highly educated in the permissible limits of radiation exposure to human physiology, craving a drink of water, but having to chose between the need to urinate as a result, or running the risk of dehydration and muscle cramping to avoid the stares of men. No wonder they separate the women from the men in the cars. I wished I had been allowed to ride in the women's car. Overcrowding seemed the lesser of the two evils. And I would have shed the damned *tarka* covering my head and shoulders, which was adding to my hypothermia. *How did women survive here?*

He was watching me, as usual. "If you cannot wait another three hours I will walk you to the door where you can step into the women's car to use the facilities. But, it will draw a lot of attention to us."

Rethinking what he had just said, he whispered "Even though we have quietly remained in our seats, I am sure the men in this car are thinking about us, and I am sure the women are talking about us in their car. Let's get you to that door, but do not make eye contact."

He rose, and I obediently followed him down the aisle with my eyes down cast. *Humiliating!*

As we walked, I could feel the eyes of the other men on me and I had a strong urge to look into the boldest of the stares and ask, "What the Hell are you looking at?" But, I realized that, given the social morays of the country and our current predicament, such a display of indignation would not play well. Women are little more than chattels in Sudan and my offense would not change that.

⤸

Having braved the stench of the train latrine, and the Arabic toilet that requires ladies to squat over a hole in the floor that rapidly passes over the tracks below, leaving one feeling totally vulnerable, I returned to the door where Shariff waited. The next three hours went by quickly and we began to organize our luggage to disembark in *Omdurman*.

When the train screeched and wheezed to a halt in the station, the team quickly threw down our stuff and Shariff lifted me to the ground. His men surrounded me, as usual, so that few others got a view of the *wahid* in their midst. Even so, I was told we would be the topic of many conversations in the *suk* and *harem* for years to come.

We had only taken a few steps toward the Russian Land Rovers waiting to take us to our plane when we were confronted by Kurt Everhart. He apologized for stopping us and introduced himself as the American cultural attaché in Sudan. Surprisingly, to me at least, he announced that he heard we were coming and gave us the traditional greeting. '*Afwan*'.

After shaking hands with the men of our team, he then turned to me. Smiling broadly, he told me that word had it the *wahid* is a CIA agent. When my face displayed my concern over that revelation he laughingly told me not to worry because all Americans are presumed to be CIA agents in Sudan until proven innocent. He told us that suspecting others as CIA spies in Sudan was a national sport. I wondered why and suspected there was a grain of truth in the suspicion."

Curious, I asked, "How did you know we were coming to *Omdurman*?"

Again, smiling broadly, he told me that he did not really understand exactly how that happens. The telephone never works so if you want to speak to someone you have to either go find them or send your *guffir* with a message. In the countryside there are no radio stations, no telegraph, not even newspapers. Yet, nothing that is going to happen goes unknown. He concluded that it must be the lorry system along the river. In addition to their cargoes, the drivers evidently carry the daily news.

Then, he asked about our destination and whether we would be staying in *Khartoum*. Shariff took him aside to explain that we were on out way out of the country and had disembarked in

Omdurman to avoid as much attention as possible. I heard him say, "We will not be stopping in *Khartoum.*"

Kurt studied Shariff for a moment and then explained to him that there had not been an operating American embassy in Sudan since the outbreak of the recent Israeli/Egyptian war. He was now based in *Nairobi* but flew in once a month to check on the embassy building and the electronic safe there. Laughing, he said that rumor had it the safe was filled with Kraft cheese and there was always the risk of a break in.

Then he turned to me and his tone grew firm as he expounded on his position. D.C. demands a report on any unusual occurrences in the country that might involve U.S. affairs. My presence in *Omdurman* would certainly qualify since I had not applied for a visa, was illegal, and probably already a diplomatic problem for my government. There was also the problem of what I knew, the reason I held high level security clearance.

My explanation, that I was just passing through, was not adequate to the task Kurt Everhart had set himself.

Nodding in disagreement, he informed me that no one is allowed in the country without a visa issued by the Sudanese government, which I could not possibly have since they are being refused to all U.S. citizens, especially U.S. government representatives. He added that he was certain Washington did not know of my whereabouts and would not approve of my entry to a country with whom it had cancelled all diplomatic relations, which I would know if I had bothered to go through channels.

He had me there. I asked to speak to Shariff privately and we stepped away from the others. I looked him firmly in the eye and said, "We have to share something with Everhart. He is a U.S. official and I am certain he can delay my departure from this country. He can probably have me arrested and delivered to D.C. What can we tell him.?'

My concern was I had overlooked the possibility that I would be considered an illegal agent. Shariff and the other members of the team would also be delayed, and the Polonium 210 was in immediate jeopardy. We could not allow it to fall into the hands of the Sudanese.

Shariff arched his eyebrows, thinking. Then said, "Let's tell him the truth, that I have just delivered the stolen submarine back to the Navy, that I am the one who killed the owner of the rotting flesh now in your Reardon lab cold storage, and that you are accompanying me to find out where the rest of the Polonium 210 will be stashed, in Cuba."

I looked at him in amazement. He turned so that Everhart could not see his smile. "Think about it. If we tell him the truth he will be compelled to allow you to proceed, not break the cover of your secret, and very critical, mission. He will also inform D.C. that you are bound for Cuba. While you are officially disallowed there, Washington officials will not interfere for several weeks, intent on giving you time to act undercover. The CIA will activate tracking immediately but they must do everything *sub rosa* in Cuba and Francesco will have such matters under control. By the time they can make any inroads, we will be out of that country."

As he suggested, I thought about it. Although I did not know that there was an "after Cuba" plan, I found the rest of Shariff's suggestion logical. Better yet, it prevented my having to mislead an American embassy official, which could be my undoing once back in the states. I nodded in agreement and Shariff beckoned for Everhart to join us.

We told him our version of the truth. His skepticism was eventually overcome by the alternative prospect; being "promoted sideways" in the ranks for wrongly interfering with a national security issue. We shook hands and our team proceeded to the waiting vehicles.

As a parting shot he warned us that we had better get out of Sudanese air space a.s.a.p. Shariff assured me there would be no problem. In Sudan, all decisions have to make their way to a tribal head with the authority and willingness to act on a significant issue.

He said it would take several hours for the news of our presence to make its way up that ladder and land in the lap of a decision maker who would be willing to direct an air scramble to stop us.

We were at the airstrip within an hour. The airstrip was not that far but the roads in the area are always packed with donkeys, camels, jeeps, lorries, English and Russian Land Rovers, and Volkswagen Beatles. Vying for space takes talent, experience, and luck.

When we got to our destination, there were two planes on the runway; both Lear Jet 23s. The execu-jets were built in 1962 and, although one of the noisiest planes to leave airports, had a range of 4,500 miles. And, they are fast. All good qualities for getting off the African continent. The flight plan was to take us south to Cape Town, with a quick stop in Nairobi for refueling. In Cape Town we would refuel again and cross the Atlantic, make a quick refueling stop in Sao Paulo, Brazil and then put wheels down in Havana. Flight time with refueling stops, meant that Havana was over 24 hours away but Shariff assured me that our route would keep us out of enemy territory. He did not want to cross West Africa.

The leather seats in the Lear's cabin were heavily padded and, after sinking into mine, I quickly fell into a deep sleep. The ride on the train had used up all the fuel in my tank.

I faintly remember landing in Nairobi. Then, I was jolted awake as the Lear's tires bit the runway at the airport in Cape Town. Everyone else had slept, too.

Our pilot put the plane down on the north side of the terminal, assigned to international flights. We disembarked and stretched our legs while waiting for the bus that would transport us to the terminal building while our jet was refueled. An efficient looking yellow and white mini bus rolled up, we loaded on, and took a quick ride across the runway where we were let out and told to take the elevator up to the 3rd level.

On the 3rd level, the doors quietly slid open to reveal the massive expanse of a Spur steak house. Spur is a franchise spread across the globe and famous for its North American cuisine and décor, American Indian themes. Mounted on the walls everywhere I looked were Dakota headdresses, quivers of bows, buffalo skulls, and the infamous scalping hatchets.

I found it satirical, given the *apartheid* policies of South Africa that are a subject of constant criticism in the United Nations. The playfully adorned room sat in juxtaposition to the brutally enforced institutionalized racism of the country. We were about to enjoy the promise of a great steak in an eatery decorated around America's 'red skinned' indigenous peoples in a land ruled by a 'whites only' dogma.

Shariff quietly said, "Let's eat and run." We all took his meaning, not feeling at all like welcome strangers. As we walked across the room to our table, I could feel eyes following us and you could have cut the suspicion with a knife. The psychological impact of *apartheid* was rampant paranoia.

We did exactly as Shariff had directed; quickly ordered and ate. The steaks were juicy and tender, accompanied by *chakalaka*, the spicy relish dish of carrots, green peppers, sliced onion, vinegar, and searing chili sauce. As an adventure into the local popular fare not normally available elsewhere, we ordered an appetizer of 'walkie-talkies', the rural dish of grilled chicken feet and heads.

As soon as we finished, Shariff got the bill, settled, and headed for the elevator, with the rest of us close behind. I was not sure which was going to be the best part of this trip. Getting out of Sudan or leaving South Africa.

15

The Sierra Maestras
A hard day's ride.

The flight to Cuba was uneventful. We had eaten well, caught up on our sleep, and Africa was in the rearview mirror. The rest of the day was spent leisurely reading, visiting, and cat napping in the padded leather seats while the Lear jet slipped through the air, eating the miles at over 500 mph.

Day 5. When we landed in Havana, an escort met us as we deplaned. We quickly piled into four-wheelers with our luggage and sped through the city. The old plantation owner's homes, lining Havana's streets, went by in a blur. I made a mental note to spend a few days in the city on my way back to the states, even though my presence there, due to no fault of my own, was not sanctioned by the U.S. government. I wanted to enjoy the spectacular architecture that raises the specter of what once had been a mecca of lavish living for the dictator, Batista, wealthy American sugar lords, and Meyer Lansky's mafia organization.

Shariff was watching me and began to explain what I was seeing. "Have you noticed all the vintage American cars?"

I had. They were everywhere, old Buicks, Oldsmobiles, Fords, and my favorite, the Cadillacs with long fins cutting along their backs. "They are a marvel."

He shook his head, "These classics are like moving paintings of Cuba's history. They are kept running on infusions and foreign invasions. They were brought here for the pleasure of Cuba's privileged wealthy and the *capo di tutti*, the mafia. Now they are anachronisms. Like the island, they are beautiful on the outside, but if you lift their hoods you will find Spanish motors, Russian gearboxes, Korean alternators, Taiwan water pumps. Much of Cuba is no longer original.

The only original parts on this island are the indigenous *Taino*. Today, Cubans even make their own musical instruments. and things like fire hydrants are collector's items. If you see trucks and tractors in the streets, chances are

they're Russian. And, the streets are full of missing pavement, but there is always music, laughter." He smiled, and said slyly, "*Cuba Libres*."

You will be meeting *Taino* soon. They inhabit the mountains where we are going. In the mountains, they have survived invasions from the Spanish, the English, America, and most recently, Russia. All of who superimposed their own brand of government on the island while attempting to exterminate the *Taino* that always lived here in peace. Not surprisingly, they fought for Guevara and Castro against Batista, and now they fight for Francesco."

We left the city behind and after two hours of bumping and swerving at high speeds along a poorly maintained highway, the vehicles turned off onto an unpaved road and headed toward the coast. Within half an hour we were looking at blue water.

The legendary Francesco was waiting for us in a quiet cove. He was standing on the dock next to a magnificent 40-foot mono-hulled yacht. She was *yar,* but he was even more so, the most stunningly handsome man I had ever seen; lean, tan, and strapping. His friends nicknamed him the Italian Stallion and it was easy to see why. Coupled with the tales of his heroism, his considerable resources, his dark and twisty powers, and his sensuality, he was the stuff of legend and took your breath away.

As we pulled alongside the yacht, he stepped down onto the aft deck and our team began hurriedly handing off our bags. These he tossed below deck through the open hatch at his feet. Motioning for us to board, he smiled at me, displaying perfect white teeth against a strong jaw line. "*Bienvenido!*" His voice was smooth, deep, and throaty. It seemed to convey many meanings, including "*Welcome to my woods.*"

Any gal not legally blind would find that eye candy. I had to remind myself who I was and what I was there for. And the Egyptian I came with.

Once our party was aboard, Shariff quickly released the fore and aft lines from the dock's cleats and jumped down beside me as Francesco started the powerful engine. The yacht surged forward and roared away from shore.

Even though we were cutting through tranquil open water at top speed, with no other craft in sight, I could not escape the uncomfortable feeling that we were being watched. Like the enemy was closing in.

Turning to Shariff, who had wrapped his arm across my shoulder to steady me, I mentioned my uneasiness, that we remained on someone's radar.

He smiled warmly, pulling me closer. "It is a feeling you will have to become accustomed to. They are always watching, from the land, the sea, or the sky. And, we are watching them." He was referring to the organizations he told me about back at *Jebel Barkal*: the *Guardians* and the *Tripartite*.

A pang of guilt ran through me, knowing that if I could lay hands on the Polonium 210 in his possession, I had to flee him and this island paradise. But for now, I leaned back, giving in to his nearness, and that warm wave when he touched me.

Palm trees fringed the beaches as the yacht pushed past through turquois waters. Behind the beaches, dense green forest flushed the landscape, gradually spreading upward toward the distant *Sierra Maestras*. The sun was growing warmer and Francesco suggested that Shariff take the *wahid* below to the cabin where I would be out of the sun and could rest in the V-berth.

We descended the stepladder into a sumptuously appointed teak and mahogany room containing a galley, chart table, and *banquet* upholstered in soft New Zealand leather the color of burnt sienna. In front of the *banquet* was a heavy mahogany table that would seat eight. Beyond the eating area was a lounge with sofas and club chairs covered to match the *banquet*.

In the galley area there was a well stocked refrigerator, full of India Pale Ales, sliced meats, cheeses, spiced olives, tropical fruits, and tea cakes. Shelves lined the starboard wall, and behind small round railings to prevent them from falling off their perches were expensive Ports, French wines, Scotch whiskies, and island rums.

On the chart table, encased in plastic sleeves, were maps of local and international waters. Francesco's yacht was built and provisioned to travel the world.

Forward, in the bow of the ship, was a V-berth and toilet. The V-berth offered a *duvet* filled with down and lots of pillows inside cases of soft Egyptian cotton. It was too enticing. I crawled up and pulled the *duvet* over me, ignoring the lustful look I knew Shariff was giving me. He retired to one of the sofas in the lounge.

I slept lightly and, when we had been running for about two hours, I heard Francesco, come down below deck. Reluctantly sliding out of the *duvet* cocoon, I joined him and Shariff in the lounge. Smiling, he asked, "How are you feeling?" The question was directed to me. I nodded, and waited for what was coming.

Turning to Shariff, he inquired, "You've told her what is ahead?

Shariff returned his smile, revealing the camaraderie they shared. Then, locking me in a warm embrace with his eyes, replied, "I have told her about the *Guardians* and the *Tripartite* watchers, and that her life must be with us from now on. But, I am not sure she is convinced of that."

Francesco looked at me sternly, then began to warn me. He said that I needed to accept that part. Due to no fault of my own, I had become involved with their organization and its mission. Now, I would only be safe inside the firewall of the *Guardians*. If I left their protection, the watchers will kill me, after I had been viciously interrogated.

He also said that he was sure Shariff told me they had announced to the world what they guard; *Kineococcus radiotolerans*. It is a system of biological warfare that, if released, will eventually destroy all sources of high-level radioactivity. The system, based on a colony of 3,000 bacteria that survives by absorbing radioactivity, is a go-no-go system, so once activated it will arm and disperse its deadly arsenal across the world.

As he spoke I began to realize that my old life was moving further and further away. He assumed Shariff had also explained that the system is controlled by a satellite in geosynchronous space and any attempt to disarm it will automatically cause it to lock, load, and fire. Since its target is radioactive material, the weapon is a threat to the *Tripartite*'s nuclear power plants, processing facilities, and massive stockpiles of nuclear warheads and waste. The *Tripartite* is rich and powerful and will not brook any threat to their kingdom.

To provide some relief to his warning, he said that fortunately, the *Guardians* are equally rich and even more powerful. Its membership is comprised of wealthy entrepreneurs, brilliant scientists, powerful politicians, military leaders, and many heads of states. So far, they had proven more than a match in Tripartite strikes against them. For now, they can only watch, and wait to strike again."

As he continued, he ran a powerful hand across his brow, saying, however, there is a down side to Guardian's arsenal. Since the human body contains potassium-40, a weak source of radioactivity, there is the chance that once all sources of high-level radiation have been absorbed, *Kineococcus radiotolerans* will go after weaker sources like human potassium-40.

He gestured with his hands and told me that then they would have killed the patient in order to cure the disease.

As he spoke, I looked from one to the other in amazement, trying to understand why two men, seemingly of sound mind and considerable worldly experience, could believe what they were telling me. I worked for the U.S. government, the most powerful nation on earth, the nation that brought Germany and Japan to its knees and ended World War II with a display of lethal weaponry that could take out population centers in seconds. Were these two men seriously suggesting that there are pan-national organizations strong enough to threaten American officials like me with impunity?

Francesco locked eyes with me and said he could tell that I doubted their veracity and he understood how that could be. Like most people on earth, I envisioned the world as it was, when social harmony was anchored by religious and ethical tenets. But the reality has changed. Many governments, formerly beneficial to the world, are now harmful, prioritizing political interests and corporate profits over their people's welfare. Science betrayed mankind by giving away, for destructive uses, the secret of nature's fission energy. Military powers increasingly lean toward nuclear warfare as winnable.

He gestured the futility with his hands explaining that it was inevitable that entities would emerge to step into the void caused by an unstable world order. The *Guardians* have become the keepers of good and the *Tripartite* is an evil conglomerate that pits itself against us for ill-gotten gain. Francesco claimed that they are all that stands between the *Tripartite* and destruction of the social contract once enacted by civilized nations.

I felt my world crumbling as I listened to him. It had been so easy to live in denial before Francesco's attack on my comfortable perceptions. What he was saying was undeniable, but it was shattering to hear him tear down, brick by brick, the illusionary wall behind which I, and everyone I know, live. How could I abjure the world in which I was taught and trained to function, illusionary or not? Until I took a hard look at it, it seemed secure.

Shariff could see the mental anguish that Francesco was bringing to me. He stepped over and wrapped me in his arms, saying, "Trust us, Cecily. We will protect you and fight for what you love in this world. But, you will have to join the fight and leave behind the role you thought you played."

I pressed my cheek to his, then pushed away from him, making my way to the ladder leading to the deck above. I needed air, and space.

Up top, Akeem was at the helm. I made my way forward to the bow where I leaned against the railing and stared out across the vast expanse of the Caribbean Ocean. The sky was clear, the air fresh, and the scene serene. How could the disarray that Francesco described exist in juxtaposition to such tranquility? And yet I knew in my heart he was right. It had just been easier to go through life taking on socially sanctioned responsibilities and ignoring the ugly truth, the threats to an orderly world. The thin line between good and evil had been erased, eliminated by politics and greed, and evil.

An hour slid by and Francesco was at my side. He spoke quietly, intending to erase some of the fear he had instilled in me. Pointing shoreward, he told me that we had passed near *Cuidad de Baracoa*, the southern most point of Cuba and would shortly be pulling into shore. His men would meet us there with horses. That was the only way up to his ranch above *Comandancia de la Plata*, He reminded me where I had heard of *Camandancia;* from news reports. That had been Chez Guevara and Fidel Castro's headquarters before the revolution. Francesco had built his ranch at an even higher elevation; *Pico Turquino*, the highest point in the *Sierra Maestros*."

He also explained that all trails to the ranch are maintained and guarded by *Taino* soldiers in the service of the *Guardians*. No one can pass them without Francesco's permission. The *Taino* are skilled in defense tactics developed from earlier times when the *Conquistadors* tried to exterminate them. They know and own every inch of the mountains. *Tripartite* forces have stopped coming against them, although they watch from above. The watchers always have eyes on Francesco and the *Taino*, and Francesco and the *Guardians* watch the *Tripartite*."

As what seemed an afterthought, he asked if I could ride. The trek up is a hard climb, steep, causing a rider to stand in the saddle off the horse's back much of the way. Without good legs, a rider's knees will be burning before reaching the top. He told me to stop when I needed.

This was not welcome news. I had not thrown a leg over a horse's back in years. It was not going to go well, but admitting it was not my style.

᪻

The yacht turned shoreward and I soon made out about a dozen heavily armed *Taino*, mounted on horses clearly built for speed. They were ponying another dozen meant to be packhorses and still others tacked for our party.

Once we were on shore, Francesco walked to a black 16-hands

mare and gestured to me. She was to be mine. He gave me a leg up."

The horses were *Cubano de Pasos*, a unique breed that evolved from Spanish *Conquistador* steeds, which were abandoned and allowed to become feral. *Cubano de Pasos* are renowned for their speed, some 13-15 miles per hour due to their four-beat lateral gait called the *Marcha*. Francesco's *Pasos* had been bred to be tall and short-backed, so they covered ground smoothly and swiftly, even when crossing difficult terrain over long distances.

Once up, I began adjusting the stirrups. He laughed and said obviously I could ride. When it was clear that I had a good seat he mounted his horse, an even taller bay stallion. The other riders bolted off into the palms and he slapped my mount on the haunch. It wheeled to follow the pack.

Francesco rode beside me. Shariff was somewhere up ahead with the other riders. He was ponying a packhorse, loaded with what I suspected was containers of the Polonium 210.

We soon caught up with him and then picked up a steep winding trail into the *Sierra Maestras*. The boat's engine could be heard roaring away.

For the next hour, as the sun grew dim through the treetops, all I could see was a blur of greenery. The horses climbed higher and higher. An hour later, running non-stop, rocking to the four-beat gait of my mount, and standing in the stirrups where the climb was hard, my knees were starting to sore. Our mounts were beginning to sweat, but we still had a lot of trail to cover.

At 2,000 feet the sub-montane forest soared a hundred feet over our heads. Tree ferns crowded together in the understory. At 6,000 feet the forests turned into *barril* and *maranon de la Maestra* trees that were not as tall as those at the sub-montane level but still loomed 60 feet or more above us. I wondered how anyone could find or watch us under the forest's thick canopy. Everything was in shadow.

We rode through the day and as evening approached we slowed our pace. Then, we began stopping the horses every hour or so to rest them and stretch our legs, sometimes still in the saddle. My knees were screaming.

I could see that we were passing small enclaves of thatched huts. Piglets ran loose, sometimes chased in fun by village *perros*. Chickens scratched in the debris beneath cocoa and banana trees. Goats ran freely, foraging at will. *Taino* Indians, obviously friends, waved as we passed. Francesco was known, and welcome, in these parts.

He saw me looking around and began describing the difficulties of living under Castro's communist government. He said that communism is supposed to result in usafructory, where everyone enjoys equal access to the resources of the land. Unfortunately, the reality of national communism is that it subjects everyone but the top echelon to equal poverty. And, under communism, people are supposed to be egalitarian. No social stratification, all men born equal, so to speak. That does not work in largo social groups, like nations, he said. In nations there is always social stratification with a few privileged and powerful at the top and the rest under their heel. Usafructuary, he contended, seems to only work in small groups like the pygmies of the Kalahari desert where everyone is related.

Then he laughed a hearty male laugh and said, that at least in the *Sierra Maestra* they are a like-minded community. They not only break Castro's laws, they do not accept them.

With *Comandancia de la Plata* well behind us, we were approaching the highest point of the range, *Pico Turquino*, and Francesco's ranch.

When we finally rode under the *porte couture* of the huge ranch house, I gladly stepped down out of my Australian saddle and its four-bar stirrups, knees on fire. Never had I dreamed of being in the saddle that long. Looking around I instantly realized that the so-called ranch was actually a well-fortified compound, complete with several barns, paddocks, assorted smaller houses, and hot-walkers on which to cool horses as they came in. Entering, we had passed through huge gates from which thick walls extended in both directions as far as I could see.

Our approach was obviously anticipated and prepared for. Food and drink were waiting and we were led to a table set out under a grove of *Copernicia* palms, endemic to the island. *Mojitos* were served first and even though it was before noon, I made quick work of mine. It took away some of the saddle fatigue but not the burning in my knees. That would take awhile.

Following our meal, I was escorted to a cabin, separated from the ranch house by only a few yards. The cabin was welcoming, a stand-alone with a cozy living room dominated by a large stone fireplace, a small but well-appointed kitchenette, a bedroom with *ensuite* bath, and a private patio accessed through French doors off the bedroom. After the last few days, it was a little piece of Heaven and I sunk into the couch to enjoy the fire someone had thoughtfully laid.

Left alone to gather my thoughts and assess my situation, no doubt Francesco and Shariff's strategy, the reality began to set in. I held no cards. To get back to *Havana* I would have to steal fresh horses, one for me and one for the polonium containers, assuming I could even locate them here in the compound. Following the trail back down to the lowlands would be a no brainer. The horses would know the way. However, the trail went by *Taino* enclaves, Francesco's comrades. They would never let me pass without his permission and he would never give that permission, especially if I had the polonium.

There was also the strong possibility that what he and Shariff had warned me of, the danger of leaving their protection and being taken by *Tripartite* watchers, would get me killed. At least the *Guardians* offered me a life, but not my life. *How could I just give up the life I knew, the life I had worked so hard to build?"*

And what of my attraction to Shariff? We had no chance. He is destined to be an ancient Mariner, roaming the seas to kill, using the *Mossad* list and the Polonium 210. The CIA would never give much priority to Nazi criminals from a distant war. They hunt much bigger game. Shariff would never let the Nazis live. By now I knew him. He could have many irons in the fire and keep each one ready to brand. Eventually, he will put to sea again and take up where the CIA failed.

By a cruel stroke of fate, I am destined to pursue him to retrieve the poison and return it to my government, which will likely hold it in abeyance for use in the same way Shariff intends. Just on a different target. Only, my government will take the moral high ground, where Shariff will be condemned. It was all mentally exhausting. I pulled a woolen throw over me and slipped into a deep nap.

Day 6. When I woke, only embers burned in the fireplace, and I was getting hungry again. I had slept through the night. Time to leave the splendid isolation of my cabin and face the controllers. Rested, my path seemed clear. My only option was to wait for opportunity to knock.

Breakfast was laid out under the same *Copernicia* palms where we dined the evening before. The meal consisted mainly of local cheeses, fresh made bread, fried yucca, and smoked ham. Something about mountain air spikes the appetite and I ate heartily.

Coffee con leche was served as soon as I finished my food and Shariff soon joined me. He looked good in jeans and a sweatshirt. We were dressed alike. Casting his eyes over me, he smiled and said, "The mountains seem to suit you more than the desert."

Nodding, I agreed. "My lab in the U.S. is in the Rocky Mountains, not as heavily forested as these. Speaking of my lab, I miss my work, my life. There is no possibility that I can spend my remaining days on this earth just lounging in a well appointed cabin by the fire."

He smiled and reached for my hand. "There will be work for you if you accept our protection and join our mission. We are hopeful that you will. Your skills are needed. And, I hope you will spend the rest of your life with me, doing what we choose."

I withdrew my hand and struggled to organize my thoughts. "Shariff, I need time to think. I am still in shock over being told that I have lost my old life and not nearly prepared to make commitments that I may not be able to keep. Before you broach that subject again, aside from your protection, how about developing convincing arguments about why I should even consider staying here at *Pico Turquino*. You must understand by now that your offer of protection is not a sufficient reason for me to voluntarily abandon my life, my family, friends, and work. The proposition that Francesco and you have put before me, death or your way, reeks of the 'Me Tarzan, you Jane' cliché. And, by the way, it does not become either of you."

He did not flinch, nor did he show any amusement at my well-aimed slash at his manhood. Instead, it was almost as if he had anticipated it.

16
The Dark Ops Program
Beware the Ides of March, 1971

It was March 15, the day that Caesar was stabbed 23 times. The day was thought to be the deadline for settling debts. At *Pico Turquino*, days had become weeks and weeks became months. Then, on the day of settling debts, the debt collector appeared on a tall white horse, under escort by a dozen of Francesco's *Taino* soldiers. The air had grown chilly as the sun began to hide behind cloud cover that was passing over the mountaintop, forming a dome over *Pico Turquino*. The debt collector's appearance added to the chill.

His eyes were unforgiving and he had an arrogant air that made me decidedly uncomfortable. We were soon to learn that he was part of a dark ops program that the U.S. government was conducting. And, he came to see if we would play.

Stepping down easily from the saddle, he nodded to me, and offered his hand to Francesco and Shariff. They shook hands with him but watched him like hunters watching their prey.

Not smiling, Francesco spoke first telling the stranger that he had us at a disadvantage and asked what we could do for him. I got the feeling that Francesco knew exactly who the debt collector was.

The man introduced himself as Dr. David Stoker. He reached inside his jacket. Instantly, two dozen weapons clicked, and took aim at his head. He slowly withdrew his hand and offered Francesco the business card and agency creds he held.

Francesco raised his hand, commanding the weapons aimed at the intruder to be lowered. Taking the card and plasticized credential, he scanned them and handed them back. Then he asked Stoker what had brought him to *Pico Turquino*.

Stoker put his identity papers back in his jacket pocket and began explaining his presence at *Pico Turquino*. According to the creds he had handed to Francesco, he was an agent of the U.S. government. His agency was a black ops program involved with Polonium 210. He said the U.S. government knew about the weapon Dr. Shariff and his team produced aboard the Scorpion before he turned her back to the Navy in Port Said. The government also knew that he had brought the weapon to *Pico Turquino*.

He turned to Shariff and told him that his team had done a pretty good job of cleaning up the sub before he sailed her into port. However, they had left enough breadcrumbs for the scientists in his program to pretty much figure out what Shariff's team had used her for. They knew the team had burned Scorpion's high-level uranium fuel to irradiate Bismuth and produce Polonium 210.

Laughing sarcastically, Stoker said they also knew that Shariff used some of the polonium to dispatch a Nazi war criminal named Alois Brunner. What remained of Brunner, some rotting skin fished from the Red Sea by Sudanese fishermen, was now in cold storage in my Reardon lab.

Looking pointedly at Shariff, he said they did not care what he had done to that bastard, but they did need control of the rest of the polonium produced aboard the Navy's nuclear submarine. Stoker claimed the need was based on the interests of national security.

Shariff's features froze for an instant. Then, he looked steadily at the man and spoke slowly. "Before we discuss this further, you need to understand that Dr. Suderman had nothing to do with our dispatching Brunner. She is here for the same reason you say you are. Your agency obviously knows that she joined me in Port

Said after I brought back the Scorpion and parked her in a berth there. Dr. Suderman simply arrived in Port Said to try and take possession of the polonium my team manufactured."

Stoker nodded and announced that his agency had no issues with me. He understood that I was on orders. In fact, he said they had no interest in taking actions against me or Shariff. What his agency wanted was to help Shariff up his game.

The CIA, he said, had turned the *Mossad* list over to Stoker's group for, 'disposition'. His bureau wanted to offer assistance with Shariff's quest to bring to justice the remaining names on that list. Of course, there were strings attached.

Glancing around at the crowd his arrival had attracted, he turned to Francesco and asked if there were secure quarters where we could talk in private.

Francesco was both amused and intrigued. He always enjoyed meeting someone with a good story. He was also sure that the man's presence offered no threat to the security of his compound there on the *Sierra Maestra* mountaintop. Not at that moment, anyway. Also, he had not been roughed up so the *Taino* scouts who brought him in did not see him as a threat. The Taino were the first line of defense surrounding the complex on *Pico Turquino*.

Francesco nodded to the intruder, suggesting that we all sit down in my cabin, if I did not mind. He looked at me for permission. I nodded, and we all walked across the lawn, passed the main lodge, and entered my quarters.

There were two servants tidying up and Francesco asked them to bring tea and beers. They quickly disappeared.

As we selected seats around the fire that had been laid, Shariff took my arm and directed me toward the sofa. Gently pushing me down into the seat at the far end, he sat beside me, Again putting as much distance between Stoker and me as the room allowed.

While we waited on the drinks, Stoker and Francesco exchanged extraneous chitchat about the ride up the mountain. Stoker complimented Francesco on the lodge and his horses. He, himself, bred Dutch Warmbloods, also a strong fast breed. That explained how he easily came down off that horse after the long and difficult ride up from the flat lands below. Stoker was no stranger to the saddle.

He then asked Francesco how it was that the *Taino* guards picked up his trail so quickly on the mountain and escorted him to *Pico Turquino*. The question amused Francesco. A small smile appeared at the corners of his mouth and he told Stoker that the *Taino* did not pick up his trail on the mountain. He was under scrutiny before he even put a foot on Cuban soil.

I sensed that Francesco was tossing out a test raison. He knew that he and Stoker were fencing and he wanted to see his opponent's reaction when he referred to the surveillance capabilities of the *Guardians*.

Stoker did not react. Black ops personnel are trained to let such blows glance off.

After the drinks had arrived, along with a tray of fresh baked Cuban bread, cheeses, and local fruits, Francesco invited Stoker to explain the reason for his journey up the *Sierra Maestras*.

Stoker began to explain that his agency was concerned about other organizations, which also have access to high-level uranium. Could they eventually achieve what Shariff's team had? Available info told them that such efforts were underway in some quarters. He stressed that they could not risk others succeeding. Or, they at least needed to ensure that the U.S. always holds the upper hand.

At that point, he leaned forward and looked at each of us in turn. Then he said he needed to reveal some pretty top secret stuff in order to explain his agency's interest in Shariff's work. However, he said laughingly, if he told us he would have to kill us.

He leaned back in his chair and smiled smugly, saying that we had an alternative. Of course, the alternative was to join them and vow to never reveal what he was about to tell us.

He again looked at each of us in turn and his eyes conveyed a steely warning. Shariff and Francesco returned his gaze, then nodded that they understood. They were confident they had nothing to lose by listening, and they were hard to kill.

Stoker's eyes then locked on me. I had not nodded, taking my time to consider the consequences. I did not really want to know about another bureau's "eyes only" program. For one thing, it was just another program that you had to remember not to remember. But most of all, I did not think I liked where this was going. And I did not like Stoker, knowing that he represented the dark matter, which was my job to guard against. I also had a secret that I was not yet ready to reveal but that secret gave me an edge the others were not aware of. And it allowed me to know that the guy was playing fast and loose with the truth. So I did not nod my head and instead, returned his steady gaze.

He coldly studied me for a minute, then sternly pronouncing my name, he said that if I had reservations I should leave the room. It was not a suggestion, more of an order. I was good with leaving, but Shariff stood before I could. He was in protective mode and, looking menacingly at Stoker, said, "It is not for you to decide who leaves or stays in this room."

Stoker stood to meet his challenge. Tension elevated in the room as the two men faced off, each taking the measure of the other. Francesco watched calmly, amused at the breast beating display of the two alpha males, being one himself. But, he was more interested in what Stoker had to say. It was proving to be something of a remarkable day. He liked remarkable days, and finding out what the other guys were up to. To cool the atmosphere he reminded them that a lady was present.

Realizing that he was not on his own turf, and remembering the reputation of Francesco Pacillo, Stoker decided to yield the field. By way of apology, and an excuse for his behavior, he explained that he had grown used to the power plays around the conference tables in D.C.

His excuse was plausible. I knew all about such power plays and decided to accept his apology because he also offered to provide enough information for me to make an objective decision about his agency's interest in the matter. I wanted more information. I needed it to decide what his game plan was.

He sat down, and Shariff followed his lead, regaining his seat beside me, but closer. I could feel his body heat and that vein in his temple was throbbing again. He was still in battle mode.

Ignoring Shariff's body language, Stoker nodded to me and continued. He said he could tell me work on Polonium 210 was being conducted in certain labs other than Shariff's. Now he had my attention. The more he spoke, the more I understood that his program was not what he said it was. And, if that was true, he was not what he claimed he was.

Turning to Shariff, Stoker said that the work his agency was involved in somewhat mirrors Shariff's own. However, Stoker's agency had taken a different tack. He noted that Shariff's team was able to convert a nuclear submarine into a production lab to manufacture Polonium 210. The work that he could not discuss in great detail unless we agreed to join it, and never reveal to any other organization, had not progressed to that point of technological sophistication. The work being conducted by Stoker's was anchored to cumbersome land-based lab equipment. For national security reasons, the government needed to expand the work of Stoker's agency to include processing aboard a sub fleet.

Turning back to me, he then struck a somewhat conciliatory note, saying that he realized I felt my work was held to a higher standard than his agency used. However, compared to their plan, my focus on retrieving the polonium that Shariff had in his possession was narrow and wide of the mark. He asked me to imagine a world in which the weapon of choice was an arsenal of Polonium 210. Imagine a world in which nations with such arsenals stood ready to release the deadly poison as offensive measures. Chemical warfare would replace existing arsenals, thought powerful enough to prevent military assaults by mutually assuring the destruction of both the targets and the attackers.

It was Stokers turn to smile. He said the current concept of détente was to become an anachronism with the introduction of the kind of chemical warfare that Polonium 210 would bring to the table. Military bases, expensive air and sea craft, highly trained fighters at great financial cost, weapons and weapons silos costing billions to build, guard, and maintain, would no longer have any efficacy. Secret agents could easily disposition deadly chemicals, or even drone fleets.

His remarks hit home. The disastrous scenario in which vast quantities of Polonium 210 were released into the world's water sources, food supplies, medical stocks, or the thousands of other potential avenues of delivery, boggled my mind. It would be a nuclear winter on steroids.

I returned his gaze as Francesco and Shariff carefully watched me. Then, I slowly nodded my agreement. I had to make it possible for them to listen and I needed to know what his real agenda was.

Stoker continued. He told us that his agency had a comprehensive plan that would provide the U.S. with an offensive option unmatched in the world. It would also function as a non-proliferation program for most radioactive materials on the planet. He claimed the plan would eliminate international stockpiles of nuclear waste that have accumulated around the globe while atom splitting was conducted to create nuclear weapons and energy. It would also remove the possibility of nuclear attacks on the U.S. by other nations or terrorist organizations. To clinch the argument, he said his agency really shared our collective goals and hoped we would join their efforts. Icing the cake, he added that they needed all of our skills, and we needed their resources.

Enjoying his current role on center stage, he revealed that in addition to developing an arsenal of Polonium 210, which would assure the U.S. offensive superiority, his agency was working on a variant, an alternative to eliminating an enemy's environment.

He paused, and gave each of us a meaningful look. Then he said that the more proactive variant would eliminate an enemy

231

population while leaving their environment intact. Leaving the environment in tact has the attraction of adding environmental resources to our own coffers. Think minerals, agricultural land, and potable water. Where we fight over oil now, we may see the day when wars will be fought over water.

To that end, his agency had taken a look back at earlier experimental findings using Polonium 210. They found that 19th century French experiments with rabbits indicated radiation from polonium settled in the liver, kidneys, and testes. Later, U.S. 20th century experiments on hospitalized patients, funded by the AEC, confirmed the French findings. After the practice of using humans in lab research came under growing public scrutiny, the focus shifted to using our primate cousins. The AEC project was supposedly shut down. However, it really morphed into another project.

His agency's scientists began looking at potential ancillary benefits of the French and earlier U.S. findings. One such benefit is the elimination of a population through mass sterilization. That work had become the major focus of their program.

Shades of the Third Reich.

We stared at him in disbelief. He misgauged our looks, thinking he was impressing his audience. Continuing, he explained that the variant of Polonium 210 which has that effect is Polonium 210^S. The S, of course, stands for sterility."

Stoker then turned to Francesco and said his oversight of the *Kineococcus radiotolerans* weapons systems was integral to their program. *Kineococcus radiotolerans* was implemented to prevent future nuclear warfare and to force the transmutation of nuclear waste. He said the agency he represented did not want nuclear waste transmutated. They needed it as feedstock for their 210 and 210^s programs. Therefore, they needed Francesco in their organization as assurance that *Kineococcus radiotolerans* is never launched.

Then, looking at Shariff, Stoker told him that because he and his team of Egyptian scientists had developed production procedures beyond the technical capabilities of the black ops organization, despite their superior resources and manpower, Shariff, was needed for the government's plan. The feds planned to enhance its capabilities by adding a submarine-based polonium production fleet. Shariff's team could make that happen.

I watched Shariff, who was calmly studying the man. He had made it clear that he did not like Stoker but nothing was betrayed behind the screen of his deep brown eyes. Over thousands of year, battling to maintain control of the upper and lower regions of their land, while repelling invading armies of other nations, Egyptians had learned well how to look into an enemy's eyes while conveying nothing. Battles are often won through cunning alone.

Stoker was not put off. He looked past Shariff to me and said that my expertise in the permissible exposure limits of radiological materials to human physiology was also needed for their program. In the entire history of atom splitting, for whatever purposes, no organization has ever been able to determine what the lower limits of such exposure are. Research has always focused on the upper limits to determine deleterious levels. Even those established limits are fuzzy. For maximum efficiency of their product, they needed to know both limits. There was no sense spending time and money on the limits below and beyond what is needed.

His tale was reading like an ethereal *sci fi* novel. I knew about the early human experiments with polonium. What I had never heard about before was any continuation of those experiments. I had definitely not heard of the subsequent program to convert America into a poison control center by producing the 210 and 210^s on an industrial scale and using it in a global aggrandizement and sterilization plan. I had good reason to know that was not true.

⤚

The *Taino* servant who had earlier brought the drinks and snacks entered the cabin and began to speak quietly with Francesco.

While they were conversing, I looked around the room. Outside, it was now totally dark but the ambiance of the room in which we sat was cozy. A warm fire burned on the hearth and reflections of the flames bounced off the handsome brass pokers hanging from hooks anchored on the underside of the thick wooden mantle. Left over crusts of bread and bits of cheese from our earlier snacks were scattered around the tray on which they had arrived. Attractive, heavily leaded crystal glasses sat empty on the coffee table in front of the sofa where Shariff and I were parked. Music drifted in from the porch of the lodge where several *Taino* guards had gathered. One of them was a gifted guitarist. From all appearances, things were well at *Pico Turquino*. But appearances were deceiving. A sickness had drifted into our midst that was even darker than the black night outside.

Francesco nodded to the servant who turned to leave. As he opened the door, we could clearly hear singing. It was *son*, the swinging musical rhythm of the island, in which an improvising singer is answered by a chorus. The warm inviting melody drifted into the room in strange juxtaposition to the cold profile of a poisoned world that Stoker had just described. We listened for a minute, then Francesco said that food had been prepared for us. He asked that we retire to the dining room.

Turning to Stoker, he smiled and told him that he did not need a food taster at *Pico Turquino*. Polonium 210 was never served on site.

Stoker enjoyed the joke and laughed, saying that was good to know.

In the dining room, wooden walls ended in a cathedral ceiling that soared thirty feet above us. The long table was laden with colorful dishes. More local cheeses and breads spread across its surface, along with assorted dishes of sautéed and boiled yucca, salted and fried fish, a goat meat casserole, and several dishes unfamiliar to all but Francesco. Dominating the scene was a tall cornucopia of vividly colored and strangely shaped island fruits.

The meal held real promise.

We sat and began to pass plates. Talk was easy and avoided the subject of radioactive material, or any plans to use it. It was as though we had entered another dimension, compared to the scene in my cabin. By tradition, mealtime in Cuba is a social occasion that takes place over two or more hours. It is never without music. The guitarist and several singers had moved into the room with us and serenaded from a corner. The pattern of food, music, and clever conversation is never broken in *Cubano*.

As we were finishing, the heavy brass clock on the wall struck ten and I was ready for bed. But Francesco directed everyone back to my quarters. He wanted to hear the rest of Stoker's plan, and get him out of camp. In spite of the late hour, he planned to send him off with *Taino* guards when he had said what he came to say. Only the trusted were welcome overnighters in the Italian Stallion's compound. Nighttime brought heightened guarding and unknown strangers were always a potential breach in security.

Walking back to my cabin, Shariff kept me close and when we began to again take seats before the hearth, he quickly guided me to the far end of the sofa where he had stationed me earlier, as far away from Stoker as you could get. Leaving little room between us, he sat next to me.

Once we were settled, Stoker began where he had left off, reiterating that their program needed the specialized skills of each of us. He briefly outlined how the plan would work. It all began with the U.S. acquisition of the world's nuclear waste stockpiles through a program introduced by President Eisenhower in the 1950s. The program was dubbed 'atoms for peace' and involved loaning out high-level uranium to other countries. The recipients were to burn the uranium in reactors to produce energy and in medical research for civilian use only. In order to receive 'atoms for peace' they also had to sign a commitment to eventually return any remaining uranium to the U.S., along with the waste that accrued while irradiating it. Eisenhower thought the plan would lead to a cleaner environment the world over, free from carbon based energy sources. It would also mitigate the threat of nuclear warfare since most nations of the world would have the same power.

As a result, there are now hundreds of reactors operating around the world in laboratories and utility plants. There is also a massive backup of lethal nuclear waste.

Stoker's agency was eventually tasked with siting, designing, and developing a geological repository for the waste. The agency quickly laid claim to a two-pronged goal: Non-proliferation and permanent safe storage of the deadly material to avoid polluting the environment and causing health problems and exposure fatalities.

However, once Stoker's agency was given the mission, the actual plan became a highly sinister black ops plot to convert the recipient nations into production centers of feed stock for Polonium 210 and 210^s. The actual plan remained sub-rosa, of course.

Over the ensuing decades, the U.S. took in the foreign receipts of spent nuclear fuel and other radioactive waste forms, storing them at various government nuclear complex sites. Since nuclear materials are highly secured, and secretive, the lack of transparency allowed Stoker's agency to gradually corner the market. Then, 'atoms for peace' waste was added to the legacy waste from the atomic bomb and Cold War eras.

According to Stoker, the feedstock plan for Polonium 210 and 210^s has been highly successful. His agency has oversight of oxide waste numbering in the tens of thousands of tons. In addition, millions of gallons in liquid form, accumulated during the atomic bomb and Cold War phases, are also under the agency's authority.

He went on to talk about the problematic storage issue, roughly reviewing its history. I was completely familiar with the issue, one of the most mismanaged and criminally neglected public health and environmental hazards faced by the nation.

In the 1950s, a plan was devised to store radioactive material in a long-term federal repository. The plan called for locating the repository two thousand feet underground in an old abandoned

Carey salt mine beneath the Kansas prairie. That plan ran off the tracks when Kansas politicians, salt corporations, and the public took their grievances to the president, pointing out that aquifers beneath the prairie regularly carry off the contents of wells and no one knows where they go. Solution mining operations in the salt beds have reported losing 350,000 gallons of water to aquifer invasions. Also, aquifer erosion beneath the surface has caused sink holes, leaving lakes hundreds of feet deep. Using an old salt mine for a national repository was the better part of insanity.

Equally zany plans emerged and failed as the search for a permanent repository continued. Stoker said his agency is quite confident that a national repository will eventually be developed. It will be billed as permanent and safely guarded, a system designed to protect the world's populations and their environments from radiation exposure. Of course, its real purpose will be to function as a centralized warehouse for 210 and 210^s feedstock. As such, the design of the repository will have to include retrievability so that the deadly waste can be accessed as needed. A bit of a technical challenge, but, he was sure they would get there.

At this point, Stoker addressed Shariff, telling him that the program had a major weakness. Its feedstock and processing operations are always at risk of being targeted in land-based labs. He went on to explain the obvious. Such facilities, while having the capacity to produce higher volumes of product, are very vulnerable. Like the nation's Minuteman missile silos, they make attractive marks for attacks by air or land.

Shariff's team was the only group of scientists that had converted a nuclear submarine into a Polonium 210 production facility and the government needed that capability. The goal was to set up a fleet of submarine-based labs, which would be outfitted with drone squad delivery systems. Polonium 210 and 210^s production facilities based in a huge fleet of fast and stealthy nuclear submarines, armed with drone delivery squads, could both elude attacks and strike with devastating capability. It would be the ultimate defense and offense system in the world. The weapons the fleet bore could be loaded and fired within minutes, poisoning any target in the sub's cross hairs; cities, reservoirs, agricultural areas, food processing plants, etc.

Stoker was especially pleased with the economy of the concept. He explained that was perhaps the most attractive of the benefits offered. The costly need for land-based defense systems, along with their production facilities, could all but be eliminated.

Just when I thought the plan Stoker was describing could not get more monstrous, it did. He explained that his agency was more and more prioritizing 210s because it was a more proactive approach. In addition to the offensive advantages it offered, it would leave the resources of targeted areas in tact while exterminating the population. Leaving the resources in tact would allow the U.S. to lay claim to any number of valuable commodities like uranium mines, precious minerals, oil deposits, water ways bearing heavy fish populations, arable land, and so on. He leaned back in his chair and smiled, pronouncing the old cliché, *To the victor go the spoils.*

The black ops plan of Stoker's agency was *Lebensraum* revisited. But he was not finished. He continued to describe an additional advantage to Shariff. The agency's proposal of a position to assist in establishing the submarine-based fleet of labs would essentially be an extension of the task Shariff had already set for himself, elimination of the men on the *Mossad* list. He suggested that goal could work in tandem with the agency's program.

Shariff was confused. "I thought you said you got the list from the CIA and were taking care of that yourselves."

Stoker nodded and told Shariff that the agency could do that but there is an option they thought he would find more to his liking. One sub lab could be dedicated as a venue for holding the war criminals he sought. Shariff's team could beta test the variant, Polonium 210s. The Nazis would first be used as guinea pigs, like they used so many victims in their camps, and then coldly eliminated by injections of 210. Sperm count data and biological termination observations would provide the basis for continuous upgrading of both 210 types.

Shariff stared coldly at the agency rep. A full minute passed before he spoke. "And when all that you have described has reached fruition, what would distinguish us from *Third Reich* Nazis?"

Francesco took another tack, describing obvious weak links in the agency's plan. For one, if there are labs outside the U.S. that are also working to unlock the secrets of producing Polonium 210 on an industrial scale, there is no defense against them if they succeed. They may even be working on marine based delivery systems. Even if the U.S. sub fleet takes them out they will be left with a window of opportunity to return the blow in kind. While Polonium 210 ingestion is methodical and ultimately lethal, it works over a period of hours, even days. The enemy would have a window of opportunity to strike back.

Stoker leaned back in his chair and confidently explained that the probability of that happening is a complex issue. It is being worked on. In the meantime, they needed the innovations that the three of us would bring to the table.

He smiled, remembering how cunning that whole plan had been. He said that no one in congress seemed to ask why the repository plan requires retrievability. The few who do are told that it was in case there is ever an emergency in the facility and a need to move the material.

He laughed, scornfully, saying that anyone dumb enough to believe that should never be turned loose to vote on bills involving America's welfare. In fact, they should not even be allowed to reproduce. If there was ever a release in a repository packed with thousands of tons and millions of gallons of high-level nuclear waste, no one could go in there, not without an instant death wish. Besides, even if they could retrieve the stuff, where would they put it? There are no other repositories, anywhere in the world.

Then he asked if we were aware that the U.S. has also been

involved in research to technologically boost transmutation of radiological material? Some quarters of the government wanted to know if we could, or should, try to emulate the transmutation process that occurs in nature as radioactive elements emit their energy until they reach stable states.

He was growing arrogant, telling us that they got the program cancelled under a policy decision that the research and development would take too long and cost too much. Driving the reason for dropping the program, of course, was the fact that the black ops operation did not want nuclear waste destroyed. They had a better use for it.

Shifting in his chair, he said the gullibility of the nuclear industry was also amusing. They were told the retrievability requirement is to ensure that when uranium ore becomes scarce, obsolete, or too expensive to use in their reactors, they could begin pulling nuclear waste from the repository for reprocessing. Reprocessing is an expensive proposition but it would become financially feasible if mining uranium cost more or was no longer an option. Believing that bill of goods, nuclear corporate heads became ardent supporters of the retrievability program and were duped into providing significant contributions for the cost of developing the repository

Francesco interrupted, saying that he would grant Stoker's point about the industry players, but insisted there must be some members of congress who question the need for retrievability. He exclaimed that they are not all stupid.

Stoker waved his hand to dismiss Francesco's argument and said that any congressional members raising concerns about the reliability of deep geologic storage of nuclear waste are shouted down. The industry pours serious money into the push for the repository. A lot of boys on the Hill are the recipients of nice perks for supporting the program. The politicians which the industry bribes are either too greedy to look closer at the issue or they believe the line that the repository is to be the global solution to non-proliferation and nuclear waste safe storage, a one size fits all radioactive landfill. They know nothing of the Polonium 210 programs. That is a need-to-know operation. Top secret.

Stoker then turned to me, still trying to sell the agency's plan and now playing the funding card. He began telling me about the kind of budget my work could have, a generously funded program that would enable me to research and determine the lethal lower limits of Polonium 210 exposure, both long-term and short-term. He said that work would meet with both of our goals. Knowing the lower permissible limits of radiation exposure will enhance the safety and health of all Americans. And, if those limits are made known, it will also allow the official recognition of much nuclear waste as harmless to humans and their environment. With that classification, the agency would gain a lot of points by demonstrating that tons of low-level radioactive material can be disposed of in cheaply constructed landfills rather than tightly controlled and expensive conditions."

My mind was spinning with kaleidoscopic images of the darker pages in America's history; Amerindian genocide, slavery, internment of Japanese Americans, the bombings of Hiroshima and Nagasaki. Somehow these got interpreted in the history books as necessary to the evolution or preservation of civilization, justifiable as freedom's cause, and the natural result of Christianity's spread across the globe. The aggression became socially sanctioned and the cloak of divine providence masked the more unseemly aspects. Even the intelligentsia gave them a pass. There were the odd scholarly protests, but lectures and print remonstrations were all eventually swept into history's dustbin. Manifest destiny marched on.

Now this! The spinning in my head stopped and I jumped into the fray. "Mr. Stoker, as a public health specialist, it is inconceivable to me that there are sectors of the government involved in the insidious chemical warfare research you have just described. Not only is it un-American, it is beyond common sense and reeks of the Germanic concept, *Lebensraum*. The government I know, and work for, would never sanction your program, a program that you are asking the three of us to join, and keep secret.

Furthermore, human physiological variability has always eluded the 'one size fits all' box that you are suggesting I design for lower level radioactive elements. In addition to gender, age, morphological conformation, general health, environmental adaptations, and a hundred other variables that are involved to precisely describe any one segment of a population, there are always two stumbling blocks to building that grey box which science cannot get around: ethnicity and individual behavior. The factors generally and vaguely describing any ethnic population always varies within and between gene pools. With individual behavior, there are the psychological factors that cannot be controlled for. Human behavior can never be precisely described, explained, predicted, and controlled, which is the goal of science no matter the subject of study.

Science can always determine the lethal levels of toxic material at the high end, but not the levels that would allow safe continuous exposure for the masses at the low end, computer models to the contrary. But, those are just pigs in prom dresses, or what honest scientists call scientific wild ass guesses.

Stoker leaned forward in his chair, the fire making one side of his face glow while the other was dark and almost featureless since no one had bothered to turn on any lights in the room. He spoke in a calm firm voice and said he understood that I found what he was telling us difficult to fathom. But, reality has a thousand faces. My reality is a thousand points of light emanating from a beneficent government in the sunny land of the free.

At this point his voice turned cold, he leaned back in his chair, and with his face now in darkness he said that the reality in which he lived and worked is equally real. There are dark forces abroad in the land. Some of us have to face that reality. The foes in his reality, he said, are of the evil sort. Because of that reality, his organization cannot afford to play nice.

Leaning forward again, so that his face was now in the soft light of the fire, he addressed my comments about his work being tantamount to Nazism, saying that while I thought his agency's weaponry is tantamount to *Lebensraum* he could assure me that if they are not victorious on the battle field, I will know evil beyond my wildest imagination. He declared that there are foes out there who fight to dominate through practices that transgress every golden rule in the book.

He turned away, dismissing me, and began to address Francesco. Apparently he thought our Italian Stallion was more likely to become an ally. He began by comparing the damage Francesco's *Kineococcus radiotolerans* weapon would do with the more localized damage that attacks with the agency's brand of chemical warfare would do. Taking the high ground, Stoker claimed that either of the polonium options his agency was planning to use would do less harm to the earth and its inhabitants than the *Kineococcus radiotolerans* weapon. The polonium attacks would be confined to targeted localities. Francesco's weapon would eventually, and uncontrollably, eliminate the radioactive energy sources of vast areas across the globe. Populations could not sustain themselves without such energy sources. Wars would breakout over what little resources were left for survivors. *Kineococcus radiotolerans* might even turn to the radioactivity inside human beings when all other sources of its feedstock were exhausted.

He said even though Francesco's stated goal is to see that the weapon is never released, the agency is left vulnerable as long as he was alive and they had no control over his actions. He also shared Shariff's belief, or hope, that Francesco may have built into the weapon's control system a back door for overriding its go-no-go trigger. Stoker guessed that he probably built it into the geosynchronous space satellite controlling the weapons. For those reasons, the agency needed Francesco on board as insurance. He seemed to think his argument won the field and insisted that

Francesco would have to give them the key to his back door.

He sat back, finished sharing the information that he obviously thought would bring all of us on board. I looked from Shariff to Francesco, trying to read their minds. But years of winning battles through cunning left them with the advantage of inscrutability, even after being told of a government program to destroy vast environments and sterilize whole populations using polonium as the latest weapon of mass destruction.

What Stoker had revealed to us about his bureau's program made me sick to my stomach. From the moment I had arrived in Port Said to confront Shariff about the grey flaccid sheet of skin I had left in cold storage at Reardon, my comfortable assumptions about the clear distinction between good and evil had been under attack. The line between them had been repeatedly thinned. My world was beginning to shake on its axis. Stoker had now stretched that thin line to the breaking point.

In a matter of a few months I had been yanked from my old world, lost my old life, and now the standards by which I had always judged objects, events, and others were becoming mercurial. My new world seemed filled with rampant insanity, a world where good can be evil and some evil is for the good.

I could bear no more, so I rose and walked to the door. "Gentlemen, I need rest. I will see you in the morning." I opened the door and signaled with my arm that they were being asked to leave my quarters. What man could argue with that. They filed out.

Late in the night, there was a soft knock on the door. I left the bed, crossed the living room, and opened the door. Shariff was standing there. As he stepped inside, he pulled me to him, kissed me hungrily on the lips, then picking me up, he kicked the door closed and carried me back to the bed. This time he met with no resistance. Close against his warm, taut body, under his exploring hands and lips and gentle lovemaking, my tension melted away. My world righted and I became the flame, not the moth.

ॐ

<u>March 16</u>. Morning came; he reached out and pulled me to him once more. His need could hardly be disguised. When he was spent, leaving me gasping for breath, he rolled over and laid quietly, his arm across my body.

After several minutes, he pulled my hand to his mouth, kissed it gently, then said, "I would love to do this all day but, unfortunately, circumstances beyond my control force me from your bed. Stoker is gone; we escorted him off the mountain during the night. We're having breakfast with Francesco to plan our next move. Obviously, we're not joining Stoker's ranks."

Pushing aside thoughts of last night's heated pleasure, and the passion we had just shared, I began recalling what Stoker had told us. The tension returned. Until he appeared on the mountain, I thought what Shariff and his team had done to Brunner was the single most horrible act I had ever encountered, not dismissing what I had heard and read about the Nazi slaughters. Now, laying next to me, my hand still in his and the faint odor of our sexual encounter hanging in the air, Shariff had become one of the good guys in spite of what he had done, and how he had done it. What Stoker's organization was postulating was the most evil use of science yet conceived. *My new standard at work.*

After showering and dressing, we stepped out into a metallic chilly morning. Clouds had settled in over the mountain and the air was heavy, promising rain at any second. As we walked across the lawn, I had to ask, "Did Stoker make it off this mountain alive?"

Shariff laughed and grabbed my hand. "He is fine. If we had bothered to dispose of him another would just take his place. That kind are a dime a dozen."

Francesco was waiting for us on the lodge's porch. A brilliant hummingbird buzzed about the bushes edging the porch, no doubt hurrying to get his breakfast before the rain hit. I marveled at its tiny physique and strength, able to beat its little wings 80 times per second while flying up or down, left or right, even upside. They could also become hovercrafts. I wondered what it would be like to live that life, flitting from flower to flower, unencumbered with concerns over the deadly issues of nuclear war, waste, and byproducts like Polonium 210. In some respects, his lot was envious.

Francesco was sitting at a large round wooden table that seemed anchored by the huge floral piece in its center. A nearby fire ring crackled as the flaming logs in its center spit sap. Heat radiated from the ring, warming the area around the table. Francesco was on his second cup of *café con leche*. His smile was warm as he greeted us, but he was clearly tense.

We sat across the table from him and Shariff asked, "When are we breaking camp?"

The answer was terse. Francesco asked that we eat first and then discuss the details.

We ate well on corn cakes sloshed with sugar syrup, fruit, and the ever present assorted cheeses and breads. I drank three cups of *café con leche* to catch up with Francesco and shake off the lack of sleep. In Cuba the cups are small and I needed the edge. It was obvious that the post-meal conversation was going to require rapt attention. And I didn't think I was going to like what was coming.

When we had finished our meal, Francesco suggested that we order more coffee brought to my cabin where we could talk privately.

After the coffee had been delivered, along with little sweet cakes, we settled around the hearth once again. The rain arrived, pushed out the cloud cover, and began to beat against the cabin's roof and windows. But it was cozy inside. Someone had again laid a nice fire for us.

Francesco had taken a seat by the fire. Stretching out his legs, he wistfully told us that we could no longer stay at *Pico Turquino*. The snake, Stoker, had told us enough that his agency would have to kill us if we don't jump behind their firewall. Also, they will worry that we could be taken by enemy organizations because of what we now know about their scurrilous plans. We all understood that they planned to get the *Kineococcus radiotolerans* weapons systems one way or another, and they were also banking on Shariff's ability to convert nuclear subs into Polonium 210 labs. Francesco warned that if we did not go to them, they would come for us.

He smiled and told Shariff that it was ironic they had become so central to the plans of organizations that they set up *Kineococcus radiotolerans* to control. Now, he said, the table had turned and the agency either had to control the two of them or eliminate them.

Shariff looked back at him for a long minute and then said, "Or we kill them. I have enough Polonium 210 to take them all out if we can locate them."

Then he leaned forward in his chair. "Francesco, did you leave a back door to the system?" The vein in his temple was throbbing again.

Before answering, Francesco looked hard at his colleague, then me. The he acknowledged that he had, and told us that was why we had to leave the mountain. That day. Unless we decide to give them the answer they wanted.

I looked from one to the other. I had already considered my answer. "I can never work for Stoker's outfit. In my mind, that would be working against humanity. I also have reason to know that he is not what he says he is, and the plan he says his agency intends to implement has not been authorized by the U.S. government."

It was time to reveal what they, and evidently Stoker, did not know about my mission, and my level of authority over Polonium 210. "The mission of recovering the Polonium 210 is mine, and mine alone. I have TS/SCI level security clearance (Top Secret/ Sensitive Compartmented Information). Because Polonium 210 is classified as having the potential to cause exceptionally grave damage to national security if made publicly available, I was tasked with bringing it in. Stoker is lying when he says his operation has been cleared to produce it in any form.

I am positive that program has not been sanctioned. My department would know if it was and I would have signature authority for any actions regarding production and use of the polonium. Who knows where their financial support comes from and what will be done with the weapons they say they have been tasked to build for the U.S. government. One thing is for sure. What Stoker told us has put us at war with them. There is no way we could ever join them.

Shariff smiled at me. "Cecily, Francesco is kidding when he suggests that is one option. Without a doubt, Stoker's organization is part of *Tripartite,* not the U.S. government. Remember Plato's *Allegory of the Cave*? He described all knowledge as shadows on a wall. Any information coming from a *Tripartite* operative fits into Plato's allegory."

Francesco laughed at Shariff's joke. He said that once they had all the information they want from us, we would be dead meat. If they had a fleet of labs like the one Shariff's team built in *Dragon,* there is no doubt they would misuse that power. They would not stop at defense. Only the *Guardians* can be trusted to objectively wield that kind of killing power. We will have to see that control of Polonium 210 is in our hands, and our hands along.

Shaking my head, I said, "Polonium 210 control will have to rest in my hands and my hands alone. Did you not hear what I just told you about my security clearance and my authority over that material?"

The two of them looked at me patronizingly. Then Shariff spoke, gently. "Cecily, remember what we have been telling you about your old life and the one you must now live? You no longer have any control over Polonium 210 unless it is given to you by the *Guardians.* That is because, as you said, that material can cause exceptional harm. The *Guardians* exist to control such threats to the world. They will see that it is controlled, that it is never to put to the kind of use that Stoker described. You will come to understand the power of the *Guardians* and relish it. But first, we have to get away from here because the *Tripartite* can never be allowed to capture and use each of us. For their purposes, we are valuable weapons."

I had to speak my mind before I finally conceded the helm. "Shariff, you, your team, murdered a man with the polonium and you planned to dispatch nineteen others. The only difference between what you did and the plan outlined by Stoker is one of quantity, not quality. Morality had been taken out of the equation. I don't know how to get around that. I don't think I ever can."

Francesco held up his hand to halt my forecast of a doomed relationship. He reminded us that we had immediate problems to attend to. He also told us that when he developed the control system of the bacterial colony in *Kineococcus radiotolerans*, he not only built a back door into the go-no-go system, he designed it so that he can independently release each of the four weapons they built and hid around the globe. He told me each of the general locations. They had imbedded one in Jebel Barkal, one beneath the ice sheet in Greenland, one here at *Pico Turquino*, and one beneath the floor of the Amazon River. He reminded us that we could not lead the Tripartite to any of those locations. But, he said, we had options because the *Guardians* are always one step ahead of a disaster.

He took a deep drink of his *café con leche* before continuing and revealed that the *Guardians'* executive committee, of which he is a member, has decided that a line must be drawn in the sand against the bureau Stoker represents. What they are proposing even exceeds the war crimes of the *Third Reich*. They would raise the bar on warfare.

Although the Nazis butcher's ultimate goal was also world domination, technology was their downfall. The Allies outgunned them. Today, guns are anachronisms. Chemical weapons are the new game.

Toxic chemicals can be produced more cheaply, delivered with greater proficiency, and have a kill rate many times higher than the weapons of war currently manufactured by the industrial-military complex. Theoretically, whole populations can now be eliminated using small inexpensive delivering systems, like drones. A fleet of drones delivering small quantities of deadly poisons can have a much higher kill rate than a bombing run due to its saturation rate.

Francesco also pointed out that there would be no need to train and field an army, or suffer battlefield casualties. One concentrated gram of Polonium 210 can eliminate millions by polluting the air, land, and waterways of an area. The immediate effect is less dramatic than a bomb but the poison is lethal and irreversible.

I gave Francesco a long look and said, "You left out the worst part of Stoker's plan, sterilizing whole populations so that eventually there would be nothing left on the land but its resources. I believe he referred to that as spoils for the victors."

Francesco nodded, acknowledging my point. Setting his cup on the table beside his chair, he responded that our first task was to escape. That the three of us could not be taken alive.

The two men, long time companions in battle, gave each other knowing looks and then looked at me. I stared at Shariff. My stomach was doing flip-flops. *Could the man with whom I had just shared several hours of passionate love making actually kill me if he thought it necessary?* I did not like the look in his eye

Francesco continued to explain the need for haste, saying that Stoker's troops were probably on their way up the mountain as we were speaking. *Taino guards* would slow their progress, and make it costly, but we could not take any chance of being captured. The *Tripartite* has ways of making people talk, including through chemistry. Francesco admitted that he would love to stay and take some of them out, but the three of us knew too much. He said we were on orders to go.

17
Run From The Mountain.

He rose and walked to the door, announcing that our horses would be ready shortly. He directed me to pack a small bag, enough to get me through the next several hours. We could pick up supplies enroute. Then he stunned me, with another announcement. Our destination was Urubamba, Peru.

I shook my head in submission. "I know what to pack. Never thought I would be returning to the Ucayali."

The two men looked at me in amazement. Shariff asked, "How do you know we are going up the Ucayali?"

It was my turn to surprise them. "I know the Amazon, and it will not be my first trip to Urubamba. I spent several years in Amazonia doing ecological research with my husband."

Shariff stared at me. "You were married, and lived in Amazonia?"

"Yes. But eventually I moved up to the *Macusani Plateau* to collect data on the health hazards of uranium mining. That was the first stone in the road leading me to radiation exposure research. My husband was Dr. Warren Jackson, the famous ecologist gone native. He is probably still wandering in the wilderness hunting bush meat with his riverine brotherhood."

Shariff continued to stare at me, no doubt imagining me married to another man. *He did not like it.*

Francesco cut in, sensing Shariff's mood and wanting both

251

of us to stay on point. He said heavy weather was predicted for the afternoon, perfect for our exit. He hoped for continued cloud cover.

He looked at me and said we were looking at another hard ride, this time down the western slope of the mountains to a lowland plateau. There, we would be picked up by boat and transported to Belize. Friends in Belize were arranging our passage to Lima. From Lima…."

I stopped him in mid-sentence. I knew well where we went from Lima and how we would get to Urubamba. "A hop over the Andes and down into Iquitos on the Amazon. After that, the rest of the trip will be by riverboat. There are only two ways to get to Iquitos, by air or the river. And only one way to get to Urubamba, up river. I have done it many times with Warren."

Still surprised, Shariff said again, "You were married and lived in Amazonia." Apparently it was a lot for him to take in.

So, I reviewed my former life for him again. "I was married. Warren and I met in college. I was in med school and he was an ecologist. I switched majors to medical anthropology and followed him to the Amazon where we were conducting research on the health of *riberenios* and their environmental adaptations. After a couple of years I relocated up to the *Macusuni*. That is where I discovered my calling for dancing with high-level radiation, recording the health effects of working the uranium mines there."

I continued describing my former life to my current lover. "Once I discovered the uranium mine on the plateau, and the disorders it causes people who work there, I fell into my current calling, abandoned Warren, and became a defender against impermissible exposure limits, the person you see before you."

Shariff was looking wide-eyed. "You cut and run?"

I had to explain further. "Warren had gone native. He no longer cared about our marriage, either. I needed to do the world a favor and focus on radiation exposure, not following Tarzan through the wilderness."

"You are full of surprises, Dr. Suderman. Some delightful, some not so much." Shariff pulled his chair closer to mine. His hand reached for my knee and I instinctively moved further from him, not used to public displays of affection. He followed with, "I trust you will not abandon us for another calling."

Apparently, our relationship, which Shariff did not seem inclined to keep secret, came to Francesco as no surprise. My guess is, he already knew, from the man who had just reached for my knee.

I waved my hand to indicate that discussion was over.

Somewhat chastised, Shariff dropped his pursuit of my past life and changed course. "Cecily, I know what it is like to suddenly have your old life yanked out from under you. That is how it was for me when Francesco walked into my *Inshas* lab and asked me to join the project at *Jebel Barkal*."

He turned to smile at Francesco. "He was really telling me, not asking. It is a jolting *rite de passage* but, as it was for me, there are no alternatives for you. You will have to turn away from the life you knew and become part of the one in which you now find yourself. You have no way out. Neither of us does."

As he spoke, I vacillated between anger and desire. His words made me angry but I also had a deep desire to settle under his wing and nest with him. I was definitely in turmoil.

Francesco was a man of few words and the clock was ticking. He brought us back to the subject of evacuating *Pico Turquino* and reminded us that the heavy weather was a godsend that we should not waste. Most of our *Taino* escorts, he said, left while we were having breakfast, as soon as the rain started. If Stoker has tried to have eyes on us from the sky, and Francesco said he would, the rain and cloud banks would give us cover while they lasted.

Walking quickly to the door, he said over his shoulder that we had to make the best use of the heavy weather.

I was growing used to throwing minimal survival gear into a small bag and high tailing it to the next stop on the next continent. But, I felt that I would never grow used to the new life that circumstances beyond my control had forced on me. How could I have known, when I first looked down on that sheet of cold decaying sheet of skin on my lab table, that it would alter the rest of my life?

Still uncertain, my bag packed, I stepped outside. One of the guards was waiting for me with my ride, another black mare from Francesco's herd of *Cubano de Pasos*. He gave me a leg up, mounted his horse from the ground and trotted off. My mare wheeled and followed.

Francesco and Shariff were waiting with other *Taino* guards. As we rode up, Francesco cautioned me again that it would be a very hard ride. That is why he had insisted that I ride every day there at *Pico Turquino*. He said I should be in shape.

He told me we would be riding down to the sea and it would take several hours, so the final part would be in the dark. I was not worried. Horses see better than humans at night but the rain would make the trail slippery and Francesco warned that some parts would be narrow. He said to pull up behind him and see to it that my horse followed in his tracks.

He laid a leg on and his horse turned into the forest, with the rest of us following. Shariff had taken a spot on the string immediately behind me. Within minutes we were in deep shade, under the canopy of towering trees. The rain hardly touched us in the arboreal canyon through which we were riding and, although it was chilly at that altitude, no wind reached us.

Within an hour, the trail began to slope steeply downward toward the coast below. Our pace slowed as the horses picked their way through rocks and roots and across areas where the deep shade had given birth to blankets of soft mosses. Francesco ordered us to lean forward and take our weight off the horse's backs, so they would not tire on the long trip ahead.

Behind me, one of the guards began to sing Cuban *Son* and the others formed a chorus. If we were not running for our lives, it would have been the ride of a lifetime.

Francesco laughed and said to us over his shoulder that you fight with the army you have, and who would not love this army.

∽

Hours passed as we slowly descended toward the plain below. The dim light of day changed to a dark curtain. My knees were beginning to burn and I spent more and more time on my horse's back. Coming to a small flat area, Francesco pulled up and dismounted. Just when I thought I would never make it out of the saddle, Shariff reached for me. With his hands around my waist, I threw my right leg over and stepped down. If he had not been holding me close, my knees would have collapsed.

Smiling, he said, "Well, that was fun." Nuzzling my neck, he whispered, "I am sure there is more fun to come."

One of the guards walked up to us and handed us some bread, cheese, and a flask of Cuban rum. "Take away the pain." He laughed.

It did. Cuban rum is like no other. Made from Cuban sugar cane and grown on Cuban soil. It cannot be replicated.

After half an hour, Francesco stepped back up on his horse and we followed suit. It was now so dark that I could barely make out his form ahead of me, but I trusted my mare. She knew what to do and how to do it. The hoof beats behind me were also a source of comfort. The *Taino* also knew what to do and how to do it, and there was no shortage of courage in the ranks. If I had to do this, I was grateful to be doing it with these guys.

A few more hours passed before we pulled up again. By now we were nearing the coast and the height of the trees seemed shorter. There were occasional openings in the canopy and quick glances of a full tropical moon. The rain had passed and the cloud cover had drifted away. Not good.

Francesco halted our string under trees and, turning, said that we should use the canopy above us as cover. If they were watching

255

us from the sky they would not see us as long as we were under the trees. He swung his right leg across the rump of his horse and stepped down easily from the saddle.

I kicked off my stirrups to stretch my legs; Shariff reached up and lifted me out of the saddle. Gratefully, I put an arm around his neck, slid down the mare's side, and let him hold me until I could stand alone. It was becoming a grueling ride, but his touch instantly brought back that energy which had always passed between us.

His voice was concerned. "We don't have much further to go. Can you sit the saddle for another hour?"

I nodded. What choice did I have?

Another thirty-minute rest break and we were back up on the horses. As sore as my knees were, it was a relief to know we were near the end of the unremitting down hill trek. I never wanted to throw a leg over a horse again.

An hour passed and the trail was steeper. We leaned forward over the pommel of our saddles and braced in the stirrups. Gradually, the heavy musty smell of the forest began giving way to the light briny fragrance that drifts in over a salty sea. We had made it down the mountain.

As we descended onto the beach, the lights of a 41-meter Long Liner vessel could be seen just off shore. The dark silhouettes of her unloading cranes rocked easily with the swells. Two *pangas* were beached, waiting to ferry us out to the ship.

We dismounted our *Cubano de Pasos* for the last time and I patted my mare's neck to thank her for carrying me to safety. She nudged my shoulder in response.

It was then I realized dozens of *Taino* guards had emerged from the forest and were surrounding us. Gerardo, head guard and Francesco's long time friend, came forward and grasped him in a rough bear hug. Francesco returned the embrace. His voice was heavy with emotion as he spoke, calling Gerardo and old friend, *cacique* of the *Taino,*

It brought tears to my eyes when he told the man that he would not get to come this way again and told him he knew why. Throwing his arm around Gerardo's shoulder he told him that the *Taino* had let him live on the mountain for many years, fought beside him, and held him safe. Giving Garardo a strong hug, Francesco told his old friend that the *Taino* are *caribe*, strong people, and he could never repay their loyalty and kindness. Then he told Gerardo to take the horses and ranch at *Pico Turquino* and use them for the good of all the *Taino*. The herd would make good breeding stock and should bring in a lot of money.

Gerardo let go of his friend and fighting companion, with whom he had long ago exchanged names in a *guatiao* ceremony. He removed the *guanine* medallion from around his own neck, and draped it over Francesco's neck. He told him that by wearing the *guanine* he, Francesco, was now chief of the *Taino*. Smiling, he assured his blood brother that the god, *Yocahu*, destines his return. The two men looked long at each other, then struck their hearts with their fists.

Other guards stepped up and took turns hugging Francesco or shaking his hand. As each stepped away, he also struck his heart. Then we were ushered to the *pangas,* pushed off, and began to ride the surf. Francesco sat at the helm of one *panga* and Shariff at the other. I was with Shariff. Our luggage was with Francesco. When the engines were started we headed out toward the lights of the Long Liner. Cuba gradually disappeared into the dark.

Looking across, I wished I had jumped into the *panga* with Francesco. Tears were streaming down my cheeks and I thought, *He could use some comforting.*

It took only minutes to speed out to the ship and we were soon aboard with our luggage. The *pangas* were quickly hauled up by the cranes and the Long Liner got underway. Belmopan, Belize was almost 800 miles to the west. We would be at sea, and out of sight, for days.

Our captain was thin framed, sun tanned and grizzled, an old sea dog. The deep wrinkles around his blue eyes attested to years of squinting against the glare off the water. He gave us a warm welcome and ordered a crewman to show us to our quarters, assuring us that breakfast would be served within the hour and urging us to rest until then. He also warned us to stay below decks and out of sight for the remainder of the trip.

Our quarters were aft where three hammocks swung lazily as the ship plowed through the quiet sea. I crawled onto one of them and fell into a deep sleep within minutes. I didn't care where we were headed, as long as getting there did not involve a saddle and stirrups.

Hours later I awoke with Shariff's hand on my shoulder. Through a nearby porthole I saw bright light and an expansive ocean horizon. It was late afternoon.

Shariff said, "I thought you could use the rest more than food so I let you sleep. How do you feel?"

I moved. Every inch of my body was stiff and my knees still burned. He laughed. "A little exercise will take care of that. Up you go."

He pulled me out of the hammock and into his arms, holding me until I was steady. He had just showered and I was immediately aroused. He sensed it and laughed again. "Don't I wish, but there is no privacy aboard ship." He kissed me on the neck and said, "Let's get some rations down you. The galley is forward."

As we made our way through the ship we passed what seemed like endless freezers and cold boxes. She really was a commercial working vessel. The sounds drifting down from the deck above indicated the crew was hauling in the gill nets.

The day turned into night, and many days and nights followed. Whenever there was rain and cloud cover the captain allowed us up on deck for brief periods. We passed our time swinging in the hammocks or eating and visiting with the crew in the galley. It became hard to remember whether it was day or night. I was beginning to champion for a horse.

◈

March 23. The far off silhouette of land appeared on the horizon. We had made it to Belize. The ship anchored off shore until darkness fell. It was a cloudy night and the tropical heat was stifling as we climbed into the *pangas*. On shore, the captain shook hands all around and wished us well. Then, the sound of the *pangas* returning to the ship were drowned out by the roar of rotator blades. Francesco's birds were back.

When the huge blades slowed, we ducked low and ran. Shariff's arm lay across my shoulders, keeping me below their orbit. He lifted me into the cabin first, then began to sling our luggage aboard. Francesco was speaking with the pilot. Once we were all on board, the bird lifted off and the lights from Belmopan, that were briefly visible beneath us, disappeared. Once again, we were enveloped in a dark world and looking at another 12 hours enroute.

March 24. It was mid morning when we landed at Jorge Chavez airport in Lima, and even hotter than Belize. Flight attendants quickly reloaded our luggage into a private jet and, as we climbed aboard, air conditioning settled around us. I had forgotten about such wonders of technology. Turning to Shariff, I started to comment..."

Before I could finish, he answered, "Port Said."

At noon, the jet dipped sharply down from its climb over the Andes and landed on a small runway in Iquitos. The co-pilot quickly opened the door and dropped the steps. As we emerged, the humidity and heat slammed into us. I thought, *Welcome back to the watery world of Amazonia.*

Another hour found us on board a large multi-hulled barge camouflaged to look like any other cargo ship on the river, but heavily weaponized. Beneath the high mounds of bananas on the fore and aft decks were Swedish Befors152 mm guns, acquired from the Peruvian navy. Our crew wore holstered .45 AMT Hardballers. Francesco and Shariff were each given Hardballers. Also, scattered about the decks were mounds of salt. The heaps of local produce aimed at giving us the appearance of normalcy. Bananas and salt are seen on almost every craft drifting on or motoring against the north flowing current.

As we settled into our room amidships, Shariff said, "My turf is the Nile. Tell me about this river."

For a moment, I thought, *Our roles may have just reversed. Perhaps, he is now the grasshopper.* But then I remembered who I was dealing with and answered matter of factly. "We are headed upriver for the town of Urubamba in the foot hills of the Andes, or at least that area. Francesco is not telling us exactly where our final destination is.

For now, we are on the main Amazon, but 60 miles south from *Iquitos* we will arrive at the confluence of the *Maranon* and *Ucayali* rivers. We will follow the *Ucayali* to the *Rio Tambo*, and then follow the *Urubamba* to the town named for the river. It is over 1,000 miles south so we will be on the river for the better part of a month."

I waited a minute, then added, "That is if we don't run into trouble."

Shariff turned and asked, "What kind of trouble?" He pulled his Hardballer from its holster and started checking to see how many rounds it held.

While I detest gunplay, I realized that he needed to know the hard facts of life in Amazonia, and the hard facts are that sometimes you need a gun. "People here are poor. They do what they can to make a living. Some turn to piracy. We should be okay since we look like a common carrier hauling bananas and salt. The pirates usually attack tourist boats where they can rob *gringos,* relieving them of their money and jewels.

There are also serious obstructions in the river. During high water the river rises thirty feet in some areas and it carries giant fallen trees downstream, along with broad islands of vegetation. The trees can ram into the hull of the ship and the floating islands can strangle its props."

He smiled. "I will take the 24 foot crocodiles and solid islands in the Nile. The crocodiles are lazy and hate to move, and boats can navigate around the islands. They don't move and everyone knows where they are."

I laughed. And, I felt better knowing he knew how to use that Hardballer.

∽

The ship we were traveling on was actually a converted two-story barge. On the outside, it appeared no different than any of the other haulers on the river. The interior was a different story. The walls and floorboards were polished teak. Aft, on the second level, there was a well-appointed dining room, modern kitchen, and reading room. The reading room opened onto the fantail, which sported a heavy white cotton canopy to deflect the sun's rays and prevent any eyes-in-the-sky from detecting our presence. The bridge and captain's quarters were forward.

Below, a series of comfortable bedrooms had small portholes to let in light but prevent observation from the shore. Broad-bladed electric fans hung from the ceilings of every room on the barge, including the fantail deck. They moved enough air to barely make the intense heat and humidity of the tropics bearable.

We moved past the shoreline at 25 knots. There was always an impenetrable wall of never ending biodiversity, except for small villages where we dropped off bananas and salt and picked up hardwoods to pull behind as more props. Our cargo maintained the ruse of being just another commercial boat on the river, we hoped.

Sitting on the fantail of the barge, watching the watery world around us, Shariff observed, "Somewhere, I read that the Amazon rainforest has almost 16,000 species of trees

It is dubbed the 'lungs of the planet'

because it produces more than twenty percent of the world's oxygen supply. The density almost makes you claustrophobic."

He suddenly pointed to the riverbank. "What are those parasitic plants growing on the trees?"

He was referring to the colorful bromeliad plants that seemed to be living on every other tree. I told him, "They hold water and are the drinking fountains for many forms of life here. Don't ever reach into one. You never know whom you will find there. Ten million species of animals, plants and insects are known to science and half of them live in the dense forest and waters of Amazonia. Many are poisonous to humans. A large percentage of them have already made their way into the pharmacology of modern medicine.

I spotted an example. "See those plants growing from the

ground beneath the bromeliads? If you squeeze their stems, liquid iodine comes out. It is a common treatment for all kinds of wounds here."

As we progressed south along the river, slow moving sloths and Monk Sakis quietly watched us from the trees, as though they knew something we did not, but should.

∽

Even with the broad-bladed overhead fans pushing the air at full speed, it was uncomfortably hot on the fantail of the barge. The almost daily rains drove the humidity higher than the temperature, which was almost always over 100 degrees. At least, the white canopy over us deflected some heat and allowed us to spend time outside, protected from scrutiny by eyes-in-the-sky.

<u>April 6</u>. Two weeks and hundreds of miles up river we were growing complacent. Always a mistake. It was three a.m. and our barge suddenly rolled violently to starboard. We had hit something, something big.

Shariff jumped from our bed, grabbed his Hardballer and pulled open the door to our room. At the same time, Francesco and the captain rushed out of their rooms, running aft to the engine room. Shariff and I followed in the dim lights of the corridor. All was in order in the engine room.

From there, we ran forward to amidships where we saw the problem. A large cruiser had bumped into us and one of our crew held a line he had thrown over its stern railing. A second crewman boarded the cruiser and wrapped a line around the boat's forward cleat. She was now moving upriver with her bow pointed downriver, parallel to our barge.

Another crewmember ran up with a large lantern and moved its beam along the port side of the cruiser. There were no hands on board that we could see. Francesco and Shariff jumped across to her deck. The lantern was passed over and I followed.

As we made our way forward, into her cabin a scene of nightmarish horror unfolded. The bodies of three men and two women lay in the main cabin. We found another couple in the V berth. All were nude, bound by their hands and feet, and drenched in blood. The walls and floor were splattered, as well. Adding to the visual horror before us, the heat and heavy tropical air was laden

263

with the stench of raw flesh.

The others stared in disbelief, trying to make sense of the horrific scene. Being a medical anthropologist, I instantly recognized what had transpired aboard that hellish ship. "You guys go out onto the deck and wait. I've got this."

They were only too happy to do so. The captain ran out to the stern, leaned over the railing, and heaved. Francesco and Shariff weren't far behind.

I stayed down in the cabin, using the lantern light to study the bodies. The massacre had been performed by river pirates harvesting organs and it did not take long for me to determine which organs had been removed. Every cadaver was missing all its major organs. Whoever did this was used to gutting animals. The only difference was they didn't bleed them before cutting out the parts they were after. They hadn't even put a bullet in their victim's brains before carving them up.

After examining each body I concluded that the bastards who had done the butchering had at least been humane enough to cut the carotid artery of their victims, presumably before butchering them. Using the standard for *algor mortis*, the death chill, I estimated time of death to be around 3-4 hours earlier since the bodies were nearly room temperature, around 95 degrees. The *rigor mortis* stage usually sets in within four hours of time of death and seemed to confirm my *algor mortis* estimate.

Another chilling thought popped into my head. *There was more than one butcher on board this vessel since all the bodies seemed to have been gleaned around the same time. Normally, in the Amazon, you eat what you kill for sustenance. Not in this case. Highly profitable organ harvesting had overtaken hunting bush meat in the upper Amazon.*

I stepped back out on the stern deck where the three others were waiting. Handing the captain the lantern, I said, "We need to keep this vessel tied to ours and haul it to the nearest police."

He was completely befuddled. "What on earth went on here?"

I answered. "River pirates. They are not just robbing passengers now. They are harvesting organs. Human organs bring big bucks in Asia."

Francesco immediately shook his head, and argued that keeping the vessel tied to ours was about nine different kinds of a bad idea. He asked how long I thought the people on the boat have been dead.

I answered, "My estimate is 3-4 hours."

All three men quickly pulled their Hardballers from their holsters. The captain yelled to the crew on the deck of our barge to arm themselves.

Shariff took my arm and began to pull me back toward the railing. "Climb back to the barge and go to our room. And, lock the door behind you."

I pulled away. "What is happening?"

With a stern voice he said, "The murderers are not far away. Given time, they would have scuttled the cruiser, counting on the piranhas to eliminate the carcass remains they left behind. They had probably off loaded their cargo not long before we ran into them and before they could sink her in the middle of the river. They're probably near. Now, go to our room."

I suspected he was planning to cut the cruiser loose in preparation for defending our own ship. I had to make them see the bigger picture. "We need to deliver these bodies to the nearest police. Whoever did this will do it again, and the police need to start monitoring the river."

He was having a hard time accepting the bigger picture

We might be in immediate danger but we also had a professional obligation to get the cruiser and its grizzly cargo to the authorities. There was no time for a standoff so I began to explain about the organ harvesting industry

"The World Health Organization has estimated that each year there are tens of thousands of black market operations involved in the sales of human organs. There are laws intended to crush the chop shops but the traffickers defy laws to cash in on a rising international demand, especially for replacement kidneys. Rising rates of diabetes, high blood pressure and heart problems in wealthy countries drive the market.

Some underdeveloped or economically depressed countries do not even have laws or do not enforce them. Lots of money changes hands where all major human organs can be sold at huge profits.

Central to the filthy business are 'transplant tourists'; the wealthy sick seeking new parts to improve the quality of their lives, or life itself. A lot of them go to China, India and Pakistan for organ replacement surgery, and pay as much as $200,000 for a kidney. The desperately poor people who undergo amputation for cash get paid as little as $5,000.

There are also people who are simply assault victims. These are kidnapped and drugged, only to regain consciousness and find they are in terrible pain and have a long jagged stitched scar where they were cut open for the removal of one or more of their major organs. Some, of course, never wake up, like the victims on the ship lashed to ours.

Physicians have been arrested in some countries, suspected of belonging to an international organ trafficking ring and committing extortion, tax fraud and bodily harm in spite of their Hippocratic oath. Here in the Amazon, physicians are not needed to support the market. Many hunters are skilled at killing, bleeding, and gleaning the bodies of their prey. Transferring those skills to human organ harvesting would not be a stretch.

Converting from hunting for survival to organ harvesting for what would be a king's ransom along this river would certainly have its attractions. A testament to the profits involved is the fact that the pirates who massacred the people of this ship were most likely willing to sink her to cover their crime. Vessels as fine as her could be cleaned up and resold for another huge profit, or kept for private use.

Shariff interjected. "Being the former pirate of a U.S. Navy submarine, so to speak, I can tell you that the main reason they would scuttle the ship is because they did not want to leave any evidence of their dastardly deed. Connections to the craft could expose their identity."

Francesco added that, as he has said, they probably intended to send her to the bottom but our arrival foiled that plan. He was sure they were close by. He could feel them in his bone marrow, which he thought they would also probably like to harvest. He insisted that we needed to cut her loose and run for it.

I continued to try and convince them that I had the strongest argument. "We have no option but to get this ship and evidence of the crime to the nearest police. My guess is that the organ harvesting industry will grow here and shortly outstrip the availability of victims along the river. There are not that many foreign travelers to prey on.

The indigenous and unsuspecting, small tribes, living isolated lives in the forest, could be targeted next. After that, riverine villagers could be culled from their herds, so to speak. The economics of the horrid business will spread like a cancer among the underprivileged here. This Garden of Eden will become a truck farm for black market organ harvesters. We are obligated to take the evidence of this crime to the nearest authorities I turned to the captain. "How far are we from the next sizable town with a police force or a detachment of river patrollers?"

He turned to Shariff and Francesco and told them he agreed with me. He conceded that we could not ignore this threat to life along the Amazon. The next town had a police force and could communicate with Iquitos, maybe even Lima authorities. He thought we could make it in two hours. If the pirates pursue us and try to board, we could hold them off with the barge's fore and aft Befors. And there were always the Hardballers.

Shariff and Francesco studied each other for several minutes, silently forming a plan. Then, Shariff turned to me. "All right. We will do as you ask but only if you do as I say and stay out of danger in our room."

I started to argue, to tell him that I was not Rosslyn, this was not like Germany, but then thought better of it. I agreed and shortly after I entered the room and locked the door behind me, I heard our engines start up again. The barge began to slide forward against the current and after a minute there was a decided pull against our motion. They had tied the cruiser on a longer line off our stern and she was being towed behind.

Hauling the yacht against the river current slowed us down to the point that we were barely making headway over the ground, but at least we had her in tow. Presumably, they had cut the line of the hardwood cargo we had been pulling.

The trip was hair raising. We had to wonder whether we were being followed and whether the men who had created the carnage on the cruiser might be planning to do the same on our barge. The captain, crew, Francesco, and Shariff took turns on watch. No one rested much after seeing the gory work of those who could be in our wake.

✍

April 27. Our barge finally docked at Urubamba, five weeks after leaving Iquitos. It seemed another life time since the day I arrived at the United Nations Peace Keeping complex on the banks of the Suez Canal to confront Dr. Mousaff al Shariff. At the time, I suspected him of producing the Polonium 210 that had polluted and almost completely dissolved the sheet of skin that landed on my lab table in Montana. Now, I knew he had done it, and why.

Before I arrived in Port Said, the why did not matter. Now, knowing what had driven him muddied the waters of my views on the permissible and the prohibited. His deed had eliminated one form of evil, but his method was another matter.

In the short space of less than a year, I had lost my life and my position at the Reardon Ridge National Lab, globe hopped with the man I was sent to out maneuver, and ended up sharing his bed.

I could not help myself. I finally had to accept that. Shariff was a magnet.

Thoreau said most men lead lives of quiet desperation. Not this man. He was a strong force to be reckoned with. It had been only months since he walked into my life, yet I knew that, years on, he would be one of those long shadows cast by small moments.

⋽

Remarkably, I had returned to the Amazon where I started my quest to track and control radiation health hazards. Now, I sat across from a Peruvian policeman trying to explain what I knew to have happened aboard the ship we had towed into port. Cognitive dissidence was the only way to describe my mental state. The policeman was even more discombobulated. The problem we had brought him was well beyond his job description.

He was taking copious notes as I described the condition of the bodies still on the ship, exactly as we had found them, except that now the carcasses were badly decomposed. We had tried not to contaminate the crime scene anymore than necessary before towing the vessel upriver to the only real port in the area.

While we were underway, we tried not to imagine the condition of the bodies as the heat took its toll and the inevitable insects arrived for the feast. The smell of blood and rotting flesh brought all kinds of other carrion and water born life to the ghost vessel. Our crewmen took turns driving away what they could, firing rounds with their rifles. That might also have kept the organ harvesters at bay.

When the policeman was finished interrogating us, he asked if we would stay in Urubamba for a few days. His superiors in *Iquitos* might have further questions for us as they took whatever actions were needed to remove the bodies to a morgue and process the crime scene. He directed us to the hotel on the little town's square.

We agreed and, checking in, found it full of charm after the hellish month we had just endured. However, that bar was not too high. Devil's Island would have seemed charming compared to our barge and the slow crawl up the Amazon towing a death ship from our stern.

On the second day, we sat in a local restaurant eating *papas a la huanciana*, boiled purple potatoes served on lettuce and topped with spicy melted cheese. Francesco and Shariff were sharing a side dish of broiled red bellied piranha, fresh from the Urubamba River. I declined, unable to get past their ugly faces and the razor sharp teeth jutting from their jaws. A tall strapping blonde man approached. Francesco and Shariff jumped up and laughingly hugged him. It was clearly a Bro moment. "*Hola!*" The three of them were obviously good friends.

Shariff turned to me and, smiling, said, "Dr. Suderman, meet Dr. Jacques Belle, another member of our Jebel Barkal team."

I stuck out my hand to shake his, but he quickly stepped forward and wrapped me in a tight warm embrace. "Sorry about the rigors of your trip, no pun intended." As I looked up into his amused eyes, blue as the Amazonian sky, I felt at ease, even deep in the Peruvian jungle. Jacques Belle was an easy man to be with.

I said, "You have already heard about the organ harvesting we came across?"

He nodded. "News travels fast on the Amazon, the same way it travels on the Nile."

Once again I was reminded that human communication systems had only used the lowly radio wave in what constituted a mere minute of our species' history. I wondered about the assumption that we would cease to exist if the current modes we thought integral to life were suddenly taken out?

Shariff pulled up another chair for Jacques and we all sat back down at our table. The men caught up on conditions at Jebel Barkal, our stay in Cuba, and the rest of the trip before our cruise up the Amazon began. Then, talk turned to our present situation, and our future.

Jacques said easily that he had cleared it with the local authorities. We were free to go with him as soon as we could get checked out of the hotel.

I asked, "Where would that be?"

The men exchanged looks. Francesco raised his brow and, somewhat mystified, asked Shariff if he had not told me. Then he laughed and said that now would be a good time

Shariff began to speak quietly to me, glancing around to ensure that no one else was listening to the conversation at our table. "We have been conscripted. Part of Stoker's reason for visiting us at *Pico Turquino* was recon. He was sounding us out to see if we could be turned. When he reported that we could not, the *Triparte* kicked the dark art of Polonium 210 and 210s production to a prioritized level. Do you remember that Francesco told Stoker he had been watched from the moment he set foot on Cuban soil?"

I nodded.

"That was not exactly the full truth. The *Guardians* are always watching *Tripartite* agents. Stoker was in their cross hairs long before he arrived in Cuba and he was under surveillance when he returned to his handlers. Our informants told us what he reported, that we declined his offer. Predictably, the *Guardians* kicked up their production plans."

I had to ask. "And, what are the *Guardians'* production plans?"

Shariff was quick to respond. "The *Tripartite* production plan necessitated producing an antidote. Always out in front of the *Tripartite*, a facility was built a hundred miles inland from Urubamba for that purpose. Jacques oversaw its construction. Our mission now is to outpace their production of Polonium 210 and 210^s with a vaccine that can be disbursed around the globe to neutralize the effects of the polonium poisoning.

Francesco intervened, his face serious. He said the *Guardians* had obtained the formula for HOE-TTC (dimercaprol) from the Brits through another member of the Jebel Barkal team, Dr. Charles Grayson. Charlie is an Oxford graduate and interceded on behalf of the dimercaprol production project. One of his Oxford classmates is now lead scientist at the Sellafield nuclear research center in the north of England. Sellafield is where dimercaprol was originally developed.

In lab experiments at Sellafield, the dimercaprol proved to be 90 percent effective against exposure to Polonium 210. We are going to bring it up to the level of industrial production. We cannot allow any depth of difference between the *Tripartite*'s production rate and ours. The *Guardians* have to be out front on this."

Again, I had to ask. "Will it also be effective against Polonium 210^s?"

Shariff gestured with his hand. "We won't know until we run tests."

Instantly on guard, I asked, "How will such tests for efficacy be conducted? We cannot expose people to the poison to see if the antidote prevents sterility. There are laws against that."

Shariff smiled and shook his head. "Not here there aren't. But before you launch into a tirade on the ethics of scientific prohibitions you need to hear all the details."

"Charlie, his wife Dr. Leslie Everly, and their daughter Dr. Cris Everly-Grayson, who is also Francesco's wife, are already here and working to bring the facility on line. They are setting up the glove boxes and robotic arms for handling the product inside the glove boxes. Most of the centrifugal pumps, and other equipment needed for the project are on line

As you have probably guessed, much of the equipment was moved from *Jebel Barkal*. Remember asking about it as we departed the temple there?

At the facility here in the jungle, there is even a huge Olympic-size pool being installed where hundreds of zyrcoid containers can be suspended in water as the vaccine we produce comes off the assembly line. Landing pads are being built to accommodate the fleet of helicopters that will convey the product off the site."

Then Francesco reached out and held my hand while he told

me two things that I was too worn out to handle. First, he said that he, Shariff, Charlie, and Jacques were going to be the test subjects for 210ˢ. It had to be done and who better to do it.

Second, he told me that I had been under surveillance since I went on the hunt for Shariff. They assumed that he would eventually bring me to them. My fate was sealed the day I walked into the United Nations complex at Port Said.

I turned and stared hard at Shariff. As usual, he was reading me and said, "Don't even think it. I had no part in planning your surveillance and I certainly did not lure you here under false pretenses."

As much as I wanted to believe him, I was overwhelmed with a sense of betrayal, and broken hearted that he was going to be exposed to 210ˢ. One minute we were deeply compatible and committed lovers. The next, I was his target. He had duped me. And, he might die.

My head began to pound and I felt sick to my stomach. Once again, my world had just spun off its axis. I stood and quickly left the square, headed back to the hotel. I was intent on grabbing my bag and finding a way out of Amazonia, and back to the U.S. I would get my job, and my life, back.

◈

The bag was almost packed when there was a hard knock on the door. Shariff's voice boomed from the other side. "Open it or I will kick it down!"

Unaccustomed to public scenes, I slid back the bolt and he stormed inside. "Where do you think you are going?"

Glaring defiantly, I told him, but my breath was coming in short spurts. He was scaring me. I knew his past and he was angry.

He glared back. "Francesco told you that when Stoker appeared at *Pico Turquino* and summarized the plan his organization intended to implement, the *Guardians* had already laid plans for our evacuation to Urubamba. That included both of us. I was brought here just like you. I may not have had your reservations because I have fought beside Francesco for so many years that it never occurred to me to resist. But I was also brought here.

Cecily, you don't just get to walk away from our relationship and the protection that you have here with me. Did you think we weren't serious when we told you that your old life is over? Do you not understand the danger if you leave here? Either the *Tripartite* killers will take you, and you will tell them everything they want to know, or the *Guardians* will kill you to prevent that."

He continued his charge. "You can have a good life here. I love you down to my bone marrow. Francesco, Jacques, Charlie and I will protect you with our lives, and that's a lot of protection. It has been tested on a lot of battlefields.

Your work here will do the world a lot more good than restricting your skills to radiation exposure in the U.S. America may need you, but the world needs you more. We have no one who can do what you are capable of."

My resistance began to erode when he started hitting on my responsibility to help the Urubamba project.

Always able to read me he charged ahead. "Dr. Suderman, you have a responsibility to save the world from the Polonium 210 and 210^s attacks described by Stoker. He felt comfortable in revealing the *Tripartite* plan because, as he told us, they will have to shoot us now that we know. Remember his saying that in your cabin up on *Pico Turquino*? What he did not say, but what Francesco and I knew from experience, was that even if we joined his organization they would kill us when our work was done.

Those evil bastards have to be stopped. You have an obligation to help us develop the antidotes to Polonium 210 and 210^s. You have to stay here and save the four us when we test the 210s antidote if a mistake is made in the plan. We could die if the test plan is not perfect or some lurking variable requires scientific back tracking of the highest order. We can produce any form of radioactive material you can name. But, none of us have the kind of exposure experience that you posses."

He pressed on. "You have another obligation; to yourself. You said you left your marriage because you wanted to prevent harm to others from radiation poisoning. Well, your work is not over, is it? The work you have been doing for the U.S. government was in preparation for the work you know you must do here. Be honest with yourself. You are not the kind of scientist who walks away from a problem of this magnitude when you know how to attack it. If you cut and run, you will be eaten alive with guilt."

He hit the mark.

But, he was not done. "And there is the issue of you and me. We are in love. You may be mad as hell at me for what you think I have done, but that does not change the fact that you love me. And I love you. Furthermore, it is not me who has sinned here. Not once have I have ever considered manipulating you. On the other hand, you have been entertaining the notion to cut and run on me. I have seen the look on your face, and in your eyes. It's like I'm inside your head, but I can always tell what you are thinking. Getting the Polonium 210 away from me and bolting with it in order to complete your mission has crossed your mind almost weekly since you walked through the door of the Port Said U.N. complex."

He had a point. In all honesty, I had pondered that prospect several times, even after we had become involved. I had been dishonest to the point of betrayal. Not without feeling guilt, but I had entertained the idea of leaving him if I got my hands on the Polonium 210 his team had produced. Returning to Reardon with it was my official mission.

As I stood in that hotel room, with a bag almost ready to hit the road, facing the man I needed to both love and flee, what Stoker had told us about the black ops program to develop Polonium 210 and 210^s began playing back from my memory banks. Shariff was right; I had a higher calling now.

Bombs, nuclear warheads, sanctions that cut hungry people's

rations even shorter, arming one side in another country's revolutionary war to up the carnage, all that was universally sanctioned or the object of political football. But, never had a nation spoke in favor of allowing war to move from the military ranks to chemical laboratories. Chemical warfare was universally banned as unacceptable.

My anger began to subside. Mentally calculating the enormity of a plan to produce the Polonium 210 and 210^s antidotes on an industrial scale, I asked, "How long do you think it will take to complete the project?"

Shariff moved closer, leaned forward, and took my hand in his. "The rest of our lives."

I shook my head. "I can't. I am still on orders by the U.S. government to obtain the Polonium 210 you used to poison Alois Brunner. If I do the research you are asking for, will you finally turn it over to me? At least they might let me maintain my citizenship. If you die during the 210s tests, I will go home."

Shariff smiled. "I will not die because I will never leave you. And, I will do better than giving you the Polonium 210 our team produced. If you lend your scientific skills to this project and help us mass produce the antidotes, I will help you destroy every ounce of that poison on the planet."

He took me in his arms and kissed me gently on the forehead. "Cecily, we have no other options. If we leave here, one faction or another will eventually kill us, including those of your government. But, if we stay behind the *Guardians'* firewall here in Urubamba and do this work, we will be doing all mankind a service. And we will be safe.

I'm hoping you will be my partner in this, my final push back against abuse of atom splitting. And I'm desperately hoping you will be my partner until the day I draw my final breath. Without you, I will have no life."

How could a girl turn down such a proposal?"

The End

Appendix

A. Concentration Camp Survivor's Testimonies.

Many of the survivors' testimonies have been documented in the Ravensbruck Archive developed by the Swedish government at Lund University. In December 2016, Lund University celebrated its 350th anniversary, having been established as a study center for Franciscan priests in 1438. The Ravensbruck testimonies are contained in 500 lengthy interviews and 20,000 pages of handwritten notes, including prisoner notebooks, diaries, poems, recipes, photos, drawings and official Nazi documents. Transcripts of the 1946-47 Ravensbruck trials at Hamburg, portraying the crimes committed by camp commanders and guards, can also be read in the archive.

The testimonies provide stark descriptions of the inmates and the mental anguish they felt. One survivor recalled that upon entering the camp she was struck by the "dead eyes" of the bald, skeletal prisoners.

The testimonies of the *Ravensbruck* survivors mirror *Dante's Inferno*.

"The camp's day began before dawn with *appell*, German for roll call, which required prisoners to stand in thin dresses for hours, even in snow. Female guards dressed in black capes lashed inmates with whips. Many women froze to death where they stood; those who collapsed from exhaustion were taken to their death. The prisoners fit for labor would then move on to grueling, often impossible, tasks in work gangs. The camp's philosophy was deliberately counterintuitive: It allowed those capable of work to live, then it worked them to death.

Breakfast was one cup of black coffee and one piece of bread crust. Later soup, made with water, cabbage, sometimes one potato, and maybe a horse bone, but mostly cabbage, or turnips. In the evening again we had one little piece of bread, nothing else.

Crematoriums were operating before our eyes. Each morning we stood
in line while the Germans looked us over. One day maybe someone's
mouth didn't look right, or their eyes, or hair, or skin. They pulled the
women out of line and sent them to the chimney. Just like that.

They might send me to take out the ashes and put them in the fields.
I did that only once, but many people did it everyday. You started
to become completely numb, like a stone, to feel nothing, absolutely
nothing. You had no idea what would happen to you the next moment.
You lived each day, each moment, one at a time.

In January or February 1945, the Germans accepted an agreement of
the Geneva Convention, which allowed the International Red Cross
to take sick people from the camp, but only those whom the Germans
allowed to go. Big school busses came to collect a few people. Again,
you needed some connections or you had to be a prominent person.
I remember they let out some Norwegians, a few professionals, and
people of well-known families.

First, the officers and higher officials vanished--escaped altogether.
Some of the others took off their uniforms and put on our camp clothes
so they wouldn't be recognized. But this didn't help. Many of them now
had to face the revenge of women they had mistreated, and it was very,
very bad. The Russian women were the worst."

The Russian soldiers were just like animals when they were drunk, and
they were always drunk."

§

Randol Schoenberg, president of the Los Angeles Museum of the
Holocaust, described the testimonies as "a lost treasure. Their
translation and preservation offers an opportunity to reclaim an
important slice of history."

Sven Stromqvist, deputy vice chancellor for research at Lund University, was recently in Los Angeles, indicating that all the written material will be translated, categorized, digitized and made available to a worldwide 21st-century audience through a searchable website and traveling exhibits.

B. Nazi Trials:

The Nazi doctors were brought to trial, many at Nuremberg. Other war criminals were tried at Hamburg, including *Ravensbruck* doctors and nurses who had participated in the medical experiments."

Dorothea Binz, brutal SS head overseer, was executed at Hameln Prison.

Irma Grese, one of the training camp graduates, was hung for her crimes at Auschwitz.

Hermine Braunsteiner Ryan, guard and supervisor at *Ravensbruck*, was extradited to Germany by the American Immigration and Naturalization Service.

৵

C. Polonium. From GNU Free Documentation License, Wikipedia, August 10, 2007
Polonium and its compounds must be handled in a glove box, which is further enclosed in another box, maintained at a slightly higher pressure than the glove box to prevent the radioactive materials from leaking out. Gloves made of natural rubber do not provide sufficient protection.

Polonium is highly dangerous and has no biological role.[17] By mass, polonium-210 is around 250,000 times more toxic than hydrogen cyanide (the LD$_{50}$ for ^{210}Po is less than 1 microgram for an average adult (see below) compared with about 250 milligrams for hydrogen cyanide[66]). The main hazard is its intense radioactivity (as an alpha emitter), which makes it very difficult to handle safely. Even in microgram amounts, handling ^{210}Po is extremely dangerous, requiring specialized equipment (a negative pressure alpha glove box equipped with high performance filters), adequate monitoring, and strict handling procedures to avoid any contamination. Alpha particles emitted by polonium will damage organic tissue easily if polonium is ingested, inhaled, or absorbed, although they do not penetrate the epidermis and hence are not hazardous as long as the alpha particles remain outside the body. Wearing chemically resistant and intact gloves is a mandatory precaution to avoid transcutaneous diffusion of polonium directly through the skin.

Polonium delivered in concentrated nitric acid can easily diffuse through inadequate gloves (e.g., latex gloves) or the acid may damage the gloves. [67]

It has been reported that some microbes can methylate polonium by the action of methylcobalamin. [68][69] This is similar to the way in which mercury, selenium and tellurium are methylated in living things to create organometallic compounds. Studies investigating the metabolism of polonium-210 in rats have shown that only 0.002 to 0.009% of polonium-210 ingested is excreted as volatile polonium-210. [70]

Acute effects.

The median lethal dose (LD$_{50}$) for acute radiation exposure is generally about 4.5 Sv. [71] The committed effective dose equivalent ^{210}Po is 0.51 μSv/Bq if ingested, and 2.5 μSv/Bq if inhaled. [72] So a fatal 4.5 Sv dose can be caused by ingesting 8.8 MBq (240 μCi), about 50 nanograms (ng), or inhaling 1.8 MBq (49 μCi), about 10 ng. One gram of ^{210}Po could thus in theory poison 20 million people of whom 10 million would die. The actual toxicity of ^{210}Po is lower than these estimates, because radiation exposure that is spread out over several weeks (the biological half-life of polonium in humans is 30 to 50 days [73]) is somewhat less damaging than an instantaneous dose. It has been estimated that a median lethal dose of ^{210}Po is 15 megabecquerels (0.41 mCi), or 0.089 micrograms, still an extremely small amount. [74][75] For comparison, one grain of table salt is about 0.06 mg = 60 μg.[1]

Long term (chronic) effects.

In addition to the acute effects, radiation exposure (both internal and external) carries a long-term risk of death from cancer of 5–10% per Sv. [71] The general population is exposed to small amounts of polonium as a radon daughter in indoor air; the isotopes ^{214}Po and ^{218}Po are thought to cause the majority [76] of the estimated 15,000–22,000 lung cancer deaths in the US every year that have been attributed to indoor radon. [77] Tobacco smoking causes additional exposure to polonium. [78]

Well-known poisoning cases in 20th century.

Poisoning of Alexander Litvinenko

The cause of death in the 2006 murder of the Russian KGB agent who defected to the British MI6 intelligence agency, Alexander Litvinenko was determined to be ^{210}Po poisoning. [87][88] According to Prof. Nick Priest of Middlesex University, an environmental toxicologist and radiation expert, speaking on Sky News on December 3, 2006, Litvinenko was probably the first person to die of the acute α-radiation effects of ^{210}Po.[89]

Abnormally high concentrations of ^{210}Po were detected in July 2012 in clothes and personal belongings of the Palestinian leader Yasser Arafat, a heavy smoker, who died on 11 November 2004 of uncertain causes. The spokesman for the Institut de Radiophysique in Lausanne, Switzerland, where those items were analyzed, stressed that the "clinical symptoms described in Arafat's medical reports were not consistent with polonium-210 and that conclusions could not be drawn as to whether the Palestinian leader was poisoned or not", and that "the only way to confirm the findings would be to exhume Arafat's body to test it for polonium-210."[90] On 27 November 2012 Arafat's body was exhumed and samples were taken for separate analysis by experts from France, Switzerland and Russia. [91] On 12 October 2013, *The Lancet* published the group's finding that high levels of the element were found in Arafat's blood, urine, and in saliva stains on his clothes and toothbrush. [92] The French tests later found some polonium but stated it was from "natural environmental origin."[93] Following later Russian tests, Vladimir Uiba, the head of the Russian Federal Medical and Biological Agency, stated in December 2013 that Arafat died of natural causes, and they had no plans to conduct further tests. [93]

Detection in biological specimens
Polonium-210 may be quantified in biological specimens by alpha particle spectrometry to confirm a diagnosis of poisoning in hospitalized patients or to provide evidence in a medico legal death investigation. The baseline urinary excretion of polonium-210 in healthy persons due to routine exposure to environmental sources is normally in a range of 5–15 mBq/day. Levels in excess of 30 mBq/day are suggestive of excessive exposure to the radionuclide. [96]

Commercial products containing polonium.
^{210}Po is manufactured in a nuclear reactor by bombarding ^{209}Bi with neutrons. 100 grams are produced each year, almost all in Russia. [97]

Occurrence in humans and the biosphere
Polonium-210 is widespread in the biosphere, including in human tissues, because of its position in the uranium-238 decay chain. Natural uranium-238 in the Earth's crust decays through a series of solid radioactive intermediates, including radium-226, to the radioactive gas radon-222, some of which, during its 3.8-day half-life, diffuses into the atmosphere. There it decays through several more steps to polonium-210, much of which, during its 138-day half-life, is washed back down to the Earth's surface, thus entering the biosphere, before finally decaying to stable lead-206. [103][104][105]
As early as the 1920s Antoine Lacassagne, using polonium provided by

his colleague <u>Marie Curie</u> showed that the element has a very specific pattern of uptake in rabbit tissues, with high concentrations particularly in <u>liver</u>, <u>kidney</u> and <u>testes</u>. [106]

In the 1940's the U.S. Atomic Energy Commission funded similar studies with similar results. Human subjects were used in the U.S. experiments. Described in Biological Studies with Polonium, Radium, and Plutonium, National Nuclear Energy Series, Vol. VI-3, Chapter 3. McGraw-Hill, New York, 1950.

www.ingramcontent.com/pod-product-compliance
Lightning Source LLC
Chambersburg PA
CBHW031254170626
46807CB00001B/134